GIRLS OF LITTLE HOPE

SAM BECKBESSINGER AND DALE HALVORSEN

GIRLS OF

LITTLE

HOPE

TITAN BOOKS

Girls of Little Hope
Print edition ISBN: 9781803362076
E-book edition ISBN: 9781803362281

Published by Titan Books
A division of Titan Publishing Group Ltd
144 Southwark Street, London SE1 0UP

First edition: June 2023
10 9 8 7 6 5 4 3 2 1

A CIP catalogue record for this title is available from the British Library.

Printed and bound by CPI (UK) Ltd, Croydon, CR0 4YY.

For Melanie and Amantha

Every thing is an attempt
To be human.
William Blake

———

To the dull angry world let's prove
There's a Religion in our Love.
Katherine Philips

ONE FOR SORROW

1. STAR FISH

DONNA RAMIREZ

I'm in the medical examination room at the Little Hope Police Department. Donna keeps saying it in her mind, over and over. Her brain can't grasp it, it keeps wriggling from her like an eel. Maybe if she says the words enough times, it might start to feel real. *I'm in the medical examination room at the Little Hope Police Department.* Over on the adjacent table, Rae seems to be having the same problem. She has a grin on her face the size of the moon, teeth bared, eyes crinkled in glee. This is not the appropriate response for where they are, *in the medical examination room at the Little Hope Police Department*, and Donna fights the urge to grab her and shake the grin off. It's too much, to be here, to have lived through what they have just lived through.

Although, if she's honest, she's not even sure exactly what it is they've lived through.

It is two days now since she came stumbling into consciousness. Literally, stumbling. Rae half-carrying, half-dragging her along a deer path, deeper into the darkness of the woods. No idea where she was, what was happening. Rae was hysterical, babbling that they had to run, her hair wet, her face streaked with mud.

The last thing she remembers before that is climbing over some boulders towards Ronnie Gaskins's cave, Rae's dark bob bouncing up ahead. In between those two moments is blank, a film strip badly spliced. It's not amnesia, everything else is still there. She knows who she is. And she knows where she is: *I'm in the medical examination room at the Little Hope Police Department.* That's a start. Hold on to that.

Rae turns to her, brown eyes sparkling from the fluorescent lights, squinting and squeezed from that too-big smile. It must be that she's just struggling to press down the panic. Find the right emotions. Or... maybe it's what Rae remembers, and she doesn't. Maybe Rae understands how lucky they are to be alive.

The doctor asked them several times if they wouldn't prefer to let her examine them separately, but they refused to be separated. They'd had to drag a second examination table in from another room.

Rae's grin seems to be spooking the doctor. She won't make eye contact with either of them, but she keeps repeating their names, tacking them onto the end of every sentence as she narrates her actions.

"I'm going to take samples from under your fingernails now, Donna."

"I'm going to check your wrists for bruises, Tammy-Rae."

"I'm taking some photographs now, Donna."

"I just need a bit of blood for the lab, Donna."

Probably something she learned in a textbook about how to calm the traumatised. Remind them they are more than a victim, they are a full human being. But Donna does not feel like a full human being right now, no siree; she feels like she's had a chunk lopped off her. Worse, she feels like the chunk that's been lopped off. Isn't it starfish, where if you chop off a leg, it can grow into a whole new starfish? That's what she feels like: a wriggling leg trying to remember how to be a person.

The hospital gown feels scratchy against her skin. Their clothes are already sealed up in a paper evidence bag, balanced carefully on the counter to be checked for hair and semen. Some scrap that can speak for them, in place of their stubborn muteness.

The doctor leans over her to photograph a mud-smear on her waist that she has no memory of getting. She smells of fruity perfume and antiseptic. Donna can make out the shape of an oversized engagement ring through her blue surgical gloves.

Not a doctor, Donna notices. FORENSIC NURSE: CARLA MENDEZ, according to the small plastic badge pinned to her white coat. Donna's never seen her before, and she's pretty sure she knows everyone in this town. They must have driven her up from Sacramento. Is Sacramento big enough to employ someone to do this full-time, comb over the bodies of girls who've been missing and are now found, to try to catalogue exactly the ways they've been violated? Seems like a weird profession. There's probably more to the job, but on this, the strangest night of her life, Donna can't bring herself to imagine what.

At least it's not Dr Abrams, the town's skeevy family doctor, who looks for any excuse to get you to lift your shirt and breathes too deeply when he holds the stethoscope against your ribs. That's something to be grateful for, that it's no one who knows her, no one who could look into her eyes and see how much is missing. What should she be feeling right now? Grief? Terror? That's what everyone around her seems to want. They seem to want her to be sobbing or screaming. But each breath feels wonderful, cold and tickling her nose, the soft rise of her chest under the thin hospital gown. It's all just too absurd, to be lying here, reminding herself over and over again that she's *in the medical examination room of the Little Hope Police Department* like that's supposed to mean something.

Sacramento's more than an hour away. They must have called Nurse Mendez just after they were found. There are no windows in this room so it's hard to tell exactly, but it can't be long since they stumbled into Louanne Martin's diner, Rae screaming for help. It was dawn. Louanne was the only person there, lining up condiments on the melamine counter before the breakfast rush. She clasped her chest at the sight of them, sending bottles of watered-down ketchup careening across the floor, splashing bright red across the tiles like some kind of high-fructose crime scene.

That can't have been more than a couple of hours ago. Maybe more. Time seems to be loping past her in chunks. Like there's an absence inside of her, a hole that things keep slipping through.

She has no sense of how long they were missing. It must have been a few days at least, judging from how Louanne gasped when she saw them, and the posters plastered up all around town. She saw them earlier, her nose pressed up against the window of the police car that drove them here. Her own face on every wall, every street light. HAVE YOU SEEN THESE GIRLS?

"I'm just checking for injuries, Donna," trills Nurse Mendez, running gloved hands gently down her arm. She frowns at a spot of bright red on her elbow and reaches for a swab. Donna starts to tell her not to worry, it's just ketchup, but she's afraid she'll laugh. She lets the nurse swab it and slip it into a baggie, which joins the growing pile on the steel trolley.

Actually, as far as she can tell, Donna doesn't have a scratch on her anywhere. Like this might be some elaborate prank they're playing on everyone.

She needs to get her face under control before she ends up grinning like Rae, leering like a loon, scaring everyone. She focuses on trying to freeze her face, keeps repeating, *I am in the medical examination room at the Little Hope Police Department* in her mind. The paint has chipped off and been painted over the metal bars lining the examination table, coarse beneath the pads of her thumbs. The air is heavy in her lungs, anchoring her back to her body. Cold in her throat. *Breathe. Just breathe. Remember where you are.*

Rae's mom gave them something for the shock, two little pills, oblong and powdery. She said it might make them feel a little sleepy. Sleepy's the last thing Donna feels. It's like somebody stuck jumper cables inside her brain, like her whole body is buzzing and dangerous to touch.

Her dad asked if he could take her home, let her wash, let her sleep a while. But no, there's too much to do. They need to catalogue and sample her. Her whole body is a clue, a crime scene. This is the grim admin of trauma. A trauma she can't even remember.

There are... fragments, maybe. Vague outlines of memories through the white mist of her brain. Crunching sounds in the darkness. The iron smell of blood. Something cold and wet on her face. And something else, nagging at her consciousness, like a memory she's not ready to look at yet.

Nurse Mendez guides Rae's feet into stirrups and begins to lubricate a speculum. "This might feel a little cold, Tammy-Rae." She pauses to look at the white scars laddering their way up Rae's thighs, but those are old.

Donna glances back at her. Rae, her best friend, her blood sister. A stranger to her now, that skeletal grin twisting her features, knees sprawled apart under a thin sheet, her normally glossy dark bob matted against her head with grime and sweat and leaves. She looks like a feral thing. Something that doesn't belong here, here in the shiny white and chrome *medical examination room at the Little Hope Police Department.*

"You look like a Troll doll," Donna tries to say. But the words come out slurred. "Ulook like a traw-daw." Rae barely glances at her. Donna supposes she probably doesn't look much better herself.

Nurse Mendez ducks under the sheet draped across Rae's

knees. Rae flinches, hisses through her bared teeth. She's crying, tears sliding over her smile.

"We're OK," Donna says, the words clearer now.

But are they? She can't be sure. If she could just remember what happened, maybe then she'd know.

Rae turns her head away from her. Donna's not sure if she's hiding the tears or the maniac grin.

There's a shriek from outside. A woman screaming. A muffled thump, raised voices, heavy footsteps pounding up the passageway. She recognises Chief Pittman's voice, yelling that she can't be down here. More shouting. A crash, and Marybeth Larkin falls through the doors to the examining room.

"Where is she?" Her face is red. A pink coat pulled on over flannel Minnie Mouse pyjamas, bottle-blonde hair tumbling out of its bun. It's the first time Donna's ever seen her without make-up, and she looks much older than her thirty-three years.

Nurse Mendez pulls her head out from under the sheet, nearly falling off her stool in shock.

Donna feels her body cringing, trying to make itself smaller. She doesn't want this, not now. Not here.

Chief Pittman runs in and grabs Marybeth, holding her tight. "Please, Marybeth. This is a medical room. Let's talk in my office."

"Where is she?" Marybeth yells again. "Where's my Katie?" She snarls and tries to fight her way out of his grip, but the chief has her tight. She collapses against him, her face crumpling into helpless, angry tears. "You left her. You left her behind. Where is she? Please just tell me, where..." And then she can't speak any more. She leans against Chief Pittman and sobs.

Oh yes, the absence. Part of what her brain has been working so hard not to remember. That she and Rae are here, found, grinning and sobbing and scaring people *in the medical examination room at the Little Hope Police Department.*

But Kat, Kat is still gone.

2. BITTERNESS BARBIE

MARYBETH LARKIN

SATURDAY, 21 SEPTEMBER 1996

Sixty-eight hours since her daughter disappeared, Marybeth stands at her own front door, daring herself to open it. A wild thought has entered her mind, that she can't seem to shake: that if she doesn't open the door, Katie might be behind it, curled in her favourite spot, legs up on the window seat, book on her lap. She might look up with a smile, ready to tell her about the latest fact she's just learned. She might just be there, and everything might be fine, as long as the door stays shut.

There's shuffling behind her. Marybeth glances over her shoulder. The two officers are squinting at her. The chief said he was sending them back with her to gather evidence from the home, but Marybeth knows what they really are: babysitters. Their job is to keep her far away from Donna Ramirez and Tammy-Rae Hooper so she cannot *grab them* and *shake them* until they tell her what the hell happened to her daughter.

"Key's sticky," Marybeth mumbles, turning back to the door. Her very hand resists her. The officer she thinks of as Sergeant Underbite clears her throat. She can't put this off forever. Marybeth fills her lungs and swings open the door.

The living room is empty. Empty as a ditch a girl might have fallen into. Empty as a shallow grave dug in a killer's backyard. Empty as a coffin sized for a fifteen-year-old girl.

The cops follow her in. The other one, Sergeant Pockmarks, pulls out a disposable Kodak and snaps a photograph of the living room. It doesn't exactly engender trust, that they can't even afford a digital camera.

"Any messages?" Sergeant Underbite prompts her.

Marybeth walks over to the answering machine and shakes her head.

"The boys will be over later to install a trap and trace," she says, adding a neat tick to the checklist that's clipped to a clipboard. "In case a kidnapper calls," she adds, to Marybeth's blank look.

Marybeth nods. There's too much spit in her mouth, like she's forgetting to swallow. She pulls her upper lip between her teeth and tongues the thin cleft lip scar that twists up to her nose, an ugly habit she thought she'd kicked long ago.

Pockmarks moves slowly through the room, photographing every corner. He runs out of film in the first camera, and pulls a fresh one from his backpack. Marybeth's eyes flick to the half-eaten chicken sandwich that Polly dropped off last night, abandoned on the coffee table next to the undrunk Slim-Fast shake, unwashed mugs and a mound of crumpled tissues. *A better woman would have cleaned up*, she thinks, *be doing helpful things, keeping it together. A better woman wouldn't have lost her fucking daughter.*

"Have you opened or shut these windows?"

"She wasn't taken from the house. The last anyone saw her was at school."

Underbite stares at her blankly, pen poised above her notepad.

Marybeth feels a vein pulse in her throat. "I haven't touched the windows."

"Does Katherine have her own key for the house?"

"Yes."

Another tick on the clipboard. Underbite picks up the notepad by the phone and holds it up to the light, examining the top blank page. "Did you find a note?"

"No."

Tick. "Have you been in contact with her father?"

"He's dead." Underbite can't be older than twenty-five. Too young to remember the scandal it caused when they found Bill's body lying in the living room of his girlfriend's house with three bullet holes in his chest. The cops were about as useful then as they're being now. And exactly as stupid.

Tick. "Are you the only other person who lives here?"

"Yes."

Tick. "Do you have a computer in the house?"

"Can't afford one."

Tick. "Have you looked through the home thoroughly?" Underbite reads flatly. "You've checked laundry rooms, the attic, any vehicles that might be parked on the property—"

"Jesus. She's a teenage girl, not a lost wallet." It comes out as a shout.

Both officers flinch and look up at her with wide eyes. Underbite's mouth opens, then closes again.

"Please, Mrs Larkin," says Pockmarks. "We're trying to help."

Marybeth closes her eyes for a second, wishing she could press some kind of button to not be here right now, for this to not be happening. She takes a deep, shuddering breath. "I searched the house on Thursday after we reported her missing. Back when you people were telling me the girls were probably just taking a joyride to the city. She's not here."

Tick. Underbite tucks the list under her arm, sheepish, and goes through to the kitchen.

"Beautiful smile," Pockmarks says, gesturing to the framed photograph above the mantel. The day Katie won Little Miss Golden State.

Marybeth nods. Feeling a surge of pride, despite the circumstances. Not just that Katie was so beautiful, but at all the work they'd put in to make her so. The little tiara perched on perfect blonde curls took a whole can of hairspray and about one hundred bobby pins. The dazzling beauty-queen smile was Vaseline on the teeth, a trick she'd learned from the other pageant moms. The bright eyes were peppermint teabags chilled in the refrigerator, left on for twenty minutes before the final make-up check. And the fact that she won, that was endless hours in the garage working out choreography, that was Marybeth's detailed notebook tracking the biases of every judge in the state, that was the thousands upon thousands of dollars she'd drained from her bank account because she *knew* Katie was special. A triumph of transformation, living proof that you can be anything you want to be, if you try.

Pockmarks smiles at her gently. "This looks like it was a couple of years ago?"

"Three years. She was thirteen." The last pageant Katie ever won, before she'd unilaterally declared she was retiring and refused to ever be on stage again. Just as she was on the cusp of making the transition from regionals to nationals and the big money. That was it, the end of all their weekends spent together, the end of her childhood.

"Got anything more recent?" He glances over at the collection of framed family photographs arranged underneath the TV, amongst the trophies.

"Maybe in her room," she says. Katie hates photographs, now. She hates a lot of things.

Underbite comes back from the kitchen. "Can you show us?"

Marybeth leads them back to the two bedroom doors at the back of the house, side by side. Hers is open, her bedspread a floral tangle on the floor, the pink sheets rumpled and sweat-stained. The other door is shut tight, like a girl's mouth clamped shut by a man's gloved hand. A small nameplate in the centre declares it KATIE'S ROOM in patriotic red, white and blue, a peace offering from Katie's grandmother just before she died.

The spit in Marybeth's mouth feels thicker. She swallows it down.

"This is as she left it?"

"Yes. Zach told me not to disturb anything." She can't bear to call him Chief Pittman, he was only a patrol officer when she was married, darkened her front door more than a couple times back then.

Officer Underbite nods, adding another tick to her list. Standing this close, Marybeth notices a nest of blackheads in the crease of her nose. She revises down her age estimate: twenty, twenty-one at best. In a flash of empathy, Marybeth realises this is probably her first missing child, too. Poor girl probably feels as lost as she does.

The door whines as it swings open. There's the faintest smell of White Musk body spray. Mid-morning light streams into the room, shimmering on the dust motes their entrance has disturbed. Bits of Katie. Bits of her skin and her hair, everywhere.

Pockmarks begins a slow circuit of the room, capturing every inch of it with his camera. Marybeth and Underbite hang back in the doorway.

"Nothing looks out of the ordinary, to you?" Underbite checks with her.

Marybeth shakes her head. The room is just as austere as always. The yellow sponged walls, the single bed, the dresser, the kidney-shaped curtained dressing table Katie uses as a desk. Two small photo frames next to her bed, one with herself and Katie eating ice creams in Bodega Bay, the other with Tammy-Rae and Donna pulling faces at the camera. Miserably bare, for a teenage girl's room. Marybeth had encouraged her to put up some posters, offered to make her a window dressing to match the bedspread. Anything to brighten things up a bit. She'd gotten nothing in response but a shrug and an eye roll.

The only real personality in the room is the bookshelf Bill built for her when she was little, which is crammed tight, books overflowing into teetering piles on either end. The whole top shelf is taken up with Katie's beloved collection of Nancy Drew books.

"What's she like?" Underbite asks.

"Smart. So smart. Top of all her classes. Never in trouble." The other pageant moms called Katie a "package kid".

"Any extramurals?"

"No. She was in a newspaper club for a while, but that stopped a few months ago."

"Friends?"

"Only Tammy-Rae and Donna." Who are sitting at the station right now, while she's here, being asked pointless questions. "It's not that she's shy. Just... always in her head, you know?" This wasn't always true. There was a time they'd been confidants. Katie would come home from elementary school and they'd sit at the kitchen counter drinking juice together, and she'd tell her everything, who her favourite teachers were, who she sat with at recess, every bit of gossip that made it round the schoolyard. A born storyteller, just like her dad. She'd add touches of drama in the retelling, little exaggerations. Scold Marybeth if she looked away, "Ma Bear, listen!" Once, when she was small, Katie had heard someone calling her Marybeth and she'd heard it as "Ma Bear", which sounded right to her, because bears were big and strong and they could protect you from forest fires. Fires had been little Katie's greatest fear since she heard about how her aunt and uncle's house burned down in a grease fire back in '89.

Where did she go, that little girl who shared everything with her? When did she begin to tuck herself away? Logically, she knows this is probably a normal part of teenagehood. But it still *hurts*. It didn't matter how hard she tried to be different to her own mother, to never be cold and scolding, Katie pulled away anyway, a thousand

thousand small retreats. And now she's gone, completely.

Pockmarks completes his catalogue of the room and waves them in. Underbite pulls an evidence bag from her jacket and starts rummaging through the clutter on the nightstand. She bags a hairbrush and the retainer that stops Katie from grinding her teeth.

"She needs those," Marybeth says, reflexively.

"I understand, ma'am," says Underbite, in the kind of singsong you'd use to calm a horse. "But we need to take samples of DNA, fingerprints, teeth impressions. That will help us to find her."

But that doesn't make sense, does it? An image flashes in Marybeth's mind. A body, lying on a cold metal table in a morgue. They don't need these things to find Katie; they need them in case they have to identify her body.

She retreats to the corner of the room, feeling conscious of the stupid cartoon pyjamas she's still wearing, tonguing the scar on her lip, watching as Underbite bags up and seals and violates Katie's things. A cold fury rises in her. They could have done all of this on Thursday morning, when she and Estelle Hooper marched into the police department saying their daughters were missing. They could have sent out helicopters. They could have called the FBI. They could have *responded*, goddamn it, instead of making her feel like she was being hysterical and overreacting to three teenage girls who'd probably taken a trip up to the city, or were sleeping off a hangover in one of the empty warehouses in Eastside. And no matter how many times she told them her daughter was a good kid, and she would *never* worry her mother like this, they placated and nodded and soothed her and did *fuck-all*. Did a cursory search around town. Spoke to some teachers. Told her to put up posters if she needed something to do.

Until this morning, when the other two came back covered in bruises and naked as the day they were born, staggering out of the woods, and they couldn't dismiss her any more.

And all she can think of is how many hours they've lost. She's counted every single one, each wasted moment. If only that English teacher had realised they weren't in class *one hour* after they skipped out of lunch on Wednesday. If only Estelle Horseface Hooper had thought to check that the girls were actually in her basement after she got home late from that church meeting, they might have realised *nine hours* later. If only Zachary Toilet-Brush-Moustache Pittman had just taken them seriously when she and Estelle told him the girls hadn't shown up for breakfast, *seventeen hours* later. If only *any one* of these supposed adults had actually looked after the children who were in their care she wouldn't be standing here, *sixty-eight hours* after her daughter went missing, watching a police officer pull the sheet off Katie's bed and stuff it into an evidence bag.

"The K9 unit can get her smell off of it," Pockmarks says quietly, sidling up to her. "They're sending a team up from the city to start searching the woods."

Marybeth nods, afraid that if she opens her mouth she'll scream.

Underbite adds the sheet to the growing pile of evidence bags in the corner of the room. She asks Marybeth to check the closet, to see if anything is missing.

"The girls have a movie night every Wednesday at the Hoopers'. She'd have taken a set of pyjamas. A change of clothing. Her toothbrush. They'd be in her school bag." They go through the closet together, Pockmarks prompting her to be sure that nothing else is gone. Everything's there, every single one of the awful flannel men's shirts she's taken to wearing recently. Marybeth can't help but feel a rush of shame, on her daughter's behalf, at how huge each one is.

Underbite finally seems to be coming to the end of her list. "Was your daughter taking any medications?"

"Nothing important."

Underbite waits, pen poised above the notepad.

"Diet pills," Marybeth confesses. She doesn't mention that Katie doesn't know she's taking diet pills. Marybeth crushes them up and adds them to her orange juice in the morning. She has no other choice. They've already tried the Ornish diet, the Zone, Jazzercize, but Katie keeps finding ways to sabotage herself. Katie calls her shallow, says things like "I'd rather be pretty on the inside," like politics will protect her. She's got no idea how cruel people can be. But this is what mothers do: they hide the ugliness of the world from their children, so they can believe in goodness for just a little while longer.

Underbite frowns and makes a note. "Did she keep a planner? A diary? Anything like that?"

"She has a journal. Thick. Black leather cover. She's always scribbling in it." Marybeth crosses her arms. "It must be here somewhere."

Pockmarks and Underbite glance at each other. She knows what they're thinking: that's exactly the kind of thing a girl running away from home would think to pack. She has to bite her lip again to keep from snapping at them.

"She might have taken it to school," Marybeth adds.

But they've already turned from her and are searching for it. Pockmarks opens the top drawer in the desk and pulls out a bright orange square of plastic cut into puzzle pieces. The pieces seem half-glued together, shrivelled. He holds it up to her in a silent question.

"No idea," Marybeth responds.

Underbite crouches by the bookshelf and starts going through the books one by one, tipping each one forwards to peer behind it. It's terrible, seeing them here, in this room she knows as intimately as she knows her own daughter's face. And it's all pointless, isn't it? There are no answers here. The answers are sitting in the police station right now, both of them, telling the chief what happened to Katie. And she has to stand here and wait until they decide what to tell her.

She walks over to the window, staring out at the peach tree in their front yard. It's heavy with fruit. She pictures them rotting on the branches, worms crawling through soft flesh.

"Your daughter was a smoker?" says Pockmarks from the floor.

It's the last straw. She turns to him to tell him to fuck off and get out of her house instead of insulting her daughter... only to see him holding a half-empty package of Marlboro Reds. The words die in her mouth.

He shows her where he found it. It's the hardcover copy of *The Catcher in the Rye* that Katie read for freshman English. The pages have been hollowed out, the remaining edges glued together. A secret storage box.

More than the cigarettes, the thing Marybeth is most surprised about is that Katie would ever mutilate a book like this. She's seen her pick up old books at the Salvation Army and sniff them.

"Teenagers keep secrets, Mrs Larkin," Pockmarks says gently. "Trust me, I've got three of my own." He pulls out a white plastic rod the length of his hand. A pregnancy test. Unused. "Do you know if she had a boyfriend?"

Marybeth shakes her head, feeling her scar tingling from how much she's chewed on it.

Underbite takes the book from him and scratches a finger into the hollow. She pulls out a piece of paper, folded up so that the corner tucks into one of the folds, a neat little envelope. Her eyebrows shoot up as she unfolds it. "And this?" She holds it up to Marybeth.

It's a five-pointed star, drawn in thick marker, crudely occult-looking, a rust-coloured splodge in the corner. At the centre of the star is a bird, like a crow, holding up its middle finger.

"Can you tell me what this is?"

Marybeth can't. In fact, for the first time, she's confronting the idea that maybe she doesn't know who her daughter is, at all.

3. YES IT'S FUCKING POLITICAL

KATHERINE LARKIN

SUNDAY, 8 OCTOBER 1995

Dear Diary,

Wait, sorry, that's too familiar of me. We've never formally met. Hello, Diary. I'm Kat Larkin. Or Kate Larkin, or Katherine Larkin, or Ma Bear's Little Katie Cub, depending on who you ask. Never Kathy, thank goat. Pleased to make your acquaintance.

I always thought that directly addressing a diary was one of those made-up things people do on TV, but Donna and Rae have both been out of town all weekend and I'm so bored I'm TALKING TO A BOOK, apparently. That's just the level of excitement you can expect from Little Hope. Like, you can't even turn the town's name into a joke, it's already LITTLE HOPE, c'mon.

It's 1995, and a new millennium is coming, and all the magazines talk about how we're living in the future, and girls have the power now and we can be anything, and capitalism won the Cold War and the whole world's just going to get *better and better* until we all get spaceships and we're all connected by the World Wide Web into one big master brain that spans the whole world (unless, you know, the planet gets fried from the hole in the ozone layer but HEY let's not talk about THAT). It's '90s energy baby!

Except all of that feels like it's happening elsewhere, to other people. Here in Little Hope we might as well be stuck in the 1890s. This whole stupid town is like a gold rush theme park even though everyone knows there was never actually any gold here. But still, we put on a mock gunfight in the town square every Saturday to keep the tourists stopping by for a couple of hours before they head on to Tahoe. It's basically the only industry left since all the factories closed in the recession. Come for the gold rush museum, stay for the alcoholism and ennui!

Only three people I know actually have a computer in their house (one of them's Rae, but her brother barely ever lets her touch it). No, here in Little Hope, girls still have to take home ec and boys get to take shop. Donna tried getting into shop, saying her dad taught her to wield a hammer better than any of the pipsqueak boys in our school, but HA HA HA, like that was ever going to happen. We get movies two years after they come out everywhere else (if ever). We have one CD shop and they have a single rack of what the owner Mr Walker calls "that grungy music" and everything else is golden oldies and pop. Donna has to get her grrrl punk tapes on mail order from Olympia, and it costs her a damn fortune. Here in Little Hope, the most thrilling change the '90s has brought us is a new portrait centre at the JCPenney.

Even our library's filled with books about the past: pioneer days, the glories of the civil war, the transcontinental railroad, but I've been waiting for a YEAR for them to stock the new Anne Rice. It's for Rae, she makes me take them out on my library card and then she only reads them at my house. Vampires are on the long list of Forbidden Demonic Things banned in the Hooper household, a list that includes *The X-Files*, "homosexuals", spaghetti-strap tops, discussions about stem cells, Judy Blume, *Aladdin*, *The Simpsons* and, for some reason that continues to baffle us all, Cabbage Patch dolls.

That dirtbag Fred Stein once tried to throw a "rave" at the old bottling factory. He said he'd managed to get some ecstasy from his brother who goes to college in Oakland, but they turned out to be caffeine pills (April Hollister recognised them, her dad's a long-haul driver). So everyone just got super buzzed on caffeine and danced around to a beatbox playing terrible club music until we were all too wired and were struck with the urge to go do something productive like homework. Some rave.

Here in Little Hope, it feels like the greatest decade in history is happening, and it's passing us by.

It's like one time I asked Ma Bear whether she was a hippie in the '70s, and she blinked and said, "No, all the hippies were in San Francisco." Jeez. Imagine being alive during Woodstock and the civil rights movement and thinking, *You know what, I think I'll just stay in my small town, thanks, and watch a lot of television.*

I really don't understand any adult who chooses to live here. But then, adults are a total mystery to me in general. It's like something happens to you when you turn twenty-five where your whole personality is sucked out of you and replaced with a sudden obsession with real-estate prices and decor from Crate & Barrel. Like you actually become a different person.

It sucks that one day when people ask me what it was like to live through a new millennium, I'll have to say, "I don't know. I wasn't really there."

Sometimes I think if Rae and Donna and I hadn't found each other, we'd be dead. Dead inside, anyway. The three of us should never have become friends. Like, in what universe would you have ever looked at us: a wannabe rebel, a preppy church girl and a wallflower nerd and thought, OH SURE, those three are going to be best friends and change each other's lives forever. But that's what happened.

It wouldn't have worked with any two of us alone. Without Donna around, Rae and I just spend hours ranting about how awful and plastic and ruined the world is. When it's just me and Donna, I always feel kind of slow-witted and dull. And Donna and Rae, jeesh. Within five minutes they're bickering and in ten minutes they've basically dropped emotional napalm all over each other. One time they had a fight about *The Fresh Prince of Bel-Air* that somehow ended with Donna throwing a milkshake over her in the middle of the cafeteria.

But together, something magic happens. Any two of us are dangerous, volatile. But as three, we balance out each other, make up for our worst excesses. Maybe that's why three is always the magic number. Three witches. Three fates. The holy trinity. Body, mind, spirit. Donna, Rae and me.

We'd known each other for years without ever really KNOWING each other, y'know? I mean, there is exactly one high school in the vast metropolis of Little Hope, California, population 8,902, so obviously we'd met. But the first time I remember actually speaking to either of them was at the inaugural meeting of a school newspaper club Rae was trying to start. Donna and I were the only two people lame enough to show up. Donna because the guidance counsellor said she had to; me because I was sick of spending every lunch break hiding in the music room with Kylie Cochrane, who's obsessed with John Stamos and would spend endless hours talking me through magazine cut-outs she'd compiled in her Stamos Scrapbook.

We were all pretty apprehensive of each other, sitting there in Mrs Green's classroom last period. I thought Donna was a poser, with her Courtney Love-imitation smeared lipstick and hand-painted rip-off Babes in Toyland T-shirt (Donna would cut off and sell any part of her body for a real one, but it's not exactly the kind of thing they sell at the Sears in Sacramento). I'd pegged Rae as an annoying suck-up: star of the athletics team, Christian youth leader, Perfect American

Girl. And I guess they both thought I was a dork probably (eh, who am I kidding, they never thought about me at all).

But then Donna pitched a super-smart story about how we should investigate which local stores sell things made in sweatshops, and Rae confessed that her main interest in starting the newspaper club was to have an excuse to skip her Wednesday after-school Bible study group, so she didn't really give a shit what we wrote about, and then the three of us started making jokes about how awful *The Catcher in the Rye* was (which we were being forced to read for English) and how if a girl had been as whiny and entitled as Holden Caulfield, no one would ever have thought it was worth writing a book about, and by the end of that hour that was it, we were friends.

Sometimes I wonder if our friendship would have meant so much to us if we'd lived in anywhere more interesting than Little Hope. That's the real thing that binds us together: all of us are determined not to be anything like the drones that live in this town. We want bigger lives than anything that's on offer here. I'll be a writer, scientist, gentlewoman scholar, Donna will be an actual rock star, and Rae's going to run for governor and single-handedly fix the hole in the ozone layer. We're going to get the hell out of here, the moment we can, and then our lives can finally begin.

Until then, the three of us keep each other sane by being our own '90s experience. We MAKE it happen for ourselves. We can't join raves and revolutions. But we can foment our own quiet revolution right here. A revolution of three.

Anyway, Diary, it's nice to make your acquaintance.

Your new friend,
Kat

FACT I LEARNED TODAY: Ecstasy was invented in 1912! Now I'm imagining what Theodore Roosevelt would be like at a rave.

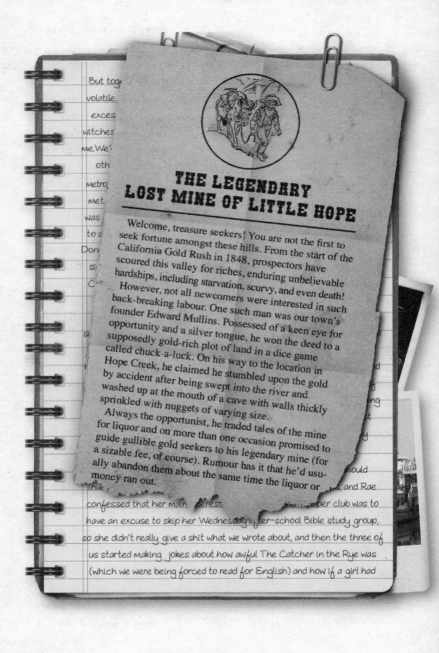

But tog
volatile.
exces
witches
me. We'
oth
metro,
met.
was
to s
Don
si
C

si

THE LEGENDARY
LOST MINE OF LITTLE HOPE

Welcome, treasure seekers! You are not the first to seek fortune amongst these hills. From the start of the California Gold Rush in 1848, prospectors have scoured this valley for riches, enduring unbelievable hardships, including starvation, scurvy, and even death!

However, not all newcomers were interested in such back-breaking labour. One such man was our town's founder Edward Mullins. Possessed of a keen eye for opportunity and a silver tongue, he won the deed to a supposedly gold-rich plot of land in a dice game called chuck-a-luck. On his way to the location in Hope Creek, he claimed he stumbled upon the gold by accident after being swept into the river and washed up at the mouth of a cave with walls thickly sprinkled with nuggets of varying size.

Always the opportunist, he traded tales of the mine for liquor and on more than one occasion promised to guide gullible gold seekers to his legendary mine (for a sizable fee, of course). Rumour has it that he'd usually abandon them about the same time the liquor or ~~s, and Rae~~ money ran out.

confessed that her main ~~erest~~ ~~per~~ club was to have an excuse to skip her Wednesday ~~er~~-school Bible study group, so she didn't really give a shit what we wrote about, and then the three of us started making jokes about how awful The Catcher in the Rye was (which we were being forced to read for English) and how if a girl had

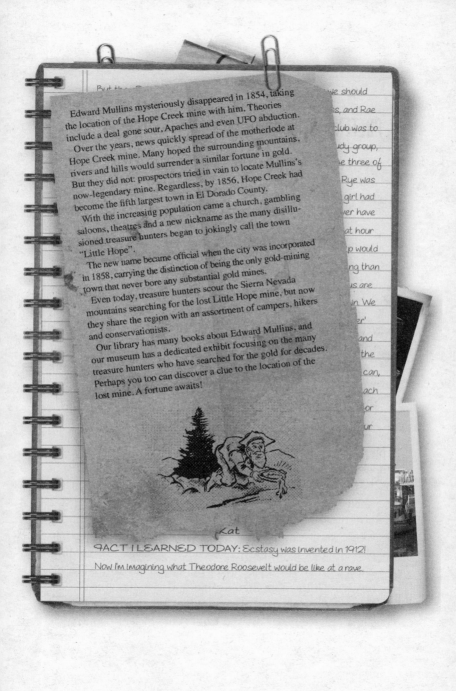

Edward Mullins mysteriously disappeared in 1854, taking the location of the Hope Creek mine with him. Theories include a deal gone sour, Apaches and even UFO abduction.

Over the years, news quickly spread of the motherlode at Hope Creek mine. Many hoped the surrounding mountains, rivers and hills would surrender a similar fortune in gold. But they did not: prospectors tried in vain to locate Mullins's now-legendary mine. Regardless, by 1856, Hope Creek had become the fifth largest town in El Dorado County.

With the increasing population came a church, gambling saloons, theatres and a new nickname as the many disillusioned treasure hunters began to jokingly call the town "Little Hope".

The new name became official when the city was incorporated in 1858, carrying the distinction of being the only gold-mining town that never bore any substantial gold mines.

Even today, treasure hunters scour the Sierra Nevada mountains searching for the lost Little Hope mine, but now they share the region with an assortment of campers, hikers and conservationists.

Our library has many books about Edward Mullins, and our museum has a dedicated exhibit focusing on the many treasure hunters who have searched for the gold for decades. Perhaps you too can discover a clue to the location of the lost mine. A fortune awaits!

Kat

FACT I LEARNED TODAY: Ecstasy was invented in 1912!

Now I'm imagining what Theodore Roosevelt would be like at a rave.

4. PRETEND WE'RE DEAD

TAMMY-RAE HOOPER

"Are you feeling calmer now?" Chief Pittman asks her.

"Yes, sir." But it's a lie. Rae has stopped shrieking, it's true, but only in the way that Lot's wife stopped shrieking when she turned to salt, mind cracked into crystals.

She tries to pull herself back to this room, to this utterly essential conversation she is having. Chief Pittman's desk is a cheap laminate thing dominated by a model steam train, a replica of the real one on display in the backyard of the Little Hope Museum, which doubles as the favourite make-out spot for the town's randy teenagers. Professional family portraits line the shelf behind his desk, all in matching outfits against a muddy studio backdrop. Those kids are grown up now, living elsewhere, some of the lucky few who got out of Little Hope. In the photographs, Chief Pittman is chubby-cheeked and smiling, the cheerful man Rae's seen every Sunday of her entire life, his job involving little more than drunks and speeding fines.

The man sitting in front of her now looks like his malnourished cousin, a refugee newly arrived from some violent country. He could fit everything he owns into the purple sacks under his eyes. Even his moustache droops, exhausted.

"I think you know as well as I do that time is of the essence here."

Rae arranges her face into the one she's practised presenting to teachers, parents and church leaders for years. Attentive. Polite. Trustworthy. But it's taking every bit of her self-control to keep that hideous frightened grin off her face, to keep the low frantic giggle stuffed into her throat. If it bubbles out, they'll all see, and they'll know that she's cracked.

Donna was so out of it. She remembers even less than Rae does. So Rae needs to *focus*. She needs her brain to stop whirling swirling hurling nonsense for a g-d *minute* so she can get this right.

"You said you last saw Katherine on Wednesday afternoon. In the woods somewhere."

Rae tucks her matted hair behind her ears, uncomfortably aware of how sweaty her face is. She tries to channel poise, calm. "Yes, sir."

"You can't tell me where?"

"Sorry, sir. We were so lost. Just stumbling through the trees hoping to get back to the trail. One minute she was behind us, then she was gone. I wish I could tell you where exactly." She allows her voice to wobble just so slightly. "I know we started hiking out towards Wildman's Canyon."

"West? The trail that starts from Black Oak Lane?"

"Yes. But I don't know where we ended up."

All liars will have part in the second death, the lake of fire, that's what the Bible says. But she'll take the lake of fire rather than ever going back into that hole.

"Don't worry, sweetheart. The sniffer dogs will find it, now we know where to start looking. What were you doing out there?"

Rae swallows. Careful, careful. "It's stupid," she says, finally. "We were looking for the mine."

"What mine?"

"*The* mine, sir. The Lost Mine of Little Hope. Kat found a map in some old brochure from the museum and we thought we'd check it out. You've seen *The Goonies*? I guess we thought we were the Goonies. I know it was foolish." The portholes of the model train stare back at her from the desk.

She is lying in the dark. A rich copper smell, sounds of crunching. There is something heavy on her chest, and she runs her hand along it until it reaches a shoe, but the ankle flesh is cold, much colder than living skin should be, and through the gloom she can just see Donna's face, right there next to her, eyes wide open and unseeing.

Chief Pittman clears his throat, bringing her back to this bright office with its model steam train and happy family snaps. "What happened to your clothes?"

Of course. Rae suspects that this fact, of all the terrible facts of this awful morning, is the one already being whispered through town, black mould rooting in the small dirty minds of every person in this whole sick sad little town: *Did you hear? They were naked. Buck naked. Teenage girls.* As though that explains what must have happened to them.

"They got wet when we crossed a river. We hung them up to dry when we slept, and they weren't there when we woke up."

Donna is still swimming in and out of consciousness. Rae holds her head up as she washes the blood off. It's thick in their hair and just starting to crust in the creases of their bodies. She thought she'd got it all, but what if she didn't? The nurse was so thorough, running a tiny spatula beneath their fingernails, taking swabs from between their toes, piling up bag after bag of evidence.

And it wasn't theirs, *it wasn't theirs*.

Chief Pittman looks up from his notes. "Did you see anyone else out there?"

"I don't know. Maybe." *Sobbing as she tried to scramble up the wall of the gully. Donna limp as a ragdoll, too heavy, Rae begging her to help her climb. She gave up; they ran the other way, deep into the ravine.*

His unibrow splits into two arches. "Maybe?"

Rae shakes her head. "No. We didn't see anybody."

"You sure?"

"Yes." *No.* She's sure of nothing, that's the g-d problem. All she has are brief flashes she doesn't understand, like a Magic Eye poster you can't get to snap into place. An image you think your brain maybe doesn't want you to see.

A shape unfolding and unfolding in the darkness.

Chief Pittman's eyebrows have pulled so close together they've met in a single furry track running along the top of his face. "OK, so the three of you skip out on school on Wednesday afternoon. And you go out into the woods to find a mythical mine. Then you got lost, and at some point Katherine vanished. Then you spent the next few days just walking around the forest. That's it?"

"Yes, sir."

"You were missing for almost three days and nights. Is there *anything* else you remember that might help us find Katherine? Any landmarks you passed? Anything at all?"

Rae shakes her head. She feels clammy, like the ice water of the river soaked into her bones and never left. "I wish I knew more." That, at least, is true.

He smooths his moustache again and locks eyes with her. Is that a flash of frustration? Bafflement? "Sweetheart, if someone threatened you, or told you not to say anything, you're safe now."

"It's nothing like that. Honestly—"

They're interrupted by a knock at the door. Detective Knox's head appears, waving the chief to come out and talk to him.

The two men have a hushed conversation in the hallway. Chief Pittman is turned away from her, so she can't see his face.

Rae sits frozen in her chair, small prey pretending to be dead in the face of a predator, but the predator's an oncoming car. Soon, they'll come back, ask more questions, and she's not confident that their flimsy story can withstand much more prodding. She needs to stop this conversation, now.

Chief Pittman comes back in. "Good news, Tammy-Rae. The K9 unit just arrived from the main county office. Sniffer dogs, just like I said. I need to brief them now. We'll talk again later."

Rae's stomach clenches. "Thank you, sir," she says, allowing her voice to crack a little. "I'm so sorry, could I see my parents first? I saw them for just a minute, but I was in shock..."

The chief strokes his moustache. "Of course, of course." A reprieve, for the moment. And maybe a gap to wriggle through.

She stands, and the floor lurches beneath her feet like a ship. She grabs the back of the chair to steady herself. She must still be lightheaded from low blood sugar. Chief Pittman puts a hand on her shoulder and guides her to the door. He gives it a gentle squeeze.

Donna is already in the rec room, wrapped in a tight hug around her dad, Hector. His thin body convulses in silent sobs. Donna's nearly a head taller than him already, stroking his shoulders gently, kissing the top of his head, whispering that she's OK. Someone's found her a beige police shirt and knee-length yellow gym shorts.

Rae's own parents are huddled together on an old green sofa, clutching polystyrene cups still half-filled with milky coffee. Her brother, Brandon, is a sprawl of pubescent limbs on the floor between them, fast asleep. Her mother smiles, and it pulls her lips so thin they vanish. Her father's jaw is clenched tight, like rictus. They don't get up.

Rae, who has learned from a lifetime of fear how to anticipate her father's anger, reads the vein throbbing in his neck like Morse code, spelling a warning. *Good*, she thinks. She can use this.

Chief Pittman hovers behind them, shifting from foot to foot. Any minute, he's going to ask Donna to go with him to his office to answer some questions.

Rae carefully avoids her father's gaze, and goes to her mother. "Mom," she says, opening the valve on her fear just a little, letting it show on her face. "Marybeth was there. She screamed at us. It was horrible."

Her father stiffens, as she hoped he would. "What's this?"

"It's nothing, Dave. She pushed past reception. She was upset, well, you can imagine—"

"She lunged at us, Daddy. I thought she was going to hurt us," Rae says, letting her voice shake. Donna flashes her the withering look she reserves for tattletales and suck-ups.

"Can we take them home?"

"I'm sorry, not yet. I've got more questions for them. I just need a few minutes with the K9 team first."

Her father's eyes narrow. "Zach, it's *my* daughter. Let me take her home so she can wash herself, put on her own clothes." He gestures to the oversized sweater that one of the detectives found for her, hanging almost to her shins.

Chief Pittman smooths his moustache. He might be the chief of police, but her father's a church elder and the town's only veterinarian, which makes him more important than the mayor. "There's still a girl out there, Dave."

"And I'm sure you'll do your job, and find her." He says this softly. David Hooper never raises his voice. He never has to: his steely gaze speaks clearly enough.

The two men stare at each other. Rae's mother stares intently at her hands, squeezed so tight together that the knuckles are white.

Chief Pittman looks like he's going to appeal to Donna and Rae directly. But he shakes his head and lets them go. "I need you back here, as soon as you've rested. Or I'm sending a car to get you." The last bit he says directly to her father, but David's already halfway out the door, waving the rest of them to follow him before the chief can change his mind.

There was an incident last year, that's how they always refer to it, "the incident", involving one of her ex-friends, Ann Mullins, that resulted in her being pulled out of school and bundled her off to "reparative therapy" faster than their school banned Pogs. This feels the same: like everyone's just trying to limit the damage.

Still, it's a reprieve from the questions.

It's brighter outside the station than Rae realised it would be. It must be nearly noon already. The glare hurts her eyes, like the start of a migraine. She still feels lopsided, unsteady. She wishes she knew why.

"Sorry to ask, Dave, but would you mind swinging past ours on your way?" Donna's dad asks. "Don't feel up to the bus, know what I mean?"

Her parents glance at each other. She suspects they were waiting for the moment they got in the car to start their own interrogation. But there's no way to decline Hector's request politely, and politeness is the true Hooper family religion.

They all pile into her mother's Audi, Donna in the middle between her dad and Rae, Brandon tucking himself into the wagon's trunk, and, for once, not even complaining about it.

Donna's head seems heavy on her neck, like she's half-asleep again. Her shirt is bunching weirdly.

"You've buttoned your shirt wrong, you clown," Rae says, reaching over to fix it for her. But her fingers aren't working right. Grasping the buttons is like trying to pick up a toy with the claw machine at the arcade. Her middle finger feels naked without the TRUE LOVE WAITS ring she's worn since she was twelve ("True Love Mates", as Donna calls it).

They hit the road, driving a little too fast, her father taking his fury out on the gas pedal. She wonders whether he thinks something terrible has been done to her, or she's done something terrible. Not that it would matter. Either way, she's shamed him. In her father's worldview, God is just, and people get what they deserve.

Her mom clears her throat and puts on the radio. Shaggy's 'Mr Boombastic'. Hardly the right music for the mood, but better than the silence.

Rae lets her head fall onto Donna's shoulder. Donna leans back, tucking her chin over Rae's hair. Close up, Donna smells of minerals and rot. She smells like the forest.

"Total dick move, by the way," Donna mumbles to her under the noise of Mr Ro-oh-oh-mantic.

"What?"

"Saving my life."

"Why's that a dick move?"

"Well, now I have to give you my firstborn."

"No thanks."

"I could give you three wishes."

"First wish: keep your leaves out of my eyeballs," says Rae, pulling one out of Donna's hair.

"I will if you brush your teeth before you lie on my shoulder again."

Rae checks that her parents' eyes are fixed on the road up ahead.

"Remember what we promised each other?" Her voice is barely a breath in Donna's ear.

Rae's head is close enough to Donna's neck that she can feel the whispered "yes" vibrate in her throat.

"Trust me." Rae closes her eyes. She feels Donna inhale, and for the first time in hours, her own breathing deepens. Tucked together like this, she imagines she can overhear the anxious whirl of her friend's thoughts, like they're melting into one body. She tries to beam the message into Donna's mind: *You're safe. I'll keep us safe.*

They stop at a red light in front of the Dry Creek Minimart. A blue Ford pulls up next to them. Rae recognises the Walkers, who go to her church. Ted Walker does a double-take at the sight of her. Rae closes her eyes until they pull off again.

Donna's head grows heavy on hers, like she's drifting off to sleep. "Promise me we'll find her?" she says, so quiet that only Rae can hear.

Rae squeezes her hand, and stares out the window, trying to figure out how she's going to explain to Donna that Kat's never coming back.

5. THE SCRATCH

DONNA RAMIREZ

"You know why the pancake king lost his kingdom?" Donna's dad asks her, using a plastic squeeze bottle to draw a smiling batter face in the pan.

Donna answers with a grunt from face-down on the pull-out sofa that doubles as his bed.

"He was u-syruped."

"Hilarious, Papi," says Donna, pushing herself to a sitting position. The joke was funnier the first sixty billion times she heard it. It might be even funnier if she wasn't lying here waiting to hear if her best friend is still alive. But she and her dad have exactly two ways of expressing emotion: jokes and food. Her dad seems to be matching the stressfulness of the situation with an equal quantity of both.

Every surface in their tiny kitchenette is already piled high with pancakes, and more batter on the walls than in the pan. Pancakes usually only happen on Sundays, because that's the day her dad has off from work. Not that she's complaining. It feels like she hasn't eaten in months, although she does have a vague memory of somebody giving her a granola bar back at the police station. The whole morning's fuzzy. She still feels weak and weird, like her memories are all there, but they're not really hers. Like a movie she read about but never actually saw. Maybe the pills Rae's mom gave them.

"You hungry?"

"I'm starved."

"Hi, Starved, I'm Hector," he answers automatically, handing her a stack the height of a small child. The grin on his face is bright, forced. His eyes are still rimmed red.

Donna shovels an entire pancake hemisphere into her mouth. It's maple-sweet, stodgy, and the best thing she's ever eaten. A bead of sweat runs down the side of her neck, every system in her body working overdrive to manage the most basic of tasks: digestion, breathing, trying not to wonder where Kat is right now.

Her dad excavates an armchair from a pile of laundry and sits to face her. He works as a finisher at a ceramics factory just outside of town, which sounds fancy until you learn that "ceramics" is just a euphemism for "toilets". He no longer owns pants that aren't covered in grey splatters and impregnated with white dust.

He watches her devour the rest of the pancakes in silence. "Bet you haven't eaten anything since Wednesday."

"There wasn't a KFC in the forest, no," says Donna, wiping a finger around the lip of the plate to mop up the last of the syrup. "And Rae and I aren't getting any Girl Scout badges."

"There's some bacon in the freezer—"

"I should probably let this settle." Although she feels like she could eat the whole meal again, right now. Donna glances at the little plastic clock on the wall, above the framed photo of Roberto Clemente sliding to the home plate at the 1966 World Series that is her father's sole attempt at home decor. "It's been hours. They'll have radios, right? So they can call as soon as they find her?"

"I'm sure they will. It'll probably just take some time for the dogs to find the trail." He leans forward and puts a hand on her arm. "They'll call soon." He knows better than to tell her it's going to be OK.

He's left his rosary out, she notices, in the little nook next to the microwave that houses their bust of *la Virgen* and a dish of stones. A bottle of Bacardi stands as a silent offering to the saints. He hasn't prayed for years, as far as Donna knows. But he's been praying for her.

She wipes a hand across her damp brow. She took a shower as soon as they got home. Jesus, how is she so sweaty already? "Did they have dogs looking for us before?"

"Things were slow. Zach Pittman thought maybe you girls had gone somewhere and forgot to tell us. They spoke to some of your teachers on Thursday, but Zach kept saying he was sure you'd turn up. That teenagers always do."

He's got a point. It's Little Hope, not New York City. Teenagers have been known to vanish for a few days heading to the city or playing hooky in one of the many abandoned buildings around the edge of town.

"The cops finally filed a missing persons report yesterday. They had every officer out looking for you. Peggy Boyd said she saw you three cycling past the Old Church into Eastside so they were checking all the sheds and factories around there. Marybeth and me went door to door, putting up posters, asking if anyone saw you. The Hoopers must have phoned every hospital and motel in the state. The plan was to start searching the forest this morning, but you came home before we could."

Donna frowns, picking up the last pancake crumb from the plate and puts it in her mouth, trying to suck the sweetness from it.

A shrill ringing interrupts them. Donna leaps for the phone so fast she nearly runs into the wall. But it's not the chief's voice on the other end. Much worse: it's her mother.

"Oh, Donna, thank God. Thank God," she sobs down the line. "I was so worried."

"Not worried enough to get in the car and actually drive down to Little Hope, though," Donna snaps.

When Donna was nine and her brother, Jay, was thirteen, their mother decided she'd had kids too young and needed to leave so she could "find herself", a mysterious process that apparently entailed eighteen months of working as a telemarketer in Oregon before marrying a blood pressure machine salesman named Sherman Miller and getting pregnant all over again, starting over with a new family, a family who were all blonde and blue-eyed like her. The first time she came home to visit, Donna poked a screwdriver through her tyres so she couldn't leave. The second visit, Donna locked herself in her room and refused to come out all weekend. There was no third visit.

"They only told me yesterday. They said you'd probably gone to the city. Of course, if I'd known—"

"It's fine. I was just kidding." She twirls the cord around her hand, so tight her fingers tingle.

"I heard you were lost in the forest. They said your friend—"

"Mom, I have to go. The police are going to call."

"The twins want to talk to you—"

"I'll call you all tomorrow."

She hangs up before the phone gets passed around to her mother's stupid upgrade family.

Her dad's watching her, with a sad expression. "She loves you, you know."

"Who gives a shit."

He shrugs sympathetically and takes her cutlery and squeaky-clean plate to the kitchen. She remembers he did this after her mom left, too: just made way too much food, instead of trying to talk to them about what had happened.

"Did you get hold of Jay?" Her brother lives in Phoenix now. Got out of Little Hope about three seconds after graduation and hasn't come back. That's the way things go in her life: everyone leaves.

"I left a message with his housemate. He's on a job. They're expecting him back next week." He waggles the bottle of batter at her. "Hey, do you know why I'm scared of French pancakes?"

"I'm going to take another shower."

"They give me the crêpes."

"Nice, Papi." She stomps to the bathroom before her father can subject her to the whole universe of pancake-related dad humour.

She strips down and catches a glimpse of herself in the mirror. Jesus, she looks awful. Her hair wild, her eyes glowing from tired sockets, skin slick with sweat, like she's coming down with a cold. She feels contaminated, dirty. "An overwhelming sense of ickiness," to quote *Clueless*. It's so much worse, not knowing what happened. What might still be on her body. *In your body*, says a sneaky voice inside of her. Would she even know if she'd been raped? Would they even tell her?

They did a module on the immune system in biology last semester. Mrs Hobbs droned on and on about how your body makes unique antibodies to fight the germs you're infected with. As your body heals, it also learns. It remembers. Even if you do not.

She turns the shower on to its hottest setting, and steps under the stream, wishing it would scald her away, get right to the infected heart of her. She'd like to bathe herself in bleach, power-hose her cells, swallow napalm.

After her shower, she goes to her room and pulls on her most oversized baggy T-shirt and the huge pair of men's jeans she found at the Salvation Army. Puberty really did a number on her, swapped out her real body with this big-boobed, big-hipped, big-lipped replacement. Hair sprouting in new and exciting places, like her upper lip, which seems to be one of those brown girl things that they somehow never mention in

Cosmo. Sometimes she can wear her body like a dare. But right now all she can think is that maybe this body is what got them into trouble. That maybe it's her fault that Kat's gone.

If she could just talk to Rae. She tried calling her earlier, and just got Mrs Hooper's clipped voice telling her, "Tammy-Rae's not up for talking right now," with a thick dollop of *why don't you leave my perfect daughter alone, you bad influence* subtext.

She lies back on her bed and looks around her room. Her dad insists that she has the one bedroom, because he gets up so early to go to work. Everything's as it was: giant jumble of hand-altered clothes in a pile on the floor next to the hand-me-down guitar she inherited from Jay. The vinyl wall cladding is barely visible behind the posters: Skunk Anansie, L7, X-Ray Spex, Sleater-Kinney, Bikini Kill. In pride of place, the poster she made herself for The Nancy Screws' first (and, so far, only) gig at school assembly. It's all the same, but none of it feels like hers any more. All of this stuff belonged to the person who existed before this thing happened to her.

She folds her legs in front of her, tracing the Sharpie drawings on her jeans. Kat always teases her about this, saying that she'll draw on anything if it stays still for long enough. She finds the little magpie on the ragged hem, K.L., D.R., T.R.H. scratched next to it.

Kat. Is she OK?

The phone rings in the other room. Donna wishes the ground would swallow her whole.

She gets there just in time to see her dad press his ear to the receiver. He waves her close, holding the phone between their heads, so they can both hear Chief Pittman.

"My deputies just radioed in. They're on their way back from their search. Look, we're going to need—"

"Did you find her?" The question tumbles out of her dad's mouth before the chief can finish his sentence.

Donna's guts are writhing. She already knows what he's going to say.

There is a long pause on the other end of the line. "We're going to need you to come back into the station."

Her dad's hand wraps around hers. "Was she, is she—"

"They couldn't find her," Chief Pittman says. "We searched where the girls told us to look. There was no trail. No anything. No sign they've been in the woods at all."

Her dad promises that they'll come straight in. He hangs up the phone and turns to Donna, his face carefully expressionless. "*Conejita*, you know you can tell me—"

"I haven't lied, Papi." She pre-empts his question. Truth is, she hasn't had to... yet. They barely asked her anything. From the moment the cops arrived, they directed all their questions to Rae rather than to her. Typical. Always the goody-two-shoes, the teacher's pet, the reliable one.

And she doesn't want to lie. But Rae made her promise.

It was their second night in the woods. They were so lost, and it was raining and mud was dripping on their faces. Donna had asked Rae a hundred times what happened, but Rae hadn't said a word all day, just kept leading them deeper into the forest like she couldn't put enough distance between them and whatever was behind, and she was all grin-twisted and dead-eyed. Then finally, when they took refuge beneath a fallen tree, Rae grabbed her shoulders and told her they couldn't let anyone find the cave. She made Donna promise. They could come back and fetch Kat themselves in a couple of days, but they couldn't lead anyone else out there. She'd never seen Rae look like that before, manic and wheezing and wild.

"But Kat," Donna kept saying. "Where is Kat?"

And all Rae would say was, "Trust me. Trust me."

Rae made her repeat their story a dozen times. Over and over again as they finally stumbled towards the lights of the town, in case they made them take lie detector tests. "It's not a lie if you believe it," Rae said.

Well, that's the problem. Donna doesn't know what to believe.

All she knows for sure is that one of her best friends is missing, and the other wants her to lie about it.

And Donna? As usual, it seems like she's in trouble.

6. EXCUSE ME MR.

MARYBETH LARKIN

SATURDAY, 21 SEPTEMBER 1996

Seventy-four hours.

A small group of journalists clusters in front of the police station when Marybeth pulls into the parking lot. They shout out at the sight of her, rush over to her car, all speaking at once, jostling to get closer. Marybeth wonders vaguely what you call a group of journalists. A gaggle of journalists? Katie would know, she thinks. She's always collecting facts like that. When they find her, she'll ask her.

The only person she recognises is Doyle Hobbes from the *Little Hope Gazette*, holding a tiny digital camera among the array of professional lenses. The rest of them must all be from out of town. This is good, she thinks. They'll put Katie's face on the national news. The more people who see it, the more likely it is that someone will recognise her, will say how they saw her travelling with a man in a pickup truck, lying face down on the side of the road, being dragged into a shed, her severed head in a lake, her body hanging from a tree, sold to a sex ring in Bosnia, her liver cut out and used in a Satanic ritual. *We found her crushed. We found her skinned. We found her dead. Dead. Dead.* She shakes the images from her mind. The private horror movie marathon playing on a loop in her brain.

"Mrs Larkin, does your daughter have a boyfriend?" asks one of these strangers, thrusting a microphone towards her face. *A feeding of journalists.*

Then Detective Underbite is there next to her, grabbing her elbow and steering her through the crowd. "The chief will talk to you shortly," she shouts. A dozen cameras *click click click* around them, like cicadas. *A dazzle of journalists.*

Underbite releases her into the police station lobby, shutting the door behind them. "I'm sorry, Mrs Larkin," she says. "They've been gathering all afternoon."

Marybeth nods, feeling unsteady on her feet. "Can I talk to Zach?"

"In just a bit. He's with the girls now," Underbite says, guiding her towards a bench facing the front desk. "Cup of joe while you wait? My cousin brought me one of those French presses when she visited from Portland. Much too bitter for me, but some of the boys here seem to like it." Underbite squeezes her hand and disappears. Marybeth grasps in her mind for her actual name. Detective Marcus? Marcy? Something like that.

The only other person in the lobby is Mindy LeBell, manning the front desk, the older sister of one of the girls in Katie's class. She's hugely pregnant and holding up a copy of *Seventeen.* Marybeth notes a tattoo on her collarbone, the word SLUT in Gothic print. The girl can't be more than a couple years older than Katie.

Her mind conjures another image. *We found her shot up with heroin on the streets of San Francisco, dying of AIDS.*

Marybeth's tongue starts seeking out the scar on her upper lip. She forces it back into her mouth. She managed to put on some lipstick this time, at least, and she's swapped the cartoon pyjamas for her more usual sequinned sweater and jeans ensemble. Typical, that they'll just leave her waiting around until somebody deigns to tell her what's going on. *Excuse me, mister, sorry to bother you, mind telling me if my daughter's still alive, thanks ever so much.*

She's sat in exactly this chair a dozen times before. In the early days of her and Bill, when she was still naive enough to think that cops were there to help you. The first time he punched her in the face. The time he stuffed all of her clothes into a steel trash can and set them on fire because they were "whoreish". The time he dragged her up the driveway by her ponytail so all the neighbours could see, yelling to the world about what a dumb bitch she was. That was the worst. You think pain's bad, but it's the humiliation that really breaks you down.

It was Chief Pendleton back then. He told her there wasn't much the police could do about her marriage problems and suggested the two of them speak to Pastor Sherman.

Katie doesn't know any of this, of course. Marybeth is determined to give her daughter what she never had: the memory of a great dad. She only tells her the good stuff about him and leaves out the rest. She tells him he was a man with a big personality (huge, it swallowed everything), that he liked to laugh (as he kicked her), that he was the life of every party. That last part is the whole truth, at least. Everyone loved Bill.

This is the great labour of motherhood, to carry all the world's ugliness and suffering so your children never have to know. To make the world beautiful for them. And how she's failed her, how thoroughly she's failed.

She glances out the glass pane of the door. The journalists are still out there, chatting with bright faces like they're waiting for a parade. *An amusement of journalists.* There are two other cars in the lot next to hers: the Hoopers' Audi, and a rusty blue station wagon. There's a shadow moving on the front seat of the station wagon, like somebody might be sitting out there, but it might just be the late-afternoon light catching the windshield.

"Mrs Larkin?" Detective Underbite pops her head out from the inner door, waving her into the back.

Marybeth follows her into the corridor that leads back to the rest of the police station. The place smells unwashed, the stink of too many people working late shifts without a chance to go home. She passes a shift roster, and a poster advertising a team barbecue that would have happened yesterday, had the whole police force not been out searching for her daughter.

Up here it's offices and interview rooms along a long L-shaped corridor, opening up into an open-plan squad room at the end.

They keep the discomforting rooms downstairs: evidence storage, holding cells, the medical examination room. They took her down there ten years ago to identify Bill's body. She almost wishes Katie's body was there now. A terrible, terrible thought. But at least she'd know where she is. At least she'd be able to hold her.

Muffled voices are coming from Zach's office. His door bangs open. David Hooper marches out, red-faced.

Zach follows him out of the room. "Mr Hooper, I have more questions for the girls." Marybeth notices he's reverted to surnames, which is ridiculous since those two men have known each other since elementary school.

Tammy-Rae is standing in the doorway. Her eyes meet Marybeth's. She's back to her usual tidy trim self, in a clean tennis skirt and cardigan, wearing an expression of bland cheerfulness beneath her glossy hair. But her hands are balled at her sides, the veins of her forearms twisted tree-roots, her forehead glistening with sweat.

"You're not going to say another word to my daughter without our lawyer in the room." David grabs Tammy-Rae's hand and yanks her from the office before Zach can say anything else. He takes his daughter by the elbow and steers her to the rec room. Detective Underbite hands Marybeth a warm mug and follows them.

Zach ushers her into his office. "Sorry about that."

"David being David." Thinks he's hot shit, but all his money comes from sticking his arm shoulder-deep into cow vaginas. He's no better than her.

Zach flops back in his chair, looking like he'd trade his entire family for a ten-minute nap. "The dogs couldn't find a trail, Marybeth. I sent my best men. Deputies told me there's not a stone they didn't turn over."

Marybeth looks down at the coffee in her hands. Improbably, there are little marshmallows floating in it like you'd put in hot chocolate. She watches them melt into the liquid. Decomposing. Like a girl's body, left at the bottom of a ravine for seventy-four hours. "Could the girls be lying?"

Zach smooths his moustache. "I don't think they're lying. But I have reason to think they might be confused about what happened."

"What reason?"

"We're exploring all possibilities, I assure you."

"I don't understand, Zach. She didn't vanish into thin air. She wasn't raptured to heaven. The girls must know *something*."

"The important thing is to stay calm. We're doing everything we can do to find Katherine."

Marybeth takes a sip of the coffee. It's as sweet as icing, with more cream than water. "What exactly are you doing?"

Zach's expression flickers. "We can't do any more searching tonight. But we're recruiting volunteers from town to start a full sweep of the woods first thing tomorrow."

Marybeth takes another sip of the syrup-coffee, trying to keep her voice from shaking. "What if she's not in the woods any more?"

"We've got roadblocks all across the state. Her photo's been faxed to every police station in the district." Zach starts reaching his hands out towards her, then changes his mind, and puts them down on the table between them.

"Marybeth, I think we both know what we're looking at here," Zach says gently.

"An abduction—" Marybeth starts, just as Zach simultaneously says, "Experimentation."

Her fingers are turning white from how hard she's gripping the mug. For three days she's listened to smug cops telling her she's being hysterical, talking about how teenage girls might run off with boys, might hitch a ride to the city, might have been *experimenting*, whatever the hell that means. And she's tired of telling them, *No, not Katie. Katie isn't like that. Katie wouldn't do that. Something's* happened.

"My best guess, those girls were out there messing around and got separated somehow. Donna and Tammy-Rae got lost. Most likely, Kat's just lost too. Now, that doesn't mean it's not serious. We'll do everything we can to find her. But there's no need to panic."

"But they were naked, they'd been attacked—"

"There was no sign of assault on Tammy-Rae or Donna. Physical or... otherwise."

Marybeth takes a deep breath, thinking of Amber Hagerman. That nine-year-old who was taken off her bicycle in Arlington and loaded into the back of a van by some psycho. How they found her body five days later in a rain-swollen creek with her throat cut. Maybe if Katie were a few years younger, they'd be taking this more seriously. And what, really, is the difference between nine and fifteen?

"All this media interest," the chief strokes his moustache, failing to keep the irritation off his face, "it doesn't help. Things get out of hand. Wild conjectures. Mass hysteria. Witch-hunts. We don't want any of that. We've got to control the flow of information. You just let me talk to the media, OK?"

"It could help. We could get the word out." Amber's mother was on the news every night, pleading for anyone who'd seen her daughter to come forward.

Zach leans back in his chair, hands withdrawn and folded on his lap. "Find Katherine's journal yet?"

"No." She spent the whole afternoon hunting for it, rooting through every drawer and cranny in the house. She's certain it's not there.

"Sergeant Mercer showed me the drawing you found in Katherine's room. Satanic symbols." He lets that hang in the air, notably not mentioning the other thing they found. "Something like that gets out, it'll be a circus. Trust me. You've got to let me do my job."

She nods, staring at the half-melted remains of the marshmallows at the bottom of her mug, wishing each one was Zachary Pittman's condescending head.

"We can't give up hope, Marybeth," he says, standing, taking the empty mug from her. "Go home and get some rest. I'll call you first thing in the morning."

Marybeth walks back towards the entrance. Mindy LeBell is still at the desk, working her way through a different edition of *Seventeen*. She pushes the door out to the street and the journalists mob her immediately, shouting questions at her.

A screeching of journalists.

A short man with hunched shoulders and oily hair pushes in front of the crowd. He has a hooked nose and reeks of cigarettes, like a chain-smoking penguin. "Mrs Larkin, did you know that Tammy-Rae and Donna were both on drugs?"

"What?" she says, stopping in her tracks.

"The patrol officer who picked them up from the diner says their pupils were dilated and they were ranting like lunatics."

Controlling the flow of information there, Zach. Even from her.

She considers the faces crowded around her. *An intelligence of journalists.* Zach be damned. She turns to the penguin. "OK, tell me everything you know."

7. BAD REPUTATION

KATHERINE LARKIN

FRIDAY, 5 APRIL 1996

Dear Diary,

We arrived at school this morning to find that some asshat had painted the words FREE PUSSY all over Donna's locker.

Before I became friends with Donna, I'd heard a lot of things about her. That she'd had sex with an out-of-town biker who came through for the Frontier Festival last fall. And our gym teacher. And Tim Knox. And half the football team.

Donna loves it when she hears these stories. She always responds with a mysterious smile, as if to say, *HOO-BOY, you don't even know the half of it.*

Of course, she's so busy encouraging these rumours of her burgeoning sexuality that she's never actually gotten around to kissing a boy in real life. Most boys our age are two feet shorter and petrified of her. Donna likes it that way. Truly, I think it's the main reason she encourages the gossip.

Donna didn't choose to look how she looks. Like Jessica Rabbit, she's not bad, she's just drawn that way. Truly, I don't envy her for it.

Rae has actually kissed a boy. Two boys at last count. But that was back when she was one of the popular girls, before she joined the DARK SIDE and embraced her inner weirdo. And I'm pretty sure that she was just doing it to fit in. Rae... well. You know, Diary. Pretty sure she doesn't actually like boys. Jury's still out on whether she likes girls either. Any real sexual feelings she might have are smothered so thick by her church's purity messages it's hard to imagine her ever being able to excavate them out. I hope she does, someday.

In fact, here's a juicy secret for you, *mon journal*: of the three of us, I'm the only one who's Done the Deed. Last summer. Me and Mickey Ramsey came to an agreement about it over IRC. We decided the time, the place, exactly what was allowed to be inserted where, the prophylactic measures to be taken, and that *no*, this would *not* mean that we were dating now, in fact, we agreed to never speak about it ever again.

It's not like I had a crush on Mickey, or any particular emotions about him really. He's OK-looking as far as teenage boys go but I mean, low bar. I chose Mickey because he doesn't have friends, so he seemed least likely to blab to anyone about it. I do NOT want a boyfriend, and I do NOT want a reputation. I don't think I could deal with randos scrawling FREE PUSSY on my locker like Donna.

I just wanted to know what all the fuss was about. An experiment, approached with the same surgical curiosity as a scientist dropping chemicals in a Petri dish. I am nothing if not a very Curious Kat and I will try anything once.

OK, OK. Between you and me, Diary, I was also horny as hell. Teenage hormones are no joke, I tell you.

Donna and Rae asked me what it was like and my knee-jerk response was "sticky". I went on to explain that Mickey had spilled 7UP on the back seat of his car but really it's not a bad description of the whole thing. The whole car fogged up and at one point Mickey's sweat started dripping on my face and he noticed, and he started apologising, but my foot had fallen asleep because of the weird angle it was at tucked under the front seat and I just wanted him to finish so I just held my hands under his chin to catch the drips and told him to keep going.

It felt pretty good (not as good as what I've been able to achieve with just the corner of my mattress). I guess I just expected it to be more... something, I don't know. Emotional? I just can't picture having sex with someone and then throwing my whole life away over it. But women do that all the time. So I just figured that sex must be something pretty damn earth-shattering. Like I expected to start sobbing and suddenly feel this overwhelming connection with him or something.

Ma Bear once told me she wanted to be an air hostess when she was younger. Imagine Ma Bear, all dolled up in a pencil skirt and heels serving champagne in first class, rolling a neat little travel bag into a new city every night, staying up late to joke around with other hostesses in hotel bars in Tokyo and Rome and Delhi and Nairobi and Rio de Janeiro and Cairo and Sydney and Amsterdam. I think she'd have loved that.

But instead, she fell in love with my dad and had me. And she says it's the best thing that ever happened to her, but come on. Sure, she did end up working at a hotel, but her job involves toilet bleach rather than champagne.

And I don't get it, Diary, I really don't. Does this happen to everyone when they grow up? Like, they're sure they're going to be different and special and then one day they're like WHOOPS, I'M DONE HAVING GOALS NOW, BEST FIND ME A MAN AND SQUIRT OUT SOME BABIES! Is everyone doomed to ultimately turn into the most boring version of themselves? Do we all end up just like everyone else?

Maybe if I knew my dad, I'd understand how he was worth giving it all up for. I have this one memory of him, I must be two or three years old, and we're in the backyard and he's lying on the grass, holding me in the air with his feet on my belly, my hands tiny in his, and we're both laughing so hard we could burst. Only... I'm not even sure that's a real memory. It's a photo from the album Ma Bear keeps under her bed. And I think all my memories of him are like that now, not memories of the real thing, just memories of the photos. Bummer, right?

But could he really have been all that great, considering he was murdered by his *girlfriend*? Ma Bear thinks I don't know that, but my dance teacher Mrs Bradley once let it slip. Ma Bear's always saying he was the perfect man but how perfect was he really, if he was cheating on her? I don't even know what happened to the girlfriend, if she's in jail now or what. I guess that she killed my dad because she was jealous he wouldn't leave Ma Bear, or something. It's not like I can just ask her. Ma Bear starts crying any time I so much as mention my dad. So, there's just this big empty space where he should be.

Maybe that's why I've always loved mystery stories. Because there's this one, at the heart of my own life. Who my father was, and why my mother loved him so much she gave up everything for him.

Ma Bear thinks love is the most important thing in the world. It's why she rides me so hard about dieting and being skinny and doing my hair and all that crap. I know that she only wants what's best for me. She sincerely believes that if I'm lovely and beautiful enough, some handsome white knight will rescue me and take me away from all this. As if! I'm the daughter, but Ma Bear is the one who believes in fairy tales. From my vantage point, romance looks a lot like consensual slavery, or slow suicide.

Every boy I've ever met was an idiot. And besides, boys get you pregnant and then you're really stuck. Ma Bear was SEVENTEEN when she had me. YUGH. Imagine being pregnant one year from now!? Sometimes I put my hand on my stomach and imagine what it would feel like to have something in there, feeding on me, getting bigger, like some humanoid chest-burster (only a uterus-burster)?? No thank you!

That's why I keep myself fat. Ma Bear thinks I have no self-control. She doesn't understand that this is ALL ABOUT self-control: it's literally what lets me control my own life. It's what finally got Ma Bear to stop dragging me to those stupid pageants every weekend where they parade girls around and judge them like they're breeding mares. The fat is my armour, fortified by every bag of Cheez Balls and P.B. Crisps, and it protects me and I love it. The fat keeps Ma Bear out of my fucking life.

That's cruel. I do love her, Diary. I just wish she would go live her own life and stop trying to control mine. Because what I want from my life is so, so much more than hers.

That's what I love so much about Rae and Donna. We're united in this: we want more than Little Hope. I can't see either of them becoming one of those dull adults who settle for love (boring) and sex (boring) and babies (triple-boring). I just can't believe that two people who are so themselves and so full of fire and justice and passion and light could just be snuffed out. Everyone says we'll understand when we're older. One day we'll meet the right guy and what we want will change. I won't believe it. I think we'll make it out of this town alive. Not just alive but Alive.

The library has a copy of Sylvia Plath's journal. I've never taken it out, but I pick it up pretty much every time I go and I page through it. It's weird seeing her write about boyfriends and dates and dirty dishes and petunias and neighbours and dresses, in between the real stuff, the parts where she practises describing trees and people, and writes about what she's reading and the art she's looking at. I think it scares me a little, seeing this ordinaryness mixed up in the magic, like it muddies it.

No thanks. I'd rather stick to reading her poems. I like 'Elm' the most, the part about tree roots probing the unknown. I like that feeling of being drawn deep into something dark... following your curiosity, no matter where it leads you (to her head in the oven, in Plath's case).

That's what it means to be Alive: facing the truth. The real truth of something. Even if it's terrible. Or just supremely disappointing, like Mickey Ramsey's penis.

Your ever-curious friend,
Kat

FACT I LEARNED TODAY: A lichen isn't a single organism, it's actually a colony of algae and fungi that live together in kumbaya harmony. Beatrix Potter (yes, the one who wrote the children's books!) was also a pioneering scientist who was one of the first people to figure this out, but OBVIOUSLY nobody listened to her because she had a vagina.

8. TYPICAL GIRLS

DONNA RAMIREZ

Donna and her father sit on one side of a metal table in a bland interrogation room. Facing them are Chief Pittman and Tim Knox, the tall skinny boy he seems to have adopted as his protégé. Of all the dozens of dudes the school rumour mill speculates she's slept with, she finds Tim the most hilarious pick. No one's had the heart to tell him that his goatee looks less *Ethan Hawke* and more *lint that's been pulled out of the dryer and glued onto a chin*.

"How're you feeling?" Chief Pittman asks her. Donna takes it from his tone that she still looks like shit, despite the second shower.

"I think I'm coming down with a cold." She hopes it's a cold, and not something nasty she picked up from drinking the water in the creek.

"She's got a fever," her dad adds.

The bags under the chief's eyes would better be described as luggage by this point, the river of wrinkles down his cheeks deepened by the bare fluorescent lighting.

"Hector, would you consider allowing us to speak privately?"

Her dad looks over at Donna. He seems to read the pleading in her eyes. "No. Sorry, Zach."

"Kids have a habit of... let's say, bending the truth when their parents are in the room."

"She's a minor. I'm allowed to be here."

The chief sighs and pulls out a small Dictaphone and puts it on the table between them. That's new. Somewhere between this morning and now, they seem to have slipped in his estimation from "survivors" to "suspects". So much for Rae's clever fucking plans.

There's a click as he pushes the red record button. Tim's got a notebook out and he's already scribbling something, even though nobody's said a word yet.

"This is Chief Zachery Pittman of the Little Hope Police Department. With me is Detective Tim Knox. Can you please state your names?"

Donna clears her throat and leans in closer to the table. "Donna. Um... Donna Ramirez."

"Hector Ramirez." Her dad doesn't lean forward. He stays back, eyes fixed on the tape machine like it's an angry rattlesnake.

Chief Pittman leans forward with his elbows on the table. "Donna, collecting evidence is a lot like building a jigsaw puzzle. You can't see the whole picture until it's completed."

"Well, you could just look at the picture on the box," Donna says. It just slips out. She gets extra-quippy when she's nervous.

The chief smooths his moustache, ignoring the snark. "Well, there are pieces of this puzzle that just don't seem to fit. I'm hoping you can help us with that."

Tim Knox flips over his notepad to start on the next page. He seems to be scribbling every single word the chief says. He'll probably rehearse this speech to himself later in front of the mirror, she thinks.

She wipes her palms on her jeans, one at a time. They leave

wet marks all over the matching trolls drawn onto each knee of her jeans. "I'll try. Everything's still a bit... warped."

"I want you to take your time now. Let's start on Wednesday. Take us through the day, step by step."

The plastic chair is sticky against her back. "Uh, I went to school—"

"Car or bike?"

"Bike. My dad's truck's broken." Although "broken" sounds like a temporary condition, when really it stopped running two years ago and they haven't been able to afford getting it fixed.

"Do you remember what you were wearing that day?"

"Jeans and a white T-shirt that says NEMESISTERS." Damn, she loved that shirt. She's probably never going to see it again.

"Mean sisters?"

"N-E-M-E." She's not going to try to explain the genius of Babes in Toyland to Zachary Pittman and Tim Knox.

"And the other two?"

"Rae, I think it was a blue sundress and hiking boots. Kat was in denim cut-offs and a flannel. Yellow and black, I think."

"Mrs Larkin mentioned that Kat wore Tibetan prayer bead bracelets. That sound about right?"

"Kat's big into 'Free Tibet'. So, probably."

"OK, go on."

Donna runs a hand through her tangled hair. "It was just a normal school day. We left at lunch. Cut sixth period."

Her dad shifts next to her. But he's hardly going to start lecturing her about truancy in the present circumstances.

"That was..." Tim checks something in his notes. "English class? Mrs Green?"

Donna nods. "It's a double. Last class of the day. We were supposed to be watching something in the AV room. Probably *Romeo and Juliet* for like the millionth time." An exceptionally boring one hundred and forty-nine minutes except for one thrilling glimpse of Olivia Hussey's right boob, where the tape warps from frequent rewinding. "Mrs Green doesn't pay attention to who's there or not. She sits at the back of the class reading Mills and Boon while the movie plays."

"So you left school at one p.m.?"

"Around then."

"Then what? Details, please."

"We, uh. Got on our bikes and cycled out to the edge of the woods. Stashed them behind a bush, and hiked out."

"Hiked out from where?"

"Um... Black Oak Lane." She tries to keep her expression neutral. "I can't remember where along the road it exactly starts. I'm a bit directionally challenged. I used to think that north was just whatever was in front of me."

Tim has covered several pages of scrawl. There doesn't seem to be much point in the Dictaphone.

"Where were you going?"

"We were trying to find the lost mine. Kat... Kat had a map in her journal." Her tongue trips over her name.

"Do you know where she found it?"

Donna shrugs. "School."

"Where at school?"

"I don't know. The library, maybe."

Tim leans in to whisper something to Chief Pittman, but he gives the tiniest shake of his head. *Not now.*

"So you had Kat's journal with you. What else?"

"Just our school backpacks. We took flashlights, snacks, first aid stuff, just in case."

Tim reads from his notes. "Donna, faded grey, covered in patches, old. Katherine, bright yellow plastic. Tammy-Rae, navy canvas, purchased recently."

Donna nods, feeling nauseous. They know so much. Every part of her wants to just get up and bolt out the room.

"You didn't pack tents, anything like that?"

"We weren't planning to be out after dark. We're not idiots." Kids in their town were taught never to be out at night in the woods from the day they were born. A few years ago, a kid called Robbie Colta got attacked by a bobcat and died three months later of sepsis. Chip Eastman, writer, editor and sole staff member of the *Little Hope Believer*, swore he once saw a pack of wolves in there, but Chip also published a monthly column devoted to local UFO sightings, so they took that one with a pinch of salt.

Chief Pittman strokes his moustache. "OK, so you hiked into the woods. Then what?"

"We followed the trail, and then we got lost, and at some point we realised Kat wasn't with us any more."

His eyes scan Donna's face. "The trail that starts on Black Oak Road."

Donna nods, not trusting herself to speak.

The chief flips back a few pages and checks something in Tim's notebook. "Your bike, that's a silver BMX with a red seat, right?"

"Yeah. It had 'Jay' written on the seat. Hand-me-down."

"And you stashed it at the start of the trail?"

Fuck.

"So why do you think it's not there any more?"

She keeps her eyes on her hands, feeling her dad shifting at her side.

"K9 units have gone over that whole stretch of road. There's no sign you were ever there. Now, why do you think that might be?"

Donna picks a bit of grime from her fingernail. "I don't know, maybe your dogs are broken."

The chief glances at her dad, then leans forward, elbows on the table in the classic *you can trust me* cop gesture. "Donna, I know it can be hard to believe that adults were once teenagers too. But I grew up in this town. I know it can feel... stifling. In my day, we used to walk up to Route 49 and hitch a ride to the coast. Things were safer back then. And, well, young ladies dressed more sensibly."

"We weren't hitchhiking—"

"These days, I know some kids, and I'm not saying you, like to break into the old bottling factory and get into a bit of mischief. So I have to ask, is anything like that going on here? If you, Tammy-Rae and Katherine went down there, maybe with some older kids, messing around and things got out of hand, I'm just spitballing here... you need to tell me."

"Nothing like that. We never did stuff like that."

"I just need to know you're telling us everything. I want to solve this puzzle. I want to find Katherine."

"So do I!" She shouldn't be shouting. She takes a deep breath and scratches her fingers on the knees of her jeans to try to calm herself before she blows up.

Her dad shifts uncomfortably next to her. His face is full of concern she doesn't deserve. "She wouldn't lie, Zach. It's her best friend."

Oof, like a punch to her gut.

She should stop this before it goes any further. Just tell the cops everything she knows. She can tell them Rae was scared and confused, she wasn't thinking straight when she told her to lie. Maybe if they leave tonight, they can still find Kat. How long can a person stay alive in the Plumas National Forest, all alone?

She wipes her brow. Somehow, it's covered in a thin film of sweat again. She doesn't know what to say. Rae would know, but Rae's not here. And *screw* her, for making her do this, and not even telling her why.

The chief glances at Tim, who pulls a sheet of paper that was tucked into his notepad and slides it over to them. Words at the top of the page say FORENSIC MEDICAL REPORT, SUMMARY. What follows is a photocopy of neat, cramped handwriting, with a section in the middle highlighted in neon yellow. Donna catches the words "recommend urinalysis to screen for barbiturates, hallucinogens…" Her dad pulls the sheet of paper away from her before she can read any more. His eyes widen.

Chief Pittman leans back, arms crossed. "It's funny, Donna. See, teenage girls wandering around the Plumas National Forest for three days, I'd have expected to see some bumps and scratches. But there was nothing on you. Not one bruise, not one scratch. Just some traces of blood, which we've sent to the labs for analysis. You know it's a crime, lying to the police?"

Her dad stands, pulling Donna's chair back from the table. "Come on, we're going."

"Hector…"

"No. Not if you're going to accuse my daughter of nonsense." He opens the door for Donna, and the two of them spill into the corridor.

Her dad squeezes her hand. He's already marching towards the lobby, talking in Spanish about how her mom's cousin is a legal secretary and might know somebody they can call.

But Donna hesitates. She's just spotted Rae and her father, still sitting in the rec room opposite them. David Hooper is having a hushed conversation into his Nokia.

Rae looks up at her, her hands twisting in her lap.

Donna shifts from foot to foot. "Dad, wait." She turns back into the interrogation room. Chief Pittman and Tim are still seated, huddled over Tim's notes.

"Talk to Ronnie Gaskins," Donna says, loud enough to be sure that her voice will carry. "Ronnie knows where the trail is."

Her dad grabs her hand and leads her away before she can say any more. But not fast enough for her to miss the shock of betrayal on Rae's face.

TWO FOR JOY

9. ARMY OF ME

MARYBETH LARKIN

SUNDAY, 22 SEPTEMBER 1996

"In the search for a missing person, time is our enemy." That's what Zach said when they first reported that the girls were missing. Marybeth had noticed then that he'd used the words "missing person", not "missing child".

It's been ninety-two hours since Katie went missing. She can't stop doing this, counting the hours in her head. Ninety-two hours. Four days. At what point will she start counting weeks? Years?

Zach was curt when she called this morning. Told her they had a new lead they were following up, promised he'd update her when there was anything to update her about, said he'd see her later with the afternoon's search parties, then left her listening to a dial tone.

It's not a surprise. The journalist she spoke to last night had a lot more to tell her about than the suspected drugs. For instance… about something called the National Child Search Assistance Act, and all the things Zach was supposed to have done in the first few hours after the girls were reported missing. No wonder he was so reluctant for her to talk to the press. He's not worried about protecting the investigation; he's worried about covering his own ass. Something she'd been happy to talk about at length, on regional television.

So no, she's not surprised she's not in his good books.

They used to put their faces on milk cartons when she was growing up. There was that girl from Los Angeles who went missing, she'd had the cutest freckles, just like Katie. They found her a year later in a shed in Ohio, pregnant at thirteen.

But she has no idea who you call to get your kid's face on a milk carton. Instead she's here, walking up Broad Street again, replacing the old posters of all three girls with a solo version. The print shop opened up an hour early for her to make them up for her. She's chosen a photo taken a couple of years ago when Katie's face was still more beauty queen than Dairy Queen. Her piercing green eyes regard them from every telephone pole. Each one an entreaty, *Don't forget about me.*

Why "missing person", though, not "missing child"? Sure, fifteen is that strange age, that in-between time. She's seen how men look at Donna, spilling out of those low-cut T-shirts she wears, strategic rips in all her clothing. If those girls were using drugs, then she'd bet her life Donna Ramirez is the one who bought them. She's always hoped Katie would take more after Tammy-Rae, who's recently picked up the incomprehensible habit of wearing hiking boots with her floral sundresses but at least has her hair cut nicely, keeps her grades straight. They're still children, really.

Time is our enemy.

She reaches the gas station on the corner and pulls sticky tack from her pocket to put a poster on the window outside the convenience store. Some of the local kids buying Slurpees inside stare at her openly, until their mother calls them to her. No one's letting their kids go anywhere alone at the moment, in a town where kids usually run around near-feral, left to themselves for hours on end. Maybe that's what she did wrong, she thinks. Maybe if she'd been the type of mom who never let Katie out of her sight, none of this would have happened.

One of her old posters is still up, the one with the three of them at a tailgate party, arms around each other. HAVE YOU SEEN THESE GIRLS? She pulls it down and tacks up the new one: HAVE YOU SEEN THIS GIRL?

She looks closer at the old poster, wondering at their arrangement. Tammy-Rae in the middle, the shortest of the three, her left hand is around Donna's waist, her right hand on Katie's shoulder. Donna, unnaturally tall, leans on Tammy-Rae. Her hand is extended past the edge of the photo, where they had to crop off the middle finger she has extended to the camera. And Katie, beauty-queen smile, she never lost that beauty-queen smile, she's standing a little behind them, to better fit her bulk into the frame.

Those girls were thick as thieves. She can understand them making up this cockamamie story about a lost gold mine instead of confessing that they were getting high. She can forgive it, even. But they'd never actually hide information that could help them find Katie, surely. She can't believe it. Which means they *must have* been so high they don't remember where they were.

But if the girls were intent on trying some potent mystery drug, why skip school to do it and increase their chances of getting caught? Why risk the woods? And, anyway, what kind of drug keeps you high for *three days*?

She checks her watch. Still a couple hours before she has to be at the school for the next round of searches. Time enough to do a little more of the detective work that she has less and less faith the Little Hope Police Department is competently doing.

She walks a couple more blocks up to the hotel. There's no sign of Polly the clerk, so she walks straight through into the wood-panelled bar in the back. Matt Wiley, her boss, is at the counter, peacocking in period-appropriate velvet-trimmed jacket and embroidered waistcoat. He always says it's for the tourists, but Marybeth has witnessed its effectiveness at seducing any attractive young woman who winds up at the hotel bar. Despite the hour, he seems to be working his way through a Miner's Revenge, the bar's signature cocktail. The "revenge" part is a sugar crash, since the thing's mostly yellow Gatorade.

Matt does a dramatic swoon at the sight of her. "Oh Marybeth, *no*. You don't have to come in until you're ready." That wasn't even a question in her mind, but it's nice of him to say anyway. She's sceptical of how long his largesse will last, though. Matt is ever the showman, great at grand gestures, but she's learned not to expect follow-through. Soon as the first toilet clogs (which won't take long; Matt's happy to spend thousands continuously renovating the bar but too tight-fisted to have updated the sixty-year-old plumbing system), she'll be expecting a frantic phone call.

"Actually, I wanted to ask if anyone came through midweek. Out-of-towners."

Matt comes over to her side of the counter. "A group of burnouts headed down to Yosemite. A retired couple doing the gold route. Encyclopaedia salesman stopped over on, oh, must have been Friday night. That's it, I think."

"Can I get a copy of the register?"

"Of course." He squints at her but doesn't ask any more about it. They head back to the lobby. Polly's appeared, legs up on the old oak front desk like she's been there all along. Her face flushes at the sight of Marybeth. She sometimes bumps uglies with Tim Knox, so who knows what kind of nonsense she's heard about her daughter by now.

"Sergeant Mercer's been trying to get hold of you," Polly says, her voice lazy. "I thought you weren't in today, sorry."

"I'm not," says Marybeth, her heart hammering as she picks

up the receiver and dials the station. She's not sure who Sergeant Mercer is, until she recognises Underbite's voice on the line.

"*There* you are. We found a trail." She wastes no time. "Zach went over to Ronnie Gaskins's for a friendly chat. He looked like he was about to go all *Rambo: First Blood* on him, yelling that it wasn't fair that he was going to be blamed for every bad thing that happens in this town 'cause of something that happened when he was a kid. Refused to let them search his house without a warrant. Couldn't stop us from searching the perimeter, though. Their bicycles were stashed behind a bush just behind his house. The dogs picked up her scent on a path that runs from his backyard into the woods."

Marybeth twists the cord in her hand. Ronnie's house is in Eastside, as far from Black Oak Lane as you can get and still be in Little Hope. A creepy old place right on the edge of the forest. She spent plenty of time there as a teenager, babysitting him when he was just a kid. Before he murdered his parents.

"Did they find anything?" she asks, her voice a croak.

A pause. "There was some kind of problem with the dogs. Followed the trail fine for an hour or so, then they got spooked by something. Might have been a bobcat. They're sending a fresh team over from Sacramento. But this is good, Marybeth. Now we know where to start looking."

"And Ronnie?"

"Zach's in the interrogation room with him now, and there's a team searching his home as we speak. Clear probable cause."

"So what should I do?"

"Just hang tight, Marybeth. I know it's hard. I'm heading to the school in just a bit to start wrangling the volunteers. Meet you there?"

She hangs up. Matt and Polly are both staring at her, failing to hide the greedy curiosity on their faces.

"The register, please," Marybeth reminds them, more for something to do with her hands than anything else.

Polly hands over the book and a blank piece of paper stamped with the hotel's letterhead. The interesting part over, Matt slinks back to the bar.

"How are you holding up?" Polly asks her, as Marybeth copies out the names.

She can't even begin to answer that.

"I've got some Zoloft, if you want. Or Chinese herb capsules." In addition to being the hotel clerk, Polly's also a one-woman black-market pharmacist.

"I'm good, thanks."

"Well." Polly blinks, all innocence. "At least you get a few days off."

10. ICICLE

TAMMY-RAE HOOPER

"Sure you're up for this?" Rae's mom asks as they pull into the parking lot behind the church.

"I said it's fine, Estelle," her dad snaps, getting out the car, shrugging his sports jacket on and hurrying towards the hall.

Her mom leans around the seat to give Tammy-Rae a conspiratorial eye-roll. Usually, when her dad's in a mood like this, he skips church and spends the morning fixing something in the garage, and they tell everyone he's got a migraine. A migraine is what you say, because of course grown men don't throw tantrums. But they'd all agreed that it was an important show of face for them to come to church together today. A united front.

Nobody asked *her* if she was up for this, she notices: the one who's actually been through something. She is *not* up for this, by the way. After they got home last night, she spent the evening being interrogated by her dad, questions she had no answers for. It was nearly midnight before he gave up and went to bed, leaving her to lie in her room in the dark trying to keep her mind from dwelling on foul thoughts.

She feels shaky now. Clammy. And ravenous, despite the four bowls of Dino Pebbles she ate for breakfast. She supposes it's lack of sleep, the stress she's been holding in her body. Whenever she's felt this wound-up before she's had to cut herself to release the tension, but she was too afraid, last night, to even get out of bed, to fetch the old Game of Life box where she hides her razor blades. Just lay there, staring into the dark, trying to make sense of the impossible images chasing each other around her brain, a toxic stew of guilt and worry and fear and *fury* that Donna can't stick to a simple g-d plan, when all she's trying to do is keep them safe.

Once, when she was seven, her parents took her to see a child therapist in Sacramento, worried that she barely seemed to speak. The therapist had cards, with little pictures on them. A girl, standing next to a broken glass with water spilled out. A girl, surprised by a mouse, shocked. A mouse, drinking water on the floor. A girl, picking up a glass of water.

Can you put these pictures into a story? That was the question.

Wednesday afternoon starts out clear enough. Skipping afternoon classes to make sure they'd have enough time to get back before dark. Hours of hiking along Ronnie's trail until they finally found the ravine, which was even harder to climb down than they'd thought it would be, Donna just about broke her leg. But the cave was there, just where they hoped: a narrow slit into rock. Rae tried to convince them to tie scarves around their mouths in case the air was foul, but Donna rolled her eyes and just ploughed in. The sharp shriek that followed is seared into her forever.

But after that... it's still just flashes. Scenes that don't connect with each other in any order she can understand.

Can you put these pictures into a story?

Donna, skin slick with blood, lolling against her as they

stumbled over rocks. Rae was begging her to move faster but it was like she was sleepwalking. Something was wrong with Rae's brain too, because the soil was alive and she could hear it eating.

Donna, running ahead of her. Bashing through bushes and howling Kat's name.

Pulling uselessly at vines to try to climb up a cliff-face, sobbing as they pulled out by the roots, roots like tangled hair.

Standing in the stream, scrubbing the mess off them.

And the worst thing. The thing unfolding itself in the dark. *The monster.*

No matter how she tries, she can't keep it out of her mind. The image gets clearer the more she thinks about it: teeth like hooks around a round gullet, hooks the size of hands, lining a window into nothing. Rearing seven, eight feet above her.

What can she do with that picture? How is she supposed to just keep going about her life knowing that *that thing* is out there in the woods, and it ate her best friend?

Brandon interrupts her thoughts, opening her car door for her, all gentlemanly. He's always on his best behaviour when her dad's in a temper. Fair, since he's most often the target of it. Brandon never learned how to surf the waves of their father's moods like she did.

The three of them follow him towards the geometric red-brick building that's been Rae's prison every Friday night and Sunday morning of her life. The New Church, they call it. The Old Church, a tiny white clapboard building in the centre of town, has no AC and is only used now for occasional weddings by out-of-towners who value "character" over air you can actually breathe.

They're quickly swarmed by her mother's friends from the various inscrutable church committees that fill her days. A blur of pastel skirts, demure cardigans. They coo over Rae, saying they prayed for her, they're so glad she's safe, it's a miracle from God. Her mother smiles at her, face full of pride, glowing in the attention. It's only among these women that her mother ever seems to come alive; at home, she shuffles around like a semi-sentient mannequin. Rae tries her best to smile and nod, play her part, be the good dutiful daughter, hoping they don't notice how pale she is, how unsteady on her feet, how broken inside.

"Did you see Marybeth on the news?" she hears someone whisper behind her.

"Terrible," comes the response. "What she said about the police keeping her in the dark. The drugs."

"If it was my daughter..."

Rae puts her arm out to steady herself against the wall, her breath shallow. If this is how bad the rumour mill is now, how much worse is it going to be when they inevitably arrest them?

Mrs Boyd, the syrupy Sunday school teacher, notices her swoon. "Oh, honey, come sit down," she says, guiding her inside the church. "You've been through so much," she coos. She guides Rae right to the front row, pride of place, places her there, where everyone can see the back of her head. Their little celebrity.

Brandon's already there. He wrinkles his nose as she slumps onto the bench next to him. "Take a shower sometime, Hammy-Rae," he whispers.

Their parents sit next to them before Rae has a chance to punch him. Her mother smells slightly sour, and Rae suspects she's fortified herself with the gin she keeps hidden in the spare wheel compartment in the trunk of the car.

Pastor Sherman gets up on stage and starts a prayer. He's got long grey hippie hair and loves to tell people he was at Woodstock (by which he means he camped outside the gates trying to convince people not to enter that pit of sin). "Thank you, Lord Jesus, for the safe return of our daughter." She hears the murmured "Amen" respond everywhere, like dozens of mouths on a single body. *Our daughter.* The word settles heavy on her. A claim, a responsibility. Her mother reaches for her hand and holds it too tightly.

The rest of the service follows a similar theme. It's the Parable of the Lost Sheep. Pastor Sherman's never had a very sophisticated understanding of metaphors, figures he'd go for the most obvious thing. He speaks about how true believers will never be forsaken by God. Rae feels her mouth screw up in distaste. Because what's the implication: that Kat isn't a true child of Christ, so she wasn't worth saving? That God chose to let her die? That God chose to let her be swallowed like a stone, a long moan, a pile of bone?

Rae lets her head tip back and feels her breathing slow as the sermon dims to a distant drone.

The blond wooden beams of the roof soar overhead, like the ribs of some giant creature. She used to sit in here and imagine that she was Jonah, swallowed up by a great white whale. She's never liked how white everything is in here, clean lines, the smooth minimalist wooden cross above the stage backlit with LEDs, the morning light shining through the clear windows along either side, as though through gills. It seems so dishonest, being in this modern clean space when all the stories they tell in here are so dark. She always preferred the way Catholics do it, worshipping beneath a life-size model of the bleeding Christ. *My God is a blood-soaked God. My God smells of guts and gore. My great God of suffering.*

But she doesn't believe in any of this any more. Not for years. Donna and Kat even held an unbaptism for her in Donna's backyard. They smoked cigarettes, burned her WWJD bracelet, made her say "holy shit" a bunch of times and drew Satanic symbols until they declared her Unborn Again. It was the day the three of them became blood sisters, deciding that friendship would be their new religion. No, she stopped believing in God and demons years ago.

So why does she have a *memory of seeing one*?

She should say a prayer to Scully, our lady of *The X-Files*. *Hail Scully, mother of sceptics, hallowed be thy pantsuits. Thy lab work come, thy science be done on autopsy table as it is in fields of creepy crop circles. Debunk this day another conspiracy theory, and save us from stretchy serial killers, gross mutant monsters and alien abduction. Amen.*

The pastor drones on and on, just background noise. She imagines herself floating up to the white beams, being cradled there in the nothing. She wishes Kat and Donna were here. The longing for them is so intense that it's like a physical buzz emanating from deep at the base of her skull. She wants them to hold her, just hold her and tell her it's going to be OK.

She has sometimes wondered, lying in her twin bed late at night, if her love for them is as wholesome as she pretends. If what she's convinced herself is the purity of friendship is something perverted, that she actually wants to *fuck* them. She cringes at the word, even just in her head. The snake in the garden, the cuckoo in the nest, that's what she is. The rotten core. The one who deserved to die.

Eventually, her mother gets up and takes the pulpit to plead for volunteers to join the searches later today. Rae turns over her shoulder to watch the rest of the congregation. They all nod in serious agreement. Rae's sure they all will be out there later, good Christian soldiers doing their duty, but secretly thinking, *This is what you get.*

It's an interminable time until the church regurgitates them onto the neat lawn out back. She notices that Chief Pittman's not here. First time he's missed a service in years. Where is he? Is he there, right now? Has he found the cave? Is he in danger?

Are *she and Donna* in danger?

Her mother vanishes, probably to the car and her hip flask. Brandon and some other boys are sitting on the low wall between the lawn and the parking lot, laughing about something crass. She envies his easy laughter. There's such freedom in being the fuck-up kid, the one no one expects anything of.

Her father holds court with the rest of the church elders. He leans over to say something to Dr Abrams, who used to lead Bible camp until one too many teenage girls said he'd "inspected their virginity", which was enough to get him removed from the Bible camp committee but not the church. Her father helped cover the whole thing up, of course, and led a sermon admonishing the young women to be more conscious of how they dress.

He was so relieved when Chief Pittman told him there wasn't any sign she'd been raped. That would have made her chewed-up gum, worthless in the eyes of any future husband.

She keeps catching people sneak glances at her like they're daring each other to go over. All of them want a piece of her. All of them would just love to ask her what happened out there. They want her to relive the gory details.

They should be careful what they wish for. She's got gore galore.

Rae figures the best way to be invisible is to look busy. She moves over to the coffee station and starts loading dirty mugs onto a tray. She's thinking that there might be nobody in the kitchen. She could just stay there, buy some time until they have to leave. There might even be leftover snacks that could quell the gnawing in her belly.

An unexpected wild-haired head appears in the doorway to the Sunday school room. Donna gives her a small wave, then vanishes back inside.

Donna's never been anywhere near the church before. It's strange, seeing her here after longing so badly to talk to her, like she summoned her telepathically.

Rae picks up the tray of used mugs and walks over, trying to look nonchalant while her heart hammers in her chest.

The room's deserted; Sunday school doesn't start until the afternoon. Donna looks terrible. She's leaning against the wall, working her way through a tub of Dunkaroos. Somehow, she seems even messier than when they got back to Little

Hope: her hair a tornado, her face covered in a thick sheen of sweat, her bright lipstick refusing to stick to the bounds of her lips ("lip-liner's for cowards", a classic Donna-ism).

Rae puts the tray down on the floor and leans next to Donna, avoiding the window, so no one will see her if they happen to glance down at the Sunday school room. Donna silently offers her a cookie, which Rae wolfs down in one bite. There are only a couple left in the tub. She immediately feels better, now that Donna's here, like the buzzing in her skull is dialled down to a hum.

"Been out here long?" she asks, gesturing to the crumbs.

"A while." She finishes the final cookie and scoops up the last of the frosting with her finger. "I tried to call you last night but your mom hung up on me. You OK?"

"Not particularly. You?"

"No, I feel like shit." Donna tosses the empty Dunkaroos tub into the trash. "And I don't understand what the fuck's happening."

Rae nods, miserable. "Tell me about it."

Donna turns to her, scowling. "I mean *with you*. Your whole stupid plan. Leading the cops on a wild goose chase."

Rae frowns back. "The plan you ruined, you mean. Thanks for that."

"Well, sorry. I'm not as practised a liar as you."

That stings. Her old friends used to call her two-faced. No one understands that Rae's had to lie every day of her life, just to survive. "Believe it or not, I was just trying to protect us."

"You're acting *deranged*." Donna cuts her off. "Which is really more my brand than yours, you know." She shakes her head. "I've tried to do what you said. But you said we could go back for Kat, and it's been *days*, and all this while she's been out there alone,"

"She's not." Rae shuts her eyes. She doesn't want to be having this conversation. She doesn't want to be the one who has to say it.

Donna's face freezes. "Because she's dead?" she asks quietly. Rae turns away.

"Is Kat dead?" Donna asks again, loudly now. Anyone walking past could hear them.

"Shh, please!" Rae says, glancing through the window, making sure no one has noticed them here.

"Rae, *tell me what the fuck's going on.*"

"OK. OK." She takes a breath to steady herself. "What do you remember?"

Donna grabs a lock of her own hair and starts chewing on it contemplatively. "Not much. After the cave, it's all a blank until we were back in the forest. And even then, that whole afternoon's... blurry."

"You went in first, do you remember that?"

Donna shakes her head.

"I said not to, *I said*, but you just barged in without thinking, and you screamed. So Kat and I rushed in to see if you were all right."

"And then?"

"I don't know. Same as you, I blacked out. That's true. But I remember...waking up." She moves away from the wall and starts pacing the room, being careful to stick to the side that's not visible through the windows. "It was dark and you were lying next to me, passed out. Then I looked up, and there was something else in there with us. Like a—" She throws a glance at Donna, who's watching her with huge eyes. "This huge thing, like a snake, but long teeth and this mouth that was round, and just... a black hole."

A creature rearing bloody, eating its way out of her belly, Kat's belly, Kat's dead body's belly.

She's too scared to look at Donna and see disbelief on her face. So she keeps pacing.

"And it was on Kat. No, it was—" She squeezes her eyes shut, feeling tears spilling out onto her cheeks. "It was coming out of

Kat. And she was dead. Like just these dead eyes, watching us.

"I grabbed you and I ran. And you were so heavy, but I had to get us away from there. We were both covered in blood. I thought we were hurt, but I got us to the river and washed it off and there weren't any cuts on us at all. Look, *I know this is crazy*, OK. But that's... that's what I saw." She stumbles into silence. Her eyes drift to the children's drawings on the walls, primary-colour gouache paintings of Noah's ark, the serpent, multicoloured stick figures holding hands around a world. There's a bright hand-sewn banner hung above them, emblazoned with the words *What Would JESUS Do?* Honestly, Rae has no fucking idea. Let people think you're dead then vanish for three days? Been there, done that.

"Are you done?" Donna is looking at her, with her brows furrowed.

"I'm sorry I didn't tell you. But I mean, how could I?"

Donna comes over to her and touches her hand gently. "Rae, you're a fucking idiot."

"I... what?"

"You know how they said we seemed high, when we came back?"

"Yeah. It's the reason I'm not going to be allowed out of the house again until I'm eighty."

"Well, I don't remember any of us being drug fiends. Unless you *really* had a secret life you weren't telling me about."

"You know I didn't."

"Right. So..."

"So you think I was hallucinating?"

Donna runs a hand through her hair, leaving it even more mad-scientist than before. "It makes sense, right? Like, maybe the creep who ambushed us in that cave, maybe *Ronnie*, maybe he drugged us. Roofies or something. And then when you woke up, you were still high and you were scared, so your brain made up this thing. It's, like, a false memory."

"I... what?" Rae takes a second to process this. It's the first glimmer of hope she's felt in days. She sits on one of the tables, pulling her knees up tight to her chest. "Or maybe a gas in the cave."

Donna pulls the hair back into her mouth. "A gas didn't dissolve our clothes, though."

"But what if it's real? What if there's actually a monster out there?"

"Dude. Come on."

Rae puts her hand on one of the kids' paintings in front of her: one of the giants from the Old Testament, holding hands with his normal human-sized wife, a Nephilim. Her mind is full of nonsense like this, littered with demons and horrors, half-remembered stories from her childhood. Creatures from Revelations, the beast full of bees with the face of a man, teeth like a lion. Biblical nightmares. There would have been plenty of monstrous raw material for her mind to draw from. And the fact that it was coming out of Kat's *belly*, well, that makes a sick kind of sense too.

But even so. Even if her mind did invent some monster, what if it was doing so to paper over some true memory, some trauma, some horrible thing? What could be worse than the thing she remembers seeing?

"But what part did I hallucinate?" Rae says, at last.

"Well, the monster, duh."

"And Kat being dead? And if there wasn't a monster, why were we covered in blood? Whose blood was it? Do you understand what I'm saying?"

Donna slumps down next to her. "When are you talking to the police again?"

"My dad's still insisting that our lawyer's there. He's coming up from San Francisco this afternoon," Rae says, checking the window again.

"Well, hooray for you. Best we managed was a ten-minute

call with someone at a legal clinic." Donna gets up, starts pacing around the room, right in front of the windows. "We should be out there looking for her."

Rae frowns. "Please, just come here."

"We should just go to Chief Pittman. We can tell them where the trail really is."

"We don't have to. They'll find it now that you've led them to Ronnie's. They've got sniffer dogs." Something she never even considered, when she first came up with their lie. Some criminal mastermind she's turned out to be. "If we change our story now, it will just make us look more guilty."

"How can you *possibly* be worried about getting in trouble at a time like this?!" Donna's voice is turning into a shout.

Rae can feel herself turning colder in response, enunciating her words. "Donna, just stop and think for a second." Then adds, "For once."

Donna's face flushes. Rae can read her mind well enough to know she's trying to stop herself from saying something, and losing the battle. She even knows what she wants to say. And she can't bear to hear her say it.

"They're going to notice I'm gone," Rae says, glancing back at the thinning crowds on the lawn.

"Rae, why would someone let us go and not her?"

"I've got to go." Her voice is wobbling. Rae slips off the table and heads towards the door. She's thought this too, of course. Even more than the monster, this is the thing that's too awful to think about.

Donna's voice calls across the room as Rae leaves. "Rae, what if she was still alive, and we left her there?"

11. WHAT ARE LITTLE GIRLS MADE OF?

MARYBETH LARKIN

SUNDAY, 22 SEPTEMBER 1996

Marybeth is satisfied at the number of cars parked outside the high school. Friday's search party was barely two dozen people. She's spent the last couple of hours calling into every local radio station she can, pleading for extra eyes and feet to join in. Probably said more than she should have. Mentioned Ronnie's name and everything. Zach won't be pleased. But whatever keeps people talking, whatever gets them here.

Now it looks like half the town has shown up. *I did this*, she thinks to herself. *I brought all these people here for Katie.* For the first time in days, there's a small flame of hope alive in her.

She makes her way through to the gym. Throngs of people are milling around, gathering in little clumps that represent allegiances and grievances built up over decades. High school never really ends in a small town. She scans the faces: Lionel Abrams, the town doctor; Louanne from the diner; the mayor (and butcher), Nate Griffis; some students from Kat's class; teachers; Pastor Sherman; even Bud Clarke, who once jokingly started a group called Drunks Against Madd Mothers. Her penguin-looking friend waves at her from the small huddle of journalists near the front doors. The sea of colour is broken up by khaki police uniforms, including a pair of out-of-towners standing near the back of the room with two Alsatians.

Hector's on the bleachers, deep in conversation with Principal Keyes. Both Donna and Tammy-Rae are conspicuously absent, but that's fair enough. Once she has Katie back, she's going to want to lock her up and never let her leave the house again. Let alone go near the woods.

She makes her way over to Estelle, holding court with a crowd of the women Marybeth thinks of as the Twinsets. Well-off housewives with manicured hands. Lucky them.

Estelle flinches at the sight of her. Maybe it's survivor's guilt, that their daughter's back and hers isn't. Or maybe what she's seeing on her face is just *guilt* guilt. Would Tammy-Rae have told her the real story? She never seemed particularly close to her parents. In fact, Marybeth once remembers her joking that she wished she could just come live with her and Katie. That was on one of the rare occasions the Hoopers had let the girls come for dinner at her house. They always said there was more "space" for the girls at theirs, but really it was clear that they didn't trust Marybeth to follow their ridiculous rules about appropriate television. Estelle's a decade older than her and acts like that makes her the only real parent.

Marybeth forces her face into a smile. "How's Tammy-Rae?" she asks, really hoping they'll tell her *where is* Tammy-Rae.

"Resting." Estelle shrugs, pursing her lips. She has a spot of mascara on her brow. Marybeth remembers how she sobbed when they went together to the police station, that first terrible morning. How she'd felt briefly like they were a team, two mothers who'd do anything to find their daughters.

"Help me with something," she starts, trying to sound as casual as she can. "The girls never told you they were going to be back late?"

"No. As far as I knew, they were safely watching videos in our basement, same as every week."

"But you didn't see them?"

"It was a miscommunication. I had a cell meeting that ran late. I called to leave a message for David asking him to make dinner for the girls and get them to bed. But he'd been called out to an emergency breach birth. Brett Collins was worried he was going to lose his best breeding mare. He only got in at dawn. I came home at around ten and caught David's message on the machine. The house was quiet. I figured the girls were already in bed. But I should have checked. I can't tell you how bad I feel that I didn't."

The girls couldn't have known David wouldn't be home. So whatever the girls were planning, they thought they'd be back by nightfall.

"If I could just talk to her directly..."

"Our daughter is not going to be interrogated by you," David says, appearing smoothly. He runs a hand through his hair, far thicker than a man his age should have by rights. An enormous silver Rolex flashes on his wrist.

Estelle puts a hand on her husband's shoulder, gives him a look. "Tammy-Rae's been through so much. She needs some time." Her voice is honeyed, polite, but the meaning is the same as David's: *Stay away from our daughter, bitch.*

Marybeth nods, hearing blood pound in her ears. "Thank you for being here," she says, stiffly.

"Of course. We all want to find Katherine."

David puts his arm around Estelle, gives a curt nod, and steers them both away.

A woman leaps to fill their place in front of her, someone she's never met before. Probably a bit older than Marybeth, and she looks it. Grey hair peppering frizzy dark curls, sun-weathered face, unfashionable blue eyeshadow. A scruffy white Maltese poodle pulls at a leash in her hand, its eyes fixed on the Alsatians. The woman is wearing a T-shirt with FBI emblazoned on the front. Marybeth's momentarily taken aback, did her TV interview last night summon even the FBI? Until she looks closer, and reads FIRM BELIEVER IN JESUS underneath.

"Laney Harring," she says, thrusting her hand out. "I saw you on the news last night. Frank and I got right in the car and drove straight down from Reno. Didn't we, Frank?" She says this to the dog.

"That's so kind." Marybeth smiles at her, gently trying to pry her hand loose. She's just spotted Zach entering the hall. Why is he here, not strapping Ronnie Gaskins to a chair and pulling out fingernails until he tells them what happened?

But Laney isn't letting go of her hand. She grips it tightly, her eyes shining. She reaches into her pocket with her left hand and pulls out a tiny plastic photo album. She holds out a photograph of a boy, nine, ten years old, face covered in ice cream. He has the same dark curls as Laney.

"My boy. Byron," she says. "Missing twelve years. His twenty-first birthday's coming up in November." Marybeth notes the present tense. "We're still looking for him. We haven't given up. But when I saw you on the TV, it took me right back. Those first few days..." She shakes her head, squeezes Marybeth's hand harder. "Well, I just knew I had to come out and help."

Marybeth isn't sure what to say. She glances at this woman's crow's feet, her brittle hair, the sadness etched into her face. *Twelve years*. She wants to shake this woman off her, get far away from her. She feels like an omen, here to shatter her optimism. A visitation, a vision of her own worst nightmare.

"You just can't give up hope," she says, dark eyes boring into hers. "That's the hard thing. Don't give up hope."

"I won't." The words catch in her throat.

Suddenly Zach's there. "A word, Marybeth?" He's all business today, gruff, no trace of his usual soothing voice, no smarmy *I'm here to help* bullshit smile. An improvement, Marybeth thinks. She'll take his anger over his condescension any day.

Laney finally releases her hand and melts back into the crowd. Marybeth shivers, like somebody just walked over her grave.

Zach guides her to the table near the back of the room where cops are dividing up small stacks of registration sheets and clipboards. Detective M-whatever with the underbite gives her a friendly wave. Zach leads her past the others and takes her to a quieter spot near the bleachers.

"Where's Ronnie?" Marybeth jumps in at once.

"I had to let him go. We didn't have enough to detain him, and Hector refuses to let Donna be interviewed again unless we arrest her."

"Zach, what the *hell*—"

"He's got an alibi, Marybeth. A good one. That mutt of his got hit by a car Wednesday morning, so he was at the vet's all day, right up until they closed. David confirmed it." Zach frowns at her. "I do listen to the radio, you know. You're making it very hard for me to do my job."

It's probably not a great idea to tell the chief of police who's leading the hunt for her daughter to go fuck himself. She takes a deep breath, and decides to just ignore his comment. "I spoke to Matt. Here's a list of all the out-of-towners who came through over the past few days. We're going to find her today, Zach. I just woke up this morning with this *feeling*. We're going to find her. And the monster who took her is going to pay."

He sighs. "Marybeth, I have to say this one last time. The best chance we have of finding your daughter is to follow the facts. Stick to what's in front of us. And we have no *evidence* that Kat was abducted, whatever you keep telling the press."

"The girls were *drugged*, Zach. You didn't think to tell me that? That's why you think they're confused about where they were."

He smooths his moustache. "Just picture it, Marybeth.

How does somebody overpower three teenage girls at once and get close enough to drug them?"

He's got a point. None of them are exactly wispy. Donna's monstrously tall, and Katie weighs over two hundred pounds. Tammy-Rae's the only one of them you could call petite, but she's the captain of the athletics team, and makes up for her lack of bulk by being pure muscle. It wouldn't be easy to manhandle them. But not impossible. *A knife held to her daughter's throat, the other two watching with big eyes. They look at each other, then they run off. Abandon her there. Katie's voice calling after them, begging them not to leave her.* She shakes the scene from her mind. "He wouldn't need to attack all three of them at once. If he threatened one, the other two would have done anything he said."

"You know how many wild theories I've heard today? The press are talking about a paedophile in the woods. Louanne told them that Tammy-Rae was mumbling about a monster, so now people are going on about rabid bears. This is exactly what I didn't want to happen." Zach shakes his head, moustache trembling in anger. "Just leave the talking to me this time, OK?"

"It's a good turnout," she says, turning back to face the gym. Even more people have filled the room now. *I did this*, she tells herself. *I got everyone here. I got them to care.*

"Yes, we'll be able to cover a lot of ground." He frowns. "I just hope it's the right ground," he adds in a mutter.

"What?"

"This town talks about 'the woods' like they're our backyard. But over north, we're talking about millions of acres of forest stretching across the Sierra Nevada. Katherine could have walked from here all the way through Plumas National Forest, up through Lassen, on to Shasta. Heck, she could have hiked to Oregon without running across another living soul. And we don't even know where to start." He glances at her and seems to realise that this is hardly the way to reassure an anxious mother.

"But we do know where to start."

He hesitates, glances over at her. "The second K9 team came back around noon. Same as before, they followed the trail some way into the woods, and refused to go further. I don't think there's anything more to find out there."

Or you're a useless cop who's not qualified to lead an Easter egg hunt, let alone a manhunt, Marybeth thinks. "Or somebody's covering up their tracks."

Zach doesn't even try to talk her out of this. He smooths down his moustache again. "Sergeant Mercer will be manning the base today, checking in on all the volunteer groups over radio." He gestures at Sergeant Underbite. "I think it's best you stay here with her. That way you'll be the first to hear if they find anything."

"I need to be *doing* something, Zach."

"I think you've done enough, Marybeth," he says coolly, marching back to the desk to talk to the other officers.

He leaves her there, seething. After everything she's done, he still wants to treat her like she's hysterical. Like she should just hang back and let the experts handle things.

The cops start fanning out, herding the crowd into smaller groups, passing around the registration clipboards. She hangs at the back, wondering if she should just ignore Zach and join one of the groups, search the ground.

An image flashes into her mind. Katie's body, half-buried behind a tree stump, white as an earthworm, dirt caking her sweet face.

Maybe he's right. Better to wait here.

Figuring she can at least make herself useful, she sets to work replacing the old flyers around the school with the new ones. She makes her way between posters of the usual school nonsense, banners about the school football team (*Let's go, Goldbugs!*), gymnastic meets, THIS IS YOUR BRAIN ON DRUGS. It's barely changed at all since her own days here. It's got the same stink she remembers: hormones and boredom.

On a bulletin board just outside the gym, she spots it. A drawing, half-hidden behind a notice about dance classes. A black and white feathery tail that looks familiar.

Her neck prickles as she unearths it from the layers that cover it. There it is: the same rude bird drawing they found in the secret box in Katie's room. It's been photocopied, and must have been up for a while. The edges are dog-eared, and it's full of pinholes where other posters have overlaid it. The only text underneath is a large *75c* emblazoned on the corner.

Marybeth peels it off, her heart hammering. What is this? She glances over at Zach, wondering if she should take it to him directly, but he's dealing with a throng of junior officers who all seem to be asking him questions at once.

Instead, she spots Alan Dunne, Katie's history teacher, in one of the volunteer groups nearby. She walks up to him.

"Alan," she says quietly. "Do you know what this is?"

He turns to her, the smile freezing when he sees what she's holding. A bright red flush creeps up his face. "Where did you find that?"

"What is it?"

"Just an ad for this stupid joke magazine the kids pass around. I thought we'd binned them all."

"Do you have one?"

"We were just heading out..." he says, glancing back at his group leader.

"Please, Alan." Why is he acting so shifty about this?

He pauses, looks at her. He must see the panic on her face. "Of course," he says finally. He flashes a *give me five minutes* signal to the group leader, who shouts after him to be quick.

"I've got one in my desk," he says, leading her down the hall in a trot. "I've had to confiscate ten of the damn things already. Kids passing them around in class. Absolutely disrespectful, and full of garbage," he mutters darkly.

He leads her to a bright classroom near the end of the hall and pulls a small booklet out of his desk drawer. "Here," he says, handing it to her with his fingertips, like it's radioactive.

Marybeth examines it. "Magazine" was an overstatement: it's a few sheets of black-and-white badly photocopied pages, amateurish drawings and cramped text, crookedly stapled along the spine. There's the bird again, on the bottom corner, below the word MAGPIES in ransom-note style cut-out letters, and below that in a scrawl, FOR CLEVER BIRDS. It's dated May.

"Caused a real stink, I can tell you," Alan says. "No names on it, unfortunately. They'd have been in big trouble if we knew who they were."

Marybeth can see why, as she pages through. The pages are full of dense text, seemingly serious articles, interspersed with joke cartoons that mostly feature the Little Hope High teaching staff. She flicks past a drawing of someone who is unmistakably Alan Dunne doing something sordid to the behind of someone who is unmistakably not his wife. The caption underneath says: "The Poophole Loophole: it's the sex Jesus can't see!" She doesn't get the joke, but at least it explains why Alan was being so weird about showing this to her.

She flips past the image, wondering why on earth Katie would have cared enough about this pornographic nonsense to hide the bird drawing in her room. Then she flicks to the next page, and it all makes sense. "TIBET NEEDS OUR HELP!" reads the headline.

Goddamn it.

Katie started talking about Tibet a few months ago after watching a *60 Minutes* segment about the Dalai Lama. She's been obsessed with it ever since. Printed out a bunch of information about it from the school computer that she kept trying to get Marybeth to read. She brings it up constantly.

She flips back to the first page and scans through it more slowly. The drawings do look familiar, actually. She's seen similar doodles on Donna's clothes, homework, backpack, anything she could take a marker to. The girls had once come over for dinner and she'd doodled a whole scene on one of her good white fabric napkins. And she's sure she's heard the three of them joking about fake Olympic sports before, and there it is, a two-page spread about the Fauxlympic Games.

She closes the pages and runs her thumb around the bird drawing. *Oh*, she suddenly gets it. A bird flipping the bird. It only makes sense if you put yourself in the mind of a fifteen-year-old.

She hasn't been able to believe that Katie's two best friends might be lying. She's told herself they were confused, that they were high, that they can't have known what was happening.

But this must be their "newspaper club". Katie told her they'd disbanded it months ago. Clearly they *had* been lying, all three of them.

And if they were lying about that, what else are the girls lying about?

12. WE'RE SO COOL

KATHERINE LARKIN

Dear Diary,

I'm not sure exactly when our sensible normal school newspaper idea turned into *Magpies*. Part punk zine, part highbrow periodical, part art project, part *MAD* magazine, all Kat-Donna-Rae mind-meld. It's like the physical embodiment of our personalities smooshed into a few pieces of paper. As politically aware as Rae, as funny as Donna, as FULL OF FACTS as me. Once we started trying to make something together, we couldn't stop. It's just too good when we throw ideas around and spark off each other and it just keeps spiralling out into weirder and weirder directions. I think it might be the dumbest, most wonderful thing ever made.

Our first edition was a surprising success, as far as those things go, proving that the students of Little Hope High School truly are desperate for quality local reading material. We printed out eighty copies of them, six pieces of letter paper folded in half and stapled down the middle (which took us HOURS to do, I might add, but we watched an *X-Files* marathon while we did it, playing the game where we sip gin every time Scully rolls her eyes). The first edition had one serious article about Tibet. A joke cartoon about what sports our teachers would compete in at the Olympics (Mrs Hobbs: competitive yelling). Parody lyrics for the Macarena (AKA the Mockarena). Some music and book reviews. Just a collection of stuff we found funny or cool.

Honestly, I didn't expect a single person to buy them, but we sold out in one afternoon. 75c each, which netted us a princely $60, which let us go see *Clueless* at the cinema THREE TIMES. The printing didn't cost us anything because Rae's mom did them for us on the church printer. And she promised not to say anything about it to Rae's dad. Sometimes I think there's more going on beneath Estelle Hooper's perma-sneer than she lets on, although Rae would never believe it.

Even better, we saw *Magpies* being passed around even to people who hadn't bought them. People kept quoting bits of it back to us. It was almost like we were popular, for a grand total of like three days. A new experience for us! For Donna and me, anyway. I've got to tell you, it was a RUSH.

Rae was unsurprised by our wild publishing success. Everything Rae ever does is a success, so I don't think it ever occurred to her that this might not be. But the money we made really seemed to get to Donna. It's like it had just occurred to her that you could sell something and make money from it. And sure, it was much easier than the odd dollars she managed to scrounge together from babysitting. She started talking about how we could save up enough money to go see a concert in Seattle, or get her dad's car fixed, or start college funds. Like she'd just suddenly realised that money can solve all your problems (a lesson Ma Bear's communicated endlessly to me since the day I was born).

For a few weeks after the first edition, Donna was full of money-making schemes. We should buy up Beanie Babies on eBay and sell them on to collectors. We should buy plain T-shirts and decorate them with markers and sell them to all the posers at school who weren't creative enough to make their own. We should try to sell *Magpies* at the corner store. Or even bigger, we could sell them on the World Wide Web to people all around the world. Other girls like us in small towns who were bored and had nothing else to do. In the end, it all got a bit irritating, to be honest, especially seeing we both know Donna's great at coming up with ideas but never has the patience to actually follow through with any of them. But Rae and I both understand how broke Donna's family is and how much it would mean to her to have some cash of her own, so we didn't call her out on it. Ma Bear says Donna's mom was always blowing the family savings on some hare-brained business idea or another, so it must run in the family.

The second edition sold out just as fast. Mrs Hooper said she couldn't print more copies for us, so we paid for that batch ourselves, self-financing the first print run with the nine bucks we had left from edition one, and printing a second batch as soon as we'd sold those out. I know this seems super-obvious now that I write it down, but I tell you we felt like Business Geniuses™ when we came up with that plan.

We all agreed that we should do another edition of *Magpies*. Do a bigger run, this time. We all want this edition to be better than the first two. We're sophomores now! If we're really going to do this, we've got to do it right. We're not going to be one-hit wonders or just make a stupid high school joke thing. We want to make something *good*.

But the problem is, nothing we could write about feels like it's important enough. We've been arguing over it all week. Rae wants to do something about why people should vote for Bill Clinton over Bob Dole in the November election (even though we're kids and can't actually vote). Donna thinks we should go bigger than that and publish a political manifesto about how the high school system creates good capitalist patriarchal drones and we need to liberate our minds from it, and the rest of the issue should be a hypothetical new school curriculum for rebels. I pitched a couple of ideas, but they weren't as bold as either of theirs. The only things I can think of are small things, secrets around our own town and our own school that interest me. And then I got kind of down and started talking about how I'm never going to make it as a writer because I've got so little imagination. Like, every thought I've ever had is just a remix of something else.

But Donna punched me and said I was an idiot, and then Rae said she's no expert but it seems like writing well isn't about making stuff up, it's about seeing what's actually there, and I see more than anyone. It was nice of her. It did make me feel a little bit better, even though it's ironic coming from Rae, who only reads books about literal dragons and vampires, and named her hamster Frodo.

Sometimes it's hard being friends with Rae and Donna, because they're both such big personalities. They don't ever mean to, but they can make me feel even more like a nobody when I'm around them. They're the two smartest, bravest, funniest, most talented, most extraordinary people I've ever met and on some level I guess I'm just waiting for them to realise that I'm none of those things and dump my lame ass.

What I really want is to write something that cracks a mystery. I guess I never got that childish idea out of my head about being Nancy Drew, brilliant girl detective, who solves puzzles and exposes the truth in the world. Except, what mysteries are there to solve in Little Hope?? Why was Suzanne Granger fired from her job at the laundromat? DUH, because she was running a profitable side-business selling pot. Why is our history teacher Mr Dunne suddenly living at the motel? DUH, it's because Mrs Dunne found out he was having an affair with Peggy Boyd, who runs Sunday school (which makes no sense to anyone; Peggy

Boyd's the most stuck-up person ever and Heather Dunne is a glamorous goddess who wears floaty kaftans everywhere). That's the problem with Little Hope: everyone's so up in everyone else's business that there are no mysteries to solve. Seriously, I don't know why this town even bothers having a police department. All they ever do is help drunks get home and stop boys from drag-racing down Broad Street.

The only honestly interesting person in Little Hope is Ronnie Gaskins. Everyone knows that he killed both his parents when he was just a kid and went to juvie for it until he got let out on some weird technicality. Everyone knows why he did it (DUH, again: because he's totally 100% fruit-loops crazy). But nobody knows why he came back after he got out of jail and kept living in Little Hope.

Ma Bear said she used to babysit him when she was my age and said he was a sweet boy, not too bright, but no one would have thought he was a killer. She said when he killed his parents it was the biggest scandal the town ever had. Their house was one of the nicest ones in town, and it burned down with them inside it. She said at first everyone thought it was a real tragedy because they assumed the fire was an accident and everyone felt so sorry for poor little orphan Ronnie, until they found out that Ronnie's mom had a bullet lodged in her skull and her dad had one in his chest, and that little Ronnie's fingerprints were all over the gun.

And then five years ago, Ronnie gets let out of jail, only he's a young man now, no trace of the pudgy cute boy he used to be, just this scrawny scary-looking dude, and he moves right back into the burned shell of the house he grew up in, there on the edge of town by the woods, and rebuilds it. The town was up in arms when he came back. Told him they didn't want a murderer living here, that they wouldn't feel safe in their beds. For the first year after he moved back, Ma Bear told me, kids would go up to his house at night and scrawl horrible things on the walls, until he started booby-trapping the whole yard and some teenager nearly had his leg taken off by one of Ronnie's snares, trying to break into his house one night. When the kid's dad tried to have him arrested, Ronnie said he had every right to defend his property, and that he had a right to be there. Chief Pittman had asked him if it wouldn't be easier for everybody if he just packed up his stuff and started life fresh somewhere new, somewhere pointedly NOT Little Hope, but Ronnie had just kept insisting stubbornly that this was his home.

Kids still sometimes go up there and taunt him. They're too scared now to go onto his property; everyone knows it's covered in booby traps. But they leave stuff on the fence. Fred Stein from our class and his gang of delinquents once made two scarecrows, one in women's clothing, one in men's clothing, stuffed with straw, and tied them up on his gate. The woman had pig's blood smeared on her stuffed-pillowcase head. The man had a hole bashed through his chest.

Fred was so proud of his prank, he told everyone it was his idea. And they didn't get into any trouble for it. I even saw some of the teachers smile when it was mentioned, I swear.

So here's what I'm thinking: how crazy would it be if the third edition of *Magpies* had an ACTUAL interview with ACTUAL real-life Ronnie Gaskins? A chance for him to tell his side of the story, and why he came back when no one wants him here. An interview with a murderer. Like how Ted Bundy gave those interviews to reporters where he just straight-out told them the sick things going through his head when he killed those people. Now wouldn't THAT be an article? That's the kind of thing that people would read, even outside of Little Hope.

Maybe this is crazy! Maybe this is just asking for trouble! But you know what, I think Donna and Rae will go for it.

And maybe that's how I'll show them that I'm not just a wimpy wallflower. I can have guts sometimes, too.

I'm pretty hopped up on excitement about this, actually! Or as Cher would say, I am TOTALLY BUGGING.

Yours,
Kat Not-A-Wimp Larkin

FACT I LEARNED TODAY: Ted Bundy chose all of his thirty victims because they looked like his college girlfriend, Stephanie Brooks. Jeez, Teddy boy, there are better ways to deal with a breakup, ya know?

Little Hope GAZETTE

Tuesday, October 13, 1981

Hometown Horror
Local boy confesses to killing parents

By Rex Cantrell - staff writer

A 12-year-old boy has been charged with two counts of murder and one charge of arson after confessing to shooting his parents in their home and then setting it on fire, authorities said Tuesday.

Little Hope Chief of Police Ray Pendleton said authorities were alerted to the murders when a neighbour called 911 last Friday after he noticed smoke billowing from the Gaskins residence.

The boy met deputies on the driveway and told them a fire had started in the kitchen and that his parents were "sleeping inside".

"Upon entering the home, we discovered the parents were deceased," Pendleton said, adding that an autopsy the next

adding that an autopsy the next day revealed they had been shot. The boy was later taken in for questioning and a few days later, "when we confronted him with inconsistencies in his story, confessed to shooting his parents." Officers were led to the handgun allegedly used in the killings by the boy. "He had hidden it in the woods," he added. The fire had been lit in an apparent attempt to conceal the crime.

Authorities identified the victims as John Gaskins, 39, the boy's father, and his mother, Mary Gaskins, 35.

The slayings have rattled the quiet community of Little Hope. "I can't remember the last time we had a murder," Pendleton told reporters. The Gaskins family lived in Los Angeles

for 12 years before moving to Little Hope in 1980. John Gaskins was a teacher at Little Hope High School.

"The whole town is an open wound right now," Mayor Joe Stanford told reporters. "We have a lot of healing to do."

Lori Griffiths, a neighbour who resides about a half-mile from the family, said she remembers the boy playing happily with his friends in the road. "He seemed like just a normal kid."

Authorities have yet to establish any motive.

13. ME GUSTA SER UNA ZORRA

DONNA RAMIREZ

MONDAY, 23 SEPTEMBER 1996

"Can't I make you breakfast before I go?"

"Papi, please, I'm fine. No more food, I'll barf." He's been buzzing around the living room for the past ten minutes, inventing one urgent chore after another. Changed a lightbulb above the microwave that burned out a year ago, dug out her thick army jacket from the depths of the closet in case she was cold, even though it's September.

Donna hands him his thermos. "You're going to be late."

"Doesn't feel right, going off to work like this. I should call in and take another personal day."

"Well, you'll be sitting here alone. I'm going to school."

"They'd understand if—"

"If I spend another day in my room, I'll go crazy." It's true. After Rae blew her off at church yesterday, she'd spent the rest of the day stuck at home. She'd begged her dad to let her join him on the searches, but he'd looked so nervous at the very thought of her going out there that she'd backed off. So instead, she just lay sweating on the bed, angriest music on highest volume in her Discman, feeling weirdly light-headed, like the room didn't have enough air, for the whole stupid day. And then her dad came home, late, looking pale, and she didn't even need to ask if they'd found Kat. All he'd said was, "Just the thought of you, lost out there for so long." Then he went to bed, and she made a blanket nest on the floor of her room, tossing and thinking, until she finally fell asleep sometime around two.

She'd rather go to putrid *school* than spend another day like that, moping around, half-formed questions chasing themselves around her brain: *Did someone ambush us in the cave? Could it have been Ronnie? And what about our clothes??*

All her thoughts, really, variations of the same question: *What happened to us?*

Her dad runs a hand through his shaggy hair. She'll have to cut it again soon. "Aren't you rushing this?"

Donna thrusts his wallet and jacket at him. "You're going to be late. I'm fine."

"Hi, Fine, I'm Hector," he answers automatically. "Let me just—"

"Papi! ¡Vete!"

He hugs her, too tight, and leaves. She peers out the window and watches him walk up the block, making sure he's not about to dash back into the house to try to make her a bowl of asopao or something. She exhales, realising she's been holding her breath.

She wanders through to her room and dials Rae. Mrs Hooper picks up the phone on the third ring, but she refuses to put her through to Rae.

"She's still upset. She needs a little space. Please stop calling." *Click.*

She leaves Donna frowning into the receiver. But that doesn't mean anything, she tells herself. She's been Estelle-blocked before. Rae's mom has never liked Donna. She blames her for Rae not being one of the popular girls any more, blames her for Rae's "moodiness", for her becoming more "difficult".

Blames her for Rae being a teenager, in other words.

That's another reason to go to school, she thinks. Mrs Hooper's force field can't keep the two of them apart there, and she *has to* talk to Rae. She's still mad with her, but she needs to see her. More than anything. She's the only one who can help her figure out what the hell happened to them, or whether Kat's even alive.

Donna stomps the whole three blocks to the bus stop. Chief Pittman still has her bike, forever probably, with her luck. Her school backpack is still out there in the woods, so she's got her stuff crammed into her ancient neon-rainbow Lisa Frank tiger backpack from elementary school. There's a slight bite in the air, the first hint of fall. It cuts through the thin turtleneck she's wearing under her Skunk Anansie T-shirt. *Dammit, Dad*, she thinks, *shoulda worn my army jacket.*

Her chest feels tight, simultaneously phlegmy and crusty, like her lungs are filled with cornflakes and milk, and she's still... spacey. Not like herself. She wonders if this is still the after-effects of whatever was in her system, or just lack of sleep, or if she caught a cold from wandering around the woods for so long.

Maybe it's grief. Of all the crazy things Rae thinks she saw, that's the part that's the most plausible, isn't it? That Kat was lying there, dead. Her brain is still refusing to believe it's true, but perhaps her body has its own ideas.

The bus is pretty full for a Monday. Every single person stares at her when she gets on. They must recognise her from the news. She has to walk the gauntlet of their eyes, all the way to the long bench at the back. There are two empty seats on either side of Sue Granger, who used to work at the laundromat before she was busted for selling pot there. Donna squeezes into the seat in the corner next to her. Sue doesn't acknowledge her, just slides silently away from her, into the other empty seat, like she's radioactive.

The bus lurches onto the road. Donna feels her face flush. Is this what it's going to be like now, everyone wanting to stare at her, but no one wanting to get too close? Is she now forever tainted as "naked missing girl whose friend vanished"? Or, actually, she realises, untucking her hair from her ear and finding her whole face is wet, Jesus Christ, is it just because she's sweating so much? She lowers her head and surreptitiously sniffs herself. She stinks.

She survives the bus trip by trying to fold herself in the seat as small as she can, hiding behind her curtain of hair, begging her body not to be so disgusting, as though she could reabsorb sweat and stink through sheer force of will alone.

A reporter is waiting for her on the concrete steps to the school building, a greasy-haired, hunched man. He rushes towards her as she steps out of the bus, the flash on his camera nearly blinding her. One of the parents yells out at him, "This is a school, are you crazy?"

Thankfully, he doesn't follow her further. She races into the hallways and directly to the bathroom before anyone else can see what a wreck she is. She splashes water on her face without looking at her reflection in the mirror, nervous about what she'll see there. She wads up some paper towels and pushes them under her shirt, stuffing them in her armpits. She leans against the wall. Her own face stares back at her from every stall, below the words HAVE YOU SEEN THESE GIRLS?

Maybe her dad was right. Maybe she is rushing this.

Once she's as fresh as she can achieve with school bathroom supplies, she finally ventures out into the halls. Kids are filtering through in twos and threes and fours. She catches them sneaking glances at her, falling silent as they walk past. Only one of them meets her eyes: Sharon LeBell, queen bee of the group of miserable airheads Rae was friends with before she grew a spine and was kicked out. Sharon is Donna's least favourite of the bunch. She's usually found draped over some or other member of the football team trying to look as vapid as possible, even though Donna happens to know that she's a secret math genius. A fact she tries to hide as much as she can.

Sharon saunters over. "I wanted you to hear this from a friendly source, before it makes its way through the rumour mill," she says, flashing a candied smile to show her deep regret, as though she isn't herself, in this exact moment, being the rumour mill. "The cops think Kat must have died of a drug overdose."

Sharon's older sister works for the police department, so she's probably not even making this up. The problem with living in a small town is it's not so much six degrees of separation as, like, half a degree. Donna feels her cheeks burning.

Sharon's friends stare at them hungrily, bunched against the lockers. So this is what's being whispered, person to person. That Kat was a screw-up, and now she's lying dead in the woods somewhere. And they're probably saying it's Donna's fault. Shit, for all she can remember, maybe it is.

Donna goes stiff, sticks her tongue out, and lets her eyes roll back in her head, and starts thrashing her arms around, faking a seizure.

"Freak," Sharon mutters, returning to her friends. Donna turns and walks away with as much dignity as she can muster, letting her head hang down so her hair covers her face, and the tears that are filling her eyes.

She slips out a side door to their secret spot by the maintenance shed, where they usually hang out before school starts. There's no sign of Rae. Time to face facts: she's not coming in. She's going to have to face this whole crummy day on her own.

She can hear the distant sounds of the band playing Bryan Adams's '(Everything I Do) I Do it For You' through the window. Badly played brass instruments don't exactly improve it, but it's hardly worse than the original. Exactly the kind of pithy observation that would have made Kat and Rae laugh.

There's a horribly familiar feeling about all this, being out here on her own, hiding from people. It feels like before she and Kat and Rae became friends. She doesn't think either of them actually realises how lonely she was before she had them. Kat thinks of herself as the big dork, but at least she used to hang out with that tiny, intense girl Kylie. And Rae had loads of friends, obviously, former Miss Popular.

Before the two of them, Donna had exactly one friend. When she was nine and her dad cobbled together enough money to send her to summer camp, and she'd agreed to be best friends with a skinny girl named Imani Williams, a contract they'd sealed with the solemn exchange of woven string bracelets. They performed all the normal rites of nine-year-old best-friend-ness. They each nominated a counsellor crush and played MASH to divine their futures. They hung out every day for three weeks, promised each other they'd stay in touch, and then in the tradition of all summer friendships, Donna never heard from her again.

Since then and now, pretty much nothing. Other kids thought she was mean so she responded by being mean. At least it felt like it was *her* choice she had no friends, rather than theirs. She was just the burnout nobody wanted to talk to, too loud and too wild, before Rae and Kat made her feel loved, made her feel like maybe she was worth loving.

She climbs onto the corner of the dumpster and hoists herself up onto the roof of the shed. From up here, the school is a patchwork of grey corrugated roofs and glimpses of asphalt, and no people in sight. There's one piece of decor: a small clay angel they've painted so it appears to be wearing a dominatrix outfit, guarding their little patch of roof like a gargoyle. Kat even made her a tiny, plaited whip out of strips of a trash bag. They've spent endless hours up here, finding the edges of their own personalities through comparison. Always so lovingly: *you are like this, we are different like this, we are the same like this, this is who I am, this is who you are.* Writing long lists together of their dreams. Things they'll do when they're old and in a nursing home together. Adventures they'll go on when they finally leave Little Hope. All the careers they'll have, the types of men they'll fall in love with, the big and small ways they'll leave imprints on the world. They've lived so many imaginary lives up here, the three of them. This little patch of nothing is Donna's favourite place in the world.

She closes her eyes, sitting with the deep hum of sadness inside of her. That's what it feels like: a hum. An electric thread between her and Kat and Rae, one end flapping loose in the wind.

The magpies aren't out today. There's a little tribe of them that roost around the vents over the science lab. They love speculating about the soap opera relationships between the six birds, the shifting loyalties and contested territories. Of course they named their zine after them.

Once, they climbed up here after school and smoked some pot Kat got from Mickey Ramsey. They had a very stoned conversation wondering whether birds *know* that they're birds. Then Kat's eyes got big and she said, "Oh shit, guys, what if *we're* birds and we don't even know it?" Rae had pulled at one of the armpit hairs growing out from Donna's tank top and said, "Yeah, see, your feathers are coming in," and they all got the giggles. They climbed over to see if the birds had stolen shiny things for their nests, but they found nothing but feathers and twigs, and a small clutch of precious blue eggs. She remembers Kat saying that the birds don't deserve their reputation as thieves. "They're not bad," she'd said. "Just curious."

Sometimes they toss bits of their lunch to them, the greasy squares of cement bread that the cafeteria tries to pass off as pizza, overcooked corn and stale Fritos. They refuse to touch the bright yellow squares of so-called cheese slices. Once, Kat cut one of the cheese slices into a puzzle and took it home. The thing oozed oil for the first few days but then stiffened and took on the texture of plastic. Never got a hint of mould on it, nothing, even after six months. They named it Mister E. Cheese. It's probably still in Kat's room somewhere.

It hurts to think of Kat. It's unimaginable that she might never see her again, that she might never know what happened to her. She could be out there alone. She might be starving and scared.

And, of course, there's always the chance that Rae's still not telling her the truth. Maybe Rae did something bad; that's why she's so intent on keeping people away.

There's no sign of the birds now. She crawls her way over to the back of the shed and checks the alley that runs behind the school building. There they are, huddled on the ground, the morning light glinting off the blue-green metallic streak along their wings, long black tails over white bellies, like a cape. Rae once noted how they always look dressed up, like they're going to a ball.

They're huddled around a bit of trash on the ground. She counts five of them. What was the rhyme? One for sorrow, two for joy, but what was five?

One of them looks up at her, daring streak of yellow below its eye. It cocks its head as though considering her. They're so smart. Kat once told them that they could recognise themselves in a mirror, you could even train them to talk, and then her and Rae got into this long debate about whether that meant magpies were conscious, and Rae said they can't be, because they don't have a soul, and Kat said she thought the soul was just an accidental side effect of neurochemistry, which was an extremely Kat thing to say.

The bird decides Donna's not a threat and goes back to investigating the dark lump on the ground. It pecks at it, and a flash of bright white appears from under a wing. It's the sixth bird, dead.

The others hop closer and peck at it, like they're trying to get it to wake up. Like a funeral. Like an omen.

14. SEETHER

TAMMY-RAE HOOPER

Everything about her dad's lawyer is the wrong size. His hair oversized for his small head, his wrists skinny but his hands huge, the shoulders of his suit far too broad but the Burberry scarf draped around it weirdly skinny. Like a person assembled out of discarded parts. His name is Bob Pelton.

He brings a sense of unreality to the room. Another point of proof that none of this can be happening, that all of this must be some kind of mad fever dream. Maybe she never woke up. Maybe she's still there in that cave.

Rae sits opposite him on the armchair in their living room. She pretends to be looking at him, but really she's staring past him through the window, watching a bird sitting on the tree in their front yard. It's some kind of raptor, a mottled red streak across its shoulder. Maybe a hawk. Kat would know.

The lawyer hasn't noticed that she's not paying attention to him. He directs his conversation to her father, who's sitting on the armchair next to her. Her mother is somewhere else in the house, ostensibly making lunch, but really avoiding the awkwardness of the whole thing. Avoidance is her mother's superpower.

Brandon's at school. There was no question of her joining him. She wonders if Donna went, though. How she's doing.

The two men are talking strategy, discussing every eventuality of what might happen. Talking about what they'll do if they find Kat's corpse out there in the woods. What they might accuse her of based on the state the coroner finds that corpse in. Words wash over her that don't mean anything: involuntary manslaughter. Culpability. Minimum sentencing. Third or second degree. Reckless homicide. She doesn't see what any of this has to do with Kat, the way her cheeks dimple when she smiles, how she smells like White Musk from The Body Shop, how she always knows things, like the names of birds.

Bob represented her dad a couple of years ago when a breeder sued him over the death of a prize stud bull that was worth a lot of money. He lost the case, but her dad couldn't stop singing his praises anyway. He's the kind of man he respects: cocky, rich, born again. She can't even imagine how much this must be costing them, to have flown him out here for multiple days, just to talk through all of these various terrible things that haven't even happened yet.

She should be grateful. Maybe she would be, if she thought for a moment that any of this was for her benefit.

The bird outside the window gives a little shake and flies off. Reluctantly, Rae brings her attention back to the room.

"What's important is that she's charged as a minor," says Bob, smoothing down the pants-leg on what is probably a very expensive pinstripe suit. "We need it adjudicated as a delinquency matter."

Her father bristles on the seat next to her. "My daughter's not a delinquent. She's on the honour roll."

"She's fifteen. Under California law, the prosecutor could file a fitness petition to argue she should be tried as an adult.

In the juvenile court, the focus is rehabilitation rather than punishment." His eyes slide over to meet hers as he says this last word. His eyes are too big in his too-small head. Bug eyes.

"California has the death penalty," she mumbles. It's the first time she's spoken in ages. Her voice feels creaky, like there's something in her throat.

Bob gives a sharp laugh, as though she's just said something hilarious. "Oh sweetheart, no. There's no chance of anything like that. Not for somebody like you. In any case, they haven't even accused you of anything yet."

She notes the *yet*. Like her father, Bob seems to take it for granted that he's here because she's done something terrible. Which, for all she knows, might even be true. When he'd arrived yesterday afternoon, the first thing he'd done was ask her parents to leave the room and told her to tell him what happened, that it was safe to tell him, and he needed to know. "Everything: the good, the bad and the ugly," he'd said. "I can't defend you against what I don't know." She'd replied that she had no idea what had happened; she couldn't remember anything more than what she's already told the cops. And he'd just smirked and said, "Clever girl."

Now, Bob gives her a toothy smile. "All this is still speculation. Chief Pittman is going to move very carefully now, after how badly he's bungled things. The longer they don't find anything out there, the less likely it is that they ever will. And who knows, maybe there really is a madman kidnapping girls from the woods." He shrugs unconvincingly. "It's just important that we figure out our plans *before* we have to, which is why your daddy was so clever to call me when he did."

It's strange how he can do this, speak to her like she's a child one moment after talking about how they might try her for murder.

Her father sits up straighter at Bob's praise. Rae notices that he's wearing his smartest blazer over his golf shirt, even though it's eighty-something degrees out. He's rolled the sleeves back to show off his Rolex.

"Let's say it was an overdose," says her father, leaning forward like an eager kid in class. "Could they hold Tammy-Rae responsible for something like that? If the blood work comes back showing she took it too?"

"In that situation, the important question would be who provided the narcotics. Donna's father, he's Mexican, right? Is he here legally?"

"He's Puerto Rican. Hence, American," Rae says, through gritted teeth.

"Well, anyway. They'd have a hard time getting a narcotics charge to stick. An OD might be the best-case scenario, honestly."

"The best-case scenario would be if they find Kat alive," Rae says.

"Well, of course." The lawyer frowns, smoothing his pants again over his too-thin legs.

Rae leans forwards. "May I be excused? I've got the worst headache."

"Sure thing, honey. Your father and I have still got a few more things to talk through before I head back to the city."

Rae stands, holding her pleated skirt down over her knees so they don't see the old scars that ladder up the inside of her thighs.

She leans over and kisses the top of her father's head on her way out of the room. His hair smells of shampoo and horses. He reaches up and squeezes her hand as she walks away. She wonders whether he'd be doing that if Bob wasn't here. He's spent most of the past two days throwing questions at her that she couldn't answer. She knows he's just frightened. Not for her, she understands, so much as for himself. What it would do to his reputation if it came out that his perfect daughter had shamed him. Again.

She slips out of the living room, hearing them return to

speculating about all the different ways her life might be ruined, like it's a friendly debate over dinner.

She does actually have a headache: a throbbing pulse behind her temples that's been building since she woke up. It might be her sinuses, because she's also felt like she needs to blow her nose all day. There's an electric prickle in her cheeks, and the back of her neck is damp against the collar of her shirt. She considers fetching the NyQuil from the medicine box in the kitchen, but she can hear her mother banging around in there, and she doesn't trust herself to talk to her without snapping at her. Her mom hasn't even tried to sit down and have any kind of real conversation with her about what happened, like she's afraid she won't be able to un-hear something Rae might have to say, and then, *Lord in Heaven forgive us*, she might have to actually deal with something instead of pretending that everything's just absolutely fine. Her father might be an egomaniac, but her mother's a coward, and that's worse.

Instead, she climbs the stairs up to her bedroom, closing the door carefully behind her. She wishes she could slam it shut, but she's not a girl who slams doors.

She takes a deep breath and wanders over to top up Frodo's food bowl. He's just visible, a tiny grey fluff-ball in the corner of his cage. Fair enough, it's, like, midnight for hamsters. But it would be nice to have some company. Ideally somebody who doesn't want to talk to her about *homicide* and *delinquency* and *being tried as a minor*.

Below the comforting sawdusty smell of his cage, she can smell something else. Rank and sweet, urine maybe. Cave smell.

She flops into the window seat. Dr Abrams's house next door is glowing in the mid-morning sun: a shabby mansion from the end of the last century, all turrets and white edging, painted an improbable pink. Clapboard confectionary.

Rebecca Abrams, their daughter, has been an object of fascination for Rae since the day they moved in six years ago from Santa Barbara. Becca's a senior, one of those girls who seems to know secret passageways through the school that allow her to get from class to class without ever being seen. Rae's never spoken to her before, but she's heard kids speculating about her stooped shoulders and short hair, her clothes that never seem to fit right, and her total refusal to wear make-up.

There are rumours about "Odd Becca Abrams", just like there would have been rumours about Rae had her father not so thoroughly crushed them. But from watching her up close through all these years, Rae knows Becca's truly thrilling secret: she is strong.

The punching bag hanging from the Abramses' front porch is still, now, but Becca's out there every afternoon, for hours, working it. She wears an old stretched-out tank top with straps that slip down her thick shoulders as she sweats.

And the real secret, the one Rae would rather die than anyone find out about it, even her friends, is that every afternoon she comes home from school, says she's going upstairs to do homework, and she sits in this window seat to watch Becca. How her shoulders turn slick and start to glisten in the afternoon sun. How the muscles in her back tighten and harden and bunch up. How she starts off with rhythmic, methodical punches, bouncing on the balls of her feet, then works herself up into a frenzy, punching and kicking in a rage. Sometimes she loses her form completely, just yells and slaps and whacks the bag.

Sometimes Rae feels so guilty and gross and wrong after leering at Becca like this that she cuts herself afterwards, just to shush her brain.

One time, she swears Becca looked up and caught her. Rae had ducked away, embarrassed at what a creep she was being. But she wonders, when Becca comes out every afternoon, if she knows Rae's there at the window. If she knows she's putting on a show for a rapt audience of one.

Rae has never been sure if the pleasure is in imagining touching Becca or in imagining being Becca.

She wishes she was the kind of person who could rage, who could tear up the stupid teen girl paraphernalia that litters her room, rip up her posters of Monica Seles and Michelle Kwan, smash her glass dolphin wind chime, slit her athletics ribbons, punch a hole through her CD player while screaming.

But she is not that person. No, as everyone keeps reminding her, *she's a good girl* who always does what she's g-d told, who stays put in her room and does what the stupid lawyer says instead of screaming at all of them that her best friend is out there, and something terrible happened to her, and she thinks her brain might be broken, and how is she just supposed to keep going on when all she can think of is a *black hole, ringed with teeth, the rippling throat-muscles, eyes that flashed in the darkness...*

She's not even sure that what she's feeling is grief, exactly. It's like Schrödinger's grief, because she's simultaneously sure that Kat's dead, and that she's crazy and hallucinated the whole thing.

The Abramses' porch swing creaks in the breeze. Their house is empty now. Becca's at school. Mrs Abrams is probably running errands.

The phone rings. She rushes out to the landing and picks up the receiver.

"Rae?" It's Donna.

"Yeah, hey." She walks to the edge of the stairs and tries to hear whether her mom is heading for the downstairs phone. It's quiet down there. Still, she has to talk fast. "Where are you?"

"I'm at school. I'm calling from one of the payphones."

"Want to come over? We could meet behind the shed—"

"Have you told the cops everything you saw?" Donna cuts her off.

"Not yet."

"Are you going to?"

Rae squeezes her eyes shut. The moment stretches out.

"There's a bunch of adults gathering in the gym. They're going back out there this afternoon to look for her. It's just a matter of time before they find the ravine."

Rae's not sure it will be so simple. The trail is well-hidden, obscured with branches, full of unexpected turns. They'd never have found it without Ronnie.

There's a silence from Donna's end. Then, "Rae, are you in trouble? I'm not going to rat you out, but you've got to tell me."

"I've told you everything."

"Then I'm going out there. I'm going to try to find her."

"Donna, no," Rae says, her hand gripping the phone. "Just be patient. I'll figure out what to do."

"You can't have seen what you think you saw. So she might still be alive out there, and I can't just sit around waiting."

"We can't. It's not safe."

"Come with me. If you're really my friend, and Kat's friend, come with me."

"Please just think—"

But the line goes dead. Donna's gone.

15. SHE SAID, "BOOM"

KATHERINE LARKIN

SUNDAY, 3 DECEMBER 1995

Dear Diary,

The Hoopers were out of town for some church leader retreat at Lake Tahoe, so I was invited to come spend the weekend there with Rae. In theory, we were co-babysitters for her little brother, Brandon, but I think I was mostly there to keep Rae from getting bored being in the house alone. Donna was pointedly NOT invited, because Rae's parents think she's a bad influence. Not like that mattered, she arrived about five minutes after Rae's parents' car left the driveway.

A whole glorious weekend, all to ourselves in the Hoopers' huge house!

But it came at a COST, Diary, which is that I had to endure Friday night dinner with Rae's whole family first (they left before sunrise on Saturday morning). An endless night with front-row seats to the Dysfunctional Family Funtime Show.

Mr Hooper spoke for like 99% of the time. He was going on about how Bill Clinton was endorsing a mass genocide of babies so he was definitely going to hell, but at least he was promising to finally kick all those "welfare queens" off the teats of the good United States taxpayers. Barf.

Mrs Hooper kept disappearing to the kitchen to "check on dessert", but dessert must have been made of gin based on the smell of her every time she came back. Not that I blame the woman. I think I'd also develop a drinking problem if I had to listen to David Hooper's sermons every day. I don't think she said ten words all evening.

Ugh, and Brandon. When Mrs Hooper came in carrying the trifle (note: not made of gin), she slipped and almost dropped it, and he quipped, "And that's why we keep Mom in the kitchen." He always looks at his dad when he says something like this, like he's hoping he'll get a laugh. But it's pretty sad because Mr Hooper really seems to hate him. He must have criticised him a dozen times over dinner. Mocked his baggy pants, the "ghetto" music he likes, his scrawny arms. Meanwhile, Rae is the sweet golden child, Daddy's girl. She and Brandon are always at each other's throats. You'd think they'd have formed some kind of alliance in surviving their awful parents, but no, just low-grade sibling warfare, all the time.

Anyway, after HOURS of this, I was so relieved it was over I didn't even comment on the fact that Rae, her mom and I did the dishes while Brandon and her dad went and watched TV. Ma Bear's always saying how different things would be if we had a man in the house and hell, if it's different like this, then no thanks.

That night, Rae and I lay on the bunk beds in her room and had a long whisper conversation in the dark, just goofing around like normal. Then Rae got all serious, and asked if she could tell me what happened between her and her old friends, the popular girls she used to hang out with before us. I was surprised because Rae's always been cagey about this. But she told me everything.

They were having a big group sleepover at Sharon's house, and she and Ann Mullins ended up alone on the porch, and

Ann confessed to her that she thought she might be gay, but she wasn't sure, and begged Rae not to tell anyone. And then Rae confessed back that she thought she might be too, or she might be nothing, because both times she'd kissed a boy she'd felt super grossed out by it. So the two of them kissed, just to check, she said, but one of the girls spotted them through the window, and Ann was mortified, so Rae just took all the heat for it. Said it was all her, she was the one who'd initiated the whole thing and Ann had tried to stop her.

But Sharon had always been a bit threatened by Rae, because Rae was more popular than her. So she made sure that word got back to Rae's parents about it. So last fall when she was away from school for a month and everyone thought she had mono, she was actually at a Christian "therapy" camp.

Then Rae went silent for a bit. Then she said, "That's when I stopped believing in God." But she didn't say anything else about what happened there.

Her first day back at school, the girls presented her with a letter. It said that it was OK if she was a lesbian but she wasn't invited to sleepovers any more, because they couldn't take the chance that she'd perv over them, but they were still happy to hang out at school as long as she promised never to try any of that "lez stuff" with them. And Rae, to her credit, politely told them they could all go stuff it and refused to speak to any of them ever again.

I asked her why she's never told Donna this story. She said Donna would blow up and immediately start plotting to put dogshit in Sharon's locker or something. "I love Donna, but she doesn't know how to just listen."

I lay awake for a long time after that.

The next morning, we were all up crazy early to see the Hoopers off. Donna arrived and started joking about getting a keg, because in movies, when someone's parents are out of town they throw huge rager parties. But we all agreed that we couldn't imagine anything that sounds less like fun than spending time OUTSIDE OF SCHOOL with the same thirty idiots we have to see every damn day, only drunk.

Oh no, Diary, we had a much better idea: because we had the house to ourselves, we realised we could rent ANY MOVIE WE WANTED. Rae's parents are normally huge sticklers for the PG-13 age rating. And when we're at my place, Ma Bear always wants to watch with us and she doesn't like anything "dark" so it's always something with Meg Ryan, yawn. And Donna doesn't even have a TV. So this was our CHANCE!

We spent like seventeen hours in the video store with that perv Jim Porter leering at Donna every time she bent over to get something on a lower shelf. Rae pointed this out to Donna so she hooked her fingers into the belt loops of her jeans and wriggled them as low on her hips as she could, so that the next time he'd get a full eyeful of the whale-tail of her G-string. They don't even sell G-strings anywhere in town! There would probably be a whole town meeting about it if they did. So Donna, get this, just cut the butt-cheeks out of all her panties. I will never understand why she does shit like this. She's so smart and talented and creative but she just loves it when dirtbags like Jim stare down her asscrack. It's like she thinks if no one takes her seriously, she can never disappoint them.

We fought for so long about which movie to get that we decided to each choose one. Donna got *Arachnophobia*, mostly to tease Rae because Rae gets super wigged out by spiders. Rae got *Body Snatchers*. And I found a movie called *Henry & June*, which I'd never heard of before, but it was about a writer, and it had an NC-17 rating. I was worried it would just be porn. The box had some pretty steamy photographs on it. Luckily Jim was too busy trying to get a look down Donna's cleavage to pay any attention to me when we were checking them out. It's nice being Donna and Rae's plain, fat friend, because it's like being invisible. Exactly how I like to be most of the time.

Back at Rae's house, we had to bribe that little shit Brandon to leave us be and promise not to tell his parents we were watching adult movies. Donna gave him two of the bottles of beer she'd filched from her dad and Rae added in five bucks as hush money. We pretended to have a negotiation over what to watch first but of course it was Rae's movie, which was hilarious, and then we watched half of *Arachnophobia* before losing interest and setting up a Christmas bed in the living room and trying to read tarot from an old deck of playing cards, but none of us knew what any of the cards were supposed to mean so we just made fortunes up for each other. I told Rae that she was going to meet the man of her dreams when she was eighteen, but then he'd turn out to be a giant spider person who'd lay his eggs in her and she'd give birth to a billion spider babies and she got so freaked out and giggly that she had to go take a shower.

We started watching *Henry & June* but the others fell asleep straight away. I couldn't take my eyes off it. I was pretty glad the others were asleep because it turned out it WAS basically porn, but it was more sad than it was sexy. It was about a real-life woman writer called Anayees Neen (spelling??) who falls in love with a dude writer and also his wife (Uma Thurman), sometime in the 1930s, and the three of them fall into this hot bohemian love triangle, and Anayees helps the guy writer publish his book but then goes back to her very boring husband in the end. And Uma gets the worst part of the deal, truly, because her husband's terrible and he's just using both of them and I kept rooting for the two women to just run away together and love each other and have adventures and be their own people living for their own purposes, not to further some dude's career. But of course that's not how life works.

I think what I loved about it so much was that I've never seen a movie before where there was so much sympathy for a woman doing terrible things. After all, she's cheating on her husband!

AND on her lover! With his own wife! But in the movie, her bad behaviour is fine, because she's doing it to experience something. She's doing it for her work and her art. So there's something pure about it. And the movie doesn't punish her for it, or make her die tragically like you'd expect her to. Her only punishment is that she has to stay married to the extremely boring Richard E. Grant. Which, OK, fair, is quite a punishment.

It made me kinda sad, because I was thinking about Ma Bear, and how at some point I'm going to leave her and try out some bad behaviour of my own, and she'll just be sitting in that empty house by herself. How do you do it, hurt the people you love so that you can do the selfish things you need to do to be truly alive?

At some point, in one of the really steamy girl-on-girl scenes (very hot, I must admit), I think I saw Rae watching the movie out of half an eye. But sex stuff always embarrasses her, so I let her keep pretending to be sleeping.

Poor Rae. Donna teases her for trying to be Little Miss Perfect but Donna doesn't get it. Donna's just a walking explosion of feelings, like a Catherine wheel at a Fourth of July celebration that's come off its pin. But she doesn't see that she *gets to be like that*, because she knows that her dad loves her no matter what. Rae doesn't have that.

It seems to me like the Hoopers' brand of Christianity is all about guilt. To be born again means to feel overwhelmingly guilty for every natural thought and feeling you've ever had and then to spend your life atoning for it. And even though she doesn't believe in it any more, the guilt hasn't gone away. All of her rage gets turned inwards. Do you know she sometimes cuts her own thighs, Diary? We've tried to convince her to stop. But there's a part of Rae that's still convinced that she's filthy and polluted. And until she makes peace with that voice in her head that says she's letting other people down, she is never going to figure out who she really is.

There's a line in the movie that I couldn't get out of my head where Uma Thurman says something like, "I want to feel free to say anything, and know that you'll forgive me."

Sometimes I wonder what it would be like if Rae stopped trying to be good, and just let herself get angry.

Sometimes I think she has so much stuff bottled up inside of her that one day she's just going to explode.

Your friend,
Kat

FACT I LEARNED TODAY: There's a way scientists test consciousness in animals called the mirror test. When an animal is sleeping, you mark its shoulder in a place where it can't see it directly, but it can see it if it looks in a mirror. You then show the animal its reflection and see if it tries to wipe the mark off. Apes and elephants can pass the mirror test, and dolphins, and even our favourite bird, the magpie. Maybe Rae's right and they do have souls.

16. SHITLIST

MARYBETH LARKIN

Marybeth is parked in the pick-up zone in front of the school after telling Sergeant Mercer that she needed to go home and lie down. Really, she's just had enough of sitting in the gym, listening to voices checking in on the radio, endless variations of "area five completed", "this quadrant clear", "nothing", "nothing", "nothing". Two days of nothing. When all the while, Katie's supposed best friends are clearly lying about what happened, searching endlessly in the woods, about as helpful as a screen door in a submarine, and nobody but her seems to have the guts to admit it. She's starting to think Zach might be right, and Katie might never have been in the forest with them at all. Are Donna and Tammy-Rae devious enough to have hiked out into the woods and back just to create a fake trail?

She's hoping to intercept the girls when they get out of school. She's willing to try a charm offensive, bribe them, damn well kidnap them, whatever it takes to get them to tell her what really happened.

She grabs the thermos from the pocket in her car door and

takes a slug, feeling like a private eye from a movie. Except instead of the thick black brew you'd expect, the thermos is filled with the over-sweetened coffee Sergeant Mercer née Underbite had pressed on her as she was leaving the school gym, complete with tiny marshmallows.

She's sitting in Fernando, her bright yellow '77 Volkswagen Rabbit. The car, too, is not exactly PI-appropriate: far too obtrusive. It's her most prized possession, covered in rust as it is. Her brother gave it to her as a hand-me-down when she was sixteen, just before she met Bill and everything changed. It's all wrapped up, in her head, with that best summer of her life, she and her best friend Jalene cruising up and down the coast, playing ABBA tapes on full blast. It's nearly two decades old now, and just about spends more time parked on the floor of the mechanic's than on her own driveway. Katie's constantly begging her to get something more practical, but Marybeth always tells her that true love lasts a lifetime.

She's a bit early for school pick-up. There are only one or two other cars. She spots Angela Bradley, Katie's old dance teacher, parked nearby. She raises a hand in greeting. Angela does a double-take, and Marybeth realises how strange it must seem for her to be here, outside a school where her daughter very obviously is not.

She slides down in her seat and shuffles the papers on the seat next to her; another batch of posters, fresh from the print shop an hour ago, and a thick spiral notebook filled with notes in her own cramped script. She spent most of last night scribbling theories. Paging through that silly magazine of theirs over and over, wondering if they might have stumbled on something that got them in trouble. Writing down motives. Unanswered questions. She'd started listing suspects, but there were too many. The whole bloody town. All eight goddamn thousand of them.

A pair of journalists walk by the car. The one who looks

like a penguin talking to a woman with bad bangs. She catches a snatch of their conversation.

"If it keeps going like this, you won't even be allowed to smoke in bars soon."

"Don't even joke, Molly. Smoking in bars is the only reason I survive this goddamn job."

"Fucking California. Did you see the museum? This town's like a Wild West Disneyland."

"With worse food."

A whinge of journalists. They don't notice her. Their voices fade into the distance.

A police cruiser pulls up ahead, driving slightly too fast. The front tyre mounts the kerb and stops with a jolt, matched by one in her chest. Is it possible that the search party found something out there? She doesn't have a beeper, so maybe Zach's rushed here to find her in the gym.

We found her body washed up on the shores of Mosquito Creek, fish-gnawed and bloated.

But the door opens, and it's not Zach, but Tim. He climbs out of the car, looking far too calm to be carrying news of her daughter. Marybeth takes a deep breath and tries to will her heart rate back to normal.

"Get lost. This is a *school*, for Christ's sake," he yells at the journalists. He shakes his head and heads into the school building. Oh yes, Sergeant Mercer said that he and Zach were staying in town today to interview more of the kids who knew Katie. Another waste of time. She's tried to tell them that there were no other friends. Those girls were a universe of three. But it seems impossible for any man to understand that teenage girl friendships are the true romances of our lives. She has never known heartbreak like the day Jalene told her she couldn't understand why she didn't leave Bill, and couldn't handle watching her destroy herself any longer, and never wanted to speak to her again.

She checks the time on the dashboard. It's nearly 3 p.m. School will be out soon. She might have a chance to get Donna and Tammy-Rae alone on their way to the bus. Surely they'd be taking the bus, with their bikes sitting in evidence? She could even offer to give them a ride home. She has before, plenty of times, the three of them belting out joke lyrics to the Rod Stewart cassette that's been stuck in the player for months.

She realises she needs to pee, and regrets the coffee. That's something else private eyes in movies never have to worry about, she thinks. None of them are middle-aged women who've had mild incontinence problems since surviving childbirth, that's for sure. Sometimes it seems that's all getting older is: just a slow accumulation of damage.

She turns on the radio to distract herself, although she suspects she knows what they'll be talking about.

"—why they haven't passed a curfew. We can't be letting our kids just walk around at night if there's some kiddie-snatcher out there." The voice sounds vaguely familiar. "I tell you, any paedophile could be out there, living in the caves probably. Are we just supposed to wait until someone else's child goes missing?"

"Couldn't agree more," the host says. "Frankly, the way Chief Pittman's handled this whole thing doesn't exactly inspire confidence. Four, five days they've been out there looking for that girl—"

"One hundred and twenty-two hours," Marybeth corrects her, automatically.

"—and what have they found?" There's a click. "Caller, you're live."

Another voice comes on the line. This one she's pretty sure is Jim Porter, who works at the video store. He starts talking about Satanic cults, about three little boys who were murdered in West Memphis as part of some ritual. "Those boys, they found them dead in a ditch, naked and hogtied with their own shoelaces, mutilated—"

The host starts talking over him, reminds him that there might be sensitive listeners on the line.

"Right, sorry. What I'm saying is the one killer, they found he was all hopped up on Ritalin. That's basically like speed, you know, except they sell it at any drugstore. Drugs like that can make you crazy. You know the girls that came back, I heard they were high as kites. And they weren't exactly saints; I knew them *personally.*" Marybeth scowls, thinking that staring down Donna Ramirez's ample cleavage at every opportunity hardly makes him an expert on their personalities.

"Interesting theory," says the host, cutting him off with a dismissive chuckle. "Go ahead!"

Another voice. A young woman. "Last month, my mother got a fax warning about a gang initiation ritual where they drive past you with their headlights off, and they wait for the first person to flash their lights at them, and then they have to follow that person off the road and murder them. It was on a police bulletin letterhead. Maybe those girls—"

"Pretty sure that's a hoax," the host interrupts. "I think we've got time for one more. I believe this is one of our *regular callers.* Chip, I'm dying to know your theory," he says, with barely suppressed glee.

"I've been saying it for years, Reg. Little Hope is built at the edge of one of the biggest meteor craters in California. That's where all the gold came from, down from space on meteors. That's a verified fact, you know, you can look it up in a book. But you know gold's not the only thing that landed in those woods; there are aliens been living out there for hundreds of years, biding their time—"

Marybeth flips off the radio. Whatever happened to her daughter, she's pretty sure she wasn't abducted by space aliens.

She bounces around in her seat, and she's just wondering whether she has enough time to dash into the school to use the facilities when the bell rings, and kids start filtering out.

Donna comes out a few minutes later, by herself, hunched over, looking furious at the whole world. The cutesy neon backpack she's wearing sits awkwardly between her shoulder blades, far too small for her.

Marybeth slouches down in the car. She'd rather not try to talk to her here, where so many people will be watching them. Donna is heading up the street towards the bus stop. Marybeth is just thinking that she'll follow her, and try to talk to her there, when Donna stops dead in her tracks.

Kids filter past her. Donna doesn't seem to be looking at anything. She's just frozen still where she stands.

Then, suddenly, she turns around, and starts walking the other way.

Shit, Marybeth thinks, fumbling with Fernando's gears in her panic and stalling the car.

Donna heads directly for her. Marybeth bends over, like she's dropped something in the footwell.

Donna walks straight by, passes the school entrance, and keeps walking the other way up the street. Marybeth sits up, watches her in her rear-view mirror, until she turns a corner and vanishes.

The girls do walk home sometimes, but Donna's house is in the opposite direction. She's heading towards Broad Street, which will make it easier to follow her, at least.

Marybeth turns over the engine and pulls her car out onto the street. She spots Donna up ahead, neon tiger simpering from her back. She pulls her hoodie up as she walks through town, but plenty of people do double-takes when they notice her. Marybeth wonders how many of them have heard Jim's teen Satanist theory, or have developed darker theories of their own.

Donna slouches past the Old Church, Louanne's Diner, then up through a side street. Marybeth follows her, but she's more conspicuous here on the quieter streets of Eastside. This would be the perfect place to stop her, get out the car and beg her to answer some questions, but she's too curious about where she's heading. She slows down and lets Donna walk ahead, until she's just a dark shape in the distance, and keeps tailing her.

They've reached the end of the bus line. There's not much past here except for a few houses, a gas station and, beyond that, the woods.

Surely not.

She must be off to join the search parties. Of all the things Marybeth has questioned over the past few days, the one thing she's never doubted is how much those three girls love each other. But how would she be planning to find the others? They've already been out for hours.

No, she's planning to go out by herself.

Marybeth realises her knuckles are white from gripping the steering wheel so hard.

Donna keeps walking. They approach the edge of town. Out here, the properties get larger but more ramshackle. Most of them mobile homes, singles, broken furniture and rusted machine parts piled around their yards. Marybeth's is a mobile home too, sure, but it's a triple volume, and she looks after it. Repaints it every few years, keeps the yard neat. These folk aren't any poorer than she is, they just don't have any damn pride, Marybeth thinks to herself.

Donna turns off the road, up a long gravel path that runs along the edge of the woods towards the sprawling property Ronnie Gaskins owns.

Ronnie Gaskins. Who supposedly had an alibi.

Decision time. She can't follow in the car any further without Donna noticing. If she's going to confront her, now's her chance. She could just pull up next to her, jump out and demand to know what's going on.

Instead, she turns off a small side road and parks Fernando. She locks up and walks back up the road, regretting the fact that she's wearing court shoes and bright pink shorts.

She can just spot the shape of Donna moving through the trees up ahead towards Ronnie's house. Marybeth hurries behind her, trying to stick to the shadows in case Donna should turn back and see her. But she doesn't. She just keeps walking towards Ronnie's, purposeful.

The house appears through the trees, shabby neo-Gothic ruin, a sprawl of rough wooden planks and plastic sheeting being eaten by the ivy. Ronnie rebuilt it himself after he moved back, since all the local contractors refused to help him. Zach said they searched the property, but how well? The house is isolated, far enough from the neighbours that they wouldn't be able to hear much from inside. *A teenage girl, shackled in a basement, screaming for help.* There's a big KEEP OUT sign on the wire gate out front. The whole thing's threaded through with chains and padlocks, no doubt since all the neighbourhood kids keep sneaking in there to pull pranks on him. The gate looks too rickety to climb.

Marybeth hangs back, sticking to the shadow of a tree, her heart pounding in her chest, wondering whether she should follow her. There's no movement from Ronnie's place. The whole thing just looks like it's a set from a horror movie about murder cannibals. She spots his dog, a small scrappy terrier, asleep on the porch. It is, indeed, wearing a cast. That answers one question in her book, at least: was David Hooper lying about seeing him at the vet's? Well, those are two names she can scratch off her shit-list.

She *does* know the hiking trail around here, she remembers with a jolt. Most people avoid this part of the woods because of the thick clouds of mosquitoes. But she walked it with her mother, a very long time ago. She thinks she can see part of it through the trees, well hidden by the copse of bushes that separates Ronnie's house from his nearest neighbours. Hard to believe that somebody might have seen three girls go past and been struck by some perverted inspiration to follow them. No, if somebody followed them, it was premeditated.

She wonders what on earth Donna's doing. Maybe she's going to confront Ronnie. The girl could be walking right into trouble. As the responsible adult, she should call for her, stop her, but she feels paralysed. Every bone in her body is screaming at her to step out into the light, talk to Donna openly.

She is just steeling her nerves, about to head up the path, when Donna stops, takes a deep breath, and bashes straight into the trees.

And what can Marybeth do but follow her?

17. TWO FACE

DONNA RAMIREZ

The sequoias grow thick here, giant columns that stretch into the deeper dark above her. Donna's hands brush them as she passes, feeling the rough fluted plates of their red-brown bark. Her hands come away damp. But it's the smells that grab her, that feel like they've turned her upside down and are shaking memories out of her brain, like nickels. The rich smell of loam, the spicy-sweet leaves, the flavour of rot.

It feels like they were just here, five minutes ago. Like Kat and Rae have dashed off around the bushes ahead, giggling, stopping to check Kat's journal for directions, thrilled to be on an adventure, about to crack a mystery.

She was worried she wouldn't be able to find the way without the journal. The path is barely a path, just a route lightly trodden through the underbrush. But she recognises each turn as she sees it. Knows that she must go left here, to get around these boulders, must duck under this branch here, must find the way along those moss-covered stones there to cross the brook. She arrives at a branch-fall, and remembers that she has to move it. Ronnie must have set this here, to hide the small path down the creek. A lot of the way seems deliberately disguised like this, erased. It's almost like the smells are leading her there, or some new sense drawing her closer. She remembers Kat once telling them about how birds can see magnetic fields; that's how they navigate the sky. Or maybe the memories of that day really are all there, buried deep in her mind, tugged to the surface by each familiar tree and stone. Perhaps the memory of what happened inside the cave will be there waiting for her, like something she dropped.

She wipes a hand across her brow and it comes away wet. Her Casio says she's three hours into her hike. She passed a couple of the search teams a few hours ago, but their attention was on the ground, and Donna crept past without being seen. She thinks. Sometimes she's sure she can hear something behind her. Snapping twigs. Like the ghosts of the three of them from the last time they walked this trail.

The straps of her stupid kid bag pull heavy on her shoulders. It was idiotic to bring it. She should have left it at Ronnie's, gone back for it later. Well, if she was *smart*, she wouldn't be here at all. She would have at least come up with a plan. She would have gone home first to fetch the two "bodyguards" her father leaves with her when he works night shifts ("my old buddies Smith and Wesson"). She would have just told the cops how to find the cave. She wouldn't be out here by herself, wandering back into a forest that she was lost in for days without any food or water. Just a loaner copy of *Intro to Calculus* weighing heavy on her back. And when has calculus ever been useful to *anyone*?

Idiot. She's such an idiot.

It's slow going. She has to pick her way around rocks, wend through tight bushes, find the gaps between the thick tree trunks that arch up to the canopy far above her.

They planned the timing so carefully last time. They knew

they needed to leave school early to be sure they'd make it back before nightfall. That was all Rae, and her clever goddamn scheming. But today, she left after school ended, which means she'll probably be stuck out here after nightfall.

Her skin prickles, remembering what it's like to be in this forest after dark. How the trunks of the birch trees glisten silver in the moonlight, their bark-like scales. How *alive* everything feels.

She could still turn back. She could just turn around, and go back, and get help.

But Kat might be out there, right now. If she goes back, they won't be able to return until tomorrow at the earliest; who knows what might happen between now and then.

More than that, she needs to *know*. She can't keep living with this hole inside.

Another *crack* behind her.

Donna whips around. She definitely didn't imagine it this time. A bush shivers, a little way behind her. She gulps, and takes a careful step towards it.

A rabbit hops out onto the path behind her. It's a small thing, mottled grey and brown. It's close enough to her that she can see the pink veins threaded through the thin skin of its ears. It doesn't run, just sits there, staring at her with dark eyes, trembling, like it's trying to warn her of something.

"Nice rabbit," she says, offering her fingers. It bounces back, gallops off into the bushes. She hears its rustles move off deep into the underbrush, but she still has the feeling that something is watching her.

The forest wigs her out. The sequoias are too tall, like something from a nightmare. She's hyper-aware of how many things in here can sense her passing. Even the trees, she feels, are aware of her footsteps pressing the soil against their roots.

She's getting close.

The ground is covered in leaves here. Each step is unpleasantly soft, unstable. Like underneath, there might be no ground at all. Just layers of leaves and soft rot, giving way to tunnels underground, weaving forever into the heart of the earth.

Her fingers tingle. Her feet know the way: over this patch of mud, around this bramble bush.

Something rustles in the trees above her. She can't see anything up there, just the dark canopy of leaves. Probably a bird. She can feel its eyes watching her.

And then it's there: the ravine.

It feels too sudden, like it wasn't there a moment ago. Like a mouth that's opened up especially to swallow her.

She peers over the edge. It's not far: can't be more than eleven or twelve feet down, to a dry riverbed about as wide. But the sides are steep, nearly vertical, a deep fissure. Kat called it a gorge; Rae called it a ravine. Donna doesn't know the damn difference. Hell, is what it is.

The trail continues to her left, following the edge. But she's never been that way. Her route is down.

Their backpacks are still right where they left them, stashed behind a convenient rock at the edge of the clearing in case Ronnie came by. Hers is sopping wet, Sharpie graffiti melting into the grey canvas. She unzips Kat's cheerful yellow bag instead, relatively protected at the bottom of the pile, and takes a few thankful sips from the half-full water bottle. Probably unwise, isn't she, what, ruining evidence? But dammit, she's thirsty.

Even better, she finds a flashlight in there, which she slips into the back pocket of her jeans, a candy bar, a disposable camera, and a sweater she expects she'll be glad for later. It's the cream one she and Rae gave her for her fifteenth with an iron-on transfer of Sylvia Plath on the back, done in Andy Warhol style, already cracked and peeling off in places, but still Kat's favourite item of clothing. Donna buries her nose in it, savouring the fumes of White Musk that still cling.

And lying right at the bottom of the bag, best of all: Kat's journal. A thick hardcover thing, plain on the outside, but crammed full of things Kat pasted in there. Kat's entire brain, captured on paper. She hugs it tight to her chest, and then slides it back into Kat's bag, promising she'll come back for it.

Her Lisa Frank bag plops heavily onto the others. How is she going to get all four of them back with her? A problem for Future Donna.

She turns back to the edge of the ravine.

Last time, they tied ropes around their waists, anchored to a boulder. Even then, Donna managed to bash her knee so hard against a rock she was sure she'd need stitches. She can't see any sign of the ropes now. But it's not that far. She'd survive a fall. *At first*, she thinks bitterly, *until I died of starvation with a broken leg*.

There's nothing for it. She made it down once; she can make it down again. She crouches over the edge and sends an exploratory foot down, looking for a ledge. Finding something that seems solid enough, she gingerly lowers her body weight onto it. Her other foot finds a root she's able to hook into.

Donna has never been good at stuff like this. She's the girl who conveniently leaves her gym clothes at home every week, who'd rather sit on the bleachers writing "I will not forget my gym clothes" one hundred times than try to keep up with the other girls who seem so naturally to be able to climb and swing and catch balls. Kat was usually right there next to her, feigning period pain (the mere mention of which made their gym teacher, Mr Philips, blush violently, even though Kat made this excuse literally every week). Rae was the only one of the three of them who liked sports. Although it was more the competition she seemed to get off on, the constant reassurances that she was better than other girls.

"Kat, you better be grateful. I'm willingly doing *exercise* for you," Donna mutters as she inches her way down the rock.

About halfway down, she gets stuck. Her left foot reaches down for another ledge, but there's nothing. She brings it back up to its previous spot and tries her right foot.

How much further to go now? Trying to look down, she has to lean away from the rock, and it makes her feel like she's going to fall. Her fingers clutch the rock tighter in panic, tiring fast. Jay's voice echoes in her head from one of their long-ago odd jobs cleaning gutters for Mrs Bradley: *Remember, it's not the fall that kills you, it's the ground.*

She's not going to be able to hold on like this. Going back up the way she came is her best bet, maybe trying a slightly different route, but there's no way her arms will pull her up. She tries her left foot again, stretching down further this time, and feels her grip breaking...

Oomf.

She finds herself flat on her back on a conveniently springy bush, rattled but fine. The ground must have been much closer than she thought. She takes a minute to catch her breath and utter a silent thanks to whatever god might be watching over her. The goddess of clumsy bitches, whoever she is.

Kat deserves a better hero than her.

It's dark down here; the meagre light that filters through the trees is blocked even further by the steep walls. But it doesn't matter; she remembers where to go. She brushes herself off and heads to her right. It's close now.

The first time they followed Ronnie out here, they hadn't been able to follow him this far. They reached the ledge, saw him descend, but there was no way they could hide from him if they followed him down. Instead they came back later, on their own. At first, they'd thought they'd hit a dead end, wandering around in the canyon, no idea where he'd gone. But they knew this must be the place, as soon as they came near it. There was a tangible heat about this place, energy radiating off the rocks.

And then they'd climbed down, into that crack, and that's where her mind grinds to a halt.

The entrance to the cave is a tight fissure in the ravine, tumbled rocks creating steps down into the darkness. It looks like a place in the earth that was sealed up, and then broke open, like an egg. The rocks are glossy, wet, rippled with strange algae.

She pulls the flashlight from her back pocket and shines it into the black crack. It cannot penetrate the dark at all, like something in there is blacker than darkness.

This place is making her feel weird. Like the cells in her body are vibrating. She's shaking too, but that could just be the nerves.

No part of her wants to go in there. It's too black, too dark. The mouth of madness.

But... Kat.

Kat, who made a point of coming by her house every single time she got back from visiting Oregon, dropping off a pack of Dunkaroos, and then leaving, because she knew Donna wouldn't want to talk about her mom. Kat, who coached her through linear equations even though her brain just refused to understand them, who spent hours drawing graphs for her until it finally clicked. Kat, who she knows almost as well as she knows herself, whose dream man is the poet Lord Byron, whose favourite food is inexplicably olive loaf, whose favourite stress-relief technique is to cover her hand in glue and peel it off, who puts paprika on everything instead of salt, who has yet to meet a book she doesn't immediately want to read, who pretends that her favourite musician is Kurt Cobain even though it's actually Bonnie Tyler...

Kat bloody Larkin. The biggest dork and the best person she knows.

Donna takes a deep breath, and she clambers down the rockfall, into the black.

All sound vanishes the moment she steps inside. The air is so humid that it's hard to breathe. Something cold oozes onto her face and joins the rivers of sweat already running down her cheeks.

The vibrating feeling in her body turns into a hum, like she's a tuning fork. She tries to steady her breathing. *Don't panic. It's just the darkness. You're not a dumb kid; it's just a cave.* But it all feels wrong.

Wrong wrong wrong.

And there is a smell. A terrible, sweet acid smell, curdling in her nose, making her retch.

She sweeps the flashlight through the dark, lighting up rough boulders covered in slimy black mould. It drips off the tips of the stalactites, like mucous off teeth.

The light catches on pale bloated lice, centipedes, wriggling in a feast of algae. An old, rusted pickaxe leans against a boulder.

Behind them, a deeper darkness, stretching far into the rock.

Then, something smooth, gently curved, lying on the ground. Mottled grey and cream. Too smooth for rock. The soft mound of an ankle bone.

A human leg.

Donna screams, dropping the flashlight in fright. It skids away from her, jams into a crack a few feet away. She crouches down, feeling blindly for it with her hands, sure that at any second something will grab at her from the dark.

"Kat…" she croaks, but there's no point. The leg was facing down, the leg of someone lying on her face. A dead leg.

Her hands touch something soft. Clothing. She pats her way along, feels them tangle in hair.

She flinches. Stretches past the body until her hands touch the cold iron of the flashlight. Then staggers back with a yelp, afraid to look, afraid not to look.

She points the beam ahead of her, finding the leg again and following it up the body to a pair of denim cut-offs. Up some more, shining on Kat's favourite flannel shirt, a mass of golden hair, face down on the ground.

And behind her, another body. This one face-up, decomposing. Brown almond eyes and a glossy dark bob. Exactly like Rae's.

There's a pounding in her ears.

Those heads are too far away for her fingers to have touched their hair.

She brings the flashlight closer, to a third body right by her feet. Over the mess of rotting meat in its middle, up to the head, face flopped away from her.

Something in her breaks.

She crouches next to the body. Her hands are shaking so hard that she is struggling to point the light. But she has to see. She has to see it.

She cups the back of its head in her hand and turns it to face her, expecting it to be stiff. But it isn't; it's far too soft. Loose. It's already begun breaking down, tissues turning to mush inside of it. The smell is overwhelming.

The face is a dark bruise of deep purple, swollen and misshapen. But there is no doubt. How could there be doubt? She's seen this face a thousand-thousand times. In photographs. In mirrors. Every day since she was born.

It's her own face, rotting dead on the floor of a cave.

THREE FOR A GIRL

MAGPIES

ZINE

For clever birds

75c

EDITION 2: JUNE 1996

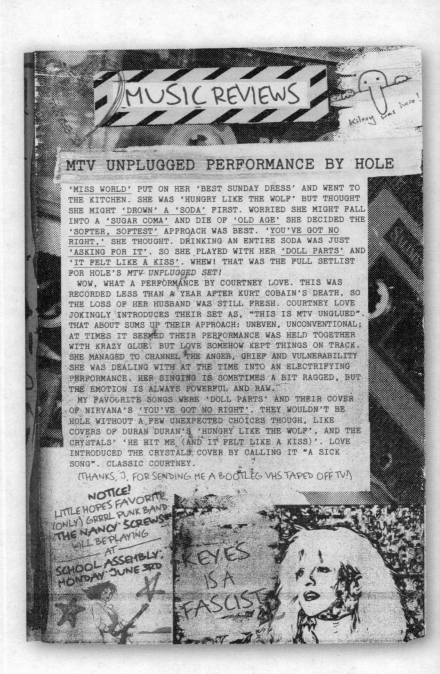

MUSIC REVIEWS

Kilroy was here!

MTV UNPLUGGED PERFORMANCE BY HOLE

'MISS WORLD' PUT ON HER 'BEST SUNDAY DRESS' AND WENT TO
THE KITCHEN. SHE WAS 'HUNGRY LIKE THE WOLF' BUT THOUGHT
SHE MIGHT 'DROWN' A 'SODA' FIRST. WORRIED SHE MIGHT FALL
INTO A 'SUGAR COMA' AND DIE OF 'OLD AGE' SHE DECIDED THE
'SOFTER, SOFTEST' APPROACH WAS BEST. 'YOU'VE GOT NO
RIGHT,' SHE THOUGHT. DRINKING AN ENTIRE SODA WAS JUST
'ASKING FOR IT'. SO SHE PLAYED WITH HER 'DOLL PARTS'
AND 'IT FELT LIKE A KISS'. WHEW! THAT WAS THE FULL SETLIST
FOR HOLE'S *MTV UNPLUGGED* SET!

WOW, WHAT A PERFORMANCE BY COURTNEY LOVE. THIS WAS
RECORDED LESS THAN A YEAR AFTER KURT COBAIN'S DEATH, SO
THE LOSS OF HER HUSBAND WAS STILL FRESH. COURTNEY LOVE
JOKINGLY INTRODUCES THEIR SET AS, "THIS IS MTV UNGLUED".
THAT ABOUT SUMS UP THEIR APPROACH: UNEVEN, UNCONVENTIONAL;
AT TIMES IT SEEMED THEIR PERFORMANCE WAS HELD TOGETHER
WITH KRAZY GLUE. BUT LOVE SOMEHOW KEPT THINGS ON TRACK.
SHE MANAGED TO CHANNEL THE ANGER, GRIEF AND VULNERABILITY
SHE WAS DEALING WITH AT THE TIME INTO AN ELECTRIFYING
PERFORMANCE. HER SINGING IS SOMETIMES A BIT RAGGED, BUT
THE EMOTION IS ALWAYS POWERFUL AND RAW.

MY FAVOURITE SONGS WERE 'DOLL PARTS' AND THEIR COVER
OF NIRVANA'S 'YOU'VE GOT NO RIGHT'. THEY WOULDN'T BE
HOLE WITHOUT A FEW UNEXPECTED CHOICES THOUGH, LIKE
COVERS OF DURAN DURAN'S 'HUNGRY LIKE THE WOLF', AND THE
CRYSTALS' 'HE HIT ME (AND IT FELT LIKE A KISS)'. LOVE
INTRODUCED THE CRYSTALS' COVER BY CALLING IT "A SICK
SONG". CLASSIC COURTNEY.

(THANKS, J, FOR SENDING ME A BOOTLEG VHS TAPED OFF TV!)

NOTICE!
LITTLE HOPES FAVORITE
(ONLY) GRRRL PUNK BAND
THE NANCY SCREWS
WILL BE PLAYING
AT
SCHOOL ASSEMBLY,
MONDAY JUNE 3RD

KEYES IS A FASCIST

FASHION AND BEAUTY

HEY GIRLS - DO YOU LONG FOR THE EMACIATED KATE MOSS LOOK YOU SEE ON EVERY BILLBOARD AND MAGAZINE?

TRY SUMMER'S HOTTEST WEIGHT-LOSS TREND: HEROIN!

THE ONLY SURE-FIRE WAY TO GET THE JUTTING CLAVICLES AND DARK EYE-CIRCLES OF YOUR DREAMS!

ALL BEAUTY IS SUFFERING!

HEROIN!

THERE IS ONLY ONE ACCEPTABLE-LOOKING TYPE OF BODY. AND IT'S THIS ONE, LOSER!

BROUGHT TO YOU BY THE SAME PEOPLE WHO BROUGHT YOU SQUISHING YOUR ORGANS INTO CORSETS AND SWALLOWING TAPEWORM EGGS.

HEROIN! NOW AVAILABLE ON ANY STREET CORNER (OR LAUNDROMAT) NEAR YOU!

*Side effects may include sores, depression and death... but who cares? You'll be so skinny!

BOOK REVIEWS

The Catcher in the ~~Rye~~ CRYbaby

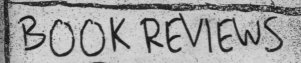

When we were assigned The Catcher in the Rye as our set book last year I was genuinely excited. I'd heard that the swearing, blasphemy, sex and rebellion against authority caused it to be banned in several countries in the world. Oooooh, forbidden fruit! This was a book that would speak to teenagers, I was TOLD. What I got instead was 116 pages about a mopey, selfish, rich, spoiled 16-year-old who acts like the universe revolves around him and doesn't even know how the world works.

The plot (or, should I say, the lack of one) follows Holden Caulfield after he is expelled from Pencey Prep. He runs off to New York where he spends the entire length of the story aimlessly wandering around the city. He meets some people, goes on some lurid escapades, gets drunk and watches his sister ride a carousel and then the story just ends!?

As a teenager, I really couldn't relate to the character of Holden. He seemed annoying, spoiled and downright awful at times, not to mention his complete lack of empathy for others. Holden blames everything on the "phoniness" of other people and never accepts responsibility for his actions. For example, after not studying, learning or even making any effort whatsoever at Pencey Prep, he expects us to sympathise with him for being expelled. Wake up, Holden! Your actions have consequences!

They say that The Catcher in the Rye is a classic. You know what else is considered a classic?
Birth of a Nation. That doesn't mean it's good. If you're looking to step into the shoes of an angsty teen, rather read The Bell Jar by Sylvia Plath. You think you have problems, Holden Caulfield? Esther Greenwood would eat you for breakfast.

You think you have problems, Holden Caulfield? Esther Greenwood would eat you for breakfast.

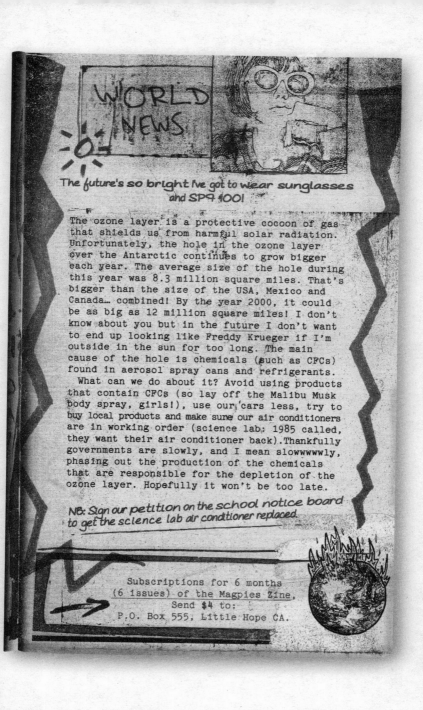

WORLD NEWS

The future's so bright I've got to wear sunglasses and SPF 1001

The ozone layer is a protective cocoon of gas that shields us from harmful solar radiation. Unfortunately, the hole in the ozone layer over the Antarctic continues to grow bigger each year. The average size of the hole during this year was 8.3 million square miles. That's bigger than the size of the USA, Mexico and Canada... combined! By the year 2000, it could be as big as 12 million square miles! I don't know about you but in the future I don't want to end up looking like Freddy Krueger if I'm outside in the sun for too long. The main cause of the hole is chemicals (such as CFCs) found in aerosol spray cans and refrigerants.

What can we do about it? Avoid using products that contain CFCs (so lay off the Malibu Musk body spray, girls!), use our cars less, try to buy local products and make sure our air conditioners are in working order (science lab: 1985 called, they want their air conditioner back). Thankfully governments are slowly, and I mean slowwwwwly, phasing out the production of the chemicals that are responsible for the depletion of the ozone layer. Hopefully it won't be too late.

NB: Sign our petition on the school notice board to get the science lab air conditioner replaced.

Subscriptions for 6 months
(6 issues) of the Magpies Zine,
Send $4 to:
P.O. Box 555, Little Hope CA.

18. MISS WORLD

TAMMY-RAE HOOPER

MONDAY, 23 SEPTEMBER 1996

Rae has been huddled in her room for hours, Discman on, listening to a mix CD Donna made her (labelled as WORSHIP MIX III, in case her mom ever found it), Skunk Anansie screaming in her ears about her tainted soul. She has a pen in her hand and is trying to conjure the shape of the thing that haunts her mind on the back of an old Spanish exam. A small head that grew straight from a long wormlike body, pale and glistening, rearing high above her. The face taken up mostly by the mouth, a huge black hole ringed with hooks. And the eyes. Green irises, but no eyelids, rolling in naked eye sockets. The strange thing about the eyes is that the more she pictures them, the more she thinks they were human eyes. Terrified or raging, she doesn't know.

Frodo has the hamster crazies. He's running over her shoulders like a circuit track, up her left arm, across the back of her neck, down her right arm, across the table and back to her left hand.

"You'd protect me from a scary beastie, wouldn't you?"

He ignores her and continues tickling her skin with his tiny feet. Round and around and around. It feels like he's charging her with electromagnetism like the solenoids from physics class. She feels wound up, dangerous. There are goosebumps all over her body, and she has to keep dabbing sweat off with a tissue. She's also starving, despite the seconds and thirds of lunch she wolfed down a few hours ago.

The drawing's no good. Wonky lines and mismatched shapes, not capturing the unworldly horror of it at all. Donna's the one who's good at drawing, not her. She crumples up the page and drops it into the wastepaper basket with the others.

It's 6 p.m. Donna must be back by now.

She slips out onto the landing and tries calling her again. The phone rings and rings.

She squeezes her free earlobe, trying to calm her breathing. *Ring. Ring.*

She puts the phone back in its cradle. She shouldn't have let Donna go. She knows monsters aren't real, *she knows*, but there is *something* out there that's dangerous, whatever or whoever killed Kat. And chicken that she is, she just let Donna go back there, alone.

She could call the police and tell them. Heck, she could even go downstairs and tell her parents, she can hear them downstairs, her dad's voice in a deep drone to her mother, probably discussing how they should ship her off to an asylum before she can cause even more harm to his reputation. Rae could go down there right now and tell them everything. But she won't. Because she's a coward. Always has been.

There was a girl in their class that they used to make fun of, back when she was friends with Sharon and the others. April Hollister. She was nice enough, just a little *off*, like she had trouble making eye contact with you, and struggled to understand metaphors. Every time they had a sleepover, they'd invite April, but they'd give her the wrong address. She never learned: every time, she'd show up, pyjamas and sleeping bag in hand, to a sleepover-free house and a confused parent. And the next day at school, they'd apologise for their *mistake*, and as soon as April left, they'd laugh until tears streamed from their eyes.

It was Sharon's idea, not Rae's, but she'd gone along with it. She'd even agreed to be the one to go over to April and invite her. A bit of harmless fun. Except that it wasn't, really. It was shitty. A real shitty thing to do. Something she can't erase, and she can't fix. Like the time they started a petition about Marcy Tompkins's bad breath. Or the time she helped spread a rumour that Jessica Daniels's mom was having an affair with their math teacher, and then Jess's parents got divorced over it. Hundreds of times she did something mean and cruel and petty. Hundreds of times she had no backbone.

Worthless. Just like now. Donna is in trouble, and Kat's gone, and here she sits in her room, doing nothing. Nothing nothing nothing.

Compulsively, she picks up the phone again, dials the first three digits of Donna's number before she slams the phone back down. No point. There's no one there.

She goes back into her room, feeling a shiver race up her body, like a premonition. Something is wrong. It's like pins and needles in her brain. Like the air becoming ash. Like something closing in on her.

The monster.

She shakes herself. Her eyes trail over the posters on the wall opposite her bed. Her pathetic attempts to curate a personality. She walks over to the poster of Monica Seles, racquet held high above her, skirts flying high, legs stretched in a frozen leap like some strange bird. She looks barely human, like she's possessed by some powerful energy.

Rae's always been terrified of the idea of possession, even though her religion talks about holy possession all the time. Other kids have nightmares about men with knives; she had nightmares about the Holy Spirit. Peggy, the Sunday school teacher, once told her that the Holy Spirit could take hold of you and give you powers, making you speak in tongues or see visions. She'd been so scared by that, because if you were possessed, how would you know if it was the Holy Spirit or a demon?

What if it's her? What if she's the monster? What if she killed Kat, and wallpapered over the whole thing by hallucinating a creature with *strangely human eyes*?

She hears footsteps coming up the staircase, and smooths Monica Seles onto the wall. There's a gentle knock on the door, and her mother slips in without waiting for a reply. She never does. The Hoopers don't believe in locked doors or privacy.

Her mother, who already struggles to find clothes in the adults' section, looks even more shrunken than usual. Her eyes are red-rimmed. From downstairs, she can hear her dad slamming things around in the kitchen.

"Your father's in one of his moods," she says, sitting on the edge of Rae's bed.

Rae rolls her eyes at her. *No duh.*

Her mom's not looking at her. She's looking down at a tissue twisted in her own hands, worked thin and ragged by her tugging.

She's actually going to try to talk to me, Rae thinks, surprised. She normally avoids Rae, after her dad's been "in one of his moods". It's weird, but whenever her dad's like that, it's her mom that she gets angry with. Her father is what he is. Rae can no more blame him for his temper than you'd blame broken glass for cutting you. But her mom chooses this. She chooses to stay here, to keep all of them here, because she'd rather put up with his disrespect than lose her *clubs* and her *societies* and her *lovely cushy life.*

She's going to ask me if I'm OK. And just at the thought of this, to her absolute horror, her eyes fill with tears. She turns back to the desk and shuffles papers around, trying to get a grip on herself. There's a lump in her throat. She gulps it back down.

I'll tell her, Rae thinks, finally. *I'll tell her if she asks.* About the monster, about Donna, about the terrible feeling she has, like she did something bad, like maybe they both did, and that she needs help. What a weight it will be, lifted from her. She could let an adult handle it.

"Do you remember when Brandon was born?" her mom says.

Rae's so surprised by this turn of conversation that her tears dry right up. She turns back to her mom, who's still tugging at the tissue, avoiding her eyes.

"Not really," Rae says. How could she? She was four.

"He wasn't an easy baby. Not like you. And I was... well, I was very sad. I even had thoughts about... about leaving." She shakes her head. To her horror Rae notices her *mother's* eyes welling up.

This is unprecedented.

"God was testing me, and I wasn't up to the challenge. I allowed my faith to be shaken. I wasn't much of a mother in those years."

She does sort of remember this, actually. Baby Brandon screaming constantly. Her father saying that if a horse had colic this often he'd put a bullet in its forehead. Having to *shh* when you went into Mommy's room because she'd be lying in bed with a headache, curtains shut in the middle of the afternoon.

Her mom looks up at her, finally. "But everything is part of God's plan. And God's plan was *you*. You were so good. You stepped right in for me when I couldn't. You soothed him and rocked him and changed him, like he was your little doll. Brandon called you his other mommy for a while, do you remember? It was so sweet how much you loved each other."

That's not the way Rae remembers it. Rae remembers being terrified that Brandon would die and it would all be her fault, this small helpless creature that needed her so badly. How she kept dreaming about murdering him, smothering his screams with a pillow until he finally shut up. Waking up and forcing herself to have extended fantasies about saving his life heroically to balance out the dreams, because God sees everything.

Her mom flashes a watery smile. "You're a good girl, honey. I know that whatever happened out there, it wasn't your fault."

It's the very worst thing she could have said. They said the same thing about Ann Mullins. *We know this was all Ann's idea; you would never do this. We love you. You're our good girl.*

They love you *so long as you stay their good girl.*

Rae turns back to the desk, flips open her Spanish workbook and picks up a pen. "I have to catch up on this before I go back to school," she says, staring at the workbook.

"I know you just want to help her. But don't ruin your life for Donna Ramirez."

Rae answers with a grunt.

Her mom gets up and heads towards the door. She pauses at Rae's posters and touches a handmade one in the middle. It says CLEANLINESS IS NEXT TO GODLINESS.

"I always liked this one," her mom says back at her.

Rae can't help but snort. She made that poster after she saw the phrase in the background of Hole's 'Miss World' music video on MTV. She's a fool to think she'll ever get any understanding from her mother. Her mom doesn't love her, only the mask of her.

She starts underlining random phrases in the workbook until she hears the door shut behind her.

Fuck her. The words flash bright and savage in her mind. *Fuck* her mother, and *fuck* her father too. *Fuck* Pastor Sherman and his holy hypocrites, *fuck* the serpents at school, *fuck* Zach Pittman, *fuck* Kat for being gone and *fuck* Donna for rushing back into danger and especially *fuck* whatever that thing is out there that won't get out of her *fucking* mind.

Fuck.
Them.
All.

She needs air. She needs to *do something.*

She slinks downstairs, carefully avoiding the creaky places on the floor. The light's on in the kitchen, so she goes out into the front yard instead of the back. The Abramses' house glows in the last of the daylight. A heavy *fwap, fwap* punctuates the birdsong, coming from their front porch.

Rae trudges into the flower bed that edges their front lawn, careful to avoid her mother's collection of homemade clay angels. One of them is missing. It's up on the roof of the maintenance shed at school, guarding their special place.

She leans over the fence. Becca Abrams is doing battle with a punching bag. One of her spaghetti straps dangles loose. She grunts as she punches, her shoulders slick with sweat, live muscle twitching beneath soft flesh, like a living sculpture, like an earthquake through rolling hills.

"Hey," Rae calls out to her, feeling reckless. "Can I have a go?" Her parents would be horrified to know she was here, talking to their certified weirdo neighbour where anyone could see. *Good.*

Becca cocks one of her thick eyebrows. "Sure." She unstraps the gloves from her hands and steps right up close to hand them to Rae. Her face is flushed.

Rae feels sweat beading on her temples, as though in sympathy with the droplets pooling in the hollow of Becca's collarbone. "Do you believe in demons?" The words come out of her, and she regrets them immediately.

Becca cracks a half-smile. "Sometimes I think all teenagers are demons."

Rae is suddenly extremely aware of the fact that there's only a few feet between them. She can smell Becca. The clean animal-ness of her. It would be so easy... to reach forwards and touch her, and kiss her, and *bite her*. Sink her teeth into that soft rippling strength of her. Take it for herself.

Becca's eyes are hazel. Rae can see herself reflected in them, two tiny dark silhouettes. Two shadow versions of herself looking back, like they've seen into her brain, into the twisted thoughts inside. The electrical feeling gets stronger, her thoughts more jagged...

Rae pulls herself away from Becca and runs back into the house, fast as she can, slamming the door tight behind her.

19. I WALK ALONE

MARYBETH LARKIN

MONDAY, 23 SEPTEMBER 1996

Marybeth's legs are starting to kill her. She's been holding a crouch for what feels like hours, behind a boulder a little way off the path. She saw Donna vanish down the edge of a ravine and considered following her into the gully, but she'd be too exposed. The girl hasn't noticed her yet, but she'd definitely spot her if she saw her dangling on the side of a sheer rock face in her sequinned jumper and bright-pink Bermudas.

So she's got no choice but to wait here, out of sight, while the girl does God-knows-what down there. She's afraid to sit down and get comfortable, because she needs to be able to get up in a hurry if Donna reappears and moves off again. But it's been a fair few years since she squatted like this for so long, and a thick band of pain runs from her hips all the way down into her screaming knees. *Jane Fonda, if you could see me now.*

But the fire in her thighs is nothing to the rage in her heart. She let this girl into her home. How many times has Donna sat there at a table with them next to Katie, shared their food, sat on their couch, *slept in Katie's room*? Donna knew where

Katie's backpack was, and said nothing. She let the cops bumble around looking in all the wrong places.

Katie might be down there right now. Her body might be rotting in the ravine, and Donna could be down there covering her tracks, destroying evidence. Or Donna could be bringing Katie food, if she's hiding out here for some reason? In that version of the truth, her daughter might still be alive, so that's the one she's hanging on to.

She tries to shift her weight a little to relieve the pressure on her knees. Maybe she should just go back, fetch Zach, bring the whole Little Hope Police Department back with her. *You see, I told you. I told you somebody was lying.*

Or she could just go down there, overpower Donna. Throw Katie over her shoulders (whatever shape she's in) and march Donna back into town, straight to the police.

But Donna's tall. Strong. And who knows what she's capable of.

No, she can wait a little longer for that bitch to show herself. Then, when Donna's gone, then she'll go down there and see for herself.

She resettles her weight. It must be getting close to sunset. The shadows beneath the trees have grown darker, like they're hungry.

There's a sharp *crack* behind her, like something stepping on a branch. The hairs on Marybeth's body stand on end. She can't see anything. But there's a rustle. Something is coming nearer.

A small shape reveals itself out of the shadows. A rabbit. It might be grey or brown, a lean, gamey thing. The shape is more hare than rabbit, ears as long as its body, but too small. It hops right up to her, nose wiggling, staring at her intently.

Another rustle in the trees, and a second one hops out to join the first. Bigger than the other. The mate? It sits next to the first one, and it, too, stares and sniffs.

Marybeth makes a shooing motion at them, but they don't budge. They stink of wet fur and are so close she can see the yellowed tips of the two front teeth poking out of the top lip of one of them. They seem entirely unafraid of her.

Suddenly, both animals tense, looking over her shoulder. Marybeth follows their line of sight, but all she sees is dense foliage beneath the tree trunks.

Both rabbits cower, frantic, and then dash away, back in the direction they came from, vanishing into the underbrush.

Marybeth looks back at the bushes, a prickling feeling at the back of her neck. The feeling that something's watching her.

The minutes tick by and nothing happens. *You're just jumpy*, Marybeth tells herself. The feeling fades. Marybeth waits.

Eventually, she hears footsteps crunching up the ravine, then the sounds of Donna puffing her way back up the cliff-face. She listens hard for the sound of a second person, but she's alone. The girl is making strange sounds, wheezing more than she should be, or laughing.

Tracking her here, Marybeth did wonder whether she's sober, from the way she weaved and wound her way through the trees. Following a hunch, not a trail.

She risks peering from a gap in the rock. Donna is pacing up and down the edge of the cliff, gripping her hair as though she could pull it out, half-sobbing, crazed, raving. Marybeth watches her crouch over a bush and heave, like she wants to vomit, but she doesn't.

Good, she thinks. *She's suffering. She feels guilty for what she did.*

It takes all of Marybeth's reserves to not rush at her, push that rotten little criminal right over the edge of the cliff, smash her guilty head into the rocks over and over again. But that's not the way. She needs to stay calm. Wait for her to go, and then go down there and see if she can still rescue her daughter.

She hides back behind the rock.

Finally, she hears the girl crunching back up the path. She slowly stands, feeling her muscles screaming at her as they stretch. Looking in the direction Donna went, she can see just the outline of the girl, through the trees, running back towards the town.

She peers down into the ravine.

"Katie, are you down there?" she hisses, scared to shout louder, in case Donna hears her. But there's nothing down there but silence.

The drop is more sheer than she'd hoped. It won't be easy to climb. She decides to follow the path a little further to see if there's another way down. It seems to continue along the edge of the gulley, to her left.

She picks her way along, pausing every few minutes to call for Katie, as loudly as she dares. The further she walks, the more she becomes aware of a bad smell, like something rotten.

Just a little further along, the pathway ends at a grass-covered clearing. There are no other trails leading out. Whoever made the trail made it to come to this place. But why?

She walks to the centre of the clearing. There are two large, squat rocks in the middle, almost equal-sized. Closer, she realises that each one has a shaky cross carved into it.

Headstones, she realises. She's standing on graves. The shiver runs up her spine again.

But these graves are old. They're covered in moss, and the grass grows thickly around her. The earth is too well-settled for these to be recent.

Even so, the smell is stronger here and she follows it to the edge of the clearing. Just there, in the trees, there's a thick pelt of fur. Grey-brown, like the rabbits. But it's huge, stretching out in front of her for four, five feet.

She bends to take a closer look. What she thought was a bunch of twiggy branches in front of her are horns. A mule deer, its face half-hidden by leaves, jewel-coloured flies buzzing around it, one eye staring blankly up at her.

It hasn't been dead long. It's still mostly intact, just bloated. There's a long gash up its belly. What could have done this? A coyote could kill a deer this size, maybe. Or a bear. But why would it just leave it out here afterwards?

She glances back at the thing's face, and, for a moment, imagines Katie's face, dead like this. *Lying in the dirt, flies clustering on a staring eye.*

She staggers back from the gory scene, almost tripping over the gravestones. She wishes she'd brought a camera. Or food, or water. Or a flashlight. Anything useful.

The little sky she can see is growing violet. There's no way she's going to make it back before nightfall, but she doesn't even care about that now. All she cares about is having enough light left to find her daughter.

Which means that she's running out of time. She has to go down there now, and the sheer rock face Donna emerged from does seem like the only way down.

She leaves the strange graveyard and returns to the first clearing. Dropping to her knees, she looks over the edge, and is about to put her first foot down when she hears heavy footsteps running up behind her.

Before she can turn, something grabs her ponytail and yanks her head back.

She screams, scrabbling behind her. Her hands grab a wrist. Padded, plasticky. *Donna?*

She's pulled back from the cliff edge and half-thrown against the leaves. Leaning her weight forwards, she tries to scramble away, but the grip on her is too strong. She reaches behind her again, goes for the wrists, tries to scratch at them to get them to release.

But another hand reaches around and covers her mouth and nose. She smells something sweet and acrid, like a disinfectant, which makes her eyes water. She twists away from it, kicking her leg back at her attacker. They stumble back from her.

Marybeth rolls over. *I'm being attacked by an astronaut.* Then realises that what she's seeing is a man wearing a gas mask and yellow rubber gloves. He's huffing, trying to catch his breath, his face distorted under the plastic. But she knows him. She's known him since he was a little boy.

He rushes towards her again, this time holding something in his hand. All of his weight falls on her, and he lifts up the thing in his hand and brings it down hard against her skull, and as the world falls away from her, her last thought is annoyance at how obvious it all is.

It's Ronnie fucking Gaskins.

20. A REAL MAN

KATHERINE LARKIN

SUNDAY, 11 AUGUST 1996

DIARY, YOU WON'T BELIEVE WHAT HAPPENED.

OK OK, but to start at the beginning: I told Donna and Rae about my idea that we should interview Ronnie Gaskins. To my surprise, they both loved it. Rae was so impressed, she said it's the kind of thing that would be *actual journalism,* maybe something so good that if we pulled it off, all of us could have our pick of any college we want, it would be our ticket out of Little Hope, to ANYWHERE.

Rae suggested that we should just spend a few days observing him first to make sure he didn't seem actively unstable. "You never know with a sociopath; they can snap at any point and just go crazy," Rae said. But Donna waved that idea off saying it would take too long and said we should just go up and ask him.

"What, like, 'Hey, Mister Murderer, would you mind telling us why you came back to the town where you killed your parents? Thanks ever so much.'" Rae mocked her.

But the more we talked about it, the more it seemed like what Real Journalists™ would do, so we did it.

We heard Ronnie had rigged up his yard with more booby traps than the house in *Home Alone,* so we figured we should wait for him to come into town. ADDED BONUS, we'd be in a public place so less vulnerable to axe-murderage. Ma Bear once mentioned he does a weekly supply run every Saturday afternoon, because he once tried stopping at the hotel bar for a drink, but her boss Matt flat-out refused to serve him. So, we decided our best chance was ambushing him outside the general store.

Rae brought along the pepper spray her mom got for the one time she had to go to Los Angeles for a Spiritual Warfare conference. I had Ma Bear's big bulky cassette recorder she used to tape me with when we were trying to improve my singing voice for the pageants (even Ma Bear finally conceded defeat in the face of my foghorn alto).

We loitered outside the store so long that the storekeeper came out and pointedly asked us if we intended to buy something so we bought his gross blue Slurpees to get him off our case.

And then, there was Ronnie!

I nearly lost my nerve, Diary. Because as he climbed out of his station wagon, Rae grabbed my hand and pointed to the back seat, and you know what was there? A GAS MASK AND YELLOW GLOVES!!!! I might have just been imagining it but I swear to goat there was blood on the gloves. It gave me the CREEPS, I tell you.

But Donna hadn't noticed; she'd pounced on him and was already gabbling on about how we just wanted to ask him some questions for a school project, and then totally forgot to open with the softball questions like we planned ("What was it like growing up in Little Hope?" and all that) and just jumped right into "I guess what I really to know is why you came back here after jail?"

And Ronnie couldn't make eye contact. His eyes were this creepy blue, like a blue that's way too *blue*. Like painted glass. And they darted around everywhere except us. To the store.

To the street. To the back seat of the car, and the POSSIBLY BLOOD-COVERED gloves.

He was rubbing his hands, and I noticed that the webbing between his thumb and forefinger was crispy, an old burn scar. And suddenly I was just very very aware of the fact that this man had spent time in jail.

Then he stepped RIGHT UP to Donna. Like, 10cm away. And Donna's tall, but Ronnie's still a head taller than her. So she had to look up at him, but Donna didn't even flinch. And those unnatural eyes of his were still flitting about everywhere except us.

Then, finally, he mumbled something. I couldn't quite catch it, but it was something about "keeping the devil in his hole". I. KID. YOU. NOT. So cryptic! Like, was he talking about himself?

Then he turned back to his car, and I grabbed Donna's hand to drag her back, because I was sure he was reaching for a knife or something.

But he wasn't, he was just getting back in his car. And he straight-up DROVE AWAY. Didn't even buy anything.

That was IT for Rae. She was convinced the whole thing was a terrible idea and we were lucky we didn't get murdered and we should never talk about it again. But honestly Donna and I were both even more hyped up and dying to know what his deal was.

So we got into the habit of going after school and taking my grandma's old birdwatching binoculars and some snacks and hiding behind a bush on a little hill near Ronnie's house, and spending all afternoon just watching him. It was SO THRILLING. It was like being an actual real-life detective. Even though we spent the whole first few days just getting twigs up our asses and eating our way through an enormous family-size box of Shark Bites. OK, to be honest, that was mostly me. For some reason I've been hungry all the time recently and I'm still losing weight anyway. And I've been nauseous, like constantly. It's freaking me out a bit.

There was nothing to see for the first two days. I actually

started to feel a bit sorry for him for how run-down his house is. Murderer or not, nobody should have to live in a house like that. There's junk and stuff lying around everywhere in his yard. We saw him come out a couple of times and check his booby traps, and he seemed to be trying to fix a hole in his roof, which seemed like a lost cause really, because we could see most of his roof, because we were sitting on a hill, and that thing was more patches than roof. He doesn't seem to talk to anybody except his dog.

The mystery of the bloody gloves was solved pretty quick, because he had a little skinning station out in the back corner of his yard where we could see two rabbit skins stretched out to dry, so we figured sometimes he ate rabbit. Donna thought this was extremely gross. She's trying to be a vegetarian because of how animals get treated, except fish because she says Kurt Cobain said fish don't have feelings. To be honest, the sad little rabbit skins freaked me out a bit too, but it seemed hypocritical to admit because I eat pigs and cows, don't I? But it was hard to look at them and not imagine what it would feel like if Ronnie Gaskins slipped a knife up my belly, cut me open, and stretched my outsides out in the sun.

Day three of watching Ronnie through the window pottering around his cabin cleaning and cooking and doing absolutely nothing interesting, we were just about to give up and try talking to him again, when we saw him pack up a rucksack and head out to the forest, dog in tow. We figured he was probably looking for his supper. A little more rabbit for the pot.

We debated whether or not to follow him. I said we shouldn't, because we were supposed to be journalists, not stalkers. But to be honest I was still thinking about Ronnie cutting my skin off and I was kind of freaked by the idea of bumping into him in the woods, alone. But Donna wasn't even listening, she'd already crammed our snacks back into our backpacks and nudged them under a bush where nobody could see them, and had darted off into the treeline. Rae rolled her eyes at me as if to say *Typical Donna,* but we both followed after her.

We followed him up a path that seemed to go directly from his house out to Mosquito Creek. Only it was barely a path. It seemed like he was the only one who ever used it. A lot of the time it felt like we were little better than just bashing through bushes.

I hadn't gone this far into the woods before. We nearly lost him a few times. It wasn't easy, trying to be quiet, staying far enough back that he didn't see us, but just far enough that we could see where he was going. He seemed kinda paranoid, like he kept checking back to see if anyone was following him. And then of course Donna started whispering jokes about how Rae's parents would be horrified to discover she WAS a bush diver after all and we got the giggles and I was sure he'd heard us. But luckily he didn't seem to.

Eventually, we realised that this was no hunt. He was still marching really fast, like he had somewhere important to be. Which, of course, only made us even more curious. We'd been walking for nearly two hours and we were starting to worry we weren't going to make it back before nightfall. I wondered if this was his plan: lure us out deep into the woods, wait until dark, and then attack us. Donna and Rae might have been thinking the same thing, because we'd all gotten real quiet, and even Donna was starting to look like she thought we should maybe head back.

Even if we did try and go back, I wasn't sure that I knew which way to go. The path had long vanished, and we'd just been making our way through trees. I had *you* with me, journal, so that I could take notes in case anything important happened, and I'd been trying to draw a little map as we walked, but I wasn't sure if I was doing a good job.

The forest was more overgrown than I'd ever seen it. Much

wilder out here than the gentle paths closer to the town. Everywhere we looked, there were thick spider webs, piles of broken branches, dark holes that looked like the dens of creatures I did not want to meet. Rae was grumbling about how nature would be fine if they just swept up all the dirt, maybe stuck a roof over it, put in some air conditioning.

Just as we were starting to think Ronnie was going to hike to Alaska, we realised he'd stopped up ahead of us. We ducked behind a rock where we could watch him. He was standing at the edge of a steep ravine, then stooped right down to the ground like he was looking for tracks. His dog was sniffing around too.

"Maybe he really is hunting," Rae whispered, but that made no sense, because why would he have come all the way out here to do so? He dropped his rucksack at the edge of the ravine and vanished into the brush. We couldn't follow him without coming right out into the clearing, so we stayed put.

Rae hadn't brought a coat and she was shivering a little from the cold. This is the advantage of bringing your own padding with you everywhere you go: I pretty much never get cold.

Ronnie reappeared. He pulled a rope out from his backpack, tied one end around his crotch and the other around a sturdy tree. Then he pulled out the GAS MASK AND RUBBER GLOVES, put them on, and lowered himself down into the ravine, carrying the mutt in his arms.

We argued, in whispers, about whether to follow him. Donna was all, "Well, we've come this far, do you really want to give up now?" and, "This could be our chance to finally do something bigger than Little Hope," but Rae and I both agreed there was no way we could follow him without being seen. "Besides, do either of you just happen to have a rope in your bag?" I added, and we all thought about the half-empty boxes of Shark Bites that we'd left back at the hiding spot by Ronnie's place, and laughed about how inadequate our supplies were.

But I was also thinking about how we hadn't brought flashlights with us, let alone a rope, so we did NOT have any time to keep hanging out here waiting for Ronnie to do something worth reporting. We needed to turn back.

But Donna had that look on her face that she gets when she gets stubborn about something. "I'm not leaving until we get something." Before we could stop her, she'd rushed down to the edge of the ravine. Rae followed her, but I was too scared, and I stayed back. They crouched down and peered over the edge, but I don't think they could see anything without risking being visible themselves.

I didn't want it to seem like I was just hiding (although I totally was) so I started pretending to look around in the brush where Ronnie had gone before he went down into the ravine.

But I did find something: another little path. You could just make out how the grass was squashed from having been walked on, but it looked like it was worn down enough that I didn't think it was the first time someone had come this way. I was pretty proud of myself for noticing all of this. Nancy Drew eat your heart out.

I wish that's where I'd stopped. I had a bad feeling the more I went. Like something was screaming in my ears telling me to GET AWAY.

But I didn't, because I didn't want Donna and Rae to think I was a wuss.

The path opened out into a little grassy clearing in the trees. And there were two rocks there, side by side, with little crosses carved onto them. And I just knew they were grave markers. And suddenly I realised that the ground I was standing on had bodies underneath.

I ran out of there, back to the clearing, and I tell you, Diary, it was everything I could do not to scream. Donna and Rae weren't there. I looked up and saw Donna waving at me frantically from our hiding spot. I could see why, the rope

Ronnie had tied to the tree had gone taught and jiggly. I rushed back to Donna and Rae, and the three of us hot-footed it out of there as fast as we could. We didn't wait for Ronnie to climb back up; we just started running back through the woods. The other two could tell from my face that I'd seen something, and I managed to whisper to them what it was, and we ran faster, desperate to get away from that place before Ronnie caught up to us. We got back to Ronnie's in half the time it took us to go out there, and we were wheezing and huffing and half dead, sure at any second that Ronnie himself would grab us from behind and then there would be three more graves out there deep in the forest where nobody could find them. But he didn't catch us and we didn't see a hint of him the whole way back.

The sun had just set by the time we got back to town. We just ran all the way back to Broad Street, to where we'd left our bikes chained up outside the Bi-Lo, and we cycled right back home. Ma Bear was mad because I was late for dinner and she asked me why I had dirt smears all over my jeans, and I told her that we'd been climbing trees at Rae's, but I could see from her face that she thought we'd been out to the old bottling factory to make out with boys or something, and she looked sad, so I asked her to tell me all the gossip from the hotel and she forgot about all that and it cheered her up.

I had to wait until after dinner when Ma Bear went to take a bath before I could sneak to the phone and call Donna. The two of us spent ages wondering who the graves might belong to. Donna thought it must be his parents, but I reminded her that they're buried in the church graveyard; we've all seen their headstones. "But what if he dug up their bodies and moved them out to the woods." Neither of us could think of a reason he might have done this, though. Then Donna said maybe they weren't graves, just memorials, and he liked to go out there and think about his parents, and "visit" with them, because people are so shitty to him when he comes into town, so maybe he likes to mourn out there where he has privacy. This was a pretty perceptive idea, but I told Donna I didn't believe it. I can't tell you why, but I'm SURE there were bodies out there. I just got a feeling, like a shiver that ran all through my body.

Then Donna asked what I thought was down in the ravine. We debated this for a while. I said maybe he had a mystery science lab, hence the gas mask. Then Donna said softly, "What if it's the Lost Mine of Little Hope?" And I told her that was just a myth, but she said, "But what if it's not?" I think Donna was imagining a big pile of gold, and how much that could change her life.

I asked Donna if she'd told her dad about what happened, and she said no, and she asked if I'd said anything to Ma Bear, and I said also no, because if I tried to explain to Ma Bear why we followed a KNOWN MURDERER into the woods ALONE I would never be allowed out the house again until graduation. Then Donna asked if I thought we should go to the police. But we both agreed that we couldn't decide anything without talking to Rae, and we can't call her this late, because her parents freak if their phone so much as rings after dinner time.

So we hung up, and I've been in my room since then, and I needed to tell SOMEONE about all this, Diary, so I told you.

And I'll tell you something else, too, that I didn't even tell Donna: there's no way I'm going to tell the cops about this. Because hell, this is the first actually exciting thing that's ever happened to me in my whole stupid boring life. An actual real-life mystery! Something I could WRITE about. Something like this could actually change our lives.

If we go to the cops with this, we'll just be three dumb teenage girls who found something weird and they'll arrest him and the story won't belong to us any more.

Diary, I want this to be OUR story. OUR mystery. OUR adventure.

We have to go back and see what's really out there.

My heart is racing. Is this the stupidest thing we've ever done?

Love,
Kat

FACT I LEARNED TODAY: Kurt Cobain (RIP) was a Pisces so Donna's theory is that when he sings that it's OK to eat fish, he's talking about himself, because he's so emotionally numb he might as well be dead. DARK. What's up with all these great artists not caring if they live or die?

Little Hope Gazette

Ronnie Gaskins' conviction overturned after discovery of false confession.

By Doyle Hobbes - staff writer

A local man's murder conviction was overturned on Friday, nine years before he would have served the minimum portion of his life sentence.

Sacramento District Attorney John De La Rocha announced that following a thorough investigation by his Conviction Review Unit (CRU), he would move to vacate the conviction of 23-year-old Ronnie Gaskins.

A 12 year old juvenile at the time, Gaskins was sentenced to life in prison for the brutal slaying of his parents in 1981.

A 12-year-old juvenile at the time, Gaskins was sentenced to life in prison for the brutal slaying of his parents in 1981.

Speaking on behalf of the committee, Mr De La Rocha said, "On investigation, it quickly became clear that Mr Gaskins didn't receive a fair trial. He was interviewed for hours without a lawyer, family member or adult present, and his confession included several statements that were contradicted by the physical evidence."

In the confession taken by Chief Pendleton in 1981, Gaskins claimed that he first shot and killed his parents, and then several hours later set fire to the house in an attempt to conceal the crime. However, the day after Gaskins made the incriminating statements and was charged for the double murder, the medical examiner reported that both parents' lungs showed evidence of smoke inhalation, indicating that they had been alive when the house was set on fire.

At the time, police claimed that Gaskins led them to the murder weapon, a .38-calibre revolver, hidden in the woods near his parents' house. A transcript of Gaskins's police interview presented during the investigation indicated that Pendleton knew of the firearm's location before interrogating him.

Several other small inconsistencies from the case cast the timeline into doubt, including the puzzling fact that while bullets were found inside the bodies of both of the deceased, forensic investigators were never able to identify entry wounds.

The investigation also cast doubt on the validity of the gunshot residue evidence collected from Gaskins in 1981. Hanna Page, a gunshot residue expert, testified during the investigation that a positive test result does not necessarily mean that Gaskins had fired a gun. "They could have come from other sources such as fireworks, brake

pads, or they could be a result of a contaminated sample," she said. Friends of the family had testified at the time that Gaskins was known to play with fireworks in the front yard.

"It is clear that Chief Pendleton teased out contradictory statements from Mr Gaskins, steering him towards his theory of the case," said De La Rocha. He added, "Whilst we cannot say for certain that Mr Gaskins was not involved in this crime, a thorough investigation by my Conviction Review Unit has concluded that he was deprived of a fair trial, thus undermining our confidence in his conviction."

In his ruling, the judge said, "The greatest care must be taken in making sure that confessions obtained from juveniles are voluntary."

Mr Gaskins could not be reached for comment.

Hope Police

21. WHAT KIND OF MONSTER ARE YOU?

DONNA RAMIREZ

It's long past dark when she finally unlatches the gate to her home. Every part of her aches from the long hike. She is shivering, parched, half-delirious and covered in scratches from stumbling around in the dark. The last hour was the worst, once the sun had set fully, and it felt like there were eyes on her. She kept tripping over roots and sliding on mud, able to see nothing but the image burned into her mind: Donna Ramirez's face, lying next to the other bodies in that dark place.

There are lights on inside the house. She'd been hoping, vaguely, that her dad would have been late coming back from work, that he might not have noticed she was gone. But she's not going to be that lucky. She can see the shadow of him through the curtains, pacing back and forth by the window.

She closes the gate behind her, pushing slowly to avoid the rusty creak, and walks up to the house as quietly as she can. The shadow behind the curtain twitches, he must have heard her coming.

Fuck. Too late, she realises that she's got Kat's yellow backpack slung over her shoulder. She left the others where they were, hidden behind the rock near the gorge. But she couldn't bear to leave this one. It feels like the last bit of Kat she has left.

But how is she going to explain it? She's going to be in so much trouble. Jesus, she's such an idiot. She rushes over to the window of her bedroom, which has mercifully been left ajar in the late summer heat, and slides the bag through it onto the floor of her room, just as she hears the rattle of the door handle, and her father spills out onto the porch.

"*Ay!*" he yells, incoherent, pulling her into the living room. He grips her shoulders, firmly, as though checking that she's real. His jaw is set in a way that she's never seen before. Furious, she realises. He's furious.

He goes off in a stream of Spanish, so fast that she only catches half of what he says. She gets the gist of it, anyway. Questions that aren't really questions. Where has she been. How dare she put him through this. What the hell was she thinking.

"Sorry, Papi, I need a minute." She runs to the bathroom and shuts the door behind her. Her father continues raving in the other room. She just hopes that he doesn't go into her room and notice the little yellow surprise she dumped through the window.

She sinks onto the toilet, gripping the seat tight, trying to catch her breath. Through the door, she hears her dad pick up the phone, and talk to someone she can only assume are the police. "It's OK, she just came home. No, she's fine. I'm sorry to bother you. No, no, of course." His voice slurs with rage.

Her back muscles are cramping all up one side. She rubs a fist into the small of her back, feeling the bones of her spine click around her knuckles. *Whose spine is this?* she thinks dreamily. *Whose fist?*

There's a hammering on the door. She goes to the sink and washes the worst of the grime off her face, afraid to look up into the mirror and see who's there. The girl who isn't Donna, who *can't be Donna*, because Donna Ramirez is lying dead in a cave in the middle of the Plumas National Forest.

She cups a hand under the faucet and takes a few merciful gulps of cold water. The hammering intensifies. She unlocks the door, and steps out into the harsh light of the living room. Her dad's eyes scan over her, as though they're taking inventory, checking that she's all here. He, at least, doesn't seem to notice anything off about her. He seems to have calmed down enough to talk to her. Barely.

"You went back to the woods." It's not a question.

Donna sits on the sofa and slips off her sneakers. Her grateful feet immediately start to tingle as blood flows back into them. She nods.

"You went to look for Kat."

She nods again.

"Did you find anything?"

"No." *Nothing I can explain, anyway.*

"And did you stop to think, *for even just one second*, what you would be putting me through?"

She has never, never seen him like this, so angry and hurt. Donna's heart is a brick, heavy in her chest.

"I came home, and you were gone. You were gone, and I didn't know..." He trails into silence. His nostrils flare with each deep breath.

Blue lights flicker through the window. She hears a car door slam, and then voices coming up the drive.

Her dad peers through the curtain. "Zach and Tim. They must have been on their way here already."

Donna feels herself shaking again. "Please, Dad." Her voice comes out as little more than a croak. "I can't."

He glances back at her, and she thinks for a moment that he'll say this is just what she deserves, she made her bed and now she must face the consequences, but then the hard look on his face cracks, he's just her dad again, and he slips out of the door to talk to the cops on the porch.

"She's fine," she hears her dad tell them. "I got a bit of a scare, is all. Overreacted." He even gives a self-deprecating chuckle, which the cops don't reciprocate. She can hear the rough rumble of Chief Pittman's voice, but not the words. He sounds ragged, like he hasn't slept in days.

What if they want to come inside? she thinks, twisting her grimy hands in her lap. *What if they search the house?*

But their voices move off, and her dad says, "Sorry to waste your time." Then she hears car doors slam again.

Her dad comes back inside, and all of the anger has burned out of him now. He sits on the couch next to her and exhales deeply. "I was so scared," he says, at last.

Donna lays her head on his knees. He lifts a hand and starts stroking her eyebrows gently with his forefinger. He used to do this to get her to fall asleep when she was a baby.

"Where were you?"

"I just needed to... I had to get away."

"It doesn't look good, you leaving. After everything. The cops already think..." He lets the sentence trail off. Sighs. "Donna, there are some things you can't run away from."

A clutch of white candles is burning in front of the small statue of *la Virgen*. It was a Christmas gift from her *tía* in Cagua. She remembers that trip in perfect detail: the sounds of tree frogs singing at night, the giant sunflowers in the yard, the smells of whole roasting pig and plantain, driving with Jay and her cousins to get greasy snacks at the *chinchorro*, Brewley MC blasting on the radio, how they teased her for her clumsy Spanish, called her a *gringa*.

But how can she remember this, if these are Donna's memories?

"They'll find her," he says, obviously misinterpreting the frown on her face. "When I joined the search party on Sunday, they had cops from all around the state. They even had those sniffer dogs. California's finest." The pads of his fingers smooth her unruly eyebrows, over and over.

Her body goes stiff. The dogs. The forest's big but it's not endless. They'll find it eventually. And she's just renewed the scent on the trail, which will lead them straight to the cave, and the inexplicable bodies.

God, Rae was right all this time. *Other* Rae. They should have kept people away from there.

Eventually, her dad's breathing deepens, and his eyebrow-stroking stops. She peels herself off him, carefully. He's fallen asleep, head flopped against the wall, worn out from stress and worry. Her heart aches with love for him. Surely he would have known, if she was some kind of imposter? Isn't this love proof of her own existence?

She pulls a blanket over her dad, turns out the lights and wanders through to her bedroom. Kat's backpack is there beneath the open window. She fishes Kat's journal from the bottom and flips through it. Kat's neat block-text, pages and pages of it. All sorts of things pasted in there between the entries: newspaper clippings, flyers, notes they wrote each other in class. The whole second edition of *Magpies* is wedged in the centre. She spots her own name a dozen times. The whole thing is a scrapbook dedicated to their friendship.

She opens to a random entry near the beginning and skims it. It's from last December, about the time the three of them slept over at Rae's house all weekend when her parents were away. Yes, she remembers that. She definitely does. Kat showed them both how to do eyeliner properly, she recalls, and that's not even in the diary entry.

She goes over to a mirror. Runs her finger along her chin looking for the flap of a mask. Opens her mouth and lifts her tongue, imagining a button underneath. Pinches herself. It's her own real body. It's her own real face.

But obviously it's not. She's some kind of imposter. Maybe

she's a clone, like Dolly the Sheep. Or a weirdly corporeal ghost. Or a body snatcher like from that movie they watched, some alien life force here to destroy all humans and take their place. But if she's a body snatcher, where's her damn instruction manual? Where's her pamphlet titled, *So you're a body snatcher, now what?*

She glances over at the phone sitting next to her bed, wondering if she should call Rae and say, "Oh hey, your monster's real after all, and whoops, it's us!"

Except, she has the feeling Rae already knows.

22. HAMSTER BABY

TAMMY-RAE HOOPER

MONDAY, 23 SEPTEMBER 1996

Long after everyone else has gone to bed, Rae lies on the floor of her room, headphones still on, staring at the ceiling, trying to figure out what is going on with her brain.

She's been trying to meditate. Since she got so into the Tibet thing, Kat was always going on about how there's actually a bunch of science supporting it, something about different brainwave frequencies or something. Well, Rae's just about desperate enough to try anything.

So she's on the floor, trying to calm her own mind, but instead… she seems to be tuning into Donna's.

It feels like Donna is lying next to her. Like if she just reaches out, her fingers will brush the soft hair on Donna's forearms. But Donna is on the opposite side of town, lying in her own bed, sleeping fitfully. She can feel her, a little point of light at the edge of her consciousness. She felt her walk back from the forest, knew the moment she got back home. She can hear her fear, like her brain is a radio and Donna's just a half-frequency off her band.

How the *hell* does she know what Donna's feeling?

There's something else, right at the very edge of her awareness. Less a single point of light, more like moonlight rippling off the surface of a lake. A dark, deep lake, with too many eyes staring back at you from the depths. It feels like the forest.

Rae rubs the tips of her fingers together, trying to reconnect with her own body. She tells herself to breathe, that this can't be happening, that her imagination's just getting carried away with her.

She gets up, slipping the headphones off her ears and tossing them onto the carpet, and stands in front of the mirror. She considers herself: the sharpness of her cheekbones, the hard edges of the planes of her face. Unpretty, a face to match her boyish hips and plank chest and the thin downy bit of hair between her legs that's nothing like the womanly bushes she's seen on Kat and Donna. Once, she read in one of those confessional columns in *Cosmo* about a girl who hit puberty and found that instead of her breasts growing, her clitoris did. It grew and grew out into a tiny penis, and then they did tests and discovered she wasn't a girl at all, but a boy that hadn't developed properly, secret testicles inside and everything. The girl kept insisting that she felt like a girl, not a boy, but they told her she was just confused and her parents made her cut her hair off and practise dressing in boy clothes.

For months after reading that piece, Rae would nightly examine herself in the shower to check she wasn't growing a tiny penis. It wasn't masturbating. Donna jokes about her lover Fabio, the rubber handle of her paddle hairbrush. Even Kat once confessed to having a technique of humping the corner of the mattress. Rae told them she masturbates too, but the truth is that she's only ever touched herself in anxiety, poking around, wondering if she's secretly a boy, if one day she'll just wake up with a giant dick in her pants and everyone will finally see how wrong she is inside.

But she never imagined this, that one day she'd wake up having spontaneously developed Donna-specific ESP and the urge to bite her neighbour.

She smooths down her hair, telling herself that she looks normal. But the stress is building up too tight inside of her, and there's only one way she knows to relieve that stress.

She keeps her cutting kit inside her old Game of Life box, in the drawstring bag that stores the life tiles. A pack of razor blades, alcohol wipes, Band-Aids. She lays them all out on her desk in neat rows, exactly the same distance between each item. This is all part of her ritual, her way to re-establish control. She lifts a new blade from the box and kisses it in thanks.

Donna and Kat were always the only ones who could talk her out of it. They had a buddy system. She didn't have to say it, "I think I'm going to cut myself later"; she could just call them and say that she was feeling a little low, and they'd know what she meant, and they'd keep her on the phone, and they'd make her talk about inane things until the feeling passed. They'd ask her pointless questions: what was her favourite toy as a kid; if she had to, *had* to marry one of New Kids on the Block, which one would she marry and why; is there any way one can conclusively prove that Bob Dole is *not* a lizard in a human-suit; if she time-travelled into Europe in the Middle Ages, how would she prove to them she was from the future without being burned as a witch. It didn't matter what the questions were; what mattered was that they made her talk until the bad feelings went away.

But Donna's asleep, and Kat's gone. There's no one to phone now. No one to pull her out of the dark place. And she just has to do *something* to quiet her mind, to break her out of this insane thought spiral.

Frodo is back in his cage, running on his wheel. The wheel's squeaking is irritating her, so she takes him out and lets him scamper around her desk. The walls in this house are paper-thin, so she can hear video game explosions coming from Brandon's room. *She* was the one who'd shown her parents all the articles about how computer skills were going to be so important for all the jobs of the future, but they put the computer in Brandon's room, where he mostly uses it to shoot aliens.

She grabs a tissue from the box next to her bed and lifts her skirt. Her thighs are latticed with thin white scars. But, of course, no one ever sees her thighs.

She slices and her heart pounds in relief. Endorphins flood her, and her mind is still. She allows herself five deep breaths, relishing the calm, eyes closed, then tears open an alcohol wipe to clean it up.

But there's no sting. The blood wipes clean off, but there's no cut underneath.

She grabs the razor and cuts again. Kat's always telling her how dangerous this is, how she could bleed out if she nicks an artery. She hisses with pain, but forces herself to go deeper, sinking the corner of the blade deep into the skin.

She pulls it along, a long two-inch slice, then out. Blood pours out, dripping down her leg onto the carpet. Then, a moment later, the sting fades, and the skin knits itself closed in front of her eyes.

Someone is moaning. A deep, animal sound. She realises it's coming from her own chest. *How*, how is this happening? She stabs the blade back into her leg, deep. Blood spurts out, splattering her skirt, the desk, but that closes too.

She holds up her left hand. Her hands are shaking so violently that it takes three attempts before she manages to cut her palm. Blood streams over her wrist and down her forearm, but the wound is already gone. The room starts to whirl around her.

She throws the blade away and picks up a pair of scissors from her desk. She plunges them into her thigh, right down to the handle. She gasps in pain, but she pulls it out, and the red mouth of flesh shuts, the skin slides back together, blood-slicked and unblemished.

Her whole desk is covered in blood now. It's pooled on the floor, running in rivulets down her body. If her parents find her, God, how will she explain this?

"Frodo, no." The hamster is sniffing at the bloody tissues on the desk, tearing a corner off experimentally. She picks him up with her free hand and puts him back in his cage. Blood everywhere. She has to clean it up before her mother sees.

The hamster shrieks. She hushes him, scared he'll wake her parents, that they'll run in here, and see what she's done... but he shrieks again, in a way she's never heard before, a creaking shriek, over and over. Did she grab him too hard? He falls onto his back and starts to twitch.

"Boy, what's wrong?"

She tries to lift him back out, but he's thrashing around in his cage now, throwing sawdust up around him. With horror, she notices that he's oozing foam from his mouth. She yanks her hand back out. Rabies, isn't that what makes animals foam?

The room spins. The blood runs down her leg, onto the carpet.

She has to go and call her dad. He'll know what to do. But she can't go like this, covered in gore. Pulling on a pair of pyjama pants, she grabs her cutting supplies and the used tissue and shoves them all back into the box, blood and all, stashing it on her shelf. But there are still droplets of blood all over the carpet.

Frodo is lying on his side now, gasping for air. His whole little body inflates and deflates like a balloon.

Then it stops.

"Boy?" She reaches in carefully and pulls him out. His tiny body is completely limp. There's no trace of the fast little flutter of his heart. He's dead.

A sob breaks from her. She lays him back on the desk, his

poor tiny body. She takes ragged breaths. Could the room stop spinning for just a moment so she can think?

The house is quiet, except for the tinny sound coming through her headphones, the distant sounds of Brandon blowing up pixellated enemies in the next room. Rae slumps into the chair and puts her head in her hands and just lets herself cry. It doesn't make sense.

Frodo lies there, dead and small and still.

Except... not still. Is he *moving*?

She leans forward to look at him carefully.

His tiny black eyes are open and blank. His jaw is slack, lips still covered in white foam, but his belly is moving. Not the twitch of living muscle. Something squirming inside of him.

She recoils so hard that she falls off the chair and smashes back onto the floor.

A voice inside her insists, *Go get Dad*. But something else tells her no. And not because there's still blood on her hands that she'd have to explain. Because something is telling her that she needs to be here and witness this.

The skin on Frodo's belly is stretched out thin, something struggling to get out. It bursts open, and a chunk sloshes out onto the desk. A foetus. A small squirming shape, covered in blood and viscera. But unmistakably, a tiny hamster, barely the size of the top segment of her index finger. Its eyes black orbs sealed with skin, its mouth the tiniest gash in its pink hairless face. She watches as it swells to the size of her thumb, hair sprouting all over its moist body. The front left leg stretches out, longer than the others, almost tipping it over. A right leg sprouts out just in time to catch it. The tiny nubs on its head unfold into ears. Nostrils unseal and quiver. The front teeth grow far too long, two curved bone-daggers piercing the bottom lip, until the head catches up, broadening to the right size and shape.

Eyes blink open.

It takes its first, shuddering breaths.

And something lights up in Rae's mind, like a new star bursting into existence, a mess of sensations and hunger and delight. Frodo. She is connected to him, like the cells in her body are vibrating in tune with his. She puts her finger out to the tip of his nose and the feeling gets stronger. His tiny black nose twitches, exploring her smell. Small dark eyes fix on hers. Both of them know: he is like her. She is like him.

She picks him up, gently. He looks exactly like Frodo, down to the one black whisker on the left side of his face, among the others that are white. There is blood on him, where he crawled out from the body. She puts him down in his cage. He sits back on his hind legs, and starts to scrub his paws over his face, washing it off.

There's too much, little buddy, Rae thinks madly, feeling the terrible laughter bubbling up in her again. The blood is everywhere. Dripping down her thighs, over her shoes, pooling on the carpet. There are blood smears on the walls, splatters across her dresser, a sticky, sodden mess between her legs. The other Frodo's body is lying on her desk, split up the middle, guts and organs spilling out all over her Spanish workbook.

It's like her brain has seized, the thoughts jammed.

"What are you *doing* in here?" Brandon's voice from the doorway. She whirls around to see him standing there, door wide open to the landing.

Her heart pounds in her chest. She keeps her eyes on him, praying that he looks at her and not the bloody mess behind her. "Get out of my room," she says, trying to sound calm. Something thrums in her bones.

"You were groaning," he says, craning to look around her. His eyes go big.

"Please," she says, approaching him, hands out in front of her.

"The heck did you do?"

"Just shh…" she says, frantic.

Brandon turns away, towards her parents' room.

She tackles him. Her hands wrap around his face, clamping his mouth shut. They're blood-slicked. She feels strong, stronger than she thought she was. He struggles against her, trying to get free. He swings his arm backwards and tries to hit her off him. She blocks the blow with her forearm.

"Please, don't," she says. She clutches his T-shirt. He lurches forward, the fibres ripping from her hand. Then she feels wet slobber as he licks her hand, trying to get her to let go. His go-to move from a dozen sibling fights.

"No," she hisses at him. She holds on as tight as she can.

Suddenly, his whole body gives a huge shudder.

Scared that she's suffocating him, she lets go. He staggers forward. He doesn't yell. Instead, he seems to be gasping for breath. He falls to his hands and knees.

"Brandon?" she says again. Her voice comes out as a croak, like in a nightmare where you want to scream but you can't.

He looks like he can't breathe. He is gasping, and there's a rattling sound in his lungs. He lifts one of his hands and starts to claw at his throat.

"Oh God, please." She finds herself praying, like she hasn't prayed in years. "Oh Lord please forgive me and protect me and those who I love. Oh Lord please forgive me and protect me and those who I love." A little mantra she used to mutter to herself when she was afraid.

Brandon falls onto his face, his limbs thrashing. An awful gurgling sound coming from his throat.

He shudders against the rug. *He's going to hurt himself*, she thinks wildly, as if *she* isn't the one who's done this to him. She rolls him over, pulls up his T-shirt. The soft pale skin on his belly is writhing and distending, like he's growing rapidly, horrifically pregnant.

You did this, says another voice. *Don't look away. Look at what you've done.*

She looks back at his face, and his expression has gone slack.

His eyes are blank, staring at the ceiling but not seeing it. He's dead. He's her brother, and he's dead. And she killed him.

No. No. No. She can't look at this. She crawls into the corner and closes her eyes.

She hears a bang from her parents' room, heavy footsteps coming towards her.

There is a wet ripping sound in front of her, and then a heavy squelch.

She opens her eyes.

Something has burst out of Brandon's body. It's about the size of her forearm, but growing as she looks at it. Writhing and covered in blood. It has the oversized head and soft misshapen limbs of a foetus, but a full set of hair, and the features are already forming into the face of a twelve-year-old boy, only in miniature. No screaming birth-cry: it's just lying there, twisting and squirming, making little squelching sucking noises as it learns how to breathe.

Her father bursts through his bedroom door holding the aluminium baseball bat he keeps next to his bed, in case of intruders. His face is red, unbelieving. Her mother screams, behind him.

Her father bellows, raising the bat high. Rae cries out, but he brings it down on the bloody lump with a heavy *thwack*. Blood splatters onto all of them.

Rae pushes her body deeper into the corner, wishing the walls would push her closed, fold her up, compress her into crystal. *This isn't happening*, she tells herself.

The creature repairs itself, inflating larger and larger. Her father hits it a second time, and then stumbles backwards into her mother, gasping for breath. He falls into their bedroom.

Rae cannot move. She sits there and listens to them die.

The creature's head lolls to face her, the bloodshot eyes locking with hers. Her body lights up, as he turns his blinking eyes on hers. In its hurry to grow, parts of it are growing at the wrong rate. Its eyeballs are too small for the sockets. They're sunken in, framed by the dark hollow of its skull. Thin fingers push through the misshapen blob that will become its hand. She can see a pale scar forming on its forearm, from the time Brandon broke his arm jumping from the tree outside. She remembers this perfectly, even though she was never there. She remembers it, she realises, because she copied Tammy-Rae's brain, just like this thing is copying Brandon's.

Its twisted mouth opens, nubs of teeth just starting to push through the gums. It seems to be mouthing something she can't make out, over and over, testing its voice. It's already grown now to half of Brandon's former height.

"Brandon," it is mouthing, the word barely intelligible in its clumsy mouth. "Brandon."

It's trying to understand what it is. It's just grabbing whatever memories are there. The memories recorded in the neurons of the body it just made.

"Brandon," it says again, its voice clearer now, the lips taking the correct shape, the tongue and teeth almost normal now.

It feels like the walls of the room are all that's holding her together. "I'm sorry, God," she whispers. "Please take it back. Take it back take it back take it back."

23. PLUMP

MONDAY, 23 SEPTEMBER 1996

The monster in the forest is hungry again.

She stretches herself long, feeling each segment click satisfyingly against the next. She is watching an army of ants march a complex path through the fallen leaves, considering the similarities between herself and these creatures. Their world is a three-dimensional olfactory map, largely untroubled by sight or noise. Their antennae read each smell and taste it. Odour receptors, but also taste receptors that read pheromones, that digest the environment. The ant eats its way through the world. She can relate.

She dips in a spindly finger and ferries a few ants to her mouth. They taste pleasantly like lemons. Little sour bursts on her tongue. But the flavour of each one is so distinct: a specific layer of acids and compounds that specific ant had made to communicate with the others. There are so many marvels in this world to discover.

The underworld in the humus is richly populated. She noses further into the leaf-litter. Trace smells of worms, beetles, aphids. Saliva drips from her lips at the thought.

She is still hungry, despite all she's already eaten today: two rangy jackrabbits, one small pika, a marmot, a blue-tailed skink, several ants and eighty-four of the fat creamy termites she patiently fished out of rotting tree trunks.

What am I? The creature has spent a lot of time contemplating the question. There wasn't much to contemplate, before, when she was trapped in rock. Her cave was a static ecosystem, tightly sealed for eons and eons. Bacteria and fungi and worms and tiny shrimp wriggling blind in that noxious damp darkness. She survived by eating gases in the air, a trick she learned from the bacteria. A meagre existence. Barely alive. Barely thinking.

Until the humans came along and disturbed everything. Cracked it open. Showed her the world.

And what a world! So much to delight in. So many new things to *eat*.

What am I? The trouble is that she has a map in her brain of how her body should be, that does not match her body. And parts of her body seem to have minds of their own.

She pulls her massive weight off the forest floor, weaving her head from side to side, trying to catch a scent, wondering what to eat next. Light-sensing cells on her back guide her into deeper shadows. It's almost midnight, and many of the smaller creatures are hiding or asleep. But she can't wait. She's just so hungry, always, so hungry. Brains are expensive machines, she is learning.

In a pinch, she can always snack on grubs. The whole forest is lousy with grubs. Millions of them, tiny bodies wriggling in every rotting lump around her. But they're her snack of last resort. They're not bad, slightly almondy, plenty of protein, but they're so bland. Boring. Taste one grub, you've tasted them all.

She'd like to find another rat. She ate a rat a few days ago. It was rangy, complex, delicious. Tough body, good strong teeth and claws. She was fascinated by the intricate machinery of its body: how the tendons connected the skeleton together, the way the ribs hugged the soft organs tight at the centre of the body, how each vertebra of tail locked so neatly into the next. She'd gotten just a sense of its intelligence before she'd started digesting it in her magnificent gut, just the briefest flash of affection and wiliness and courage that made up its consciousness. What a mind.

Almost as good as the girl she ate.

Maybe it's something about being an omnivore, she thinks to herself. Most creatures are perfectly attuned to eat one thing. But rats and humans, they can eat anything. That's why they have to get smart.

She drags herself along the edge of the bushline. It is a joy to move, to sniff and follow these scent trails. There is such abundant life here, life tangled in death. Choking vines, colonies of lichens spreading like veins along dead bark, exploring the nutritious rot. Caterpillars turning through stippled leaves. A gilled yellow fungus punctures the body of a dead moth, exploding an ecstatic release of spores into the air. She can smell burrowers and climbers, parasites and hunters. A thousand different strategies to eat and reproduce, nature's high-stakes games of hide and seek.

A smell catches her attention. Something she hasn't smelled before, musky and a little damp. She raises her head and spots a delicate basket of dried grass and twigs nestled on the branch of a nearby tree. A nest.

She'd like to try a bird. A new flavour. Might be interesting.

The nest isn't too high. She's spent a fair amount of time in the trees, these past few days. Her body's a conundrum: powerful digestive system, strong jaws, but under-developed limbs that don't always seem to do what she wants them to do. With her pathetic legs, she's no good at running, but she's developing a way of hunting, ambushing prey from above. She managed to get a good bite of a bear like that, the other day. It ran off before she could attach herself to it with some of the suckers on her face, pity.

She's not very strong, but her nails are sharp. She hooks them into the bark and tries to drag herself up the trunk. But she's been greedy; she's so much heavier than she was. The bark comes off under her left hand, but it holds under her right. She reaches up to a firm-looking knot and is able to swing some of her long body over the branch.

Leaning forward, she peers into the nest. Three tiny, featherless bodies huddle together in the dark, eyes still closed. Warblers.

She salivates. It drips off the hooks around her mouth and onto the branch.

She slips one baby between her jaws, and feels it squirm for a moment before she crunches it dead. There's a flash of its character before she swallows it down. The bird mind is two minds, she discovers. Two halves of a brain barely connected to each other, a collaboration. Curious.

Am I like this? she ponders. *Or am I one?*

She reaches forward for another mouthful.

But she's overestimated the branch or underestimated her weight. There's a cracking beneath her, and then they come crashing down, branch and birds all. She feels a sharp pain in her belly and looks down to see that a branch has pierced her between two of her segments. Hissing, she tugs it out. It stings, but it's only moments until the hole closes up again. She doesn't like pain. This has been a consistent feature of all the minds she's tasted.

She scratches around in the leaves beneath her and finds the nest. Squashed flat by her weight. She finds the head of one of the tiny birds, bloody, beak cracked down the middle. She throws it from her in disgust.

Small matter. Plenty of other fish in the sea. And birds in the trees, and rats in the forest.

But she's so, so hungry.

Oh well, nothing for it.

She untangles herself from the branches and slinks over to a rotting branch nearby. Dips in a long finger, hooks out some grubs, and swallows them down.

FOUR FOR A BOY

24. DOUBLE EDGED KNIFE

MARYBETH LARKIN

Marybeth draws her shoulder blades together, hoping to get some blood to flow into the knots around her collarbones. Her hands are tied around her back with some kind of elasticated cord, the kind you'd use to tie boxes down on the back of a pickup truck, wrapped tight around an iron pipe that runs up the wall behind her. Tilting her head back, she can just make out the dark shape of it running up the bare concrete wall of the cellar she's trapped in.

She's been down here all night, tied in this awkward seated position against the wall, and she can feel every hour of it in the screaming ache of her shoulders. Her mother warned her that the women in their family were cursed with arthritis, but she didn't expect it to happen so soon. Old age has a way of sneaking up on you.

Old age, and Ronnie Gaskins, apparently.

She twists her hands, first one way, then another, moving the ropes down to the narrowest part of her wrists. There's only a little give, but it might be enough. She was still pretty out of it when Ronnie led her down here and tied her up, but she'd had just enough presence of mind to ball her fists and tense up her arms as much as she could, bunching her muscles so there would be more slack in the bonds when she relaxed. Getting out of bound hands is a special skill of hers. Thanks, Bill.

Times when she'd been especially wilful, when Bill felt like she needed an extra reminder of the respect he was owed, he'd tie her to the bedpost when he went to work. She learned how to free herself, so she could go about her day and slip her wrists back inside her bonds just before he returned at lunchtime, having picked up Katie from kindergarten himself. The other moms were always talking about what an *involved* father Bill was. How lucky she was to have him.

Just this once, it turns out they were right.

Inch by inch, she twists the rope closer to her hands.

Ronnie must have injected her with something, because there's a sore patch on her arm. She half-remembers some parts of the hike back to town. But she felt weird, dissociated, like she was there but didn't care about anything that was happening. She must have wet herself at some point on the walk, because she smells like stale pee now. She doesn't know if she screamed, when they got close enough to the edge of town that someone might have heard her. She hopes she did.

This is why the girls don't remember anything. Ronnie must have injected them with this stuff, too, made them confused about where they were. They were telling the truth. After all this time she spent obsessing about that joke magazine, wondering about Satanists and drug addictions, it was the simplest answer all along: a madman attacked Katie in the woods, and he took her to his basement, and then he killed her.

He must have been waiting for them in the cave. Injected them with roofies and Lord knows what else. Somehow, Tammy-Rae and Donna managed to escape, and they left Katie. Maybe they thought she wouldn't have been able to keep up if they ran. Donna must have seen Katie's body down there; that's why she looked so shaken when she climbed out of the gorge. Marybeth hopes she is ashamed. She hopes it burns her up for the rest of her life.

But why did David Hooper lie about Ronnie being with him all afternoon? Zach said if the girls were kidnapped, it was most likely by somebody close to them. But *David Hooper*? Stealing girls with Ronnie Gaskins? It doesn't make sense. And how did Ronnie cover up his tracks so well that the dogs lost the trail?

Not that she's going to have much longer to puzzle over these loose threads. If she doesn't get out of this basement, she'll be dead soon, herself.

She's surprised by how calm she feels. It might be the remnants of the drug in her system. But it's more that there's no point in being afraid, now. It was always like this with Bill, when he got into one of his moods. Just when she should have been most afraid of him, when he would get that dead look in his eyes that she knew meant he was about to teach her a lesson, she'd feel a peacefulness come over her. Because it's out of her hands now. *No use putting your raincoat on after the rain*; that was something her mother used to say. Or the best compliment Jalene ever gave her, the time she said, *Marybeth, you're a good man in a storm.*

Besides, in some sick way, she got what she wanted, didn't she? She wanted to know what happened to her daughter. Well, now she knows. She's living it.

It must be close to morning. Around dawn, she'd guess. There aren't any windows down here, just the smallest amount of light coming in through the cracks around the hatch door. She can't hear any birdsong, but the cellar seems well insulated. She tried to scream plenty of times through the night, working herself up to the loudest pitch she could, and repeating the shriek for as long as she could bear, until her throat burned. Over and over. Nobody came.

She wonders how long it will be before anyone notices she's gone. Zach would have phoned her when the volunteers came back from the searches yesterday, wouldn't he? Her heart sinks when she thinks of him, how furious she was the last time she spoke to him. He'll think she's not taking his calls because she's sulking.

It took her seventeen hours to realise that Katie was missing. But her own mother is long dead. It might be days until somebody cares enough to go and check on her home, notice she's not there, start wondering where she is.

There's not much down here. A wooden staircase leading up to a hatch door, the kind that you enter from outside the house. In front of the stairs are dark crouched shapes that she can't decode. In her worst imaginings, they keep morphing into Katie, tied down here with her in the dark. But she's alone and there's no movement in here beyond the barely perceptible scuttling of insects. No bad smell beyond damp. No, Katie's body is probably out there in the woods, somewhere in the gorge.

She thinks back to the smell of the rotting deer that she found in that strange graveyard. Is it possible that Katie was out there too, her smell mixing in with the deer? She might have been just a few feet away from her body, and not have known.

When Katie was born, it was terrible. She'd been in labour for eight hours. She'd begged for death. But they pulled Katie out of her, that snarling furious thing, and she'd been so astonished at how small she was. She held her close, licked the gore off her the way animals do. She wouldn't hand Katie over. Refused to let the nurses take her away. After everything, after Bill, and her mother, and Jalene, and all that had been taken from her already, all the ways she'd been loved so badly, from that very first moment Katie was *hers*, and she'd promised then that she was never going to let her go. Never going to let her down. Protect her until she dies.

And how's that going, Margita, she chides herself in her old name, the one her mother gave her, the one she cast off as soon as she could convince the kids at school to stop calling her Margherita Pizza and call her Marybeth instead. Her mother was heartbroken, like it was a personal betrayal. She'd tried to make up for it by naming Katie after her, Americanising the Katalinka, but it didn't make up for all the ways Marybeth had already disappointed her by then. Getting pregnant at seventeen, refusing to give up the baby, filing for emancipation so she could marry Bill. In the end, she and her mother were strangers to each other.

This is how girls become women, by hating their mothers. It's just the way of the world, a stage of development. A long legacy of ingratitude.

She's thought about her mother so much tonight. She's been dead for thirteen years, and they barely spoke for the last few before that. But she supposes, at the end of everything, that's what everyone does: wishes for their mama.

The ropes have reached her wrists. There's more room now to explore her binds. She runs her fingertips along the ropes, figuring out the pattern. There's just enough of a gap. She takes a deep breath, holds the rope in the fingers of her right hand, and pulls her left as hard as she can. Her shoulders scream in pain, the skin burns, but the rope slips, little by little, and she's free.

Her entire left arm immediately comes alive with pins and needles. She works her right hand into her shoulder, moaning. Holding the cold wall for support, she stands and feels her way across the room until her feet find the stairs, crawling up them until her head thumps the hatch door. There's only the thinnest sliver of weak light coming in through the cracks. She listens for approaching footsteps, but the world is silent.

Chains clank on the other side when she pushes against the hatch door. It lifts an inch, but no further.

Getting up closer, she crouches down, and then rams against the hatch as hard as she can with her shoulder. She yells out in pain, then clasps her hand over her mouth, realising she might be alerting Ronnie that she's awake.

What are her options? She could try to scream again, press her face right up to the gap in the door and yell, pound on the wood, hope that somebody hears her. But she remembers how far Ronnie's house is from his neighbours. She'll summon him long before she summons them.

And even if she gets out, even if she gets to the police station and reports him, then what? She's got more hope of getting justice from the Abominable Snowman than from Zachary Bottlebrush Pittman and his clowns at the Little Hope Police Department. No. There's nobody left to fight for Katie but her.

She finds her way back down the stairs and approaches the jumble of dark shapes. Maybe she can find a pole, something to wedge into the door to pry it open. Taking a deep breath, she reaches her hand into the darkness and feels a textured plastic surface, maybe a cooler box. She slides her hand along it until she finds a pole leaning against it, but it's flimsy plastic, perhaps a mop handle.

Something tickles her hand and she flinches away, feeling a dozen tiny legs scurry up her arm. She gasps and shakes them off.

It's just insects, she tells herself. *Probably silverfish, or roaches. Nothing that can kill you. But if you don't find a weapon, then Ronnie will.*

She braces herself and plunges her hands back into the jumble. They decode a wooden ladder, a pile of soggy cardboard boxes. They slide onto the surface of an old oil drum, rough and rusted through in places. She nearly cuts herself against a tear in the side, a shard of metal barely still attached. She pulls on it, and it snaps off in her hand, a jagged blade. Just long enough for her to plunge it into Ronnie's neck if she can get close enough. She grips it tight, feeling it bite into the palm of her hand, a double-edged knife.

That's fine. It doesn't matter how much it cuts her up, or if she even survives this. As long as she can kill the man who murdered her daughter.

She always regretted not being the one who finished Bill, in the end. She was still too young then, too afraid. Somebody else had the pleasure of putting a bullet through him and watching him bleed out on the carpet. It should have been her. No one had earned it more.

She's not making that mistake again.

25. SECOND SKIN

DONNA RAMIREZ

"*Conejita*? Sorry to wake you."

All Donna can manage in response is a groan into the pillow. She lay awake until long past midnight, reading snippets of Kat's journal, brain spinning with frantic questions. Questions about who she is. What she is.

Her dad puts a hand to her head. "You're burning up," he says, sounding concerned.

Donna pulls away from him, replying with another groan.

"Work called. They're having some trouble mixing the glaze. Asked me to come in for just a couple hours to get them going."

Donna manages to sit up. The air in the room is far too hot. Her pyjamas feel sticky against her skin.

"I won't be out long. We've got an appointment with Chief Pittman at eleven. He's got some questions about where you went last night."

Donna nods miserably.

"I'm sorry, *cariño*. You know how it is. Work's asking a

favour. They've been good giving me time off, with... everything that's happened."

With a monster having murdered your daughter and left her to rot in a cave while she steals her life, you mean, Donna thinks.

"Go, Dad. I'll meet you at the police station later."

He sighs, gives her a sad little smile. "I'm sorry I lost my temper with you last night."

"I know."

"I was scared."

"I know."

"So I'll see you at the police station? At eleven, no?"

"Yup."

His eyes are narrowed, like he can sense something else is wrong. "No school today, OK? You're not well."

He puts his hand on her head one last time and gets up to go.

"Dad—" Donna begins. She wants to say, *I'm sorry*. Or just, *I love you*. Because whatever she is, whatever she's about to do, she knows that's true. But she can't get the words out. Instead, she says, "Go be a hero."

"Oh yes." He smiles. "I will be the Batman of toilets."

He disappears, and in the living room she hears him gather up his things and leave, shutting the door gently behind him so as not to disturb her.

She wonders if she'll ever see him again.

Dragging herself out of bed, she grabs her mom's old duffel bag from the closet in the living room. She goes back to her bedroom and starts cramming it full of clothes from the chaotic piles on the floor. She fetches her toothbrush from the bathroom, this time refusing to face the girl in the mirror, the reflection of Not-Donna she'll see there. Back in her room, she stares at the mess, trying to imagine what else she'll need for her new life as a runaway. After some consideration, she loads her guitar into its canvas carrycase. It's going to be a bitch to carry, but she can't contemplate life without it.

She hoists Kat's backpack on her bed, where it will be the first thing the police see when they search her room after she's reported missing. It's as good as leaving a confession note, she figures. She fingers the tiny magnifying glass keychain attached to the zipper, saying a little goodbye to Kat in her mind.

She can't bear to leave the journal. All these memories of Donna and Rae and Kat, and the friendship they had. All that's left of the real them. She tucks it into the kangaroo pouch at the front of her hoodie.

Rae will come with her, of course. What other choice does she have? They'll have to steal Mrs Hooper's car, sell it for cash in Nevada and switch it out for another one. Maybe the two of them can get to Phoenix, try to find Jay and ask for his help. Get jobs clearing tables or something, save up enough money to buy fake identities that might let them live some kind of normal life. They'll need new names; they can't keep using these ones that they stole. Rae won't be able to graduate, which means she'll never get to go to college like she wanted. But they'll figure it out, somehow. They'll get to reinvent themselves, away from Little Hope. They can be whoever they want to be.

In a way, it's what they always wanted, isn't it?

But as she walks into the living room and sees the blanket that she covered her dad with last night, she starts crying anyway. There's an oil stain on his pillow. She begs him to wash his face before he gets into bed, but he says he's always too beat. The room smells of him: Old Spice and sweat.

You're not even his real daughter, she chides herself. *You're like one of those cuckoo birds that invades a nest and grows too big and takes over. You killed his daughter. You have no right to love him.*

She hoists the duffel bag over her shoulder, grabs her guitar bag, and leaves, not bothering to lock the front door of the house that is no longer hers.

It's already seventy degrees out, and not even eight in the morning. Their neighbour Bud is standing on his front porch, already working on his first beer of the day. His eyes widen at the sight of Donna. She hisses at him like a cat until he has the good manners to look away.

Rae's house is all the way over on the other side of town, but there's no way she's going to take the bus. She has no choice but to walk. *No problem*, she thinks. Nobody's going to notice she's gone for a few hours yet. She's got plenty of time.

She hasn't gone ten steps out of her front gate when a man's voice behind her says, "And just where might you be off to, little lady?"

Donna whirls around, nearly dropping her guitar, to see Tim Knox unfolding himself from a nondescript pickup parked across the street.

Shit. She sees his eyes flick over the duffel bag and guitar case.

"Sleepover," she says, her mouth dry. "At Rae's."

"And here I thought it was a school day," he says, fingering the radio on his hip, giving her a disbelieving smile. "Gave us all a bit of a scare last night, you know. Zach asked me to keep an eye on you. Make sure you don't *forget* your appointment with him later."

"I won't. I'm just dropping these off at Rae's first." So much for sneaking off unnoticed.

"Excellent. Why don't I give you a ride?"

"I like walking," Donna says, aware of how totally idiotic this sounds. She can feel the sweat running down her neck. It was bad enough thinking she was a teenage girl; now she's some kind of clammy clone. When the big change came, wasn't she supposed to mature into a beautiful young lady, or some crap like that?

"Oh, I insist," Tim says, through a toothy grin.

Donna throws her bags onto the bed of the pickup and climbs up into the passenger seat. "This yours?" she asks, gesturing to the plastic sunflowers tacked onto the dash, the matching floral pill box lying in the seat well.

"Polly's," he says, pulling onto the street. He must have thought he'd be too visible in his police cruiser.

He doesn't have to ask Donna where Rae's house is. She wonders if they've been tailing her, too.

"Looks like you girls caught a lucky break," he says, like he's just making casual conversation. "The lab rats called this morning. They said there's been some kind of outbreak, some weird fungus contaminating every sample they had. They've had to incinerate every bit of organic material in the place. How convenient, no?"

Donna gives a noncommittal grunt, keeping her eyes on the road.

"Problem is, I got a pretty fine-tuned bullshit detector. And ever since I laid eyes on you two girls, it's been ringing off the hook. It's hard enough for one person to keep their lies straight, but two? Sheesh. It's just a matter of time before you turn on each other. I've seen it a hundred times."

"Where, on *Law and Order*?" Tim's barely a few years older than Jay.

"It's not too late to come clean," he says, still through that horrible grin. "Negotiate a plea deal. Maybe save your missing friend."

"What's your game here, Peach Fuzz?" Donna asks him, her heart hammering. "Hoping I'll give you a confession and you can go be the big man who solved the case?"

Tim keeps smiling, gives a cocky shrug.

"Sorry to disappoint you," she says, leaning her forehead against the window. It's deliciously cool. A bead of sweat condenses between her forehead and the glass, and then slips down like a tear.

The houses become larger, the yards more manicured the further away from Donna's they drive. Finally, the tall dormer windows of the Hoopers' house loom ahead.

Tim turns to face her, the grin still plastered on his face.

"I'll be right out here when you get back, sweet cheeks."

Donna can't help herself. She takes a deep breath, and then blows him an enormous raspberry, but overdoes it a bit. Flecks of spittle fly out and hit him on the face.

"Classy as always," Tim says, wiping spit off his face.

Donna gets out of the cab, moving quickly, half expecting him to follow her. But he doesn't. Donna grabs her bags from back of the pickup. She glances back. Tim is bent over, coughing. It doesn't seem like he's about to follow her.

Well, there goes her whole plan of convincing Rae to meet her in the garage, loading up Mrs Hooper's car and hitting the road. Tim's probably on the radio right now, telling every cop in California where they are. She and Rae are going to have to sneak out the backyard, figure out another way to get to Nevada without being stopped. Rae will come up with something, Donna reassures herself.

They're so close, so close to getting out. She just has to keep it together.

She tries to make her body language communicate *everything's totally chill* as she walks up the neat pathway to Rae's front door. Mrs Hooper's clay angels line the path, glass eyes glinting at her.

Both of the Hoopers' cars are parked in the drive. Surprising. She was hoping that Mr Hooper would be out at work, and she'd only have to get past Rae's mom.

Donna steels her nerves and rings the doorbell. "Please be Rae. Please be Rae," she mutters to herself.

The door swings open. And of course, because Donna's the unluckiest bitch ever born, it's Mrs Hooper.

26. RID OF ME

KATHERINE LARKIN

FRIDAY, 7 JUNE 1996

Dear Diary,

For a couple of days this week, I legit thought that Rae and Donna might never talk to each other again.

It started on Monday. Donna somehow managed to convince Principal Keyes to let The Nancy Screws play a song at weekly assembly. Apparently, she described their sound as "rock music", and Principal Keyes misheard the name as The Nancy *Drews*. Poor man was probably imagining something a bit more demure than Donna's riot grrrl screamo punk.

Donna was SO nervous. Rae and I helped her set up and she was shaking so bad she couldn't plug in the amp. The band is Donna (guitar, vocals), Miguel Garcia (bass) and April Hollister (drums). I don't think either Miguel or April have any particular feelings about the type of music they're making. Miguel's there because he's painfully in love with Donna, and April's there because she's painfully in love with drumming. April struggles to talk to people, but damn she's an incredible musician. The best of the three of them by miles, if I'm honest (NEVER tell Donna I said that, Diary).

Rae and I sat right in the front of the gym bleachers so Donna could see us. We even made a sign, like proud moms! There were all the normal boring announcements about bake sales and prom elections, mandatory tepid applause for the Mathletes and the dance club, a snoozefest "say no to drugs" play from the sophomore drama class, and then Donna and Miguel and April got up and started playing.

Donna told us that they were going to play one of their covers. They do a pretty good 'Rid of Me'. But instead, they got up and launched straight into their original song 'I Fucking Hate Everything (Especially You)'.

Understand, nobody's ever WHISPERED the f-word in assembly before, let alone screamed it repeatedly over a guitar chord in front of the whole school. Nobody can say that Donna doesn't have guts.

At the first mention, there was sniggering. By the second, the sniggering had blossomed into full-blown laughter. At the third, Principal Keyes leaped up to the microphone and told The Nancy Screws to stop playing.

The laughter carried on for a while. I don't even think people were being mean (OK, some people were; Fred Stein yelled, "I fucking hate you too, Donna!" super loud). I think people were just shocked, and maybe kind of thrilled. But as the laughter went on and Principal Keyes was trying to get everybody to calm down, Donna's face just went expressionless, like she was withdrawing into herself. Her whole face was red. And then Principal Keyes turned to the band and asked them in a very calm voice to keep profanity out of the assembly, and invited them to play a different song.

Donna just stood there, holding her guitar, for so long we didn't know if she'd even heard him. April and Miguel were just looking at her waiting for her to tell them what to do. I felt so bad for Donna. I wanted to get up and just start singing FOR her, even though being on a stage while people look at me is literally my worst nightmare. The minutes just stretched out, the whole school trying to keep quiet, and UGH it was awful.

Then, next to me, Rae started clapping and whooping. Others started clapping too. It started spreading through the crowd, encouraging them.

April started counting down, and then she and Miguel launched into their song 'Venus de Milo'.

But Donna just kept standing there. And then after another few endless seconds, she put down her guitar and she ran off out of the gym. Miguel waited a moment, and then he stopped playing too and followed her out. April just kept playing. Drummed the whole song through, and everyone sat through and listened, and we clapped politely, but I think all of us wanted to just DIE on their behalf, basically.

'I Fucking Hate Everything' isn't even The Nancy Screws' best song! Definitely not worth the bazillion hours of detention it cost her. Donna's best songs are actually the sappy ones, like this sad ballad she wrote about missing her brother, but she'll never play those in front of anyone except us. Donna's secret soft underbelly is the best part of her, really.

After the assembly broke up, Rae and I raced off to try to find Donna, but she'd actually *left school and gone home.* We went through the rest of the school day without her, wondering if we shouldn't have done more to try to help. Donna pretends she's such a tough guy, but she's so sensitive really.

After school, we biked straight over to her house and found Donna sitting in her backyard, sketching punk birds. We sat out there with her and told her we were sorry for what happened, and Donna shrugged, but she still looked pretty upset about it. Then she said, "You know what we should do? We should go back to school after dark and paint 'KEYES IS A FASCIST' all over his precious football field."

I ran with it, saying that we should paint it on his Volvo instead, but Rae immediately got defensive. She was like, "You're already in so much trouble, and I'm not going to get dragged down with you and spend the rest of my sophomore year in detention."

Donna looked pretty hurt at that. Like, she was never going to actually graffiti the football field! She was just embarrassed about what happened and she was trying to turn the whole thing into a joke. But then she snapped back, something like "Oh, I'm *soooo* sorry, I would never want to do anything to risk ruining your *perfect school record* for something unimportant like artistic expression, Tammy-Rae."

I tried to interrupt them, get us back to joking about Principal Keyes, but Rae just talked over me. "You could have just gone up there and played a cover like you said you were going to. Everyone would have liked it! It would have been fine! I don't understand why you always make things so hard on yourself."

And Donna mumbled that she doesn't want The Screws to just be some lame cover band. And Rae rolled her eyes and was all like, "I don't know what you expected. You do things to piss people off and then you act all righteous about it when they *do get pissed off*. You can't just throw tantrums and then run away."

And then Donna said something about how she was just being herself, and then she said, "Maybe you'd get that if you weren't such a two-faced suck-up." And then she clamped her mouth shut, like she realised she'd gone too far.

It looked like she was about to apologise, but then Rae got really still and quiet and said something like, "One day, Donna, you're going to have to grow up and realise that sometimes you get more done playing by the rules than thrashing against them." It was creepy; it was like Rae was channelling her father.

Donna couldn't stop herself; she leaned over and pulled up Rae's skirt and said, "How's that going for you? Is it making you happy, or is it making you so crazy that you've got scars all over your legs?"

Rae just got up and left.

I didn't know what to do. I stayed with Donna and told her she'd crossed a line, but she was too mad to talk about it and just asked me to leave so she could take a shower. Then I went home and tried to call Rae but she wouldn't talk to me.

I hoped they'd just have gotten over it the next day at school, but they refused to talk to each other. I've spent the whole week trying to split my time between them, listening to each of them bitching about the other on and on and on and on. Eventually I told them I was sick of it and if they had any more to say about it they needed to say it to EACH OTHER because I was sick of being their go-between. So they agreed to meet each other after school so that they could hash it out.

I was really worried it was going to erupt into another blowout. I had this whole speech planned reminding Donna that Rae was the one who pushed her to take the band more seriously in the first place, and reminding Rae that Donna was always the first person she called when she was feeling low, and that the three of us NEED each other, and our differences are what make us work. It was a good speech, Diary!

But before I could even say anything, both of them just immediately burst into tears and started hugging each other and apologising for being assholes and saying how much they love each other.

Ugh.

Figures.

Your friend & secretary of The Nancy Screws fan club,
Kat

FACT I LEARNED TODAY: The Nancy Drew books were written by a bunch of different people. Carolyn Keene was just a collective pseudonym they used over the years. The original creator was actually a DUDE who, get this, believed a woman's place was in the home. Good thing he didn't actually write any of the books (women did all the actual work, typical).

THE FORBIDDEN KNOWLEDGE CHRONICLES

THE TRUTH NEVER DIES

The Gaskins Murders: California's Very Own Amityville Horror?

By Gregory Bartlett

Tape an "X" onto your bedroom window, slip on your black trench coat and turn on your flashlight! It's that time again, Forbidden Knowledge believers, where I shine a light into the dark corners of the unknown. This week your resident Fox Mulder examines the infamous Gaskins murders and their strange connection to *The Amityville Horror*.

Let's rewind to 13 November, 1974: 23-year-old Ronald DeFeo Jr. uses a high-powered rifle to shoot and kill his parents, two younger sisters and two younger brothers, while his victims lie sleeping in their beds. He ends up confessing, but gives a strange reason. He says that "the voices from the house made me do it". It is a crime that grips the country and inspires one of the scariest movies ever made: *The Amityville Horror*.

Fast forward seven years later to 8 October, 1981. Twelve-year-old Ronnie Gaskins sets fire to his home at no. 1 Edgewood Road and uses his father's .38-calibre revolver to shoot and kill his parents. Both parents are found dead in the living room. He also provides a bizarre confession: he testifies that "monsters replaced my parents". The crime shocks the usually sedate town of Little Hope and the trial that follows keeps its residents transfixed.

The parallels between these two cases go beyond the similarities in their first names, and their surprising connection may reveal what really happened on that fateful day in 1981.

Four years ago today, Ronnie Gaskins was released from prison after serving only eleven years of his life sentence. He was freed on a technicality:

they decided that his confession had been coerced and was full of false facts. Doubt was also cast on some of the other evidence that was collected. Which raises the question: who really killed John and Mary Gaskins?

Local News

Ronnie remains the prime suspect, despite the conviction being overturned. His case isn't helped by the fact that he moved back to Little Hope after his release, right back into his childhood home, which he rebuilt himself. This reporter has heard more than one local resident comment that "the murderer always returns to the scene of the crime". Many other people will tell you that Ronnie is as guilty as sin and if Ray Pendleton had not botched the investigation, little Ronnie would still be behind bars.

Well, I am not one of them. I believe Ronnie is innocent, in a manner of speaking. Allow me to explain.

Chief Pendleton came down with a big case of confirmation bias during the Gaskins investigation. Did they look for other suspects? No. Did they entertain any theory other than "Ronnie did it"? No. It's hard to solve a crime with the blinders on, Ray. This is the problem with people who choose to engage with the world in an entirely pragmatic way. Now, I've heard your theories through the years, dear readers – a second shooter, Ronnie being mind-controlled by aliens, even a Satanic connection. All valid theories in my book. However, today I'd like to offer another. You see, Chief Pendleton overlooked a prime suspect: the Gaskins house itself.

Before you call me crazy, hear me out. The Gaskins house on Edgewood Road is one of the oldest in Little Hope and a bit of an architectural oddity. The sizable farmhouse was built by Orville Brock, a wealthy entrepreneur who moved to Little Hope in the late 1800s from Vermont. It is, by all accounts, an ordinary-looking home except for one distinct and curious detail: if you were to gaze up at the second floor you'd notice a singular window at a 45-degree tangle. This is a "witch window". According to an old superstition, these windows were built to keep witches out. It gives the house an air of the supernatural.

Brock, by all accounts a very superstitious man, had fled Vermont to escape a "curse". His entire family had succumbed to a mysterious illness a year earlier. It seems the witch window kept him safe while indoors, but outdoors was another matter entirely.

Chief Pendleton overlooked a prime suspect: the Gaskins house itself.

Local News

In 1904 he was found in the woods, dead via a gunshot to his right temple. It was alleged that the wound was self-inflicted, but who can say for sure.

After his death, the house cast a dark spell over its future inhabitants. This truth-seeking reporter visited the local library and, after hours examining newspapers on microfiche, discovered a slew of peculiar cases related to the Gaskins property at 1 Edgewood Road. 1911, a father and son venture into the woods surrounding the house and are never seen again. 1937, a woman was found drowned in the bath. Her husband was suspected of murder but never convicted. 1953, a woman believes her husband has been replaced by "a demon" and tries to poison him. She is committed to an insane asylum. That sound familiar? In 1981, Ronnie testified that "monsters" replaced his parents. Swap "demon" with "monsters" and it is eerily similar to Ronnie's testimony during the 1981 trial.

My theory is that, like Amityville, there is an evil entity inhabiting the house on 1 Edgewood Road.

Let's examine the facts in the Gaskins case. 1 July, 1980 – the Gaskins family move into no. 1 Edgewood Road. This reporter has it on good authority that Mrs Gaskins confided in a local resident about hearing strange sounds in the house at night. In the months that follow, the family dog disappears, John Gaskins breaks his leg falling from a ladder, Mary Gaskins miscarries and the trees on the property mysteriously die. 18 September, 1981 – Ronnie mysteriously disappears while out hiking with his parents. Two days later he wanders into the Little Hope Police Department claiming he had been lost in the woods. The officer on duty, Officer Oldham, reported at the

time that Ronnie was spouting all kinds of bizarre theories involving his parents. Most notably that his parents were "monsters".

Following that, teachers say Ronnie began to withdraw socially. In the weeks leading up to the murders, it is reported by friends and neighbours that Ronnie started behaving strangely. "As if something had taken hold of him," a close friend had testified at the trial. Around 3 a.m. on the morning of 1 October, the murders take place. Our most attentive readers will recognise 3 a.m. as the "witching hour" or "devil's hour", a time of night associated with supernatural events. Now here's the kicker – *The Amityville Horror* murders also took place at 3 a.m., also involved a young son, also involved the death of two parents by shooting, and also involved weird statements by the killer about possession.

Like the previous occupants of the house before him, I believe Ronnie had been slowly corrupted by whatever evil force dwells at no. 1 Edgewood Road. Like Amityville, there was an entity that twisted him to its will. That morning he snuck into his father's office, retrieving the .38-calibre revolver stored in his desk. But perhaps, just for a moment, he broke free of the house's influence and tried to burn the house down instead. The smoke woke his parents and they tried to stop him. A struggle ensued and, in the tussle, he shot them both. Or perhaps the entity regained control and made him do it.

We may never know for certain. Not unless Ronnie shares the truth of what really happened that night. A prospect that now seems unlikely since Ronnie has refused to be interviewed after his release, even by a truth-seeker like myself. I assure you, readers, I will continue trying. The truth will, after all, always reveal itself.

Why he chose to move back into his childhood home, on that, I can only theorise. Perhaps he sees himself as a guardian against the dark forces that lie in wait there? That by residing in the house he ensures it will claim no further victims. That no one else will suffer the tragedy he has. As they say, "Only by confronting your demons can you hope to overcome them."

NEXT ISSUE

We examine a bizarre new story about two hikers who disappeared in Owens Valley. Could this be another case of alien abduction? Your resident truth-seeker is on the case.

27. OH BONDAGE! UP YOURS!

DONNA RAMIREZ

TUESDAY, 24 SEPTEMBER 1996

Mrs Hooper doesn't even seem surprised to see Donna. "Rae will be down in a minute," she says, ushering her inside. "Let me take those." She grabs Donna's bags and stashes them in the hall cupboard. Mrs Hooper's hair is wet, tied up in a neat bun.

As Mrs Hooper's hands brush against her, the skin on Donna's arms erupts in goosebumps. Something feels... off about her. No, that's not right. Something feels *on* about her. Extremely *on*.

There's nothing out-of-the-ordinary-looking about her. Same old petite frame. Same old gold crucifix hanging over a modest neckline. Same old pursed lipsticked lips.

Donna glances back to see if Tim's still watching, but Mrs Hooper swings the door shut. "Tammy-Rae will be down in a bit," she says again, leading Donna through to their overstuffed living room. Everything in here is covered in floral print and lace. Donna's barely spent any time in here before: it's always been so much Mrs Hooper's space. When they come over, they're usually relegated to the rumpus room in the basement, or Rae's room.

Brandon and Mr Hooper are on the sofa. Both of them smile to see her, like she's their favourite person, not the girl they've teased and shunned, respectively, for as long as she's known them.

She was supposed to grab Rae and run. None of her plans involved a police escort, or being welcomed by a super-friendly Mrs Hooper into her fancy living room, like she's arrived at a family meeting. Nothing about today makes any sense.

"Juice?" Mrs Hooper asks. Donna nods. Mrs Hooper heads to the kitchen, leaving her facing the two Hooper men, who smile at her with vacant cheerfulness, each holding a glass of OJ already.

Something in Donna's brain is screaming at her. She clears her throat. "I just need to talk to Tammy-Rae."

"You're always welcome here, Donna. We're practically family," Mr Hooper says. He takes a sip of his OJ. Brandon matches the movement perfectly, like they're training to be synchronised swimmers.

"I'm just going to, uh... I'll see if she's upstairs." She backs out of the living room and heads for the stairs.

The old house creaks and groans as it warms in the morning sun, like it's alive. She can smell somebody cooking breakfast, something meaty and sweet.

Rae is sitting on the bottom of the staircase, hair wrapped in a towel, Frodo scampering around her shoulders. There's a box of Cap'n Crunch next to her. Her eyes are red-rimmed and puffy. She doesn't look happy to see Donna, just infinitely tired.

"Can we go outside?" Donna whispers.

"We can talk here." Rae's voice is flat.

"Your parents—"

"It doesn't matter."

Donna sits next to her on the step. Frodo seems hyperactive. He leaps from Rae's shoulder to hers and runs around her neck. His tickly feet send shivers up the back of her neck, into her hairline. Frodo jumps back to Rae.

Rae leans into her shoulder, tucking her head under Donna's head. They fit together so well, Donna tall, Rae compact. All the ways they're different, the three of them, but it's like they slot together. Her and Rae and Kat.

Donna tugs on the end of a lock of her hair, trying to keep her voice steady. "Rae, I went. Back up the trail. All the way into the forest."

Rae's face feels damp against her shoulder.

The words tumble from Donna before she can think how to make them not sound crazy. "There were bodies in the cave. One of them was Kat's. And Rae... oh God. Yours was in there, and mine." She's trembling, but she has to get it out. "It was us. The three of us. The real us, I'm sure of it. Something happened in there that's not... that's not *human*. I know this sounds nuts. But we are not who we think we are. We're some kind of copy. I am not Donna. And you're not Rae."

Rae pulls away from her and wipes a tear from her cheek. "I've been thinking about that a lot. Whether I'm Tammy-Rae Hooper. And I think I am. I've got her memories, and I've got her face. If that doesn't make me Rae, then what does? I think I'm also just... more than her."

Donna shakes her head, mystified. "You know."

Rae starts pacing back and forth across the hall, not bothering to keep her voice down. "I've gone over it in my mind, again and again. I think I've figured out most of it. I must have been the one who woke first, after we changed. I saw our bodies, but I didn't understand what I was seeing."

Donna glances over at the kitchen, where she can hear the distant sounds of Mrs Hooper clinking glasses.

"I panicked. I just knew we were in danger, so I grabbed you and pulled you out of there. You were so out of it. You were still... waking up, being born, whatever. I just wanted to get us as far away from that place as possible, I didn't realise how lost we were getting. By the time you came to, I didn't know where we were. We were covered in blood from climbing out of our bodies. I was confused, and I guess I was worried about getting in trouble, because that's the first thought Tammy-Rae Hooper always has. We found a stream and we washed most of the mess off. You were still only half-conscious. But you trusted me. Because you were already starting to be Donna."

"What are we?" Donna says softly.

Rae stops pacing, finally, looks her full in the face. "I don't know. Clone people. Body snatchers."

Donna blinks at the word. Like they're talking about some cheesy B-grade horror movie. "It's the cave, isn't it? The cave changes you. Or that monster you saw—"

Rae starts shaking her head. "I think something went wrong with Kat. When she changed. Like there was too much of her."

Donna frowns.

"I mean, what if she *was* pregnant? Like maybe it couldn't figure out if it was supposed to be a foetus or a person."

"I don't get what you're saying."

"Donna. There wasn't a monster in the cave. It was Kat."

"But you said it was huge, long like a snake…"

"Like I said: something went wrong."

Donna runs a hand through her hair. "We've got to leave. Kat's… gone. The cops will figure it out eventually. They'll realise we're not who we say we are. Let's take your mom's car. Thelma-and-Louise it out of here." She gives a gulping laugh.

Another tear rolls down Rae's cheek. "It's too late," she says softly.

Mrs Hooper walks in, holding two glasses of orange juice. She holds one out to Donna. The prickly humming feeling in Donna's body intensifies. She glances at Mrs Hooper's hands. The tips are brown. There's something caked under her fingernails. Dirt, or…

Donna takes a step back. Rae is trembling. She looks behind her, up to the landing, like she can't say the words.

Donna walks up the stairs slowly, like walking in a nightmare. The smell she thought was coming from the kitchen grows stronger. Metallic, sweet, like the cave.

There's a hand draped onto the top step. Grey.

She takes another step, and sees them: the bodies of Rae's mother, father and her brother, lying with wide staring eyes in pools of their own blood. Torn up the middle, like something has climbed out of them, discarded like banana peels.

Donna stumbles back, almost tumbling down the stairs, but Rae is there to catch her. "It's not just the cave that turns people. It's in our blood now," she says. "It's us."

Donna rips herself away and races down the stairs. There's a humming in her ears, a buzzing in her bones, like there's an electric current running through the room. She staggers back and runs right into Mrs Hooper. Mr Hooper and Brandon appear behind her. All of their faces are identically calm. Only Rae is crying, her chin wobbling as tears run down her cheeks. "The more of them there are, the stronger it gets. Can't you feel it?"

The Hoopers take a step towards her. Donna bolts. She skids down the hallway, turns sharply and runs through the front door. There are heavy footsteps behind her. She can't tell how many. She flings open the front door and runs outside.

Tim's pickup is still parked across the street. "Help me!" she screams. There's no movement. She runs towards the passenger door and tries to open it. It's locked.

Tim is slumped against the steering wheel, squirming slightly like he's in pain.

"Hey!" Donna yells, hammering on the window.

Rae's voice echoes in her head: *It's in our blood now.* She got her spit all over him. Did she...

She looks back at the house. Rae and her mother have nearly caught up with her. Rae's eyes are wide, her face pale.

"Please," Donna babbles, backing away from Rae. "Let's just leave. Let's get in your mom's car and go."

"That's always your plan, isn't it?" Rae's voice sounds dreamy, far away. "It won't undo it. I killed my family, Donna. I killed them." Rae's mom hovers behind her, face impassive.

"You didn't mean to."

"Didn't I?" Rae's face is crumpling. Her forehead creased, her lips pulled back and trembling. "I hated them."

Donna takes a step back. Her eyes dart between the cars in the driveway, wondering if she could grab the keys before one of the Hoopers could stop her. Unlikely.

"Don't look at me like that," Rae says.

"Like what?"

"Like you're disgusted by me. Please. I don't think I can take it."

Donna runs a hand through her hair. "Well, I can't pretend that I understand you right now."

A single ugly laugh cracks out of Rae. "Did you ever? Did you ever even like me?"

"Fuck you, Rae."

"Be honest. If this town wasn't so small, would we even have been friends?"

Mr Hooper steps up behind Rae and puts his hand on her shoulder. Frodo runs from Rae's shoulders up his arm, and from him to Rae's mother. Brandon steps forward and holds Rae's hand. She's never seen the Hoopers look so like a happy family.

Donna wipes her brow. "Why are you doing this *now*, idiot? We've got to *go*!"

"Because this is all your fault!" Rae bursts out, tears spilling over her already-glistening cheeks.

It feels like being slapped.

Rae continues, relentless, her father's hand still resting protectively on her shoulder. "*You're* the one who talked us into going back to the cave. *You're* the one who just dived into the dark. You never stop to *think*. And now they're all dead. Kat's dead. My family's dead. My mom was right. You're every bad thing that happens to me."

She can't listen to this.

Donna takes one last look at the Hoopers' identical cheerful, mad expressions, eyes fixed on her, looming behind the girl she thought was her best friend. She starts to turn, ready to flee.

Then... something shifts in Rae's face. She steps forward, just a single step away from her family. She tugs her hand away from Brandon, gives a slow shake of her head, almost dazed, her face a mess of tears and snot and sweat. "No. I'm sorry," she splutters. "Donna, I can't think. I'm sorry."

Donna's eyes skip over to the pickup, where there are terrible squelching noises coming from the front seat.

Rae's voice is barely a whisper. "Please don't leave me."

Donna turns, and she runs.

She hears Rae calling her name, like a drowning girl. Donna doesn't look back.

28. CALCULATED

MARYBETH LARKIN

Marybeth has been waiting for him to come back for hours, considering the most effective places to stab a man: neck, groin, heart, stomach. Neck sounds good.

She found her way back to the far wall and now stands against the pipes, hands clasped behind her back. *Helpless little me!* Except now those hands are unbound, clutching a sharp shard of metal.

She considered hiding on the stairs and rushing him the moment he opens the doors. But it's too risky: what if he sees her and shuts the doors on her before she can get past him? He's scrawny, but she doesn't know how strong. If he manages to take the knife from her, she won't stand a chance. She tongues the scar on her lip and thinks, *I've only got one shot at this.*

Finally she hears the key in the padlock holding the trapdoor closed, then the scrape and clatter of chains being pulled through the handles. She checks that the rope is tucked under her butt where he won't see it, and tightens her grip on the blade.

She hears a gruff voice. "Ewok, stay!" Then the door bursts

open, letting in morning light that's brighter than she expected. Ronnie flicks on a naked lightbulb hanging in the corner of the room, illuminating a bare concrete floor and crumbling brick walls hosting innumerable spiderwebs. Really sticking to that murder-chic decor theme. Most of the basement is crammed full of junk: an old stepladder, a rusty old barbecue, a pile of mouldy cardboard boxes, some greying wooden pallets. Her heart sinks when she spots a gleaming axe in a pile of tools. It looks sharp, and much more solid than the shard of rust she's holding.

Ronnie pulls the doors shut behind him, and shambles down the stairs. He's wearing the gas mask again, and bright yellow work gloves. The mask makes him look like some kind of bug-eyed, long-snouted creature, an apocalyptic badger. He's carrying a tray piled high with peanut butter sandwiches, and a plastic tumbler with cartoon Smurfs dancing round the edges.

He puts the tray down on the floor and sits on the bottom step.

"Could have cut the crusts off, at least," Marybeth says. When she used to babysit him, when he was a kid and she was barely a teenager, he'd throw a tantrum if she didn't cut the crusts off his sandwiches. Maybe this nod to their shared history might humanise her, make him reconsider whatever he's considering. But he just continues to stare at her through the plastic visor of the mask.

He's blocking her only way out, and she's not sure enough of her surroundings yet to take a chance at rushing him. No. If he wants her to eat, he'll have to lean in nice and close to untie her. Close enough for her to plunge the shard into his neck. She'll just sit here, bait. She's got all the time in the fucking world.

"What did you put in me?" she asks him.

"Ketamine," he says, flinching a little. "Horse tranquilliser. I had to make sure you weren't going to try to run."

"Gave me a hell of a headache."

He nods, brows knitted.

"Look," he says, finally. "We're going to have a conversation. And you need to tell me the truth."

"Well, if you want to talk, it would only be polite of you to take that off." *All the better for me to stab your neck with, my pretty*, she thinks.

He hesitates, then pulls the mask up to the top of his head. There's just a trace there of the little boy she used to know. Thick, dark eyelashes, sun-bleached hair, those hazy eyes. He was such a dreamy kid, always reading fantasy books, playing that *Dragons and Dungeons* game with his friend Manuel. All that softness has been burned out of him now. He's grown lanky. He keeps tugging at the neckline of his T-shirt, like he can't get comfortable in himself.

"What were you doing there, where I found you?"

"Going for a hike." She half-smiles at him. A dare.

"Wearing that?" His eyes flick to the sequinned sweater she's wearing, now covered in mud and leaves.

Marybeth shrugs.

Ronnie scowls. "Nobody knows that path. I've worked hard to keep it that way."

"I was following Donna Ramirez. I hoped she'd lead me to my daughter." She says Donna's name slowly, looking for a reaction in him. A flash of guilt.

He doesn't respond.

"You know Donna Ramirez. She was one of the three girls who went missing. With Tammy-Rae Hooper. And you might have heard of the other one. Katherine Larkin. My daughter. You heard of those girls?" That's all she can do: say their names. Force him to see them as human, to confront the true horror of what he did.

He is watching her with a deep frown. "Those girls are dead."

"You're saying my daughter's dead."

"All of them. They're dead."

Relief blooms in her chest, momentarily pushing back the

dread. OK, so he's crazier than she thought. Maybe he left them all tied up somewhere, and just assumed they'd died? But no, that makes no sense: Donna and Tammy-Rae coming back has been all over the local news for days. There's no way he hasn't seen. There's no other explanation except that he's lost it completely. People around town joked for years about how Ronnie Gaskins had finally blown a gasket, how prison took him halfway to crazy town and living by himself on the edge of the forest drove him the rest of the way.

She wanted some kind of explanation from him. But it doesn't look like he can give her even that.

"How many others are there?" he asks.

Why is he asking *her* this? Has he been blacking out while he kills? "Other... girls?"

"Others like you."

Marybeth is utterly nonplussed. None of this is going how she expected it to be going.

"You're going to burn up either way. You might as well tell me. Do one good thing."

Burn up. The words catch in her mind. Just like his parents. Is that what he did to Katie, immolated her? *Flames whipping around her sweet face, hair catching fire, a halo of heat and pain, hot air filling her lungs in a final scream.*

Marybeth starts to tremble. But it's not fear, no. It's hatred. Madman or not, she wants to stick this knife right into his eye.

Just come. Lean in close.

Ronnie is staring at her, like he's trying to read her mind from across the room. "You really don't know," he says. Then he shakes his head, mutters, "But of course that's what one of them would say," like he's having both sides of an argument with himself. "Did you go into the cave?"

"What?"

"Down the gully. When I found you, were you coming up, or going down?"

"I was just about to go down. That's where Donna went. You caught me before I could."

He bites the corner of one of his plump lips, still so boyish.

"Can I get some water?" she asks.

He doesn't answer. He reaches into his jacket with his left hand and pulls out a stack of paper. He leans down and fans it out on the floor in front of her, staying well out of her reach. He seems more scared of her than she is of him.

They're photographs, black and white, blurry, printed on large sheets like they were developed in a home darkroom.

Marybeth leans forward, careful to keep her hands well hidden behind her back. The first photograph is of a mule deer. A buck. The same one she saw near the gully, she thinks, but pulled out of the bushes and stretched out across a boulder. Something has taken a single clean bite out of its back. Something enormous.

Her eyes skip from photo to photo. The bottom half of a skunk. A coyote. A black bear. Each one with a hole in it, like something took a single bite and then left the rest. *Predators don't do that.* What does any of this have to do with Katie?

"She's out of control, isn't she?" Ronnie mutters. "She's not doing what she's supposed to. And she's getting bigger."

"Please, I'm so thirsty. I'll tell you anything you want. But I need some water first." *Lean in, so I can sink this piece of metal into your throat, you crazy piece of shit.*

He pulls the gas mask back down. She can no longer see his expression through the glare on the plastic, but his chest heaves in a heavy sigh.

He reaches into another pocket in his jacket and pulls out a can of WD-40 that has duct tape wrapped around it. "How many of you are there?" he asks, his voice muffled by the gas mask. "I need names."

Marybeth shifts her body weight, ready to lunge at him. *Just a little closer.*

He aims the WD-40 at her, and gives it an experimental

squirt. She realises that the duct tape is fastening a plastic lighter onto the front of the can, base against the can, tip lined up along the nozzle. He takes an elastic band out of his pocket and hooks it onto the lighter's gas trigger, keeping it squeezed. The smell of gas fills the room.

Marybeth's eyes grow huge as she finally realises what he's planning to do.

He takes a second plastic lighter from his pocket and lights the gas on the lighter attached to the can. He points the can a few feet to her right, and presses the nozzle on the WD-40. A burst of hot flame licks the wall next to her, singes the hairs on her face. A warning shot.

"Last chance. Tell me how many. Tell me who." The oil slick on the wall keeps burning.

She's forgotten the knife, forgotten her whole plan. Her whole world has narrowed to the size of the small blue flame of the plastic lighter against the nozzle of the can, now pointed directly at her body.

"Tell me!" Ronnie says, his eyes wild and desperate.

Marybeth can't talk. Can't think. Just cringes against the wall, frozen.

The seconds stretch out in silence.

"I'm sorry, Marybeth," he says. "I always liked you."

He presses the nozzle, engulfing her legs in flame.

She can't breathe. There's no pain yet, only panic. She can't think, just screams and pulls herself as far away from him as she can. The oil splatters on her pants continue burning. Frantic, she bats at them with her hands, until they go out.

And then the pain comes, searing through her.

Ronnie drops the can and pulls the gas mask off his face. He is wide-eyed, looking at her in horror.

He is still just out of her reach, but she doesn't care. She roars and lunges at the only part of him she can get to, stabbing the knife deep into his calf.

Ronnie screams, and staggers back, the knife still embedded in his leg.

She's weaponless, in agony, but superpowered by rage. She gets to her feet and runs at him. He dodges. The momentum carries her past him; she trips and falls into the pile of rotting boxes stacked against the wall. Her foot catches on the edge of the stepladder as she falls, bringing the whole thing down onto her. The wood slams against the ruined flesh of her leg, sending a bright shock of pain up her spine.

She's face down in the pile of damp cardboard. Insects scuttle away from her. She gasps, and lifts herself, trying to turn around. She's expecting Ronnie to be there, looming over her, ready with his DIY flamethrower, about to finish her off.

But she rolls onto her back, and there's nothing but the naked bulb hanging from the ceiling. Sitting, she sees Ronnie, collapsed at the other end of the room, tears streaming from his face. He's probing the skin around the knife, but seems afraid to pull it out.

"I'm so sorry..." he says to her. "I... I thought..." He shakes his head and touches his calf again. He hisses in pain.

"You shit!" Marybeth screams. She gets to her feet and picks up the axe. It is heavy in her hands, just as heavy as she hoped. He looks up at her with his little-boy eyes, huge, red-rimmed.

"It's my fault," he murmurs. "I led them right to it."

"You killed my daughter." She hoists the axe over her shoulder like a baseball bat.

"I didn't mean to," he says, squeezing his eyes shut. "I promise I didn't mean to."

He looks so small, beneath her. Not that much older than Katie. Hurt, defenceless. And obviously crazy.

She drops the weapon, and screams. It is an endless ululation, all of her grief, her pain, her self-loathing. All the ways that she has failed her daughter, again and again and again.

She turns, and runs up the stairs, through the doors, and out into the bright sunshine.

29. HUMAN BEHAVIOUR

KATHERINE LARKIN

TUESDAY, 17 SEPTEMBER 1996

Dear Diary,

Uggggggggggh Ma Bear and I had a huge fight this afternoon. It's been happening a lot recently, but this one was a doozy.

All I asked was that she take down some of the photos from my Glorious Pageant Years from the living room. It's so embarrassing when my friends come over and there's me all primped up like a Barbie. She was like, "It reminds me of happier times." For her, obviously; who cares about my feelings.

I told her it's MY FACE so I think I have a right to decide where it's displayed. And she said, "Well, it's my house and my photographs." Teenagers don't have rights apparently.

So I asked her to at least take down the star-spangled bikini that's framed and hung above the mantelpiece (from when I was SEVEN, by the way, have you ever heard of anything more vomit-inducing) and she started going on about how it was one of the first outfits she ever made for me, and then she said, "Did you know that your grandmother was a dressmaker? I made it on her old sewing machine. I could teach you! It will be fun—"

And I cut that right off, because I can just see how that would become a whole new chance for her to measure and probe my body and make all these sneaky comments about how beautiful I could be if I just stuck to the Weight Watchers programme with her, so I said, "Thanks but I'm going to hang out with my friends."

Then she got all morose and said, "Remember when you used to say I was your best friend?"

And I was all, "Yeah, when I was a kid."

And she said, "You're still my best friend."

I couldn't help it, Diary, I rolled my eyes and said, "Like yeah, that's the whole problem." I guess it was a bit mean, but come on. It's true! Ma Bear has NO FRIENDS. Zero. Zilch. She's super judgemental and always going on about other people's flaws and she never spends time with people her own age.

Then she shrugged and she said something like, "I know it seems now like your teenage friends are forever, but I promise you, they're not."

And I said, "Maybe for some people. Not for us."

Then she said, "You'll see. Boys will hurt you without thinking about it, but girls will find your deepest most vulnerable places and rip you to shreds." Projecting, much?

Then I maybe said some more things to her. Pretty bad things.

Ma Bear always says that I'm an old soul but she's forever young. Sometimes I wish we could just swap, and she could be fifteen again like she wants, and I could be thirty-whatever and just live my damn life and be an adult and get to make the choices I want. I think we'd both be so much happier.

Uggggggggggggh. I guess I have to go and apologise but I'm just so PISSED. What would it be like to have a mother who actually gave a shit about you?

Kat
Too mad for facts today.

30. SHE'S CRUSHING MY MIND

TAMMY-RAE HOOPER

TUESDAY, 24 SEPTEMBER 1996

Rae watches Donna race down the street, long hair bouncing against her back, feeling like her heart is in a vice. She calls her name, but Donna never looks back.

Her mother walks up next to her, smelling of shampoo. Her face still has that vapid, half-there look. Secure in its own righteousness. Not that different from Estelle Hooper's real face, honestly. She takes Rae's hand and the pain subsides a bit.

Her mother leads her to the pickup that Donna arrived in. Tim's body is slumped in the front seat; a bloody mass of cells on its lap is squirming into existence. *Typical Donna, leaving a giant mess for somebody else to clean up.* She's not sure if that thought is hers or her mother's.

"Get the car into the garage," her mom says. It's a relief, having someone else take control. She was such a fool, thinking she could handle this on her own, a stupid fifteen-year-old girl. Her father opens the door of the truck, heaves Tim's body over to the passenger seat, and climbs inside. A curtain in their neighbour's house twitches. Angela Bradley.

Probably in there right now, getting an eyeful.

Her mother ushers her and Brandon back inside. The engine of the pickup roars to life behind her. Rae can still feel Donna, like a beacon moving off into the distance. She can feel the panic beaming from her, like an electric current. It occurs to her that she could follow this, track Donna through her feelings, like a bloodhound following a scent.

But it's over. Donna hates her. She saw who Rae really is, and was repulsed.

Rae crumples onto the floor of the living room, drawing ragged breaths. Her family is dead. She killed them. And *they're not even her family*, because she's a monster wearing a human suit.

And Donna left her.

She cannot live with this. *How* is she supposed to live with this? She wants to walk upstairs and lie down with the bodies of her parents and slit her own throat. She wants to douse herself in gasoline and set fire to herself. She wants to destroy herself, utterly. But there would be no point. This body she's wearing would just fix itself.

It's too much. It's all too much, and *Donna just left*, and she's heartbroken, and she can't—

Brandon touches his forehead to hers, and it's like all her thoughts are instantly debarbed, like the volume is turned right down on her feelings. She takes a deep, shuddering breath. She and Brandon have never been close, but there is something in him that reaches something in her, now. Something not human. Something peaceful, and enormous, and so much bigger than either of them.

They sit there, head to head, until her breathing calms. She hears the garage door closing and her parents banging around back there, but she's not particularly curious about what they're doing. After this, the worst night of her life, she just wants to sit here for a minute and be at peace.

"She's not your friend," Brandon says. She's not sure if he means, literally, she's not Donna Ramirez, or that she's their enemy. Either way, it feels true. Donna was always too cool, too funny, too bright to be friends with cowardly, cowed Tammy-Rae.

She puts her hand on Brandon's cheek. It's sweaty, hot. She feels a pang of sympathy for him, for this imperfect body. *Family can never leave you*, she thinks.

They pull apart, finally. Thoughts start whirring again, but less frantic than before, like she's taken a sedative.

Brandon picks up the Cap'n Crunch box and shakes it.

"I finished it, sorry," she says.

"I'm starving."

"Of course you are. You just built a whole body out of air." She is suddenly certain of this, some part of her remembering what it's like to survive on chemosynthesis, grabbing whatever gases are available and transmuting them into atoms. It *is* pretty incredible, she thinks, looking at him. He is exactly as Brandon was, down to the whorl of hair behind his ear. She runs her fingers up the scar on his forearm. The scar's there because Brandon had it before he was copied. It's not based on Brandon's DNA; it's a perfect copy of his body as it was at the moment he died, down to the memories etched in his brain.

He's the same age Brandon was. Maybe he always will be.

She can *feel* her parents moving around in the house, like she can feel Brandon in front of her, like she could feel Donna running from her, on some electric or chemical level. Last night, when she'd told Brandon and her parents everything she knew, they'd been so much faster to accept it than she was. This is why, she realises. The force between them is growing stronger. She didn't realise with Donna, because on some level it's *always* felt like that with her, that immediate connection. But this buzz between her and her brother, it's like being drunk.

Brandon continues her thought. "It's pretty gnarly."

"Tell me about it."

"Why is Donna fighting it?"

"Donna fights everything." But that's not quite right. It's just that Donna was always so sure of herself, so willing to do her own thing. Thinking about Donna makes her heart feel like it's being clamped again, but Brandon slips his hand into hers, and it eases.

"She wasn't good for you," he says.

The two of them walk hand in hand through the house. Brandon's hand is sweaty in hers. Everything is far away, like she's watching the earth from the window of an airplane.

"What are we going to do about the bodies?" she asks, nodding up the stairs.

"Burn the house down?" Brandon says.

"Wouldn't work. They caught Ronnie, remember?"

"Serial killers really don't get enough credit."

"Don't joke about it. They were our family."

Brandon shrugs. "Not really."

Their parents are in the garage, pulling a half-formed Tim Knox out of the car. He's already heavy, his limbs lengthening. Rae rushes to help them, noticing the shadow of a goatee already sprouting on his face.

It is so easy to just do what they want her to do.

The muffled sound of a voice coming through a walkie-talkie comes from the car. Somebody checking in on Tim. How long before they send out more cops to come looking for him if he doesn't answer?

The doorbell rings. Rae sleepwalks through to the entrance hall. Angela Bradley is there, a large white greyhound standing behind her, looking even more fidgety than greyhounds usually do.

"Oh, good morning, dear. I was just taking Lily out for a walk but I noticed, silly me! I forgot to bring any baggies." The thinnest of excuses to come and snoop.

Rae looks past her. Next door, Mrs Abrams is standing on her front porch now, still in a dressing gown, gawking at them openly.

"We don't have any, sorry, Mrs Bradley," Rae says, managing to twist her features into a pleasant smile.

"Did I see Donna Ramirez?" Angela prompts.

"Yes. But she's gone now," says Rae, arranging her expression to look sympathetic, tinged with conspiratorial. *Oh, you know how Donna is.*

But Angela is staring at her, with a concerned look on her face, her eye line fixed somewhere lower than Rae's face.

Rae looks down and realises that her T-shirt is covered in Tim's blood.

The greyhound cowers away from her, straining at the leash. Her nose is twitching wildly. She's not sure if that's because of the blood, or some other smell that she can sense in her. The other part of her.

She continues smiling at Angela. "Come on in," she says, in her sweetest voice. "My mom's in the garage. She might be able to help."

Angela walks inside. She almost has to drag the dog, who has sunk her claws into the boards of the front porch and doesn't want to go anywhere.

"Mom!" Rae calls out. Her mother appears in the doorway, red stains all up and down her torso. Angela starts babbling nervous questions at her. Rae sighs, and wanders past them into the living room. She hears a sharp scream, a heavy thump, the whine of a dog.

Rae sinks onto the sofa, closing her eyes. She is so, so tired. But she has to make a plan. They're in so much trouble.

She sits there for several minutes. At some point, she hears the engine of Tim's car roar to life and drive away. She wonders vaguely where he's going, and finds she doesn't care.

The problem is the math, she considers. Mom, Dad, Brandon, Angela, Tim. That's already five. Angela's husband will notice, or Tim's girlfriend. If each of them takes another five, that's twenty-five. How many steps away from the whole population of Little Hope?

"No, no, my girl. Don't you see?" her mother interrupts her. She's pulled on a coat and has her bright-blue handbag slung over her shoulder. "It's beautiful. I waited so long to hear something. I tried to have faith and it was so hard. But now he's speaking to us." Her eyes are shining. Rae has never seen her so animated. "We have to spread the good news."

"God's army has been called up," her father says, throwing a sports jacket over his shirt and grabbing his briefcase.

"What are we going to do?"

"What we were born to do," her father says, patting her hair. "What each of God's creatures is born to do. 'Be ye fruitful, and multiply.'"

Her mother completes the scripture. "'Fill the earth, and subdue it.'"

"Now. Come on."

Rae follows her parents out to the driveway, blinking in the sun. "I'm not going to kill anyone else," Rae says. But her family don't respond. Did she even say it out loud? She's not sure. Maybe she doesn't need to.

She imagines all the bodies, all eight thousand inhabitants of Little Hope, lying in a pile. They could throw Astroturf over it and pretend it's a hill. Put a big sign in front that says, *Nothing to see here, folks!* She laughs, a bark that echoes into the madness of the morning.

"Estelle, you and Tammy-Rae should go door to door. Work your way through the neighbourhood. Keep it quiet, for as long as you can. Tim's going to start with the cops so we don't run into any trouble. Brandon and I will get Angela and start working Broad Street."

She remembers Kat once telling them about a type of mould that could solve mazes. A single-celled fungus that can live freely, or aggregate together. No single organism was intelligent, but they could communicate with each other, and it was the communication that allowed them to be intelligent.

There is some kind of communication happening now, between her and her family, happening on a level far below human thought. And with Tim and Angela, and with Donna. Something so much bigger than her. And the more of them there are, the less she thinks the small electrical signals firing in the human brain she's wearing will matter.

Wouldn't it be a relief? says a sneaky voice in her mind. *No more worrying, or obsessing about everything bad. No more hating yourself. No more having to be Tammy-Rae Hooper.* She could surrender, finally, to something bigger than herself.

Her mom holds out the coat she bought Rae for her last birthday. It's dusty pink, knee-length, something that looks like it should belong on an American Girl doll. Rae hates it, but she doesn't fight as her mom pulls it on for her and carefully does the buttons up to cover Rae's bloody T-shirt.

"There. All clean." Her mom smiles.

"I'm not going to," Rae manages.

"It's God's will."

"How do you know?"

Her mother smiles. The most peaceful smile Rae's ever seen on her. Absolutely certain. "Because I can feel it. Finally."

Hand in hand, they walk over to the Abramses' front door and ring the bell. Becca Abrams cracks open the door, still wearing flannel pyjamas and clutching a toothbrush. She looks wary. "You all OK? Thought I heard someone shouting over there."

"Are your parents home?" her mother asks.

"They've both just left."

Her mother nods, pushing into the hallway without waiting for a response. She clicks the door closed behind them and carefully reaches into her handbag for the kitchen knife she's stashed there.

Rae stands there and does nothing. A stubborn voice inside her is saying, *No. I'm not going to do this.*

Bemused, Becca steps back into their lilac-painted hallway, her eyes scanning Rae's face for any clue about what's happening.

God, Becca's hazel eyes are so beautiful, like a blackwater stream stained with tannins, like scumbled fall leaves, like the wild moist things that live in loam.

Her mother freezes, hand still in her bag. She grabs Rae's wrist and scans her face, eyes narrowed.

Something twitches in her mother's face. She *knows*. She can read Rae's mind and *she knows*. Rae feels like her skin has peeled off and she's more naked than she's ever been in her life.

Rae raises her chin, defiant. Hoping she looks braver than she feels.

Her mother cups her chin. "It's OK, my girl," she whispers. "God forgives everything." Then Rae feels something heavy thrust into her hand. "Be brave now."

The deep humming all around her grows stronger. If she tries to fight it, will she turn into a monster like Kat? Or, worse, will she be alone?

"Go on," her mom says, like it's the first day of school, and Rae's afraid to make friends. "Repent."

Becca comes closer. She spots the knife and gasps, backing away.

Her mother puts her hand on the top of Rae's back, gentle.

Does she even have a choice? Did she ever?

Rae plunges the knife into her own palm, throws herself on Becca, and her mind goes blank.

31. HERJAZZ

MARYBETH LARKIN

TUESDAY, 24 SEPTEMBER 1996

Mid-morning heat is beating down by the time Marybeth stumbles back into town, wheezing and limping from the pain in her legs. She's been sticking to the back roads in case Ronnie comes looking for her, so it's been slow going. The more her adrenaline subsides, the more the pain comes into focus. The fabric of her pants half-melted to her legs and every time the loose fibres brush her wounds, it's like an electric shock. The skin she can see is a bright pink and starting to swell. She'll have a few more scars by the end of this.

There aren't a lot of people out and about on Broad Street at this time of the morning. A few people in Louanne's Diner, a small crowd in the bakery. Marybeth considers rushing up to any of them, screaming that a madman just tied her up in his basement and tried to barbecue her, but it's all just too crazy. She sets her sights on the police station and hobbles towards it as fast as she can.

Zach. She needs Zach.

But the station, too, is quieter than she expects. A grey

pickup is parked right in front of the doors, not even in a parking bay. Closer, she sees that the door has been left wide open, like whoever was driving it got out in a real hurry. There's a police radio on the dashboard, squawking unintelligibly, next to a plastic sunflower.

She opens the door to the front desk area. It's eerily quiet. Mindy's not at the front desk, although the neon-green handbag under the chair must be hers. There's no one else here. No sign of the reporters who've been hanging out here for the past few days, none of the usual bustle of residents coming in to complain about their neighbours being too loud, no cops at all.

"Hello?" she calls out. She's surprised by how out of breath she is, from running halfway across town. The pain in her legs seems to be throbbing in time with her pulse. She should have run straight to the doctor's first, maybe, but Ronnie could be making a run for it right now. That stab wound in his calf wasn't that bad. He might have crawled into his car and driven halfway to Mexico already. Then there will be no justice for her daughter.

"I need help!" she calls out again.

There are noises coming from somewhere in the building. She goes to open the door that leads through the hallway to the rest of the station, ignoring the OFFICIALS ONLY sign, when she's startled by a loud hammering sound behind her.

She turns to see Donna, pounding on the glass of the front doors. She's wearing a motorcycle helmet, with the visor up, and is shaking her head frantically.

Marybeth doesn't have time right now to consider where she stands on trusting Donna Ramirez. She needs to find Zach.

She turns back and pushes open the door to the hallway. Now she can definitely hear movement: thumping noises, several people yelling.

"Hello?" she calls out again. Where the hell is everyone?

Most of the doors back here are wide open. She walks past the interview room where she and Estelle sat on that first terrible morning, telling them that the girls were missing. There's nobody in there now.

She walks past a kitchenette, the bathrooms, Zach's office, the briefing room. The station is still plastered with photographs of Katie, maps of the woods annotated with markers. Each room she walks past is empty.

The noises grow clearer. There's a crash like a piece of furniture breaking. Someone repeating "Stay back! Stay back!" over and over again, then a sharp scream, then silence.

The noise is coming from the large open space near the back where most of the sergeants have their cubicles, behind another door at the end of the hallway.

Marybeth slows, her hand shaking. But she can't turn back now.

The sounds are quieter. Squelching noises. The sucking sound of something wet. She hesitates with her hand on the handle, then opens the door to a bloodbath.

It takes her a moment to understand what she's seeing. Her eyes fixate on the smallest detail: a dark smear against the wall, four streaks from fingers grabbing for support against the beige wallpaper.

She stares at that, because it makes more sense than the bodies slumped across desks, strewn across the floor like discarded toys, the strange foetus-like creatures squirming between them in pools of blood.

No, those things are too absurd, so she finds her eyes returning to the streaks on the wall. They are so neat, the distance between each of the four stripes an even distance from the others, even as they arc down onto the floor, where Chief Pittman's body is lying on its side, a deep gash up his torso that one of those creatures is in the process of climbing through.

There seems to be a bite mark on Zach's cheek, exactly the same size as a human mouth.

There is one man standing, leaning against the wall on the far side of the room. Marybeth's numb brain recognises Tim Knox, blood dripping from the pale skin of his skinny naked body. There's a small chunk of bloody tissue dangling from the tip of his goatee. The look on his face is entirely serene.

Their eyes meet. Tim gives her a lazy smile. "Good morning, Mrs Larkin. Come to chat about your daughter?"

A hand grabs Marybeth's ankle. She looks down to see Sergeant Mercer, foam bubbling from her mouth, staring up at her, unable to speak. She is holding something out to Marybeth: her gun.

Marybeth reaches for the grip, surprised at how heavy it feels.

Sergeant Mercer gurgles. She flicks her eyes back towards the hallway in an unmistakable signal. *Run.*

It's enough to shake her from her stupor. Marybeth stumbles back, just as Tim takes a step towards her. "We've got a lot to discuss, Marybeth."

The door hits her back as she stumbles away, afraid to turn away from him. He keeps advancing even as she screams at him to stop.

She fumbles with the gun, looking for a safety switch. She's only fired a gun a couple of times in her life. There's nothing that feels like the safety.

She pulls the slide back to cock the gun, and points it at him, hoping to frighten him.

He keeps advancing, arms outstretched now. She panics and squeezes the trigger. To her surprise, the gun bucks in her hand, shattering the quiet with a loud *crack.*

Tim stops. He looks down at the bloody blossom in the hollow of his shoulder.

Marybeth cocks the gun again. "Stop!" she screams at him. But after a second, he takes another step towards her.

She fires again. This one goes straight through the centre of his chest.

Tim seems more curious than perturbed. He halts, looking down at his wounds. Before Marybeth's eyes, the flesh knits back together, leaving nothing but two more bloody patches on unmarred skin.

Well, fuck.

Marybeth turns and runs back up the hallway. His heavy footsteps pound up the passage behind her. Her fingers touch the cold metal of the door back to reception, then a muscled arm snakes around her throat.

Then Tim is on her, choking her. The gun drops from her hand and skids along the floor. He pulls her to the ground and straddles her, leaning over her face, a bit of tissue wobbling from the tip of his goatee. Marybeth twists and screams, the pain in her legs an agony where Tim's legs are pressing against her raw burns.

Suddenly, there's a heavy thump, and the weight is off her.

Marybeth gasps as she watches Donna tackle Tim and knock him back up the hallway. They grapple, but Donna is firm on her feet while Tim's half-slumped against the wall. She shoves him hard into the interrogation room and pulls the door shut behind her, twisting the key in the lock. A moment later, the handle begins to rattle.

Donna looks back at her, sliding the visor of the helmet down over her face. Marybeth puts out her hand, hoping she'll help to pull her up. But Donna just stares at it.

"I can't touch you," she says, voice muffled by the motorcycle helmet. "Come on!"

Donna heads for the entrance, and Marybeth gets up off the floor, grabs the gun, and follows her through the empty front desk area, out the front door, and into the dazzling sunlight.

Hector is there, shifting nervously from foot to foot. He looks about as confused as Marybeth feels.

A small crowd has gathered across the street, watching them. They must have heard the gunshots. They seem reluctant to come closer.

"What's happening?" Marybeth splutters out.

"There's no time. We've got to go."

Donna climbs into the driver's side of the pickup and starts rummaging on the ground. Her father leans over to help her. Donna flinches. "I said don't touch me!" The girl seems deranged. In addition to the helmet, Marybeth realises she's also wearing yellow rubber gloves, and a trash bag over her clothes. She looks like some alien creature made of plastic and rubber, its one huge eye glinting in the sunlight.

Marybeth reaches into the passenger side and picks up the radio from the dashboard. Tim's voice is crackling out of it.

"All units, report to the station immediately. Repeat. All units, report to the station."

Another voice on the radio. "Uh... this is unit one four. Say again, please? Over." Marybeth recognises the voice: Sergeant Pockmarks.

Marybeth presses the button on the side. "No!" she yells into it. "It's not safe. Stay away. Call for help."

"The keys aren't here," Donna says, still scrabbling madly around the footwell.

"We have to go," says Hector, grabbing Donna's shoulder and pulling her out of the car.

Marybeth looks back at the station. Through the glass of the door, she can see the silhouettes of people shambling into the front room.

The crowd of people across the street has grown larger. They're staring openly.

"Help!" Marybeth calls to them.

No one moves a muscle to help them.

"Where do we go?" Marybeth asks Donna. The gun is still clutched in her hand, useless.

"I don't know," says Donna, through a sob.

Hector grabs her hand, and they run out onto the road. Marybeth follows, wanting to put as much distance between herself and the horror-show behind her as she can.

A blue station wagon careens up towards them, driving much too fast, weaving slightly. It skids to a halt right next to them. The passenger door is flung open.

"Get in," calls Ronnie, from the driver's seat.

"You just tried to kill me!" she screams at him.

He throws open the car door. "There's no time."

Marybeth can't process this, on top of everything else that's just happened. But right now, it feels like she has no choice but to do what he says. She climbs into the passenger side. Hector climbs in behind her.

"Not her," he snarls, pointing at Donna. "She's one of them."

"It's OK," Donna says, trying to close the door on her father. "Just get them safe," she says to Ronnie.

But Hector's already trying to climb back out of the car. Donna tries to push him back in. "Dad, please, just go," she says. Through the visor, Marybeth can see tears streaming down her face.

Behind her, she sees Tim burst through the front door of the police station, coming after them.

And she just saw Donna try to push her father back into the car after saving her life. Her daughter's best friend.

"Jesus, Ronnie," Marybeth yells at him. "All of us or none of us."

Ronnie shakes his head, looking incredulous. But there's no time to argue. He lets Donna and Hector climb into the back seat, and they drive away.

FIVE FOR SILVER

32. PANIK

The monster scrabbles at the hole with her spindly fingers. She can smell baby rabbits in there, maddeningly close. Pads on her fingertips feel disturbances in the air as they tremble. But she can't reach them.

The trouble is, the more she's eaten, the bigger she's become, and in all the wrong places. She's twenty feet long now and fat as the trunks of the sugar pines, but all she's got in the way of limbs are two pathetic front human arms that have barely grown at all. Her segments are fat with eggs. Her mouth is enormous, her belly infinite, and it's becoming harder and harder to fill.

She reaches her arm in again, hoping to widen the entrance enough that she can force her way just a few inches deeper and grab one of the squirming tender hairless bodies cowering in there.

There's a sharp nip on her elbow as the mother bites her. The rabbit is frantic, leaping from side to side at the entrance to the hole. Her whole arm is covered in its bites and scratches.

She will eat the mother too, once she's done. But she wants the veal before the beef.

"They'll die without you anyway," she tries to reason with the rabbit. It's the first time she's spoken in days. She's been forgetting words lately. There's only a little bit of human mind left, crowded out by the parts of her that are just hungry all the time. Her voice is a sonorous growl coming from a wide larynx in the neckless transition between neck and body. The words are a slur through hook-ringed lips that are the wrong shape.

She bats the mother away. It rushes right back, nipping at her arm again, this time biting in and trying to drag it out the burrow. The rabbit must know that it's dying. Flecks of blood mar the warm brown of its fur. Its eyelids are drooping. But the eyes beneath them flash yellow, furious, using every last bit of energy it has to defend its babies.

But she's so hungry. It's not *fair*.

The monster groans, stretching her arm as deep as she can into the hole. Her fingertips brush the velvety warmth of baby rabbit skin.

The mother rabbit growls and throws its body against her arm, wrapping its front legs around her elbow, and kicking its hind legs hard against her, slicing her skin. Milky-pink fluid seeps from the wound.

The monster hisses and concedes, pulling her arm back to the safety of her body. It stings.

Exhausted, the mother rabbit collapses in the hole of the burrow. The monster watches as it struggles to draw its final breaths.

"Were they worth dying for?" the monster asks her, irritated. Waste of time. Waste of life.

The rabbit falls still, the eyes fixed on some far distant place.

A new rabbit begins to squirm in its belly. The monster sighs, wondering if she'll swallow this one down, or let it go off into the woods. She's let some of the copies go before, curious to see what would happen. Other rabbits, a couple of lizards, some of the ants. She'd half-hoped they'd be obedient to her, their sire, little scouts that might run off into the woods and report back to her. None of them did. She can sense them, sometimes, when they come near. Who knows where they are now, or what kind of strange little lives they're living out there. It can hardly be as strange as her own.

The rabbit splits in two, the new creature falling out of it, glistening in viscera. It's already fur-covered, unlike the babies in the burrow. The monster eyes its muscles as they thicken, the lovely Z-shape of its hind legs.

That's what she needs, she muses. Rabbit legs. Strong and sharp. She could leap through the forest, instead of dragging this long slithery body that goes on forever, on puny legs grown far too small to carry her weight. She would be fast. Nothing would be able to escape her.

The spark of an idea forms, somewhere in the muddiness of her mind, built on a long-ago memory of riffing on wild jokes with her friends, photocopying, cutting and pasting, remixing. Combining the old to make something new.

She is already half one thing and half another. What if she could be… more?

She rears around and takes it into her mouth. All of it: rabbit carcass, and the mass of cells that is straining to copy it.

The urge to swallow is strong. The powerful digestive juices of her stomach would dissolve it in minutes, ruin the strange microscopic alchemies that are turning air into body tissue. It would become just another meal.

Instead, she holds it there in her mouth, her maw filling with saliva. It drips down onto the hooks surrounding her face and coats the bloody mass on her tongue.

The substance creating this new body mingles with whatever created hers. Suddenly, it's like a light turns on in her mind, a second consciousness. Information: the shape of rabbit, the blueprint for each cell and nerve ending. Like a perfect map, on the level of atoms and electrons. Millions and millions of copies of this thing, writ in miniature. Instructions to be executed.

Well now, that's interesting.

The oldest parts of her remember what it was to live in the cave for all those centuries, to communicate as yeasts and moulds and fungi. This is like that: communication through chemicals, mind without consciousness. Letting her saliva mix with this thing, tasting it slowly, she knows that they understand each other perfectly.

She can feel the will of it. The clear logic of its imperative: reproduce. It wants to suck in air, reshape whatever molecules it can find into this rabbit. It *must* become this rabbit.

And she is made of the same stuff as it; so much of her wants to obey. But other parts of her used to be a girl named Katherine Larkin, and those parts are curious, and powerful, and powerfully curious.

And that part of her wants to know what it would feel like to be a rabbit.

What if... she thinks, holding the open-endedness of that thought for a moment.

What if... instead of reproduction, we tried evolution.

She holds the map in her mouth, considers it. She has more interest in some parts of this rabbit than other parts. Best to just borrow the good bits and discard the rest.

She focuses hard. Her spindly legs begin to thicken, lengthen. The muscle fibres multiply. She sprouts a thousand-thousand new mitochondria. They fold into a new shape, a shape better for leaping, better for slashing.

Interesting.

Her legs swell until they are huge, strong enough to lift her long torso. Strong enough to allow her to jump to the top of the redwoods, maybe.

Very interesting indeed.

She flexes one of her new legs, marvelling at the amount of energy stored in there. *Now what am I?*

She crouches deep, and then she leaps.

It all whips past her, air and branches and leaves. She flies high into the canopy of the forest, to where the light filters more brightly through the trees. She lands back down with a thud that makes everything near her scurry and flee.

Yes, this will do just fine.

She's still holding the rabbit in her mouth. Some of it refuses to die, and it jostles against the tough walls of her mouth. Her tongue probes at it as she wonders what else might be fun to try. A little fluffy tail, perhaps. Ears that can pick up movement from miles away.

Her tongue feels out the little helmet of its skull, the dense fatty brain nestled inside. What would happen if she copied its brain? Would she become the rabbit? Could she steal its memories of forest and small warm babies and whatever complex warfare is waged by rabbits against other rabbits?

She breathes deep and feels a little rabbit brain begin to bloom at the base of her thick head, attached to her own spinal cord.

Oh, no.

A new feeling washes over her, of being a small, frightened thing in a world where larger things want to kill you. A bright yellow feeling. Sharp. Hot.

Panic.

Every muscle in her powerful new limbs tenses. Before she knows it, she has started to run on those fast new legs of hers, awayawayawayawayaway.

Her human mind tries to wrestle back control. It tries to shut down the rabbit brain, detach it from herself. But it is part of her now. And there is no arguing with panic.

AWAYAWAYAWAYAWAYAWAYAWAYAWAYAWAY-
AWAYAWAYAWAYAWAYAWAYAWAYAWAYAWAY-
AWAYAWAYAWAYAWAYAWAYAWAYAWAYAWAY-

AWAYAWAYAWAYAWAYAWAYAWAYAWAYAWAY-
AWAYAWAYAWAYAWAYAWAYAWAYAWAYAWAY-
AWAYAWAYAWAYAWAYAWAY...

The burrow is far behind her now, the rabbit babies probably beginning their slow starvation.

33. SURVIVE

DONNA RAMIREZ

Donna expects Ronnie to head straight for Route 49, drive them as far away from Little Hope as possible. Instead, he winds the station wagon through the back streets to his house.

"Where are we going?" her father asks, from the back seat next to her.

"We need weapons," Ronnie answers. He meets Donna's eyes in the rear-view mirror as he says this.

Donna rearranges the neck of her hoodie to ensure the fabric is tightly bunched around the bottom of the motorcycle helmet, forming a seal. A jolt of pain runs up her back from the awkward angle she's holding her body at, leaning as far away from her father as she can. She can't be *that* contagious, seeing as she's been walking around town for days without killing anybody, as far as she knows, but she's not taking any chances.

Her dad keeps throwing her worried looks, but for now, he's being surprisingly accepting of what's happening. She was so lucky to have found him when she did, when he was walking from the bus stop towards the police station to meet her there for their appointment with Zach. She doesn't want to think about what would have happened if she'd been too late.

He is definitely himself. Sitting next to him, there's none of that magnetic feeling she got from being in the room with Rae and her family. That's all she's holding on to, now: that he is still him, and somehow, because the universe has a strange sense of humour, she's the only one who can protect him.

Marybeth, on the front passenger seat, is chewing on her top lip, worrying a small scar Donna's never noticed before. She smells like piss and oil, but there's something fierce in the set of her forehead. It's exactly the same look Kat gets when she's concentrating. A stubborn Larkin look.

They bump up the drive towards the old Gaskins house. The gate is standing wide open, which is unusual: Ronnie's famously paranoid about security. It looks like he drove out in a hurry.

"How did you find us?" she asks.

"I was following Marybeth."

"Wanted to finish me off?" Marybeth mumbles, staring straight ahead.

"To see if you were OK."

Ronnie parks the car just in front of the house. They all climb out as Ronnie limps over towards the gate and starts securing the half-dozen chains and padlocks that hold it closed. There's a strip of fabric tight around the left leg of his cargo shorts, a makeshift tourniquet, and a knife handle wobbling around in the calf of his leg.

Marybeth wanders over to help him. She, too, is limping, and one of her pants legs seems to have been scorched. The two of them seem to be doing everything they can to avoid making eye contact with each other. Ronnie's dog yaps around their feet, a hideous creature that looks like he was assembled out of enthusiasm and steel wool scouring pads.

Donna's dad seems less interested in this mysterious drama

playing out between Marybeth and Ronnie. His eyes are fixed on her. "I need you to tell me what kind of trouble you're in," he says finally.

"Actually, we'd all like to know that," says Marybeth, walking back towards them. "I think it's past time that we all have an honest conversation."

Donna nods. She's fucked up every single step of this. Time to let the grown-ups take charge.

They start towards the front door. "I don't want *it* in my house," Ronnie protests, gesturing to Donna.

Marybeth ushers Donna inside, regardless. Ronnie grumbles but follows them in.

———

Donna always expected Ronnie's house to be as run-down on the inside as it is on the outside, but it's not. There's a vase of wildflowers in the hallway. The living room has been painted a cheery green, although it wasn't done neatly, and there are occasional brush marks on the ceiling. Beneath two 1970s-style overstuffed armchairs is a thick shag-pile rug, flanked by little end tables holding picture frames and ceramic birds. He has put care and love into this place.

Donna sits on the armchair in the furthest corner of the room, trying to keep as much distance between herself and the others as she can. Ronnie vanishes, and comes back offering an ice pack to Marybeth. Her dad and Marybeth sit on the sofa opposite, and Ronnie stays on his feet, hovering anxiously near the doorway. The dog curls up on the rug and falls asleep immediately.

Donna starts to talk, words streaming out of her, like a flood she's been trying to dam up with cardboard boxes. She tells them everything, from the beginning. Waking up in the forest, Rae leading them to safety, washing off the blood.

About the monster Rae was so sure she saw out there, that they thought had killed Kat, how weird she's been feeling since she came back, how her whole body feels contagious and sweaty and out of control. *Different.*

She fingers Kat's journal in the kangaroo pocket on the front of her hoodie. It gives her strength.

And then she tells them about finding the path back out to the cave, and what she found out there.

Her father covers his face with his hands at this. Marybeth's expression is more puzzled than frightened. Donna supposes that after what she saw in the police station, this can't be as much of a shock to her as it might have been.

Ronnie is still watching her with open hostility, shifting from foot to foot. The knife handle in his calf twitches as he moves. Luckily, it doesn't seem to be bleeding very much.

Donna goes on, the full awful truth of it. Her slow realisation, at last, that they can spread it. And that Rae already had.

"Tim Knox," Marybeth chimes in. "I shot him. Twice, right in the chest. The skin just closed right up."

"That's not how you kill them," Ronnie says. "Trust me."

Donna glances up the stairs, where the bedrooms must be. Pieces click into place. They are not the first.

Marybeth gives him a slow nod in return. "They burn," she says, lifting the ice pack from her ankle to show them scalded flesh. "Faster than normal people, I assume?"

"Light right up like kindling." Ronnie glances back at Donna as he says this. "They aren't human."

"Then what are we?" Donna asks him.

Ronnie scowls. "You can play innocent all you want—"

"Use your eyes, Ronnie," Marybeth cuts him off. "Look at what she's wearing. She's trying not to hurt anyone else, and she saved my life back there."

"I'm telling the truth," Donna says. "Please. I don't understand any of this. I just want to know what I am."

Her dad has dropped his hands to his lap, but his expression is stony, unreadable.

They all look at Ronnie, waiting.

"There's a cave in the forest," he says finally. "Anyone who goes inside changes." He picks up one of the ceramic birds and weighs it in his hands. A rich dark blue, not too dissimilar to their magpies.

"We moved here when I was ten. My dad got a temp job at the high school. He was a science teacher, but he'd been out of work for a while. And my mom was pregnant. Little Hope was supposed to be a new start for us."

He turns the bird over in his hands, places his thumb in the thumbprint of the maker. "I guess luck just doesn't stick to some people.

"They didn't renew my dad's contract. My mom lost the baby. They were both just sitting at home all day. Fighting a lot."

Donna's eyes wander to a photograph on the end table nearest to her. Ronnie and his parents. He's a sad-looking kid, wearing a Scooby-Doo T-shirt. She wishes Kat could hear this. They're finally getting a proper interview with Ronnie Gaskins, after all.

"My dad started reading up about the lost mine. He took out all the books about it from the library. We thought it was just a hobby, something to pass the time. But it became... like, an obsession. I think he got it into his head that he'd find it and we'd be rich, all our problems solved.

"He pulled my mom into it. She read this theory somewhere that all the gold in California comes from meteorites that hit the Earth a long time ago. The two of them started going out into the forest every day, collecting rock samples. They'd bring them home and test them for iron and nickel. We'd all go out together on weekends, like little family field trips. It was the first time I'd seen them happy, for so long." He strokes his thumb on the little bird. Donna wonders if he's ever told anyone this story before. This is not the polish of a story told many times, given shape and meaning. It's a rush of words, like a poison he's trying to vomit up.

"My dad borrowed this radar thing from a friend of his who worked at the science department at Sac State. It could sense cavities under the ground. They took it out to some of the places where they'd found a lot of space rock. That's how they found the cave. Sealed up, but they thought they might be able to get into it with pickaxes.

"We all went out there together. They wanted to share the discovery with me, I guess. But I couldn't get down the gully. I was a short kid, and the handholds were too far apart for me to reach. They left me waiting out there, at the little cliff." He squeezes his shoulders together, like he's trying to hold off a shiver.

"Hours went by. I called for them, but they didn't come out. I tried climbing down again, but I was afraid. I just kept sitting there, calling. Sometimes I thought I could hear someone moving, but they never answered me. I was just starting to think that I was going to have to go and get help, when I heard something coming up the gully, and I looked down, and I saw it."

He swallows. "Naked. Covered in blood. It was carrying my father's body in its arms. And then it looked up at me, and its face looked exactly like his.

"I ran. But I was panicked, and I got lost. When it gets dark out there, it's like the trees stalk you."

Donna remembers birch trunks glistening silver in the moonlight, the feeling of a thousand eyes on her.

"A search party found me after two days. I was babbling, trying to tell everyone that my parents were dead, but everyone just kept telling me to calm down, that I was traumatised. They got me back to town and old Chief Pendleton drove me home. Two people opened the door who looked like my parents. But I knew they weren't.

"I was twelve," he finishes. He doesn't have to say the rest. They all know what happened next.

Donna's dad turns towards her, brow furrowed. "So that's what happened to you, when you went to the cave. You... died."

"Donna died," Ronnie corrects him. "This isn't her. This is an extra-terrestrial creature that has made itself look like her."

"*Locura*," her dad mumbles.

Marybeth's brow is furrowed. "Say that again. You're saying that space aliens that can mimic human faces are hiding in the cave? Little grey men with big eyes. Shapeshifters from space. You see how crazy that sounds, right?"

"No, not like that. I've been in there a couple of times, with protection on. There aren't... creatures living in there or anything like that. Just a lot of mould on the rocks, slimy algae. This black liquid that drips down from the ceiling. Whatever's in there, it's ancient. It might have been biding its time, or maybe this has happened before, who knows? I experimented once, very carefully. I put a rat in a cage and threw it in, pulled it back out with a rope right away. It died in less than a minute, as the copy burst out from its body."

Marybeth and her father both flinch at this.

"Once it's formed itself into a body, it doesn't seem quite so spreadable. It needs blood or spit. Body fluids."

"Tim was biting them," Marybeth says, shuddering.

"They went into the cave and they died," her dad repeats, looking numb.

"It's my fault," Ronnie says. "All my life, I've guarded it. I go out there every couple of weeks to check that it's still hidden. It never occurred to me that..." He gulps. "I led them right to it. I can't tell you how bad I feel about that."

"Hang on," Marybeth says, looking back at Donna, brow still furrowed. "You said you saw Katie's body in the cave. So why didn't she come back like you and Rae?"

"Something went wrong," Donna says. "Rae said the monster she saw was this long skinny thing, like a worm, but it had this huge mouth and too many teeth. At first, she thought it was eating Kat's body. But I think the monster was... what came out of it."

"Show me those photographs again," Marybeth says to Ronnie. "The ones of the dead animals."

"They're still in the cellar," Ronnie says, running his hand through his hair.

"It must have been something huge, to have made bites like that—" Marybeth says.

"If we're some kind of alien life-form like he says we are, then who's to say what we can do." Donna shrugs, half-laughing despite herself. It's all just too damn weird.

"We've got to stop them before they can spread," Ronnie says, putting the ceramic bird back on the table.

"Didn't you *hear* what I told you about the police station?" Donna asks. "It's too late for that. I can feel them out there, multiplying. There's like this web that gets stronger the more of them there are. If you stay here, you'll all just get taken too. We have to leave. Now."

"You'll only spread it further."

"I'm not trying to spread anything!" Donna snarls. "I never asked for any of this! I don't want to hurt anyone. I don't want to be a *body snatcher*, for fuck's sake. I'm *sixteen*. All I want is to live my goddamn life."

"It's not *your* life—" Ronnie starts.

"Stop saying that," her dad says, getting to his feet. "I don't understand half of this. But I know my daughter, and I tell you, that is her. If she says that we must go, then we're going."

Donna's heart explodes with love.

"Come on, *conejita*."

Ronnie storms from the room, disappearing somewhere deeper into the house.

"Take my car," says Marybeth, handing her dad a set of keys

from her pocket. "It's parked one street up, to the right. Yellow Rabbit, you can't miss it. His name's Fernando. Take care of him."

"You aren't coming with us?" Donna asks.

She shakes her head. "I have to keep looking."

Donna takes the keys. She remembers thinking what a wet sap Marybeth was. But she doesn't see any of that now. This is a lioness. "If you find Kat, tell her I'm sorry."

"Stay safe, Donna," Marybeth says.

Donna follows her father back to Ronnie's front yard. "We should stop by the house," he says. "Pick up my passport and your birth certificate. We're going for the border?"

She hasn't thought about that. She's planned as far as getting to Sacramento, where there would be uninfected police they could go to. But then what? Tell them that the whole of the Little Hope Police Department are alien doubles? Oh, and by the way, she's one too, but a *good one*, she swears.

She can't think that far. "Let's just get you out of Little Hope. We'll figure out the rest on the road." She and her dad trudge towards the gate, side by side.

It looms over them, threaded through with thick chains and padlocks.

Donna's dad groans. "I forgot the gate's locked. Is Ronnie still sulking?"

"Not sulking," says Ronnie's voice, behind them. They turn around to see him holding a can of spray lubricant, with something duct-taped onto the front. He presses the nozzle, and a burst of flame fires out ahead of them. He points it at Donna.

Donna gasps, stumbling backwards.

Marybeth runs up behind them, holding a gun. "Drop it!" she screams.

Ronnie keeps the nozzle of the can trained on Donna. "Think about what she could do. We can't let her go."

Donna's dad rushes in front of her, shielding her with his body, hands in the air.

"I'm not going to let you kill her." Marybeth fires another warning shot into the bushes. "Drop it, I'm warning you." She cocks the gun again.

Ronnie's eyes are wild. He rushes at Marybeth, trying to knock the gun from her hand. Marybeth tries to twist herself out of his arms, but she doesn't shoot.

Donna's father pushes her away from the danger, thumping her back against the chain-link fence.

Then Ronnie has the gun, and there's another *crack*.

A mist of blood explodes from her father's neck, two feet ahead of her.

"Dad!" Donna screams.

He slumps down against her onto the ground.

Donna collapses to her knees next to him. "Dad, Dad..." she sobs. Bright blood puddles in the three-inch hole in his clavicle. He takes a shuddering breath and clutches at the bloody mess of his throat. His eyes roll in his head.

Marybeth is there, next to her. "Put pressure on it," her voice croaks.

But Donna is still afraid to touch him. Marybeth pushes past her and presses hard on the wound. Her father gurgles in pain and tries to twist away from her. Blood spurts up between Marybeth's fists, pooling on the floor beside him.

"Dad, Papi..." Donna moans.

Ronnie is pacing up and down nearby, hands locked in his hair. "Stop confusing them!" he screams at Donna. "You're not human!"

Donna grabs her dad's hand in hers. His grip is weakening and his eyes are focused on something far in the distance. His breathing grows shallow.

He is slipping away from her, and Donna knows there's only one thing she can do to save him.

She has to kill him.

34. CHERRY BOMB

KATHERINE LARKIN

TUESDAY, 17 SEPTEMBER 1996

Dear Diary,

Tomorrow's the day. We're going to go back out into the woods where we followed Ronnie, down into that ravine to see what's there. We've got it all worked out: we're going to skip school at lunch. That will give us an extra couple of hours to get out there and back before sunset. Just in case we're back late, Donna and I have told our parents that we're sleeping over at Rae's. Rae's mom's got a church thing, and her dad never actually checks if we're in the basement (he refers to parenting his children as "babysitting", what an ass), so that should buy us some time, if we need it.

Eat your heart out, Nancy Drew!

We've each packed supplies into the bottom of our school bag. Rae gave each of us a list of what to bring. Donna's bringing a disposable camera, and I'll be bringing you, Diary, to document whatever MYSTERIES we discover. I just hope that the little map I drew is going to be good enough. It was a really complicated route, and the idea of being lost in that forest after dark is pretty nerve-wracking.

There's just one little snag, which is that I haven't been feeling so great recently. I barfed twice today already, and most days for the past week or so. I went to see the school nurse on Monday and she said it was probably just a stomach bug and it would work its way through, but it's not like I've had the runs or anything. It's only coming out one end.

When I got home from school, I was putting on a sweater, and I looked in the mirror, and realised that my belly's kind of swollen. Normally, my fat sits mostly on my hips and below my belly button. But this morning it looked like I'd swallowed a volleyball: my whole torso was weirdly distended and round.

And then I started thinking... what if I'm pregnant?

HAHAHAHA wouldn't that be hilarious? SO FUNNY. I'M LAUGHING, NOT HUDDLED IN A BALL WANTING TO SCREAM MY HEAD OFF, NO SIREE.

But seriously. What if I am??? Preggo. Eating for two. Up the pole. Harbouring a fugitive.

In other words, *fucked*.

I mean, Mickey used a condom. Well, he SAID he did. It's not like I checked. It was pretty hard to see what was going on there in the romantic love chamber of his sweaty Yugo.

And the true cherry on the shit sundae is that it was more than three months ago since we did it. My stupid period is so irregular I honestly can't remember if I've had it since then. So, if *I am* knocked up, I don't even think I could un-knock myself any more.

That would be it for me. Worst nightmare come true: I'd have turned into my mother. Only worse... Ma Bear at least waited until she finished high school before she got up the duff.

Ma Bear spent literally her whole life living in one dumb town. She never did anything in her life that mattered, just raised me and made beds and filled her brain with trash TV. She tried to live THROUGH me instead of living her own goddamn life. It's not like I ever wanted to be a child beauty star, SHE did. She's so obsessed with looks. All she ever wants to watch are those stupid makeover shows on TV, like you can fix your life by looking the way people want you to look. She has a TINY SCAR on her top lip from when she had a cleft palate as a baby and she talks about it like she's gravely disfigured, Quasimodo. But no wonder she's so melodramatic, she has no sense of perspective because her life has been SO SMALL.

I ruined her life, that's the truth. And idiot me, what if I've just gone and done the same thing? What will I do, Diary, marry Mickey and live in Little Hope forever while Donna and Rae go off and live their whole lives without me??

Anyway. I was feeling so freaked that I called Donna and told her. And she didn't say much, just kind of said "uh-huh" a few times and then hung up. So there it is: even Donna thinks I'm an idiot and that this is everything I deserve. *That's Kat for you, she'll do anything for a story!* I bet that's what she's thinking.

Ma Bear has to work late tonight because she has to clean up after some engagement party or something. Not that I could even stand to look at her right now.

So I guess I'm just going to sit here, and re-check the hiking supplies I've packed for the seven hundredth time, and think about what a stupid loser I am. Who knows, maybe tomorrow we'll find a real scoop and take some photos we can sell to *Life* magazine and be millionaires, and then it won't even matter that I'm a teen mom.

Nice talking to ya, Diary.
Kat Fucking-Idiot Larkin

FACT I LEARNED TODAY: Babies cry in the womb. And I'm crying in my room. Hey, I'm a fucking poet.

———

Later

I do not deserve my friends.

About an hour after I wrote my last entry, Donna and Rae showed up at my front door. They both told their parents we needed to have an emergency meeting of the school newspaper club. They'd brought soda and frozen pizza. We reheated the 'za, climbed up onto the roof and hung out there for hours, until long after the sun set and the stars came out.

Donna was cracking dumb jokes to make me feel better, describing this elaborate scheme where we pretend the baby is Prince Charles's lovechild and that's why he really divorced Diana, so we can sell the story to the tabloids and retire off the profits. Rae had already made a list of people we can call, including her cousin in San Francisco who's a doctor who can help me end the pregnancy if I want to (who she PROMISES would never tell our parents), and the psychologist she saw in Sacramento who could help me decide what to do if I decide I want to keep it. But they were both also extremely reasonable and reminded me that I'm not even sure I'm pregnant yet, so I should also just calm down until I take the pregnancy test Donna shoplifted from the drugstore for me.

We bounced a cigarette, read poetry to each other, and started making lists of all the stuff we're going to do when we're grown up and our lives can start. Rae's suggestion. I knew she was reminding me that we've still got a whole life ahead of us.

I wanted to cry, I was so full of love for them. How absolutely, improbably lucky am I, to have met these two extraordinary people, right when I'm still becoming who I am? They've imprinted on me so deeply that I literally don't even know who I am without them. I can't imagine ever not having them in my life.

Everyone says you don't stay friends with your high school friends forever. We're going to be the exception. I'm determined.

Even today, so much of American girlhood is still about training you to be pretty and compliant so that one day you'll make somebody a happy little wife and mother. Like your teen girl friendships are just supposed to be a practice run before you start a REAL family.

So maybe loving each other is the most radical political act of our lives.

We're going into the woods tomorrow. I'm not afraid. With Rae and Donna by my side, I'm not afraid of anything.

KL

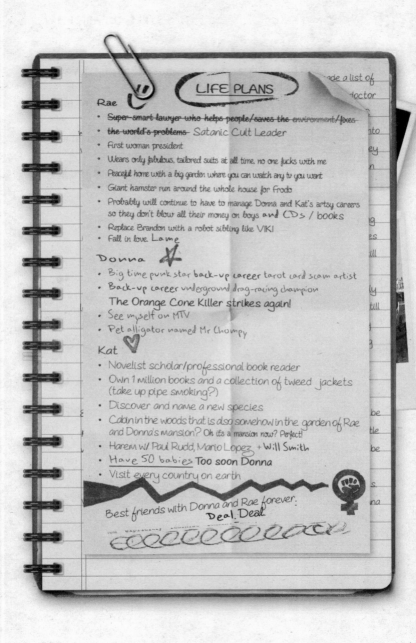

LIFE PLANS

Rae

- ~~Super-smart lawyer who helps people/saves the environment/fixes the world's problems~~ Satanic Cult Leader
- First woman president
- Wears only fabulous, tailored suits at all time, no one fucks with me
- Peaceful home with a big garden where you can watch any tv you want
- Giant hamster run around the whole house for Frodo
- Probably will continue to have to manage Donna and Kat's artsy careers so they don't blow all their money on boys and CDs / books
- Replace Brandon with a robot sibling like VIKI
- Fall in love. Lame

Donna

- Big time punk star back-up career tarot card scam artist
- Back-up career underground drag-racing champion
  The Orange Cone Killer strikes again!
- See myself on MTV
- Pet alligator named Mr Chompy

Kat

- Novelist scholar/professional book reader
- Own 1 million books and a collection of tweed jackets (take up pipe smoking?)
- Discover and name a new species
- Cabin in the woods that is also somehow in the garden of Rae and Donna's mansion? Oh its a mansion now? Perfect!
- Harem w/ Paul Rudd, Mario Lopez + Will Smith
- Have 50 babies Too soon Donna
- Visit every country on earth

Best friends with Donna and Rae forever.
Deal. Deal.

35. ALIEN SUMMER NIGHTS

MARYBETH LARKIN

TUESDAY, 24 SEPTEMBER 1996

"This would be easier if you stopped writhing," Marybeth scolds.

Ronnie's lying on the floor, leg propped up next to Marybeth on the sofa, holding the dog in his arms. She'd said that they should try to elevate it above his head in case it bleeds when they pull out the knife.

She'd wanted to leave the knife in and take them straight to Doctor Abrams, both of them. Ronnie wouldn't hear of it. "We don't know who's safe any more," he'd said darkly. And if they go hiking with the knife still in, there's every chance it might get knocked about and do even more damage in there.

"You're hurting me on purpose." The dog whines in sympathy.

"I swear I'm not." Tempting as it is. He's still furious with her for forcing him to toss her the gate keys, at gunpoint, so that Donna and Hector could leave. She's still furious at him for shooting Hector, for kidnapping her and burning her leg. But right now, he's the only ally she has, so she needs him mobile.

"Stop moving!" she berates him. His calf around the entry wound is swollen, but the wound itself has clotted. There's a

SAM BECKBESSINGER & DALE HALVORSEN

torn-up bedsheet soaked in antiseptic, a bottle of superglue and a roll of duct tape at the ready. Still, Marybeth hesitates.

"Just do it," Ronnie says through gritted teeth.

"OK," Marybeth says, gripping the knife handle. "Five, four, three—" She yoinks it on three. The same trick she used pulling Katie's baby teeth.

Ronnie gasps in pain. Blood oozes from the wound, but it doesn't gush. He'll live.

Marybeth pats at the wound with the antiseptic. Ronnie flinches away from her. "Stings," he mutters.

"I know. But we've got to clean the wound," she says in her most patient voice.

"Just close it up," he says, holding out the duct tape.

"Try five seconds. If you still want to stop after five seconds, I promise we'll stop." Something else that used to work on Katie. Trying a new vegetable, performing on stage, whatever it was. She could always count on her daughter's curiosity to overcome her fears. "Just see what it's like."

Ronnie scowls at her, but allows her to pat the wound until it seems clean. "See? Not so bad." She dabs beads of superglue along the rim of the wound, then pinches the skin closed until the glue dries. Some more torn-up bedsheet works as a bandage, bound closed with the duct tape.

"Where did you learn first aid?" Ronnie asks her.

Marybeth shrugs. "Nurse is one of my many mom jobs." *Along with coach, teacher, chef, cleaning service, psychologist, chauffeur, dressmaker, last-minute school project diorama expert...*

Ronnie pulls himself up and tests his weight on his foot, gingerly. The dressings seem secure. They really should go to a hospital, both of them. She promises herself that if they survive the next twenty-four hours, she'll make sure they do.

If there are still hospitals, and the whole world hasn't been taken over by alien body doubles, that is.

They both hobble to the kitchen. The cabinets are rustic, handmade, but there's another cheerful vase of flowers on the kitchen table. Ewok follows them expectantly, tail wagging. Ronnie throws a handful of kibble into his bowl, then digs out some expired-looking painkillers from the back of a shelf, offering one to Marybeth, which she isn't quite ready to accept.

"Where did you get the... horse drugs?" she asks as he gulps a palmful of pills down with a pitcher of water.

"David Hooper sells it to anybody who asks," he mutters. "And fentanyl, tramadol. A lucrative side-business, I believe."

"And I thought Polly was bad."

"It's a small town. People escape however they can."

Ronnie crouches in front of a closet under the staircase and starts pulling out an arsenal. A crossbow, several more of his makeshift flamethrowers, a large canister labelled WELDING GAS. The mutt sniffs the recesses of the closet, trying to help. Ronnie throws a gas mask and plastic hazmat suit at her feet. "Put that on."

This seems like as good a time as any to broach the question she's been burning to ask, the real reason she's still here. "I want you to take me into the woods. To where you found the dead animals."

"Why?"

"Because if there's any chance that my daughter's alive, I have to find her."

"I'm sorry." He looks up at her. "She's not. When those girls were reported missing, I knew in my gut what must have happened. I went up to check. Her body's in the cave."

"But... even if she's like Donna. I need to see her. Fuck, Ronnie. You owe me that much, at least."

"We've got more important things to do," Ronnie says, adding a baseball bat to the pile.

"Nothing's more important to me." The gun is still in her handbag, sitting on the corner of the couch. But she doesn't particularly want to march him into the woods at gunpoint.

Ronnie huffs. "We might already be too late to contain it. I can't waste any more time."

"So, what's your plan? Go around burning everyone in town and see who's flammable? You'll get arrested in two minutes. The cops have already changed, remember."

"Well, sure, we can start with them," he says, checking the nozzle on one of his flamethrowers.

"You mean, just kill them?"

He gets up, looking incredulous. "Are we really debating the right to life of an alien species?"

"You saw Donna, how upset she was when you shot Hector."

"We shouldn't have let them go." He shakes his head, drags his haul to the kitchen table and starts cramming it into a backpack.

Marybeth follows him, talking to his back. "How would you feel killing a bunch of them only to learn that they can feel and think, just like us? Why are you so convinced they're evil?"

"Because if they're not evil, then that means I killed my parents," he explodes.

Marybeth doesn't know what to say to that. Ronnie sinks onto one of the kitchen chairs, his head in his hands. The dog rests his chin on Ronnie's knee.

They stay like that, in an uncomfortable silence, for many long seconds.

"OK," Ronnie says at last, his voice thick. "I'll take you." He wipes his face. His shoulders are still trembling slightly. "But we can't leave until the morning. It's been moving deeper into the woods. We're talking a seven, eight-hour hike. Trust me, you don't want to be stuck out there in the dark." He gets up, still averting his face from her. "You sleep on the sofa tonight. It's not safe to go home."

"OK." She's impatient to get going. But it's been one hundred and forty-five hours. What's a few more?

"Stay away from the windows." Ronnie's voice is gruff. "We'll leave at dawn. Then you can see for yourself." He starts up the stairs. It's not even 2 p.m., but he seems eager to be away from her. He pauses. "Just know, you might not like what you find."

———

Marybeth spends the rest of the afternoon alone downstairs, the occasional creak of floorboards above the only sign of life from Ronnie. She considers asking him if he wants to play a game of cards or something, but they're a long way from being friends.

Instead, she occupies herself by snooping around the house. It's a cluttered place full of wood and wonky corners, most of the furniture handmade. There's a collection of books about science, geology, the history of California. She finds a Walkman and a collection of tapes that's like a time-capsule from the late '70s, and passes some time lying on the rug listening to Phil Collins. The mutt tucks himself into the crook of her arm, poking her with his cast, and farts cheerfully as he naps.

A little after three, she hears footsteps crunching up the gravel outside. Crouching beneath the living room window, she peers through the grimy glass to see two kids creeping along the boundary of Ronnie's property. They're teenage boys, kids she recognises but doesn't know.

They hang back in the shadows of the trees opposite the house, watching Ronnie's yard, conversing in whispers. Marybeth is just debating whether she should go and fetch Ronnie, when they shrug and walk back up the road. Maybe they're just regular kids here to torment a loner, or maybe they're something else, she doesn't know. The rumours of Ronnie's booby traps seem to have scared them off, either way.

She picks up the phone, thinking she might try dialling 911, but the line's dead.

36. KILLER ON THE ROAD

DONNA RAMIREZ

The sun sits low on the horizon. Donna keeps angling the rearview mirror away, trying to avoid the glare, only to become paranoid that a car could be sneaking up behind them and flipping it back into place. She was afraid they'd be caught on the interstate, so they're sticking to back roads, weaving their way through the desert. She has no idea where they are. She's just trying to keep the sun behind her as much as she can, heading east, hoping that eventually they'll either hit a town or drive straight into the Atlantic.

The man sitting in the passenger seat looks like her father. He's already grown into the right size and proportions, but he hasn't said much. Occasionally, he mumbles something she can't make out, turning around to look at the back seat, then turning back, his eyes big.

Donna can't bear to look back there herself. Every time she thinks about what's there, it's like the ground falls away, like the world turns into a yawning maw that could swallow her up; it stops her heart and makes her insides scream.

So instead, she keeps her eyes firmly away from the rear-view mirror and on the cracked road. Marybeth's yellow car, having nothing that resembles decent suspension, shudders across every groove in the surface. Rod Stewart's voice belts out of the stereo, asking if they think he's sexy (*we've got bigger things on our mind right now, sorry, Rod*) and the car smells of pennies.

Her left leg has been hovering over the clutch since they started driving and it's starting to cramp. Donna only got her learner's permit a couple months ago, and that was an automatic. She hadn't done much more than a few hours going round and round the empty parking lot behind a disused warehouse in Mrs Hooper's car, Kat and Rae heckling her from the back seat. They called her the Orange Cone Killer, from the number of them that she mowed down trying to figure out parallel parking.

She has to keep reminding herself that these aren't her memories. That she only knows how to drive because of instincts she copied from Donna's brain.

They're instincts that are serving her well, so far. The fake cops were setting up a roadblock on the edge of town that she got past through dumb luck. She'd gotten such a fright when she saw the police cars lined up across the road that she'd spun the wheel without thinking, and ended up on the verge, trees and bushes flying past her in a blur. It was sheer panic that got her back on the road, and a happy surprise when she saw the cruisers in the rear-view mirror, falling behind her.

She could feel the pull of them as she drove away, the others like her, the feeling getting stronger and stronger as more of them bloomed into existence. Dozens of them, maybe hundreds. Rae's been busy. So like her, to never do something by half measures. It felt like a race to pull herself out of their orbit before they could lure her back into it. One consciousness spread out across multiple host bodies. But the thing is, Donna's quite attached to *this* host body, and the distinct thoughts and memories it has. She'd rather be a dumb teenage girl than one neuron in a big hive mind, thanks.

And what if it works the other way around, and they can feel exactly where she is, as if she had a tracking beacon on her? What if they're just biding their time before they come and fetch her? Their prodigal daughter?

Every time they round a bend in the road, she holds her breath, afraid they'll be there waiting. It would be just as bad to run into a real roadblock. Driving without a licence will be the least of her worries when they see the mess on the back seat. They'll arrest her on sight, lock her up forever, and she'd deserve it. It's bad enough that she's not human, but it's worse that she's a murderer. A triple murderer. First Donna, then Tim, and then her own father.

She still doesn't have a plan outside of: get as far away from Little Hope as possible. Far away from Ronnie Gaskins and his MacGyvered flamethrower, far away from the thousands of new replicants swarming the town, far from Rae's sad eyes and freaky family, far from whatever monstrous thing Kat's become, and far, far away from her own mistakes.

She never forgave her mother for leaving her, yet here she is, leaving everyone she knows. But what the hell else is she supposed to do? It's survival.

The man sitting next to her turns around in his seat again to look back. He touches Donna's shoulder. "Hector," he says clearly.

She's not sure if he's talking about the body in the back seat, or himself. But she nods, anyway. "Yes, that's right. You are Hector. Hector Ramirez." Maybe if she says it enough times, they'll both start to believe it.

"Hector," he says again. He turns back to the road, leaving a bloody handprint on her shoulder. The once-blue blanket on his lap is tie-died red. They'll have to find a place to rinse themselves before they get to a town.

He's still got the puckered scar on his upper arm from his

polio vaccine, she notices, but no fresh bullet wound in his neck. Some types of damage become part of you.

Up ahead she spots a green board announcing that they'll hit some place called Eureka in half a mile, and below that, a smaller blue sign with a white telephone.

Bingo.

The rest stop is a small sandy patch off the road with a bright yellow call box mounted halfway up a metal lamp post. They pull in and park the car. Rod Stewart cuts out, leaving just the ticking noise of the engine.

"Wait here," she says to the passenger. He is turned around in his seat again, staring at the back seat.

Gravel crunches under her sneakers as she walks up to the call box. A notice on the top reads: 24-HOUR EMERGENCY LINE. No dialling pad, just a receiver, which means she can't call Jay, or even her mother. She stares at it, shuffling from foot to foot.

She picks up the phone. It's heavy. There's just half a ring before the line clicks.

"This is Ely dispatch. How can I connect you?"

"Uh, hi. I need help," she says.

"What's the problem?"

"It's... you need to go to Little Hope."

"I'm sorry, ma'am, please repeat?"

"There's been an accident at Little Hope."

"Is that a joke?" There's a mumble on the line, tapping noises. "Oh, I'm sorry, ma'am. Is that the Little Hope township off Route 49?"

"You need to send help."

All business now. "What's the emergency?"

"There was an accident. A man, Sergeant Knox, he was... A bunch of people died." None of this is coming out right.

The tapping intensifies. "Are you in danger right now?"

"No, I got away."

"And what's your name?"

Could the cops be looking for her? "Kat Larkin." She says the first name that comes to mind.

"Please hold, Ms Larkin. I'm contacting one of the officers in the area."

"Don't, they—"

The line goes dead for a minute. Donna glances back over to the road. Nobody's chasing them.

The voice comes back on. "I'm sorry, I'm not getting through. I'm going to try the backup number."

"No! They won't... The cops are all dead. We need, like, the army."

"I'm sorry, could you repeat?"

She leans her head against the post. What is she doing? Even if she can convince them to send more people over there, the colony will just absorb them too.

"Ma'am?" The voice is saying something to her through the line. Waiting for the answer to a question she didn't hear.

"It's nothing. This is a prank call. I'm sorry."

She clicks the phone back into the cradle. It immediately starts ringing. She ignores it and makes her way back to the car. She flops back into the driver's seat, and sighs deeply.

The man in the passenger seat is watching her with a serene look on his face.

"How are you feeling?" she asks him.

He seems to consider this for a moment. "I have very intense emotions."

"What do you mean?"

"I am beside myself." His smile cracks open wide. "Get it?"

They stare at each other. Donna starts to laugh and cry at once. She collapses into his chest. "Dad," she says, into the warm familiar smell of him. "Daddy."

He wraps an arm around her and pats her back. "I'm having a very strange afternoon."

She laughs, feeling a big bubble of snot come out of her nose. But it's OK, she can't hurt him any more. "Tell me about it. I had to kill my father."

"I'm not feeling very dead."

She laughs again, sitting up and wiping her face. He watches her with that small smile still playing on his lips, and even though he's covered in blood, even though she just watched him crawl out of a body and be born less than an hour ago, she knows it's true. This is her dad, in every way that matters. Whether that makes sense to her or not.

And if he's alive, then how can she be a murderer?

"I don't understand what's happening," he says.

"You don't remember earlier? Ronnie Gaskins? Marybeth's handgun?" She explains as best she can. He accepts it more quickly this time, with the evidence sitting on the back seat behind him. It still takes her a few minutes to get through it all. She finally runs out of things to say, and they sit there in silence for a minute, while he processes it.

"Why did you bring him?" he says, gesturing at the back seat.

"I couldn't leave him behind."

"He's an ugly bastard." He runs his hands through his hair. "And you're a mess," he says eventually.

"You're the one wearing entrails."

"This is Marybeth's car? Maybe there's a towel or something in the back."

"Good idea." She finds the little lever next to her seat and pops open the trunk.

Donna avoids looking at the dark hair of the head slumped against the back seat. There's a lot of junk back here: old magazines, a Thighmaster, some dirty Tupperware. And right at the bottom, a small pink bag with some nut bars, wet wipes and a change of clothes. Thank God for moms.

She pulls out a couple of the wipes and hands the rest of the bag to her dad. He starts to clean the worst of the gore off himself, while she picks through the clothes. It's meagre pickings. She hands him a pair of high-waisted floral Bermuda shorts and a sequin-trimmed green sweater, swapping her blood-soaked hoodie for a dark tunic that looks like it's part of Marybeth's work uniform.

All her beloved handmade T-shirts are sitting in a duffel bag in Mrs Hooper's cupboard right now, she thinks ruefully, along with her guitar and everything else in the world that she owned. At least she still has Kat's journal, which she pulls from the pocket of her hoodie and tucks into the waistband of her jeans. A comforting talisman, pressing into her skin, filled with echoes of Rae and Kat, and all the dreams they once had.

Donna's dad eyes her as he chews on a nut bar. "You need a break."

"Well, we can't exactly pull up to a motel with Ugly in the back seat. Unless you want to do a whole *Weekend at Bernie's* thing."

"We could bury him out there in the desert."

Donna shudders. "I can't."

"Then I guess we're camping."

———

She drops her dad on the outskirts of Eureka and waits anxiously on the side of the highway. He trudges back half an hour later, carrying what looks like the whole town's supply of food in brown bags emblazoned with MARTIN'S FOOD AND HARDWARE. "Never shop when you're hungry," he says, by way of explanation. Donna laughs, remembering her own constant gorging for the first few days. Her hunger has been slowly abating, she realises. She's getting the hang of this body.

They turn onto a back road and drive until the sky turns violet. Then they leave the road and drive directly through the brush. Fernando screams at them with every bump and scratch on its undercarriage. It's hardly an all-terrain vehicle.

Finally, they stop in a patch of desert that's especially middle-of-nowhere-ish, where the land dips into just enough of a valley that the Rabbit won't be visible from the closest road, half a mile away.

They find a box of matches in the trunk and make a small fire. The twigs out here are as dry as bone, and the star-splashed sky is larger than any sky Donna's ever seen. The world is so big. It never really sank in how big the world is, before.

Well, she finally made it out of Little Hope.

Her dad leans back against Fernando and stretches his legs out in the sand. Donna tucks herself against his shoulder.

Her heart aches thinking of Rae and Kat. She's probably never going to see them again.

But Rae was right. *Be honest. If this town wasn't so small, would we even have been friends?* Now she has the whole world ahead of her.

"So, kiddo," her dad says. "Thought about what you want to do for the rest of your life?"

"Sleep. Forever," she mumbles against his shoulder. "Dad?"

"Donna?"

"Will you be here when I wake up?"

His lips tickle the top of her head. "Always, *conejita.*"

37. CONNECTION

TAMMY-RAE HOOPER

TUESDAY, 24 SEPTEMBER 1996

Old Mrs Griffiths's body is slumped across her front porch. Rae's mother tucks her hands under the body's arms and is telling her to grab the feet so they can drag it inside before anyone hears

———

Screaming coming from the high school, but her mother grabs her hand and pulls her up a side street just as a police car careens around the corner, siren-blaring, and she can smell gunpowder, and

———

Principal Keyes is cowering under the desk in his office; Rae is flanked by her English teacher and a lunch lady and they move as one towards him, a school of fish perfectly in tune with each other, then

———

She's alone, stumbling up the street near the clinic. A woman she doesn't recognise is trying to hotwire a car, while a small white dog yaps frantically at her feet, and the woman sees Rae and screams, but

———

The chorus of 'Jesus Wants Me for a Sunbeam' wakes her up.

Somehow, she is in the church, kneeling in the middle aisle, Jim Porter's body lying open-eyed beneath her.

Rae blinks.

The singing comes from Pastor Sherman, who has Peggy Boyd cornered behind the organ. He's wearing nothing but a crucifix over his silvery rug of chest hair, splattering the Sunday school teacher with blood from self-inflicted stigmata on his palms. She is screaming the worst profanities back at him, but her words are lost in his shrill singing.

> "A sunbeam, a sunbeam,
> Jesus wants me for a sunbeam,
> A sunbeam, a sunbeam,
> I'll be a sunbeam for him."

It's one of Kat's favourite songs. The Nirvana cover version, anyway. She sings it whenever she's concentrating on homework, her voice syrupy and warm. And it feels like that's what brought her back to herself, that memory of the three of them squished onto Kat's couch watching that *MTV Unplugged* VHS for the seven-billionth time. It's not Pastor Sherman's off-key caterwaul, that's for sure.

Rae pulls herself to her feet. The cross above the pulpit is decorated with bright splashes of the pastor's blood. There are a few more bodies slumped here and there, new creatures growing from them. She recognises Louanne Martin, naked, trying to re-learn how to stand, awkward as a newborn lamb. Jim Porter, growing a brand-new face. There are more people than should have been in church on a Tuesday night; people must have rushed here to pray once they started seeing the world go mad around them.

Mrs Boyd isn't screaming any more, just gurgling as she dies. Pastor Sherman places his hand on her forehead and starts intoning one of the psalms. The wounds on his hands have already closed up. "For the angel of the Lord encampeth round them that fear him, and delivereth them. O fear the Lord, you His holy ones."

Peggy Boyd's body squirms and begins to split.

Reality starts to swim again in front of Rae's eyes. Rae picks up the next verse of the song, singing it in her own ragged alto.

"Jesus wants me to be loving
And kind to all I see
Showing how pleasant and happy
His little one can be."

The world comes back into focus, like the flat tune is all that's keeping her tethered to herself. Music was always her favourite part of church. The only time she ever felt certain she felt the Holy Spirit was singing as one voice amongst four dozen others. After she lost her faith, she realised it was just music that gave her that feeling of rapture, not God.

Now she's wondering if there's really any difference. Rapture is rapture. One of the many miracles humans can do. Beautiful, terrible, miraculous humans.

She lurches up the pews, letting her hands linger on the smooth polished wood. It's dark out. What happened to the day? Her dress clings to her legs, damp from blood and sweat and spit. Probably not her own.

It's like she's woken up halfway through a zombie movie. She hears smashing glass, distant screams, the roar of car engines firing up as people try to hurry out of town. And what's the point? This isn't going to stop at Little Hope, oh no. That's just not how exponential curves work, sorry, everybody not paying attention in pre-calc.

She wonders where Donna is now. Far away, she hopes. She and Kat, she hopes they get to live good lives, wherever they are. While they can.

She feels a tickle in the pocket of her sundress. Frodo pokes his little pink nose out and sniffs at the air.

She can feel each and every one of them out there. So many of them, a chattering at the edges of her mind, a thousand radios tuned to the same station, trying to hook her back into the stream. She switches to humming a Nancy Screws song, 'Medusa', which turns down the buzzing in her brain a bit.

Look me in the eyes
When you try to bring me down.
Now you're just a statue
Crumbling to the ground.

Donna used to play private concerts for her and Kat in Rae's rumpus room. They'd call them RH1 Storytellers, for "Rae's House". Donna said this one was a song she wrote for Sharon LeBell, which really meant a song she wrote out of affection for Rae.

People are running helter-skelter across the street. As she watches, Fred Stein smashes through the window display of the Dollar Tree, tossed like a doll. He rolls across the asphalt of the road. Before he can get to his feet, three of his friends from the swim team swarm him. They pin him down. One of them leans over and spits square in his face.

They just meander off, leaving him lying there, twitching and transforming in the middle of the street. Secrecy's over. This is their town now.

Well, you can't gather up water once it's been spilled on the ground, as the Bible says.

She turns onto Main Street. Matt Wiley, who owns the hotel, is walking up the sidewalk wearing a green velvet smoking jacket and nothing else, blinking at the mayhem. But when Polly Jones runs past him, still human, he falls onto her and licks her face, out of pure instinct. Chip Eastman, their local conspiracy nut, is stumbling up the road looking dazed. He was always going on about aliens and UFOs in the hills around Little Hope. Guess even a stuck clock's going to be right eventually.

There are two loud *cracks* behind her. She whirls to see two men dressed as cowboys, holding the antique pistols they use for the mock gun duel they put on for tourists every Saturday during the summer. They're usually loaded with blanks, but both gunslingers sport bloody holes in their torsos. They laugh, already reloading the guns, as the wounds close.

Rae ducks into the museum. It's quieter in here. Pleasantly dark. She wanders through the unkempt dioramas, the history of their strange little town told through wax models and painted backdrops, the site of so many boring field trips. A wax model gold prospector with a plasticky beard pans gold in a river while a painted Chinese mine worker simpers behind him. The prospector's been dressed in a full gentlemanly getup: riding boots, straw hat, suspenders, unrealistically clean beige pants. The Chinese mine worker is depicted topless, his muscles rippling like the cover of a romance novel. Little care has been taken in painting his face, like the bones are crumbling beneath his skin.

Medusa, yeah yeah yeah.
I'm a witch, whatever.
I'm a bitch forever.

She considers the wax prospector. Maybe creatures like her have always been a part of this town, for all she knows. Maybe the world was always so much weirder than she thought it was.

Frodo gives a little squeak from her pocket, sniffing at something in the courtyard out the back, where there are replica Native American bark houses, a wooden mill and the rusty old steam train. There's a heavy feeling nearby that pulls at her, like gravity.

It's funny: she has so many memories of walking through this musty room, Kat and Donna on either side of her, chatting about math tests and the zine and the petty politics of high school. But the truth is that she's never actually been here. The girl who those memories belonged to is long dead.

She walks further back, to a scene of Miwok women tending their babies. Unrecognisable remains lie in a puddle in front of it, like an outfit that's been dumped onto the floor at the end of a long day. Its wearer is already long gone.

Her instinct pulls her out the back door.

A mob of kids is shouting and hooting up at something stuck up a tree. The buzz is coming off them in waves. Rae walks over and spots Sharon herself, clinging to a branch above them, sobbing. She is still human.

Rae's vision starts to warp again. It's being among this crowd of other kids, tangled in the web of their minds. She keeps singing, remembering the way Donna's face would screw up when she performed it, how she lost herself in a song.

I hear them talking.
She's got snakes for hair.
You're all gonna get bit
Because what do I care.

April Hollister has two hands on the lowest branch and is about to pull herself up when Rae touches the bare skin of her shoulder. The current between them lights up her mind. It's like touching the surface of a star. She flinches away, before they pull her back into the current and her singular mind fades out again.

"Don't," she says to April. She means to say more. She means to say, *Don't kill her* and *Sharon was my friend, once.* But the words don't come out her mouth. There are hands on her, encircling her waist, and it's like the good days of church when she still believed, it's *ecstasy*, it's *oblivion*, and time skips and

———

She's sitting on the branch. She looks down at them, a crowd of hungry eyes.

Go get her, the other children think through her, from far below.

A small voice inside Rae answers, *I don't want to.*

She crawls along the branch, trying to get closer to Sharon, who's one level higher, scrabbling at a branch further up, just out of reach. Foolish, there's no exit up there. But if she comes down to this branch, she might be able to jump onto the platform of the mill, get from there onto the museum roof before the others can swarm her.

"Sharon, the mill," Rae manages to say. But Sharon whimpers at the sight of her, stops reaching, and scuttles on her butt far to the edge of the branch she's already on. It bends under her weight alarmingly. Mascara runs in two thick smudges down her cheeks.

"I don't want to hurt you." And it's true. She's spent so long hating Sharon. But she's just a girl, and she's scared, and she doesn't want to die.

Rae reaches out her hand. "Jump onto the mill." But her mouth feels cottony. The buzzing in her ears is back, and she can't sing to keep it at bay and try to convince Sharon to trust her at the same time. "The mill," she tries again, already feeling the world growing distant.

Sharon stares at Rae's hand like it's poisoned. Rae's seen that look before.

Sharon's eyes narrow. "Don't touch me, freak!"

And then she has leaped onto Sharon, and they are falling together, but it's OK, because she knows the others will catch her. They'll catch her, and touch her, and hold her, her new family, and she is

SIX FOR GOLD

38. MILES PER HOUR

DONNA RAMIREZ

Donna wakes before her father. He is stretched out in front of the smoking embers, grains of sand crusting his stubble. The sky is huge and magnificent, billowing streaks of pink and orange that stretch from horizon to horizon, and she feels humbled that she gets to witness such a world.

Their backseat passenger is starting to smell, even through the closed doors of the car.

She stands and stretches, and wanders a little way off to pee behind a bush. A tiny bug with a ridged iron shell watches her from the leaves, sniffing her with curious feelers. *Is there anything quite so zen*, Donna thinks sleepily, *as peeing under a sunrise?* This is what she'd lose if she got sucked into the hive mind: everything.

Once, Kat and Rae and her stayed up all night to cram for a history exam, and ended up climbing onto the roof of Kat's house to watch the sunrise. They'd sat there, the three of them, in the silence of the dawn. She remembers Kat asking them if they thought they'd still all be friends when they're old, if they'd be watching the sunrise from the front porch of an old-age home. Your eighties seem like exactly the time to take up cocaine, Donna had joked, so they'd probably see plenty of sunrises. But then Rae got serious, saying that they had to stay friends, always, because one day they'd go out into the world and they'd change, and they needed each other to remember the people they'd been, to understand how they started.

Rae and Kat. She doesn't really know who she is without the two of them.

She heads back to her dad, who's awake and wiping the grime off his face with another of Marybeth's wet wipes. It's the same gesture she's seen him make a thousand times, coming home from a long day at work, wiping off ceramic dust with a facecloth. He is completely himself, and if he is himself, that means that Rae is Rae, and Kat is Kat.

She doesn't want to be a body snatcher. She just wants to be Donna. The most Donna-ish Donna she can be. That means she needs her friends. Even if they're monsters.

She takes one of the wipes from him and cleans up a spot he's missed by his ear. He yawns. Achingly human.

She's made up her mind.

"I have to go back," she says. "I have to get Rae and Kat."

"Weren't you telling me that Rae's lost in a hive mind? And Kat's turned into a monster?"

Donna meets her dad's gaze. "But we're still us."

"For now. Who knows what will happen if you go back?"

"Look, we all share some kind of brain connection thing, right? And the more of us there are, the less we can think for ourselves. The Hoopers, they seemed *mindless*, like drones. But separate a drone from the hive mind and it can think for itself. Like you know those cyborg aliens on the TV show Jay used to watch—"

"This isn't a TV show," her dad cuts her off, getting to his feet. "You can't defeat them."

"I'm not going to *try* to defeat them, honestly. I just need to pull Kat and Rae out of there. Far enough that they'll remember who they are." She bunches up the grubby towelette and throws it into the embers.

Her dad smooths down the sequins on Marybeth's sweater. "OK," he says at last. "Let's do it."

"No, you don't understand. If you go back there, you might turn into a drone."

"And you won't?"

"I don't know. Maybe."

"I won't let you just walk into danger alone."

Her dad reaches out to grab her hand. Donna yanks hers away. "I just got you back. I can't handle losing you again."

"You are sixteen, so that's not up to you," he says, angry now.

"Technically, I'm six days old, and you were born yesterday."

He shakes his head. "I'm your father. It's my job to protect you."

"It was. But that's not what I need any more. I need you to support me."

Her dad is about to say something else, but she cuts him off. "No, Papi, listen. Remember when you told me there are some things you can't run away from? This is one of those things. Rae and Kat are my friends, and I have to try to help them."

He stares at her, morning light glinting off his sequins.

"Trust me," she says.

He shakes his head. "No hero stuff, OK? In and out."

"Puh-lease. You know I don't have a heroic bone in my body."

She climbs back into the car. Her dad leans in through the open window. "Want me to drop you off somewhere?" she asks him.

"I think I'll enjoy a walk, actually. See what these legs can do. I'll head back to town and find a way to get hold of Jay. You call him when you've sorted things out, OK? I'll make sure he knows how to reach me."

"OK. Just promise me you won't, like, lick anybody."

"I'll try to resist."

"I'll call you soon as I can."

"You'd better. You know how I worry."

"I know."

Donna hesitates. They both know this might be the last time they see each other. But there are no words for something like that.

"You're a hell of a person, Donna," he says, resting his hand on the top of her head.

"I love you, Dad."

"I love you too, *conejita*."

He steps away from the car. She turns on the engine, stalls, turns it on again and manoeuvres the car in an awkward sixteen-point until it's facing the way they came. She drives towards the road and watches her dad shrink until he's nothing but a tiny multicoloured speck in the rear-view mirror, and then he's gone.

She lets herself cry, because that feels like what Donna Ramirez would do.

39. CARRION

MARYBETH LARKIN

Ronnie has barely spoken to her all day. Marybeth can read the anger in every gesture of his body as he stomps and hacks at the forest path up ahead of her. Both of them are covered in sweat. The skin on her burned leg itches like hell, and it seems like it snags on every single bush they walk past. Ronnie is limping too, keeping as much weight off his bad leg as he can. A fine pair of heroes they make.

He slows down to move a pile of branches blocking a gap between some boulders. Marybeth rushes forward to help him.

"This is a waste of time," he grumbles.

Marybeth shrugs it off. They're both exhausted after a long day of trudging through the forest. There's not really a trail out here; Ronnie's just leading them towards the places where he found carrion. It's hard going. The trees don't seem to want to let them through.

She reaches into her backpack and pulls out a water bottle, grateful that they're better prepared for this hike than she was for her last one. Ronnie's is a proper hiking backpack, well

313

worn. Hers is a leather satchel-type thing that looks old enough to have been his school bag once. Each of them has their own supply of water, peanuts, flashlights and a gas mask. Ronnie had ignored her protests and insisted that they each carry one of his homemade flamethrowers. She also has the gun tucked into her waistband, but she has no idea how many bullets are left in it. If only she were somebody who knew about guns, rather than make-up and mops.

It's peaceful out here. She runs her hands along soft furry moss growing on a boulder. Incredible how much life there is in this forest. The roots of trees, chattering to each other through chemicals in the soil. Even the moss is thinking, in its own way.

Her mother used to love hiking. She said the forest reminded her of home, of the Nyírség forests in Hungary. She dragged her and her brother Deco out here every weekend when they were small, until they both got old enough to hate it. They'd complain ceaselessly, drag their feet, beg her to let them go home and do any of the things they'd rather be doing. Teen Marybeth never wanted to be here, mucking around in the dirt. She wanted to be off having adventures with Jalene, making up dances and listening to records. Her mother always said Marybeth never understood the beauty of Little Hope, how lucky they were to be surrounded by nature.

Why did she never take Katie out here? She'd always take time off work for the pageants, but never for the things Katie wanted to do. Katie loved the outdoors. She knew the name of every kind of bird, could identify a tree by just looking at a fallen leaf, collected facts about insects. She was an extraordinary child. She was an extraordinary person. And that person is gone now.

She feels a tear carve a path down her cheek. *Now is not the time*, she scolds herself. But it's the first time she's cried, she realises. The first time she's just let herself mourn, and now that the tears are starting, she doesn't think she can stop them.

Katie, who always seemed so much older than her, somehow. Who she used to tease for being three going on thirty-three. So wise and strange. Marybeth always knew, on some level, that she was going to grow up and be too special for her one day, something she wouldn't understand any more. A stranger she'd see on Thanksgiving. On some level, all motherhood is mourning, because the child you love dies every day and is replaced by someone a little bit older, someone who needs you a little bit less. She'd expected her to go off to college. She'd expected her to leave her and get married and have children of her own one day. She'd braced herself for it. She's been preparing to lose Katie since the day she brought her home from the hospital.

But not like this. Not rotting in a cave. Not turned into something her own best friend described as a monster.

A high wail escapes her, shattering the peacefulness of the afternoon. It breaks into a series of ugly sobs. She puts out a hand to steady herself, and crumples against a rock, and cries.

She feels a hand on her shoulder: Ronnie. He doesn't try to comfort her, or tell her everything's going to be OK. He just stands there, with his hand on her shoulder. Someone who knows what it feels like to have lost the person you love the most in the world. It helps.

They stay like that for many long minutes, until the tears run dry, and Marybeth is finally ready to walk again. Now, Ronnie doesn't rush ahead so quickly. He hangs back, so that the two of them walk almost side by side along the path.

"You still play that game with the funny dice?" she asks him, after a while. "Where you pretend to be a knight?"

"*Dungeons and Dragons*? No. You need friends for that. People haven't exactly been clamouring to hang out with me since I got out of prison."

"Must be lonely," she says.

He shrugs. "I heard you married Bill Larkin."

"Yup."

"Tell you the truth, I never liked him much."

She laughs. "Well, you're a better judge of character than me."

"He was mean."

"He was worse than that."

"You regret it? Marrying him?"

"I don't know. You start picking at what you regret, and before you know it, you've unravelled your whole life."

They follow the stream in silence, passing a family of geese, bobbing and diving in the shallows. Ronnie glances at her, through long blond eyelashes. "I'm sorry I burned you," he says.

"I'm sorry I stabbed you."

"And I'm sorry I attacked Donna."

"Why don't we both just agree not to attack anybody else until we figure this all out."

He grins, looking more like the boy she once knew. "Deal."

They scramble up a small ridge where a patch of spicy cedar trees grows thick. Ronnie pauses, thinking, then leads them north, deeper into the underbrush.

"Do you know where she is?"

"Not exactly. Just where it's been... hunting," he says, keeping his voice low.

They trudge deeper into the forest, slower going now, bashing their way through shrubs. A bush catches on Ronnie's bandage, and she sees him wince in pain.

———

They don't spot the corpse until they nearly walk into it. Larger than a dog but smaller than a cow, draped on a low branch of a pine tree, folded in half like a pair of pants on a hanger, the head and hind legs touching. Even up close, it's hard to tell what it was. It has the elongated jaw of a deer, but stubby hind legs like an alligator. A soft pelt of spotted fur runs up its spine, like a bobcat. The belly is split open, entrails draping down into the grass below like vines.

"Leftovers?" Marybeth asks, feeling woozy at the smell.

"Or discards," Ronnie says, running his hand on the fur, brow furrowed. "At least we know we're getting close." He squints at the eyes, blank jellied discs staring at nothing. "Are you sure you want to keep going?"

"She's my daughter."

"Parts of her, maybe."

He crouches down to take a look at the underside. "Shit!" he shouts, falling backwards onto his ass.

"What?"

Ronnie gestures at the corpse mutely, shuddering.

She pulls a dry branch off a nearby bush and uses it to lever the animal off the pine tree. It plops to the ground, releasing a fresh stench, landing with the viscera exposed.

"Oh God," Marybeth says. The rotting innards squirm inside.

The belly is stuffed full of worms, long and white, writhing. She dips the edge of the branch into the mess of them and hooks one. She pulls it, and it keeps coming, and coming: three feet, four feet, five feet long. An endless long segmented worm. One of dozens.

Finally, it all clicks into place.

It was months ago. Polly, one-woman drugstore, said her cousin had brought them back from Mexico. Said they were miracle diet pills, guaranteed to make you lose twenty pounds a month. Marybeth had paid $50 for two measly tablets, dissolved one in Katie's cereal milk, and then felt so stupid about the whole thing she immediately regretted it. It seemed so obvious that she'd been taken advantage of.

She'd told Polly off the next time she saw her at work, and she protested, said no, they were tapeworm eggs, they'll make you lose weight no matter what you eat. And Marybeth had laughed at her, told her either she was a thief or a fool herself, and assumed she'd given Katie nothing but some extra sugar in her cereal that morning.

Of course she knows it was a terrible thing to do, slipping diet pills to somebody without them knowing. Her own mother used to call her shallow. But Marybeth knows how cruel the world can be to a girl who doesn't fit in. How you'll grab on to any kind of love you're offered, even love that's offered in a fist.

She was only trying to give Katie a better life than hers.

She imagines it: Katie walking into that cave. Something in the air scanning her body, trying to make a map of her to duplicate. But there are two sets of instructions. A second mass of body tissue that isn't human. It gets confused about what to be. It becomes half Kate, half worm. A Kateworm.

She has been such a fool.

She stands and looks at Ronnie. "I know what happened to my daughter," she says finally. "I turned her into a monster."

40. HEY YOU WITH THE CRUMBY FACE

TAMMY-RAE HOOPER

WEDNESDAY, 25 SEPTEMBER 1996

donna donna DONNA DONNA DONNA'S COMING

A single thought of her own, enough to untangle her from the *we* for a moment.

They are in Doctor Abrams's offices, six of them. They can hear him moving around in the ceiling vents where he has been hiding. Some of their fingers are unscrewing the gates that cover the vent plates and some of their fingers are opening the packaging on a smoke bomb for rats and some of their fingers are wrapped tight around a scalpel.

Did she just feel Donna nearby?

No, Donna left, remember? Donna hates you.

The thought scalds her mind and then she

41. THE DAY THE WORLD TURNED DAYGLO

DONNA RAMIREZ

WEDNESDAY, 25 SEPTEMBER 1996

Little Hope lies at the bottom of a valley, hugged in tight by the mountains of the Sierra Nevada. Normally when you're driving in, you round a corner on Route 49 and suddenly it's there, cheerful pastel-coloured buildings huddled below you, like ice cream in a bowl. Today, there's a cloud hanging over the valley, a brown-grey smear glowing with the single rail of street lights that runs along Broad Street. But still, Donna's heart gives a little skip at the sight of it.

Home.

There's a jam of stationary cars where the roadblock was, but no sign of the cops now. Cars block both sides of the road, some of them crashed into each other. It doesn't seem possible that many people could have escaped. Maybe there is still a chance to contain this.

She's got no choice but to get out and walk the rest of the way. It's a relief, really. Both of her legs are fully cramping now, not used to their position hovering above the pedals. The passenger on her back seat has developed an unmistakable aroma too. Plus, if she has to listen to one more minute of Rod 'Do Ya Think I'm Sexy?' Stewart, she might just drive the car into the woods and go full monster herself.

She gets out of the car and puts her hand on the back window, where her dad's head is leaning against the glass. Whispering a silent goodbye, she hopes that the other version of him is safe.

She makes her way through the gaps between the cars, avoiding looking into the windows. She's had her fill of seeing dead bodies today, and for her whole lifetime, thank you very much.

The others are a pull at the pit of her stomach. They have an almost physical weight dragging her forward, like she's tied to the end of a pickup. The strength is incredible. Fuck, there are so many of them. Hundreds already. No, thousands, and new ones blooming into existence every second. She can't discern Rae from the general din.

Donna makes her way along Black Oak Lane, the road that cups the town along its western boundary before looping up to become the bottom of Broad Street. She hugs the edge of the woods. Better to stay away from the others until she can find Rae. But how the heck is she going to do that?

The elementary school is eerily quiet, for a weekday. Quiet, but not empty: she can feel plenty of others like her flitting around. Usually, around this time, it would be full of the screaming joy of kids at play. Instead, she rounds the corner and finds dozens of children neatly sitting around the playground equipment, barely moving.

Every head snaps up to look at her. They can feel that she's one of them, and they can feel that she's resisting.

One of them stands. A tiny six- or seven-year-old with white-blonde hair pinned up in elaborate butterfly clips. She considers Donna with fierce blue eyes. There's an answering echo in Donna, a *command* to join them in the playground.

Hell no. Donna takes a step back.

The others get to their feet in perfect unison. Thirty, forty kids between the ages of five and nine.

"Leave me alone, you *Children of the Corn* creeps!" Donna yells.

They all run at her at once, like it's been choreographed.

Donna turns and races into the trees, running as fast as she can up the steep rocky bank. They're right behind her. Her longer legs are no match for their boundless kid energy.

Something happens to her brain. It starts flickering out, losing every third second, like falling asleep in a movie, blinks becoming micro-naps, then

———

Butterfly-clip girl tackles her shin. Donna kicks her off but

———

She's almost at the top of the hill, slowing, like her legs don't want

———

No.

Reality crashes back at her, bushes racing at her face; she's tumbling down the other side of the slope and thank fuck, because it's putting enough distance between her and those prepubescent demons to give her her own brain back.

Butterfly-clip girl falls with her, screaming as she goes. The scream is stopped by a hard *crunch* as the unstoppable force of her body hits the immovable object of a large boulder at the bottom of the hill.

Donna is luckier, skidding to a slow stop in the muddy leaves. She clambers to her feet.

"Hey, you OK?" she wheezes to the girl. The child's head is crushed at an impossible angle between her limp body and the boulder, and a flash of vertebra is visible in the bloody mess of the side of her neck.

But she's already lifting herself up, clicking her head back into place like she just slept funny, the skin of her neck knitting closed.

With just the two of them, Donna can force herself to ignore the humming feeling, the urge to hold her close and clump into one creature. It helps that the child's face is crusted with snot, the tips of her blonde hair now sodden red and muddy.

The little girl looks up at her with accusing eyes. "Stop being bad. Come back," she orders.

"Make me."

The girl looks like she might throw a tantrum. But she clearly recognises the stubborn set of Donna's chin, and gives up, running off back to the others. That's one lucky break, Donna considers: they don't seem to be in a huge hurry to spread all over the world. They mostly seem to want to be together.

Donna *floomphs* down onto the bloody rock, wondering what she's going to do. Ugh, she's in so far over her head. Such an idiot to think she was so special she'd somehow be immune to the hive mind.

She seems to have fallen right onto the well-trodden hiking path that leads to the lookout point over Wildman's Canyon. The very one she and Rae pretended they'd gotten lost from, what seems like a very long time ago now. There's a flyer flapping against a tree trunk nearby, ink gone all blotchy from the damp. HAVE YOU SEEN THESE GIRLS? The three of them huddled together, smiling and happy.

She pulls Kat's journal from the waistband of her jeans. All those moments in their lives. She remembers saying she couldn't understand why Kat wanted to write it all down; it wasn't like anything ever actually happened to them. It was just their boring stupid lives, joking about school and arguing about music and talking about all the things they'd do when they were finally grown up. Now they feel like the most precious thing in the world to her, these memories.

She wishes she'd written some stuff down, herself. Things that had happened only to her. *Poorly Pig*, the story her mom used to read to her when she was a kid, about a pig that had a different accident every day of the week. Ulu, the stuffed owl that her *abuela* bought her, that slept in her bed every night until seven-year-old Jay vomited all over him on a road trip to visit their *tío* out in Arizona. The smell of her dad's pancakes, the gentle feel of his fingertips on her eyebrows. Late nights alone in her room, Lunachicks or Babes in Toyland on full blast on her Discman, sketching, feeling understood. Memories written only in her brain. The million tiny things that make Donna Donna.

She runs her hands along Kat's precious handwritten lines. Maybe she can absorb all this Kat-Donna-Raeness into herself. Maybe the words will seep into her bones and somehow make her strong enough for what she has to do.

42. BE YR MAMA

MARYBETH LARKIN

WEDNESDAY, 25 SEPTEMBER 1996

They smell the nest a long time before they see it. Ammonia and iron and rot, dug into a hollow at the base of a huge sequoia, a bowl shape of knotted branches, fur and rotting vegetation, the size of an SUV. A clear, sticky secretion glistens in the dim light that filters in from the dense canopy above.

Scattered around it is a grab-bag graveyard of animal parts in various states of decay. Legs and heads and antlers and tails and torsos and fur and skin and scales and feathers. There seems to be some mad kind of order to them: Marybeth spots a collection of tongues laid out on a rock; wings hung around the edges of the nest; different-sized torsos laid neatly in a row, bird and bear and bobcat. Like the nest of a dark-minded magpie.

She can feel Ronnie trembling at her side. He nudges her and gestures up at a ridge ahead of them. It's deep in shadow but there's a faint scuffling sound from among the bushes there.

Ronnie reaches slowly into his pocket and pulls out his makeshift flamethrower. He looks at her expectantly. She shakes her head: she won't. That's her daughter.

A muscle in Ronnie's jaw twitches. He unclips a small flashlight from the side of his backpack and clicks it on, moving the beam towards the ridge, catching on the tips of hooves, claws, elbows.

When the beam lands on one of the rattling bushes, it comes alive with red glowing eyes, six of them.

Ronnie grabs her hand. She can feel the strength of her own pulse against the squeeze of his fingers wrapped around her wrist.

A tiny creature hops out of the bush. Small, tawny brown. A rabbit. It sits on the ridge, staring at them. Another follows it. More of them appear from the bushes, until there are eight of them watching from the edge of the ridge. Each one intent. Each one watching them with unflinching faces.

Ronnie stumbles back in fright, nearly falling. Marybeth steadies him, their hands still connected. He has thrown his head back and is watching the tree canopy above them with an open mouth.

The leaves shake in the trees, somewhere far above them. Like something is moving up there. Something enormous.

For the first time in this whole terrible week, it occurs to Marybeth: what if she *doesn't* want to find her daughter?

There's a heavy *thunk* on one of the lower branches of the sequoia. Dead leaves float down on them like confetti.

Marybeth cranes her neck far back. She sees nothing but tree.

And then a head lowers itself from the tree branch, just a few feet above their heads. Thick and glistening, hairless. It hangs upside down from the branch, attached to a long segmented neck, until its eyes are nearly in line with theirs. Beautiful green eyes. Katie's eyes.

But the rest of her face is wrong. Her head is bulbous, fleshy; it merges directly into her body, which is still hooked onto the branch above them. Her mouth is a jagged grin that splits her face nearly in two, her lips encrusted with hooks. It splits open and becomes a hole, lined with teeth. Marybeth can see straight into it, down a gullet that seems never-ending. A dark, mad hole, the walls contracting in waves, several long tongues twisting around inside.

The mouth closes, the hooked lips twisting and contorting. Finally, a half-formed growling word emerges. "Mommy?"

There's a strange echo behind the sound, like the screech of a bat and the buzz of a wasp, simultaneously.

Ronnie tugs at her hand but Marybeth resists him. She reaches out to touch Katie's cheek and the skin on her face ripples at her touch. Her skin is hot, tough like cured leather, and her green eyes flicker between the two of them.

"Get back!" Ronnie says, tugging harder. They stumble backwards over the limbs and tree litter on the ground.

"She's alive."

"That's not your daughter," Ronnie shouts at her.

"It's her. That's her." Marybeth tries to squirm from his grasp, but he keeps pulling them away. Katie's eyes follow them as they stumble and trip backwards.

Katie's face turns like a dial until it's the right way up. It remains perfectly still, suspended there, as the rest of the body spills out of the tree onto the ground beneath her. It just keeps coming and coming, coiling onto itself like a snake, fleshy segments as thick as a bear. Each segment holds a pair of legs, thickly muscled, each one ending in a long-fingered paw and four-inch talons. There is a ridge up the centre of her belly like a seam, and tumour-like lumps protrude across her front shoulders. She looks like a creature assembled from a lucky bag of animal parts and nightmares.

Her eyes are still watching them, as Ronnie yanks at her wrist.

The lips are moving again, struggling to form words. "You found me, Ma Bear," she says, sounding a little more like Katie.

"I found you, baby," Marybeth sobs. "We can go home now."

But Katie's eyes are fixed on Ronnie. He drops Marybeth's

hand and stumbles backwards again. He half-trips over a tree root, but just manages to stay on his feet.

Katie's eyes follow each movement, her pupils growing larger until her eyes turn black. She crouches, the muscles in each leg bunched tight like a cat.

Ronnie moans, scrabbling in his pocket for a lighter.

"Ronnie, stop moving," Marybeth says.

Katie's black eyes are trained on him; her muscles quiver every time he moves.

Ronnie drops the flamethrower and it skitters away behind him, tumbling down the hill.

"Stop!" she shouts.

But Ronnie turns and dashes after the can.

There is a blur of colour and Marybeth is thrown to the ground. There is a sharp, short scream. Katie's body keeps coming, spilling through the trees like a Chinese paper dragon. There is so much of her. Legs and claws and body and body.

Then it's gone, back up into the trees. Ronnie has vanished.

Far above her, she hears the branches rattle, a wet ripping sound.

Marybeth hauls herself to her feet and runs.

She slips out of the clearing and moves as quietly as she can through the trees, straining to listen for the sounds of movement above. There's silence. Discomforting silence.

Leaning against the rough trunk of a tree, she tries to quiet her breathing. A bird calls in the distance and it sounds like a shriek. Everything in this forest sounds like a shriek. That's what nature is, isn't it? Hunt-kill-maim-eat, and that, clearly, is what Katie has been learning.

She misses the days she just had to worry about Donna Ramirez's bad influence on her daughter, not the influence of the whole of the forest.

"Ma Bear..." calls a voice. It seems to be coming from everywhere, reverberating through the trunks of the trees, deeper than any voice she's ever heard. It sings in a symphony with shrieks and growls and hoots and yaps.

Marybeth whirls around, looking for movement. Everything is still, except for the pounding in her own chest.

"I finally got that makeover," the voice growls, sparkling with mischief. The harmony of fox calls and bear cries answers her.

"Where's Ronnie?" Marybeth calls back to her.

"I strung him up along some branches like a pretty garland." A wild giggle that seems to bounce and echo through the trees, breaking into bird chatter. "Want to join him?"

"Are you going to use him for parts?"

"I've learned my lesson about eating prey. Fear tastes horrible, Ma Bear. One must be picky." There's a slight lisp in the voice, like it's still trying to figure its way around a new voice apparatus. "Can't be shoving any old crap in your mouth. You are what you eat, after all. Predator minds, on the other hand..."

Marybeth's mouth is dry. "Stop this, Katie. Just come down and we can figure this out."

"Don't try to mother me," the voice says. "We're long past that."

Marybeth pulls the gun from the waistband of her pants. She aims it at the trees above her, looking for any sign of movement, not sure she could bring herself to shoot, even if she did.

"Do you want to kill me, Mommy?" the voice rumbles.

Her finger finds the trigger. The gun is cold in her hands. "You're my daughter."

A dark shadow twists in front of her, Katie's long body pouring down onto the ground. She rears up in front of her, eyes glinting green in the meagre sunlight.

"I'm so sorry, Katie," Marybeth says, willing her finger to squeeze the trigger.

The mouth breaks into a horrible grin. "You don't get to be sorry." She rears up high. The seam in the front of her body splits apart, revealing a hundred more mouths and eyes, clustered on inner flesh, different sizes, beaks and snouts and eye clusters glistening like fish eggs. "Open your eyes, Ma Bear." The creature chortles, deep and rumbling. "You always wanted to steal my life. Couldn't just get a life of your own." The mouths move in unison, squawks and tweets, bat cries and chatters, all saying the same thing. "*I* did this. You didn't make me. I am made of bobcat and beetle. I am made of tapeworm and jackrabbit, of kingsnake and pika and bat, of lichen and coyote and beetle, of mule deer and mushroom, and yes, I am made of a girl named Kat Larkin too, who was already weirder and more terrible than you could ever imagine. I have tasted everything in this forest. I am the best parts of all of them." The creature sways in front of her, like a snake charmer. "Just leave, Ma Bear. Go home. Let me live my own fucking life for once."

Marybeth lets the gun drop to the ground. "I can't do that. Sorry."

Katie rattles the hooks around her largest mouth, a warning. Her face twists into a snarl, bestial. But there's still something familiar about it. Not so different, after all, from the look Katie got in every one of their tearful teenage fights. Nature might be savage, but is it so different from the wild cruelty of teenage girls?

Staring up at her awful face, she understands what she must do.

"Katie, listen to me," Marybeth says, setting her shoulders back, pretending she is brave, pretending that she is taller than this creature who is her daughter, who looms a full six feet above her. "I know you think you're smart. But I've lived longer than you, and I know things you don't know. I'm not afraid of you."

Katie opens her mouth wide into a full dark O. A shriek rumbles out of her, piercing and terrible, huger than the forest.

Marybeth screams back. "You want to rip things up? You want to have some *experiences*? Well, try this experience." She unthreads her arms from the straps of the backpack, letting it drop to the ground behind her, knowing that the flamethrower is inside, any chance she might have had to defend herself. She stretches out her arms. "Think you know everything? Why don't you try knowing me? Eat me!"

The Kateworm's eyes narrow. "I already know you. You're a small-town nobody who never did anything with her life except try to live through mine."

"Turning into your mother is your worst nightmare, right? Oh, my Katie cub. You don't even know how normal you are."

A heavy bead of saliva drops from the hooks around Katie's mouth. Her body is dropping low again, the muscles bunching. Marybeth only needs the creature to absorb her, rather than just killing her. She only needs her curiosity to override her urge to destroy.

"Don't you want to know who your father was?" Marybeth says.

Katie rears up, holding six of her front arms out, thirty claws as long as knives flashing in the dappled light.

"Try five seconds," she says. Marybeth closes her eyes. In that moment, she doesn't care what happens. She doesn't care if she dies. If there's even the smallest chance she can save her daughter, it's OK.

A hot wetness engulfs her. A deep crunch, and a burning heat along her torso. She tries to run, only to find that her legs are not attached to her any more. Tongues wrap around her. The teeth crunch down again, into her chest this time, and her insides unspool into the darkness.

It is too fast for pain.

The only thing she has time to think is, *I hope it didn't hurt for you, my girl.*

43. WE ARE FAMILY

She holds her mother's body in her mouth, resisting the urge to swallow. Blood mixes with her saliva, creating a perfect map of her. She swallows the rest down, where she knows the juices of her powerful digestive system will make quick work of her. Waste not, want not.

A new brain begins to grow among the others she's collected around the base of her neck. The others are simple predator brains, sharp and snarling. Full of daring, the pure knowledge that not to attempt is death.

This mind is so much more complex. She feels neurons branch and bloom, billions of them, assembling into a three-pound mass on the edge of her collarbone. Signals begin to leap from tip to tip, tracing excited circuits. Such a small, squishy, electric thing, and yet it contains a whole person. Remarkable, really. As remarkable as any process in the universe, alien or not.

She grows a thread out from her spinal cord and wires it in, and Ma Bear's mind begins to unwind before her.

The smells come in first. Paprika. Cigarette smoke. Hospital anaesthetic. Anaïs Anaïs perfume. Ice cream. The ocean.

Then images, beliefs, ideas, sounds, impressions. It all comes rushing at her in a blur. She tries to make sense of it, but it's like trying to take a drink from a fire hydrant.

Woah, woah. She severs the spinal cord, takes a deep breath. *Slowly.* No, a human mind is not a buffet. She needs to be orderly. *Try again.*

She reaches for a single smell. Paprika. She ignores everything else, and focuses only on that until it unfolds into a memory.

She is four years old and her name is still Margita Horvath. Paprika fills the kitchen of the house she grew up in, in the small yellow mobile home on the other side of Little Hope. Her mother is singing an aria from *La Bohème*. She only sings when she's cooking. She and Deco are sitting under a Formica table, while her mother holds a wooden spoon out to each of them in turn, asking them if the stew needs anything else. She and Deco take their tasting duty very seriously. Each time they're asked, they think of a new suggestion for the soup. More carrots, some pepper. It's the only time their mother is so happy, and they want to keep this going as long as they can.

Another memory. She is five. She goes to day-care while her mom is at the doctor's office working as a secretary, because she can't make enough money as a seamstress. Day-care is four children who eat biscuits and play mostly unsupervised in Mrs Leland's front yard. One of the other boys asks her who her father is. She tells them that her mom said he's a rat, and that he went back to Hungary after she was born. She knows this is just a way of talking, and her father wasn't *really* a rat, but the other kids start teasing her, saying the reason she has a funny face is that she's half girl, half rat.

She is eight. They are going to do surgery on her face because her cleft palate makes her talk funny. She's had three surgeries already, but she was too young to remember them. The doctor explains to her that they're going to take a piece of bone from her hip to fill a hole in her mouth. Her mother keeps disappearing and comes back smelling of cigarette smoke. When they come to wheel her out, her mother isn't there, and she's afraid.

She is nine. She comes home from school in tears. She tried to drink a soda but some of it came dribbling out of her lip. The kids at school spent the whole day taking sips of things and then spitting it out onto her, calling her Dribbly Margibbly. She crawls onto her mother's lap and begs her for another surgery to fix her face better. Her mother strokes her head. "The world is cruel to ugly girls. But I can't fix the world for you, *édesem*. You must learn to be stronger."

She is eleven. She's just started middle school, and a new girl has joined their class. Her name is Jalene, she has blonde curly hair and she is the most beautiful person Marybeth has ever seen. On the second day of class, Jalene slips her a note saying she likes her yellow headband and asking if she wants to be friends. Marybeth has to look around the room to check that there's not another girl wearing a yellow headband, sure this is all a mistake, or some elaborate prank.

She is twelve. They're on Jalene's mother's couch watching *American Bandstand*. ABBA comes on, and they start singing 'SOS' and it's amazing, and she and Jalene are so hyped about it that they get up and start dancing along in the living room, only they start singing the lyrics as S-E-X, which strikes them both as screamingly funny. Jalene wraps her up in a hug afterwards and makes her pinkie-promise that if ABBA ever come to America, they have to find a way to go to the concert together, and then they spend the rest of the night talking about how great it would be if Dick Clark was your dad.

She is fourteen. She decides that high school is her chance to reinvent herself. She learns to do her make-up so that it hides her scars. She tells her mother that she's changing her name to Marybeth. Her mother looks like she's slapped her, and asks what's wrong with the name she gave her. It devolves into a screaming match. "If you didn't want us to be American, then why did you bring us to America?" Her mother doesn't respond, she just gets up and walks out the door into the night. Marybeth bikes over to Jalene's, sobbing. Jalene holds her, and says, "It's OK, I'll be your family." She smells like Anaïs Anaïs roll-on, floral and comforting.

She is sixteen, and it is the best summer of her life. She and Jalene don't spend a minute apart. They spend their time cruising around in Fernando, smoking pot, talking about their future, plotting their escape from Little Hope. They're going to be air hostesses together and travel the world and marry film stars they'll meet in first class. The two of them drive up to San Francisco in Fernando to see ABBA at the Concord. They spend the whole concert gripping each other, tears streaming down their faces in joy. Afterwards, they strip down to their shoes and go streaking down the Embarcadero. It is the dawn of a new decade, and everything feels possible for them.

She is still sixteen, but summer's long over. Bill Larkin comes up to her one day as they're leaving school and invites her to come watch kung fu movies in his basement. She's never thought much about Bill before. He's three years older than her but still in junior year, held back a couple times because of his dyslexia. He gets into a lot of fights, but he's also popular and funny. Most importantly, he's the first boy who's ever asked her out.

She goes with him to his parents' basement. They don't get through ten minutes of the movie before they start making out. At one point, he traces her scar with his fingertips and asks where she got it. She flushes and wants to leave. But he says, "It's sexy." And that's all it took. After that, she would have let him do anything.

The teasing at school changes after that. Peggy Boyd comes up to her in the cafeteria and asks her loudly if she split her lip sucking Bill's big dick. Jalene walks right over and punches her in the nose. Later, she corners Bill and berates him for telling everybody they had sex. He blushes, little-boy-naughty, and says it was just because he was so proud that she went with him, such a beauty. Fool that she is, she believes him.

She's seventeen. She is four months pregnant, and everybody seems to know it. Her history teacher asks her to stay after class one day. She tells her that she's a smart girl, that she could get a college scholarship if she wants to. She tells her about a clinic in Sacramento that can help her. She tells Bill. He begs her not to. He asks her, "But what if this is the only child God will ever give you?" He buys her a ring and promises her the world.

She's seventeen, and she has slept a total of six hours over the past four days. She thinks she is losing her mind. The screaming infant they sent her home with hasn't stopped crying. She can't get her to latch on her nipple. Bill is at his mother's, saying he needs peace and quiet to study for finals. She thinks the baby might just die of starvation, and that it might be a relief for both of them if she did. Katie screams and screams. Marybeth falls asleep anyway, right there in the chair, holding her daughter in her arms. She wakes up to find that Katie has found the nipple on her own, and she's gazing up at her with soft eyes as she eats. Marybeth feels a rush of love she never expected. "Maybe we can do this," she says to the small mewling creature at her breast. Just two kids, figuring it out together.

She's nineteen. Jalene's birthday party. She's determined to go. Jalene's just back for her birthday weekend, visiting from Berkeley. They haven't talked in months. She leaves Katie with Bill and meets them at a bar off Broad Street. Jalene's brought two of her college friends and the three of them spend the whole night making fun of Little Hope. They talk about books she hasn't read, campus parties, kooky lecturers, college boys. They might as well be talking about another planet. One of the other girls asks Marybeth what school she goes to. Jalene jumps in. "Marybeth's studying at the school of life!" Jalene reaches under the table and squeezes her hand. Marybeth drinks too much to cover her awkwardness. She's late coming home. Bill is waiting for her in the living room. He punches her in the face and then hands her the baby. It's the first time he's ever hit her. The strange thing is how expressionless his face is as he does it, like this is all just a big hassle for him. She is too shocked to be angry.

She's twenty, twenty-one, twenty-two. The years blur together. Bill gets worse. A hundred punches, slaps, kicks. Lessons. What hurts is the humiliation of it. Once, he drags her out into the street by her ponytail. "Show them what a pathetic mess you are," he screams at them. That's what hurts, that everyone knows, and no one comes to help.

Once, in an argument, she threatens to leave Bill. He reaches up and fingers her scar, the same way he'd touched it so lovingly before. "Who else would have you?" he says gently.

But he's a wonderful dad. With Katie, he is all jokes and piggy-back rides. When he comes home from work, she runs up to him and scrambles up him, like a climbing gym. And girls need their fathers.

She stops seeing people, because she's ashamed of the bruises. If they see them, they'll know how cowardly she is, that she stays. She sits at home every day, playing with Katie. They make up worlds together, tell each other fantastical stories. Being a mom is the one thing she's good at.

She finds herself sleeping a lot. One day, she's watching a news report about an oil spill near Chile. They show footage of birds lying dead on the shore, coated in black. That's what it feels like, she realises, like drowning in blackness, like if they pulled out her heart it would be heavy with viscous oil. Some days, she can't drag herself out of bed, until Katie starts jumping on her begging her to come play.

Her mother dies. Emphysema at fifty-five, but she looked

eighty. Deco flies down from Portland for the funeral, and it's the first time she's seen him in years. From his eulogy, she learns that their mother had a masters degree in engineering back in Budapest. Deco says nice things about her, how she gave up everything she knew to give her children a chance of a better life. He doesn't talk about how disappointed she was by the life she got instead. Afterwards, she and Deco go back to her mother's junk-filled house and drink pálinka in her honour. Deco asks if she's OK. She has no idea how to answer the question.

Two weeks later, she drops Katie off at Mrs Leland's daycare and goes home. She swallows an entire bottle of Benadryl and a quart of vodka and climbs into bed, hoping she never wakes up. But she does, lying in a pool of her own vomit. There's just enough time to clean it up before Bill gets home.

She's twenty-three, and Katie has just turned six. She begs Bill for a piggy-back ride. Bill's watching a football game, and he's not interested in being her horsey right now. Katie pesters him. Bill snaps. He stands and lifts her up like he's about to put her on his shoulders, but then tosses her across the room like a rag doll. Marybeth scoops her up. Katie is gasping from fright and confusion, and hasn't started crying yet. Bill has never lost his temper with her before, never. Marybeth carries her daughter in her arms right out the door, and gets in her car, and drives away. It's the off-season, so Matt Wiley is happy to give her a hotel room in exchange for her labour. For the first few weeks, she's afraid that Bill will come for them. She pulls Katie out of school, and won't let her out of her sight. She lives on a knife edge, but he never comes for them. She feels even worse realising she could have left sooner.

A month later, two officers knock on her hotel door to tell her that her husband's dead. Shot by his new girlfriend, self-defence. She surprises herself by crying for him.

She is twenty-four. Everything should be better now. They're safe. She and Katie have moved back into the home she and Bill bought. Between Bill's life insurance and the money she makes at the hotel, they're getting along OK. She starts a college fund for Katie. But the oil spill feeling is back, and that's terrifying, because it means that the sadness wasn't because of Bill, it was *her* all along. She is broken. It feels like something died in her after that night streaking down the Embarcadero with Jalene and she will never get it back. She starts thinking about sending Katie to live with Deco in Portland and making another date with the Benadryl. Katie will be better off without her.

Katie sees a poster advertising a pageant at a mall in Santa Rosa. The prize is a Barbie Dreamhouse that Katie has been eyeing desperately in the window display at Toys "R" Us for months. She begs Marybeth to let her enter. Marybeth consents despite her better judgement. She stays up all night hand-sewing one of her mother's long ruffled skirts into a tiny ballgown. The two of them prepare a dance routine to 'Walk Like an Egyptian'. Katie is effervescent, a born performer. She places third, winning a $50 gift card to Macy's and a pink satin sash. The two of them are over the moon. They drive to Bodega Bay afterwards and get ice creams and sit on the beach. The ocean smells like hope, and Marybeth sees it, Katie's whole future unfolding ahead of her. She is so beautiful and smart, she could be Miss World, she could win a scholarship, marry a president, have anything she ever wanted. She can have the life both of them deserved.

The two of them commit to pageants with an ambition neither of them knew they had. They learn how to do make-up and hair. They practise dance moves until their muscles ache. Marybeth digs up her mother's old sewing machine and learns how to use it. She empties the college fund to pay for the pageants, because Katie loves them, and she sparkles, and it's impossible to imagine that she won't win them all.

She's popular among the pageant moms. None of them knows that she's the fool who let herself be terrorised by Bill Larkin. None of them knows her as Dribbly Margibbly, or Rat-Face, or Margherita Pizza, or the lisping girl who wore homemade clothes. She and Katie get to spend so much time together. For the first time, both of them experience what it feels like to be a winner. Marybeth starts to believe again. In transformation, in bettering yourself, in Katie.

Katie is nine. They are in Fernando, on their way to a pageant in Nevada. Katie asks what her father was like. She remembers her own mother's words to her. *I can't fix the world for you, édesem.* Her mother was wrong; she can make the world beautiful for her daughter. She can carry all the world's ugliness and suffering so that Katie never has to know. "Your father loved you so much," she tells her.

Katie keeps winning and winning, and grows more beautiful every day. Bill's life insurance money is gone, and Marybeth has to double the shifts she works at the hotel. It's hard work, scrubbing toothpaste flecks from bathroom mirrors and shit-stains from toilet bowls, dodging snark and groping hands from drunks at the hotel bar. But it's worth it. She starts giving cruel nicknames to everyone who's mean to her, in her head. She spends the whole time thinking up new moves for dance routines, costume designs, strategies. She hasn't thought of oil spills or Benadryl in years.

Katie is twelve. She declares that pageants are stupid and she's too old for them. Marybeth begs her to consider doing just one more year, and Katie punishes her by pretending to be deaf for the rest of the afternoon. It's like a punch in the gut: Bill used to do exactly the same thing to her.

Marybeth suggests other things they can do together. She tries to sell Katie on dance classes, aerobics, tennis club. Katie only wants to be by herself, nose in a book. She starts gaining weight, and Marybeth is scared for her. She knows how cruel the world can be to an ugly girl, the depths you'll stoop to if you're starved for love.

Katie is fourteen. Her new best friends Tammy-Rae and Donna are over for dinner. The three of them are planning Halloween costumes. Marybeth suggests one of them go as Frankenstein. Katie rolls her eyes. "God, Ma Bear. Frankenstein was the name of the *doctor*, not the monster. Read a book sometime." She knows Katie's just trying to impress her friends, but it stings. She goes through to the kitchen and starts washing dishes so that Katie doesn't see the tears in her eyes. Tammy-Rae follows her. "I wish my mom was like you," she says. The two of them clean the kitchen together while Katie and Donna make more and more outrageous jokes from the living room. She watches bubbles slide down the dishes, and for the first time, she starts to think about what she'll do after Katie leaves for college. Maybe she'll track down Jalene's number, or drive out to Portland to visit Deco. Or maybe, without Katie, she'll fall apart again, and try to die.

Isn't that what you just did, Mother? The voice of Kat reasserts itself, against the swell of Ma Bear's memories.

Kat shakes her huge head, overwhelmed by this knowledge. It wasn't fair of her mother to lie to her, to keep so much from her. It's so much more than she bargained for, and she can't hold all of it.

The creature considers herself, her several selves, her strange composite self.

She is trying to figure out what to keep and what to prune. There is so much here she doesn't want. So much pain. A thousand rejections. So many times Marybeth wasn't loved as well as she should have been, as she needed to be. She wants to cut it out, like she cut out the weak parts of the other creatures she consumed. Keep only what will make her stronger.

But it's all so mixed up, the good and the bad.

A human mind is a story, she realises. You can't just chop out the bits you don't like, because it all fits together.

Jalene's voice on the phone saying she can't keep watching her destroy herself; Jalene saying, "I'll be your family."

Her grandmother singing opera in the kitchen; a tombstone behind the Old Church.

Herself rolling her eyes; leaning over to steal a lick of her mother's ice cream; giggling and three years old; laughing at one of Ma Bear's stories; screaming at her to get out of her room; nuzzling into her breast; asking her how to spell "lemon"; smiling at her from a poster saying HAVE YOU SEEN THIS GIRL?

No big moments. No big dreams realised. Just a small normal life. But the love inside it was huge.

This love, it drowns everything else out. All the other noises in her, the ones urging her to catch and kill and eat and destroy, they are nothing compared to this. Marybeth knew every inch of Katie, loved all of her, and her mind, newly reformed inside of Katie's body, is full of longing to see her again.

What is left of Katie obliges. It can't help itself. How can anyone turn away from being so loved?

The last segment on her tail detaches and falls to the ground with a heavy thump. Milky pink blood oozes from the wound. She lets the clear fluid inside her seep out, holding the hot blood in.

She wants to see Katie again, so badly.

She wants to be Katie.

Segment by segment, the body falls apart. Limbs drop off. Lumps of brain tissue fall out of the lumps on her shoulders and fall to the ground. Extra muscle tissue peels off. Eyes fall from the dark place inside of her and tumble out onto the grass. Lips slide off mouths; teeth clatter to the ground.

She breaks back into a human shape.

The last extra part she has is Marybeth's brain. She considers keeping it. She could keep it attached to her spine, like a huge tumour. Heck, she could just grow a second head, share a body with her mother for the rest of her life.

But that's not the stunted half-life Marybeth wants for her daughter. Not really.

She takes a deep breath, severs the connection and lets the brain fall. It lands on the other tissue with a plop. That small thing, that blob of fat and veins and connective tissue. It was a whole personality, a whole person.

She still has her own experience of learning her mother's memories. They're part of her now, always.

"Thank you, Ma Bear," she whispers, her mouth parts returned back to a shape she's more familiar with. The grief is a deep oil well within her.

On two tottering human legs, Katherine Larkin starts the long walk home.

44. WE THREE

TAMMY-RAE HOOPER

Time skips again.

It's already dusk when Rae finds herself outside Kat's house. Usually, lights would be flickering on behind windows right about now. Families gathering for dinner, the soft glow of TV lights through curtains. But tonight, except for the odd street lamp, most of the town is dark.

The Larkins' is the best-kept house on a bad street: lilacs lining the driveway, pear tree shading the front porch, two matching concrete cherubs framing the door, big American flag hoisted proudly out front. She thinks of all the times the three of them lay on that roof, making up names for the constellations. The hamster. The hag. The Olivia Hussey's Magnificent Right Boob.

Like all the other houses, it's dark now.

She pulls her denim jacket tight around herself, shivering. Frodo's gone from her pocket. He must have jumped out somewhere, gone on to live his own hamstery life without her.

She can see the shapes of people in the distance, others like her, peering in windows, looking for human stragglers. None of them close enough to hijack her thoughts. Proximity seems to matter: like it's easier for the stuff in her to communicate with the stuff in them if they're close. Maybe if she runs away, she could keep her own mind. For a while, until the spread reaches her, until it swallows the whole world.

But why? Why be Tammy-Rae Hooper? It would have been better if that girl managed to kill herself a long time ago. It wasn't true, when she told Donna this was all her fault. Because it was Rae's idea to start the stupid zine in the first place; Rae who brought the three of them together; Rae who is the reason all these people are dead.

There's so much blood on her. She can never scrub it out. If she does have a soul, it's damned.

Her stomach gives a miserable rumble. At least she hasn't gone full zombie and started eating human flesh. There's a pizza place round the corner from Kat's, where there might be something she can scrounge. What's a little light theft after a day of butchering a whole town?

She wanders right up the middle of the street, enjoying the feeling of the cold air on her face, the unusual quiet, her hand in her pocket missing Frodo's soft little body. More alone than she's ever felt.

On a wooden bench outside Jimmy's Pizza, she finds a man rummaging through the pockets of a corpse. She doesn't recognise him: he's squat with rounded shoulders, a long beaky nose beneath greasy dark hair. He is like her. There's that comfort of being with one of her own kind, that instant sense of connection. The hum starts up in her spine as she walks up to him.

He looks terrible. His eyes are bloodshot, and sweat is running down his face in rivulets. The pants he's wearing are bunched up at the bottom, far too long for him.

He looks up as she approaches. "Hey, kid. Got a light?"

"No, sorry."

"Goddamn figures. Managed to get myself caught up in an apocalypse and I lost my lighter." He holds up a crumpled box of cigarettes. There's a smear of blood on the wrapper.

"You're not from around here."

"I, young lady, am a reporter for the *Sacramento Bee*. Originally from Ecorse, Michigan. Even more of a shithole town than this one."

"That doesn't seem possible." Rae sits at the bench.

"Ha. Wait till you're older, kid. You'll learn that the whole world's garbage." He starts digging through a handbag, its former owner face-down in a pepperoni pie at the table next to them.

"I don't think we're going to get any older."

"How you figure that?"

She picks up a pizza wheel from the table and runs it up the skin of her calf. It stings like a bitch. Immediately, the skin knits itself closed.

"Well, fuck me," the penguin says. "Eternal life, huh? Well, that's an upside. But if it's eternal life without nicotine, I choose death." He returns to the handbag. "Are you also this sweaty? Ever since I came back, I've been sweating like a cow in a slaughterhouse."

Rae frowns. She hadn't even noticed. "Actually... not any more. I was, the first few days. I guess eventually you get the hang of it. The body."

"Eureka!" he says, holding up a plastic lighter. "Thank God. I found the last smoker in California."

He sits at the table opposite her, pulling a cigarette out of the pack. His eyes narrow. "Oh shit, you're her," he says.

"Who am I?"

"You're one of those girls. They sent me up here to cover your story. Your father threatened to call the cops if I didn't get off his lawn."

"Sounds like him."

He clicks the lighter. It sparks, but doesn't light. He shakes it. "Where are your friends?"

"Gone, I don't know. Kat and Donna always had their own minds."

"You don't?"

She shrugs. "I'm here, aren't I?"

He tries the lighter again, still nothing. He tips it over, letting the gas run right up against the flint. "Good for them, getting away. Feels like if you stay too close, you go a bit dippy. Might be nice. Just wanted to have one last smoke first, see if it feels as good in this new body as it did in my old one."

She nods, wiping off the thin line of blood on her skin where she cut herself.

"I guess you three started all this, huh?"

"I guess. We didn't mean to."

"If I were still a journalist, I'd have a hell of a story on my hands."

He clicks the lighter again.

This time it catches.

One moment, Rae is sitting opposite a short, dark-haired man. The next, she's sitting in front of a column of fire.

She leaps back, tripping over the bench and landing hard on her butt. He burns like he's been doused in gasoline. The dark shape of his mouth opens in a scream, but there's not enough oxygen in his lungs to power the noise of it. The burning man falls to the floor, writhing, rolling, trying to put himself out.

Rae screams. It's like a part of her is being amputated. His pain is awful. It echoes in her own body, like a bright searing light. She can feel the flames tearing through him and it's excruciating.

There are running footsteps behind her. A boy, another one like her. He joins in her screaming. Both of them are afraid to get too close to him. They stand there, helpless, immersed in his pain.

Both of them feel the exact moment when he dies, when his consciousness snaps out, and their connection is severed.

The shock of it reverberates through the mind-mesh. She hears distant keening from deeper in town. The others feel it too, this pruning of their network.

Mr Dunne, her history teacher, joins them, out of breath. "What happened?" His voice is high-pitched in panic. The boy shakes his head, trembling violently, eyes fixed on the pillar of flame in front of them.

Rae can feel others drawing closer. *No.* She starts humming to herself, trying to keep herself together. They all feel the danger, and, like a herd, their urge is to huddle against attack.

The flames subside. The man's body is still burning, but it's burning like flesh would, rather than fuel. Whatever was in his cells that wasn't human has burned out, leaving nothing but a human carcass behind.

Like an exorcism.

There is a verse in the Gospel of Mark where Jesus performs an exorcism on a possessed man in Gerasenes. He asks the demon for its name, and it says, "My name is Legion; for we are many." Jesus drives the demons out and puts them in the bodies of pigs, and then drives the pigs over a cliff and into the ocean.

She doesn't have any pigs, and she's certainly not Jesus. She's just a demon who stole the body of a girl, one of many. Powerless against the will of the hive.

But maybe she can do the right thing anyway.

More of them are gathering now. "Hide!" somebody whispers, and this gets taken up by the others, whispered from mouth to mouth. "Hide." "Hide."

The boy tries to tell them that he did it to himself, it was an accident, but they're tied up in their panic. They grab hands, start pulling each other away, moving in a mass of bodies towards the centre of town where there are larger buildings, a place they might be safe. The gravity of them pulls at her like a bowling ball in the middle of a trampoline. She will have to follow. She has no choice.

But what if she does?

It doesn't matter what she does now. She is damned. A good deed does not erase a bad one. As Pastor Sherman liked to say, if half an apple's rotten, it's a rotten apple.

But she can still do something good. Even if it's not for her.

The boy tugs at her jacket. "Come on!" Rae shrugs him off. Wailing, the boy runs after the others, his footsteps echoing into the night.

Rae crouches over the smouldering corpse. The plastic lighter is lying a few feet away from it, bright pink against the asphalt. She puts it in her pocket and turns towards the centre of town, where the force pulling her has become too strong to resist.

———

DONNA RAMIREZ

WEDNESDAY, 25 SEPTEMBER 1996

Something has happened.

The pull of the others has been growing stronger all afternoon as they multiplied through Little Hope. Donna's continued hiding in the woods, paging sadly through Kat's journal as the day faded.

But quite quickly, over the last half-hour, the force has grown irresistible, like a rope tied to her stomach and the other end an anchor that's just been thrown into the ocean. The strength is incredible. It's very concentrated now, all of them gathered together somewhere in the middle of town, she's sure of it.

She lets her feet take her back up the hill, down along Black Oak Lane. The elementary school is empty, one swing creaking in the breeze.

She makes her way down to Broad Street, passing places she's known her whole life. Emptied and wrecked, they all seem strange to her now. The glass windows of Louanne's Diner are all smashed out, dark shapes slumped across the tables. The old wooden wagon that used to stand outside of the museum is lying on its side, riddled with bullet holes. Jim Porter from the video store lies dead in the doorway of the jeweller's, pockets bursting with gold.

It always was an odd place. She spent her whole life desperate to leave it, but for a hundred and fifty years, people came out here because they were searching for something. Fortune, jobs, purpose. Hope. But there was something else here, lying in wait all along. This new thing that she is. Is it good? Bad? She doesn't have a damn idea.

But maybe that's the point: the unknowability.

Maybe that's the reason to keep living, whether you're human or not.

She steps over other bodies lying in the street. The pull of the hive is stronger. She can feel panic radiating from it, palpable. Something has made it afraid, and the fear flows into her, too.

She clutches hold of Kat's journal for strength.

The school looms up ahead of her in all its squat concrete glory. She can sense them, crammed in like sardines. It's the biggest building in town. They must have hoped to hide from something. Her heart sinks, imagining how hard it's going to be to find Rae in there, a body pressed up against so many others. How will she get her out without getting sucked into the madness?

Then she sees her, a skinny figure standing at the front doors, threading a heavy chain through the handles, dark bob a curtain over her face. Rae.

"Whatcha doing, guy?" Donna says, stopping halfway up

the steps, so she can run if she needs to.

Rae ignores her. Her lips are moving, like she's muttering something under her breath. Her dress is covered in dark stains.

"Nice look. Like Carrie, but on a casual day."

No response. Rae reaches into her jacket pocket, pulls out a huge padlock and clips it onto the chain.

"I'm sorry I left, OK? You can be mad at me later. Right now, I need to get you away from here, and then we need to find Kat."

Rae walks off, not saying a word. Donna chases her around the side of the building and grabs her arm. "Hey!" Rae's face is blank, her eyes staring right through Donna to some deeper distance. She's there, but she's not really there. Her lips keep moving. Maybe it's a prayer.

Rae shakes her off and marches around to the back of the gym. The world feels like it's spinning around her. There are so many of them in there. But Donna keeps her eyes fixed on Rae's skinny outline, doing her best to stay focused.

The gym door is already chained closed, iron links obscuring a SAY NO TO PEER PRESSURE! poster. There's a pile of stuff lying on the ground. More chains, padlocks, and two steel jerry cans.

"Rae, you can't. They're human. Well, maybe not human, but they're people."

Rae picks up one of the gas cans and starts splashing the contents onto the door. The smell hits her: acrid, deadly. She remembers Ronnie's words: *They light right up like kindling.*

"No!" Donna rushes at her, shoulder down. She takes Rae by surprise, whacking her off her feet. The two of them tumble across the grass. The gas can clatters to its side, liquid spilling out across the pathway.

"Rae, it's me!" Donna says, straddling her, shaking her. But her face is a mannequin. Only her lips keep moving. Donna's bigger, but Rae is so much stronger than her, toughened up by afternoons playing volleyball while Donna was picking at her guitar. She pushes Donna off her, picks up the second gas can, resumes wetting down the door.

Donna rushes at her again. This time, Rae's expecting her. She braces herself, legs wide. Donna bounces off her uselessly. She tries to grab Rae's hand, wrestle the can from her grip, but Rae swings the can up and brings it down hard on Donna's face. The corner of it hits her on her upper lip, a blast of pain that sends her reeling.

Donna staggers back, gasping for breath. Her mouth is full of iron. She spits, and a bright splatter hits the concrete, her two front teeth scattered there like dropped Chiclets.

"Fuck!" Donna yells, bringing her hand up to her lip to feel the damage. Pain blooms across her face, but two new teeth are already pushing their way through her gums.

Rae doesn't look back at her. Doesn't turn to check if Donna's OK. She pours the last few drops out of the can, and then reaches into her pocket, and pulls out a pink lighter.

"It'll kill you!" Donna yells and throws herself at Rae again. She manages to knock the lighter from Rae's hand. It goes flying across the lawn, and lands under a bush.

There is finally the flicker of an emotion on Rae's face: irritation. She storms off towards the bush, and drops to her knees, scrabbling around underneath.

She can't beat Rae. She has to find a way to reach her.

Donna pulls Kat's journal from her waistband. It falls open to the zine stapled into the middle. Their zine. The words they made, together.

"When we were assigned *The Catcher in the Rye* as our set book this year I was genuinely excited," she starts to read. "I'd heard that the swearing, blasphemy, sex and rebellion against authority caused it to be banned in several countries in the world. Ooooh, forbidden fruit!"

Rae stops scrabbling for the lighter. She slumps on her knees, facing away from Donna.

"This was a book that would speak to teenagers, I was told. What I got was a hundred and sixteen pages about a mopey, selfish, rich, spoiled sixteen-year-old who acts like the world revolves around him and doesn't even know how the world works."

She reads on, the whole review, to Rae's silent back. She gets to the last words, the ones Rae wrote herself, a lifetime ago. "If you're looking to step into the shoes of an angsty teen, rather read *The Bell Jar* by Sylvia Plath. You think you have problems, Holden Caulfield? Esther Greenwood would eat you for breakfast."

Rae makes a choking noise. Donna sidles up to her and puts her hand carefully on Rae's back. It convulses and then settles into a rhythmic sob.

"You have to let me fix it," she says.

"I think we're pretty far past being able to fix things."

"Then why are you here?"

"I came back for you, dingus."

Rae turns to face her. Her eyes are focused now, her face full of feeling. But that feeling is pain.

"Screw you, Donna. You left. You ran away and left me to sort everything out, as usual. I messed it up. I know I did. But this is me putting things right. We can't let these things run wild. They'll eat the world."

"Yeah? Well, I don't care about the world."

"You don't care about anything."

"I care about *you*, idiot. I don't want you to burn down the school because of what it will do *to you*." She grabs Rae's hand. There's a thrill in the touch, skin on skin, belonging. "Yes, we killed a bunch of people. But they're all still here. The memories, all the things that make them who they are. If you burn them, that's all gone. Then they're really dead. I don't want you spending the rest of your life trying to live with that."

"There's no rest of our life," Rae says. Starlight glistens in her eyes.

"Not with that attitude!"

Rae snorts, then shakes her head. "Stop joking about this. This is serious. We're evil. We're dangerous, and we're not in control of this. Can't you feel it? This is the last thing I can do to redeem us."

"Stop this Calvinist self-hatred crap. You didn't mean to do anything wrong. You've got the half-formed brain of a fifteen-year-old girl who was in an impossible situation and you did your best. You're not *broken*. I love you and I'm not going to let you destroy yourself. I'll fight you if you try."

"I'll win."

"Definitely. I'll still fight you, though."

Donna scoots over and leans her head on Rae's shoulder. They never do it this way round. Donna's so much taller than her that she has to twist her neck wildly to fit. It's uncomfortable. But it's home.

"I'm still mad with you," Rae says, cupping the top of Donna's head with her chin.

"I deserve it."

There's a rattle at the door, somebody trying to get out. But it feels like the hive's growing calmer.

"What are we going to do?"

"Hell if I know. Kat might have an idea. I think... I've got this feeling she's on her way home."

"I can feel her too. Close, now. She's just a presence at the edge of my brain, but I still wouldn't confuse her with anyone else."

"Yup."

"What if she's still a monster?"

"We'll love her anyway."

Two of their magpies flutter over to a body in the parking lot and start joyfully tugging at the meat. It's a great day for them.

"We're pretty terrible without her, aren't we."

"Yeah. I killed my dad today."

"Amateur. I body-snatched a whole town."

"Show-off."

"Father-killer."

"Pyro."

"Runaway."

Donna pokes Rae in the ribs. Rae responds by blowing a raspberry on her forehead. The two of them sit in silence, waiting for Kat.

———

KATHERINE LARKIN

THURSDAY, 26 SEPTEMBER 1996

It's been a while since her body has been this shape, so she finds it difficult to walk. She shuffles along slowly, keeping her legs stiff so she doesn't fall over. It takes her a long time to walk home, but she knows the way.

Rae and Donna are on the steps of the school. The sky is just starting to go grey, and it's still dark, but she'd know them anywhere. They are the two missing pieces of her heart.

They race out to meet her, and the three of them put their arms around each other, their heads touching in the centre. The three of them stand there, just happy to be breathing the same air. There are no words that seem like enough; it's like there's a current that flows through them, arm to arm to arm. It's hard to break apart again, but they do. The two of them grin at her.

Donna reaches up to touch her face, brow furrowed. "Your mother found you."

She nods. That's too painful to think about right now. "How long was I out there?"

"Like a week?"

"Sorry I took so long. I got a bit... caught up in stuff."

"What was it like?"

"Interesting at first. I was experimenting. Then it got scary. I think I did some bad things."

"We all did." Rae takes off her denim jacket and hands it to her.

Donna grins. "So... quick update from us: we turned the whole town into aliens, and now we're trying to figure out how to avoid winding up in some Roswell-type facility for the rest of our unnatural lives."

"Wow. I can't leave you two alone for five minutes."

"Any ideas?" Rae asks.

She looks up at the school. "They're all in there?"

Donna nods. "When too many of them gather, the communal mind seems to take over."

Oh, like a slime-mould," she says. "I read about—"

"—it in a book," Rae and Donna finish her sentence in unison.

"We talked about getting them to scatter," Rae continues. "I think if they're apart, they might start to think like individuals again. We could tell them not to spit on anyone, or bleed on them. They might be able to go out and live normal lives."

"Tell them to never kiss anybody? Or have sex? Or get into an accident? Have you met people?" Kat says. "I know your church is big on the abstinence message, but I've never seen it work in the real world. They'll replicate. It's just biology."

"There's also the small matter of a town full of dead bodies we have to worry about," Donna adds. "Rae and I didn't manage to cover up our *own* deaths."

"Although I think it's safe to say that Chief Pittman is no longer investigating us," Rae says. "Last I saw him he was pressed up against Principal Keyes and my mom under the gym bleachers."

"Hot," says Donna.

Kat considers the problem from all angles. There are a lot of angles she knows how to consider, now.

Finally, she knows what she has to say. But she doesn't want to.

The three of them stand in silence, as the sky slowly turns lilac.

"Come with me," she says finally. "These weirdos aren't going anywhere." She leads them to their spot behind the maintenance room where they whiled away so many endless hours. She pushes the dumpster up against the wall so they can get onto the roof. Rae and Donna follow her. The magpies are squawking happily to each other about food and territory and whatever else happens in the minds of magpies.

The three of them lie on their backs and watch the sky wash out into yellow, and then transform into a neon orange. It's better out here. Away from the crowd, they can hear their own thoughts.

"We've got to hide them," Kat says eventually. "Some people will have escaped. They'll get help. The authorities will be all over this place soon. We have to get them away from here, before they do."

Rae rolls onto her stomach to see her better. "Where?"

"Back where we came from."

"You want to send them to spaaaaaaaace?" Donna says, wiggling her fingers.

"I meant the caves. There are miles and miles of them under the forest. Some of the things that I was... they lived in them. I remember the ways in. There's plenty of room in there for all of them."

Rae frowns. "We can't be sure they won't search the forests. They had whole search parties out there looking for you. Dogs and everything. And that was just for one missing girl."

"But there's no one missing this time, see? Just a big mysterious accident, but all the bodies are present and accounted for."

"And how will they explain that?"

"Who knows. Who cares? Let it be an X-file."

"There are animals in the woods that are like us. We'd have to track them down too."

"Won't be hard. When they're afraid, their instinct is to gather."

Rae's eyes meet Kat's. Rae, at least, understands where she's going with this. Donna is still looking at both of them like they've lost their minds.

"You're talking about just cramming eight thousand people underground and letting them live like mole people. It's cruel."

"Sorry to sound melodramatic, but it's literally the only way we can save humanity."

"It would be better to burn them."

"I can't do that. Could you?"

"OK, so we cram them in some caves with a bunch of animals," Donna says. "Then we change our names and move to Mexico, and just forget about them. Nice going, us. Real heroes."

Donna smooths down the very un-Donna-like tunic she's wearing. Kat recognises it as part of her mother's work uniform, and her eyes fill with tears, but she blinks them away. There will be time for that later.

"They'll never be safe," Kat says at last. "There will always be the danger of somebody finding them. We'll have to guard them."

"Like Ronnie Gaskins." Rae nods.

Kat is about to ask, but Rae waves her off. "Tell you later."

Donna's face flushes. "Stay in Little Hope forever? Are you kidding? The thing we *literally* said was our worst nightmare."

"It was my mom's worst nightmare too," Kat says. "But it wasn't so bad, in the end."

"I know it sucks." Rae nods, her eyes glistening. "There was stuff I wanted to do, too. But Kat's right."

"No way," Donna says. "Let the hive mind take over the world, I don't care."

"Six billion people would die."

"I can't. I won't."

Kat shrugs and lies back on the roof. Donna stares off into the distance.

Rae chews her lip. "How can we trust ourselves not to go brain-dead? It's still in us, and we'll be together. What if three of us is enough to make it take over?"

Kat shrugs. "I don't know. Three always felt like the right number, and we three... I think we're different enough that I trust us to stay ourselves."

Rae leans back next to her. "So, forever in Little Hope."

"Maybe we can make it fun. We can grow our own vegetables. Learn to make potions. Live the witch fantasy life, like *We Have Always Lived in the Castle*."

"As always, I have no idea what you're talking about."

"That's because you're a jock."

Rae elbows her. "You know what, Kat, I've changed my mind. I think I'd rather let the hive take over the world than have to spend eternity with you dorks."

Donna's back is still turned to them. She lifts a hand and wipes her face on the sleeve of Marybeth's tunic. "I might never see my dad again," she says softly.

Wordlessly, Kat reaches for Rae's hand, and Rae rests her other palm on the small of Donna's back. Three tips of a perfectly balanced mobile. They come to a silent agreement.

Kat watches the clouds catch the edge of the sunrise. "OK, an article for the next edition of *Magpies*: sports played at the alien hive mind Olympics. Go."

"Spit wrestling," says Rae.

"The three-legged race, only it's the seven-million-legged race," Kat says.

Rae prods Donna's back. Donna turns back to face them, her eyes rimmed red. "High-stakes fire-juggling," she mumbles.

They lie like this, the three of them, talking shit until the sky bursts into a brilliant orange. Bathed in the morning light, Donna and Rae look like they're glowing. She has no idea what the future will look like any more. But right at this moment, she wouldn't be anywhere else.

SEVEN FOR A SECRET
NEVER TO BE TOLD

Little Hope: A Trip Through California's Weirdest Ghost Town

By Pete McGloster

You will find it hard to believe that there stood at one time a fiercely flourishing little city, of two thousand or three thousand souls, with its newspaper, fire company, brass band, volunteer militia, bank, hotels, noisy Fourth of July processions and speeches, all the appointments and appurtenances of a thriving and prosperous and promising young city, and now nothing is left of it all but a lifeless, homeless solitude. The men are gone, the houses have vanished, even the name of the place is forgotten. In no other land have towns so absolutely died and disappeared, as in the old mining regions of California…

Mark Twain

Follow Route 49 past El Dorado County, through Comptonville, towards Oak Valley. If you look closely after the Mosquito Creek campground, you'll see the remnants of a road that winds into the mountains. It's more pothole than road, really, littered with fallen tree branches and dead deer, so drive carefully. You'll lose cellphone signal just as you come over the rise. Nestled there between the hills, you'll find one of Gold Country's lesser-known ghost towns. The sign at the entrance reads, WELCOME TO LITTLE HOPE, CA! POPULATION 8,902. But the sign is sun-worn now.

And it's a lie.

Drive on, and you'll find that the town is boarded up, abandoned. The only sign of the terrible thing that happened here is the sprawling graveyard on the edge of town, identical headstones, overgrown now. The date on every headstone is the same.

Welcome to Little Hope indeed: a ruin porn mecca, a nineties time capsule and a mystery, all in one.

***

With international travel restrictions still too unpredictable for even this adventurer's tastes, I've had to look closer to home to get my dark tourism fix. Regular readers of this blog know that what I look for in a destination is the abandoned, the haunted, the morbid or the bizarre, and Little Hope is all that and more. Plus just three hours' drive from SFO to boot. What's not to love?

Little Hope was an old gold rush town founded in the

1850s. Once one of the most bustling towns in El Dorado County, its fortunes dwindled throughout the twentieth century until it was propped up by a tiny tourism industry and the handful of local factories that managed to survive the decline in manufacturing in the early nineties. If its luck had been better, Little Hope might have ended up a lot like better-located Placerville, also an old mining town supply centre, now one of the hippest towns in the region mixing frontier tourism with indie shops and coffeehouses in rehabbed historic buildings. But true to its name, Little Hope's never been lucky. Always *just* too far off the major highways to be an easy stopover, its economy was already on life support when a bizarre disaster snuffed it out for good, including, tragically, the lives of most of its inhabitants.

The official story is that on one fateful summer's day in 1996, a fire started underground in the extensive network of disused mine shafts that run under the town, which leaked carbon monoxide up into the air and suffocated everybody. A similar thing happened in a town called Centralia, Pennsylvania, in '62.

There were plenty of bewildered think-pieces about it back in the nineties, and the strange rumours have never entirely stopped. You can still find breathless conspiracy theorists in some of the more obscure corners of the internet that are obsessed with it. They cite a number of facts that don't quite add up: that the few people who escaped told stories about a madness that made people attack each other; that the whole town was shut down for months afterwards by some shady government department; that none of the forensic reports was ever released and no relative ever got to see one of the bodies before they were buried. A couple of years ago, a thread got to the top of Reddit's r/UnresolvedMysteries claiming that the whole thing was a cover-up for an experimental bioweapon the US government didn't want anybody to know about. Of course, there's no real proof, but it's a heck of a story.

Alyssa Morgan of the *Mystery Junkies* podcast claims that in the mid-2000s, back when anybody and their dog could get a mortgage, a group of property developers rolled in and started talking about buying up the town. They were hoping to revitalise it just enough to turn it into a tourist attraction. Repair the electrical lines, get the water flowing again, fill the road in, refurbish the crumbling hotel. They tracked down the deeds and found that every bit of land, every yard and stone, had been bought in 1997 by a San Francisco lawyer named Bob Pelton. They contacted him and he refused to sell, for any amount of money. "Don't you understand what we're offering you here? That town's worth nothing. We'll give you ten times what it's worth," they'd said.

"Ten times nothing's still nothing," he'd chuckled before hanging up. He refused to take any more of their calls, and the property development company folded two years later after the subprime crash of 2008.

I don't think we'll ever know exactly what happened here. The mystery only adds to the sense of strangeness that pervades the place.

***

I park on the edge of the town and make my way up through the hollowed outbuildings. You might be walking through an American Chernobyl, a twentieth-century Pompeii, everything frozen at one moment in time: rusted-out cars, still right where their drivers parked them before they popped out and never came back; a plate of fossilised waffles on tables in the diner; a garish lime-coloured handbag lying empty on the sidewalk. Bittersweet and gruesome, quality Instagram opportunities at every turn.

I wander through some of the stores on the main road. They're mostly picked clean, hipster kids from San Francisco and Portland who've emptied them over the years of all the trendy nineties kitsch. The three clothing stores have been emptied out of fanny packs and hammer pants. The CD and video store shelves are empty, as well as certain shelves at the toy store. I imagine that most of the knick-knacks have found new homes through eBay and Vinted.

In the shell of the high school, I finally strike gold: an original zine. It was tucked into a teacher's desk drawer, probably confiscated from some delinquent kid, protected enough from the elements to have survived mostly intact. I tuck it carefully into my backpack for later perusal (it turns out to be nothing interesting, just a bunch of schoolkid in-jokes).

DARK ADVENTURER

Grass and wildflowers push through what used to be the road. A huge colony of black-and-white crows has made its home in the ruins. There must be hundreds of the bastards. They sit on every rooftop and watch me walk through town, with eerily intelligent eyes. You don't get the sense that they're glad you're here. I think of all those Covid memes that joked about how "nature is healing, we are the virus". In some ways, Little Hope feels less like you've time-travelled back into the nineties, and more like you've travelled into the distant future when climate change has got us all and humans have inevitably perished.

Following this line of thought, I decide to walk among the tombstones for a few minutes. They're simple white marble slabs, in rows, identical, like the military graves at Arlington. The full names carved into the front of each one in identical block letters somehow make them seem more anonymous, not less.

But something surprising: on the back of each one there is a crude portrait done in what looks like Sharpie. The style is amateurish, but there's something distinct about each face. Some of them have little objects drawn around them, like things they might have loved. I spot a football, a Christian cross, a guitar. I walk to the back of the rows and look out at them, and every single headstone I see has one of these drawings on the back. Some art project, clearly, but who'd have stayed out here long enough to do it? There are no facilities in this ruin of a town, no running water, electricity, Wi-Fi, or any other of life's other essentials.

It's hard to imagine anybody lasting out here for long.
Mysteries upon mysteries.

***

I spend a pleasant afternoon photographing the scenes
of decay, trying to ignore the curious stares of the birds.
Golden hour comes and goes, and I'm just heading back
to my car when I spot the glow of a campfire at the edge
of the woods.

Ol' Petey's never one to ignore the call to adventure,
so I stash my valuables in the car and make my way over.
I'm expecting a group of hikers doing a multi-day trip
through the Plumas National Forest, so I'm surprised
when instead I come across three teenage girls.

They tell me they're camping, but there's no sign of
any tents or sleeping bags nearby. They've got some
branches rigged up in a homemade roasting spit. My
stomach grumbles, until I look closer and realise that
they're cooking a rabbit.

The girls might be homeless, or runaways. Their clothes
are clean but hard-worn. I ask how old they are and they
say eighteen, but they're at that age when it's hard to tell.

They look nothing alike, but you still might think they're
sisters. They just have that vibe about them, some kind of
deep kinship unintelligible to outsiders. One of them is
tanned and lean, dark hair and sharp angles and strong
arms. Protective and fierce, undoubtedly their leader. Her
mischievous friend, long hair cut in messy grunge style

that's almost, but not quite, fashionable. Ripped jeans and a homemade T-shirt featuring a slogan I don't recognise. And the other one, the strangest of them all. Shy. Huge green eyes, only in some lights, you'd swear they're brown. Sometimes it feels like there's something else in her smile, something predatory. Still waters, undoubtedly.

It feels equally plausible that they're about to rob me, or tell me I'll be the next King of Scotland.

They've got a dog with them who's cheerfully asleep, contributing smelly farts to the smell of cooking rabbit.

We talk for a while. They evade any direct questions I ask them but are very curious about me. What do I do for a living, what brings me to Little Hope, am I married, what do I do for fun? They want to know what's happening in the world. They don't have a TV, they say. I pretend to be better informed about current affairs than I am and give them a summary of the various ins and outs of world culture and politics. The girls seem honestly curious. They seem to be entirely unaware of the fact that there was a global pandemic. Like people who've been stuck on a deserted island, or sailors who've been at sea too long. But they're teenagers, I remind myself, so it's more likely that they're just messing with me.

The one topic they don't seem remotely curious about is the one I've been puzzling over all afternoon: what happened in Little Hope. I ask if they've got a theory. They shrug. "It was before our time, duh."

I ask if they're not worried they'll run into trouble out

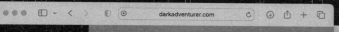

here, three girls on their own. They laugh at me. I ask them how long they've been out here.

"A while."

"Seems like a lonely life," I say. They smile at each other, some secret joke I'm not in on.

***

Little Hope, California. It's hard not to get obsessed with it. It's been two weeks since I went out there, but I must have sunk twenty hours since then spiralling down the rabbit hole of conspiracy theories.

I went back over that old Reddit thread. Buried deep at the bottom is a link to a poorly scanned biography of somebody named Edward Mullins, the town founder. The weird thing is, it suggests there never were any gold mines in Little Hope, that the whole thing was a lie. There's an old saying that in a gold rush, you want to be the person selling shovels, and Edward Mullins was selling directions to a mystical lost mine that probably never existed. But tell me, if there were no mines running under the town, then where were all those fires? What killed all those people?

It's like a Lovecraftian monster: you can't look at it for too long, or you'll go insane. I'm trying to let it go, before I become yet another Little Hope truther sacrificing my sanity and my job and my girlfriend (who tells me if I bring up Little Hope one more time she's moving back to her mother's) trying to solve an unsolvable mystery.

Why do mysteries grip us? I guess, like those nineteenth-century miners, we're all looking for something. Maybe some kind of meaning. Maybe some sign that the world's a more interesting place than you thought, that there's something more than the humdrum of our jobs and all the disappointments of our boring adult lives. Maybe the reminder that there are other ways to live, like grabbing your two best friends and a dog and living wild on the edge of a forest. So many ways to be human.

And that's why we travel, isn't it?

While morbid, Little Hope is an essential visit for any dark tourist that likes their ghost towns with a side order of mystery. Be warned, it gets hot in summer so bring water with you. There are no toilets or other public facilities. Also, there's a fairly good chance that the trip will turn you into a babbling obsessive and a bore at parties.

If you go, and you meet three feral teenage girls living in the woods there, tell them Pete says hi.

***

Join us next month for a tour of an
abandoned Victorian-era aquarium in London
(pandemic permitting).

***

Follow Pete on YouTube | Twitter | Instagram
Subscribe for dark adventures in your inbox

ACKNOWLEDGEMENTS

When you're so much of an outsider that you feel like an actual alien sent from space, what gets you through is finding other weirdos. *Girls of Little Hope* is a love letter to the teenage friends who helped us survive our own monstrous adolescence.

Specifically, we'd like to thank the many friends who helped us shape this book. Lauren Beukes, for being our hero and our mentor and our favourite-favourite, for making us tapeworm talismans and helping us find the right ending, we love you dearly, always. Hayley Tomes, for letting us pick her brain about parasite facts. Anja Venter, for being one of this book's earliest readers and for "shut up and write" Fridays. Jared Shurin, for insights about American high school assemblies. And Charne Lavery, for small-town anecdotes and *gees*-boosts when we needed them.

Meghan Finn and Maya Jaffer, thank you for being the first people we trusted to read a whole draft of this novel, for being treasure troves of legal and medical insights, for your unfailing support and boundless generosity and impeccable literary judgement. You helped make this book into what it is, and we are so grateful. Also, did you know that you are both huge dorks? You are both huge dorks.

Bringing a book into the world is significantly harder than birthing a clone from your abdomen. Thank you to the many people at Titan Books and Jonathan Ball who believed in us and in this story. Especially, thank you to Cat Camacho for seeing the potential in a rough early manuscript, and to Daniel Carpenter for helping us to close plot holes and tighten the prose, and being a bottomless well of hilarious '90s facts.

Thank you to our agent, Oli Munson, for his wisdom and faith in us (and for helping us choose the right title!). And to our film agent, Angela Cheng Caplan, for always having our backs.

Thank you to Peter Godfrey-Smith, Jonathan Birch, Merlin Sheldrake and Rachel Carson, whose books helped us to imagine radically different minds. And thank you to *The X-Files*, William Blake, Anaïs Nin, Sylvia Plath, J. R. R. Tolkien and the many bands we mention in this book. When we were lonely teenagers stuck in our own small towns, you helped us to imagine bigger lives for ourselves.

Dale would also like to thank the following people who made possible this book's journey from idea to publication. Sam, for being the *Xena: Warrior Princess* to his Gabrielle. This book would not exist without her brilliance, fearlessness and unwavering belief in the original idea. Amantha, for being his anchor in life. And his mother, for encouraging him to always follow his dreams no matter where they led.

Sam would also like to say thank you to Dale, for being the other half of her brain, for being our plot-whisperer and dialogue fiend, and the best collaborator a girl could have asked for. Making this book-length zine with you is the most fun I've ever had. Thank you for trusting me with your idea. To my mom, who licked the afterbirth off me and has loved me without limit my whole life, even when I least deserved it. To Matt, who gave me the immeasurable gift of the time and space to do the thing I've always dreamed of doing, and whose fingerprints are all over this novel. To my own teenage friends Zani, Xoli, Jet, Monique and Josie, I'm so grateful we got to be awkward and odd and hide out in the music room together. But most of all, thank you to Melanie. We made it out of Pretoria Alive! Thank you for helping me to grow up without growing less strange. I choose you, forever.

Finally, both of us would like to thank our readers. We are so grateful you chose to spend time with this book. Thank you for allowing us room inside your brain.

ABOUT THE AUTHORS

Dale and Sam are best friends and horror dorks who collaborated on a short story called 'This Book Will Find You' (along with our third best friend, Lauren Beukes, who IS NOT missing in the woods, we promise) which is now being developed as a TV series.

Dale Halvorsen co-created the Vertigo Comics horror series *Survivors' Club*, along with Lauren Beukes and Ryan Kelly. He collaborated with Lauren and Carlos Ezquerra on the one-shot *Durham Red and Strontium Dog* comic for 2000AD and *CHUM* in *Strange Sports Stories* for DC Comics. He is also an international award-winning book cover designer, graphic designer, and illustrator. He cannot remember loved ones' birthdays, but he can embarrassingly recall horror movie run times, facts like Count Orlock blinks only once in *Nosferatu* and the voice of *Scream's* Ghost Face Roger L. Jackson is the voice of Mojo Jojo in *The Powerpuff Girls*. Proudly autistic. He lives in Cape Town, South Africa.

You can find him on Twitter at @JoeyHifi or reach him at dalehalvorsen.com

Sam Beckbessinger is the bestselling author of *Manage Your Money Like a Fucking Grownup*. Her interactive story about climate change, *Survive the Century*, was featured in *New Scientist* and *Gizmodo*, and she was one of the writers on Realm and Marvel's *Jessica Jones: Playing With Fire* serialised novel. She teaches creative writing at Bath Spa University, writes kids' TV, and is weirdly obsessed with spreadsheets. She grew up on a farm near Durban, South Africa (where she had a pet donkey named Mr Magoo) but now lives in London. You can find Sam online at sambeckbessinger.com

For more fantastic fiction, author events,
exclusive excerpts, competitions, limited editions and more

VISIT OUR WEBSITE
titanbooks.com

LIKE US ON FACEBOOK
facebook.com/titanbooks

FOLLOW US ON TWITTER AND INSTAGRAM
@TitanBooks

EMAIL US
readerfeedback@titanemail.com